I0654147

Blood of a Boss 4

Askari

**Lock Down Publications and Ca$h
Presents**

Blood of a Boss 4

A Novel by *Askari: The King of Philly
Street-Lit*

Lock Down Publications
P.O. Box 944
Stockbridge, Ga 30281
www.lockdownpublications.com

Copyright 2018 Askari
Blood of a Boss 4

All rights reserved. No part of this book may be reproduced in any form or by electronic or mechanical means, including information storage and retrieval systems without permission in writing from the publisher, except by a reviewer who may quote brief passages in review.

First Edition 2018
Printed in the United States of America

This is a work of fiction. Names, characters, places, and incidents either are products of the author's imagination or are used fictitiously. Any similarity to actual events or locales or persons, living or dead, is entirely coincidental.

Lock Down Publications
Like our page on Facebook: Lock Down Publications @
www.facebook.com/lockdownpublications.ldp
Book interior design by: **Shawn Walker**
Edited by: **Shawn Walker**

Stay Connected with Us!

Text **LOCKDOWN** to 22828 to stay up-to-date with new releases, sneak peaks, contests and more...
Thank you!

Submission Guideline.

Submit the first three chapters of your completed manuscript to ldpsubmissions@gmail.com, subject line: Your book's title. The manuscript must be in a .doc file and sent as an attachment. Document should be in Times New Roman, double spaced and in size 12 font. Also, provide your synopsis and full contact information. If sending multiple submissions, they must each be in a separate email.

Have a story but no way to send it electronically? You can still submit to LDP/Ca$h Presents. Send in the first three chapters, written or typed, of your completed manuscript to:

LDP: Submissions Dept
P.O. Box 944
Stockbridge, Ga 30281

DO NOT send original manuscript. Must be a duplicate.

Provide your synopsis and a cover letter containing your full contact information.

Thanks for considering LDP and Ca$h Presents.

DEDICATION

This book is dedicated to the big homie, CA$H. Thanks for believing in me, bro, and for helping me make a way when things were dark and it was hard for me to see the light. Your loyalty and love is bulletproof, my brother. Not only did you keep it 100% since day one, you've blessed me with many jewels as an old head and a big brother. Even when I wanted to branch out and create my own company, you had my back and helped me to see the game from an executive's point of view. You constantly challenge me as an author, motivating my drive to one day be considered one of the best in street lit. From the bottom of my heart, beloved, it's an honor to be your protégé.

LDP, WE IN THE BUILDING!!!!

ACKNOWLEDEMENTS

Shout outs to my babies: Dayshon, Kenyonti, Diamond, and Quamar, I love you all so much, and I am so very proud. Keep up the good work and stay focused. The best has yet to come.

Shout outs to my right-hand man, Michael "Abdur Rahman" Grant. I love you, bro. Blood couldn't make us any closer. Thanks for always having my back, bro. I couldn't ask for a better comrade.

Shout outs to my day one rydas, Eric "E Class" Stubbs and William "Billy Bear" Taylor. I love y'all dudes to death. Two of the realest n****s I know. When it was it time to ryde out and put the money where their mouth was, they stood tall like city hall. No rap and no questions asked, the same as always. I know it's hard for y'all right now, but keep y'all heads up and stand firm like the soldiers y'all was bred to be. If I make it home first, y'all know what is. Crew Love, DSE forever!!!

Shout outs to my little brother, Fat Mitch and Scrap. I'm proud of y'all, man. Keep that drive and focus, one day it's gonna pay off. Just remain patient, prioritize, strategize and keep y'all foot on the gas. I love y'all.

To my big bother, Cheese. I love you, bul. You're father of the century, my G. I admire your dedication to your children. I'm 34, and I still look up to you. Thanks for always having my back. You was the ONLY one who believed in my aspirations as a writer from day one, and bought me my first typewriter. I love you, Puppy Nuts! LMAO!!!

Shout out to my cousin, Lance "Big City" Lindsay. I love you, cuzzo, and I'm proud of you. Thanks for having my back and for believing in me. You was another one who put that bread up when it was time to move. Get wit' me, cousin. I love you.

Shout outs to my Aunt Dee, Mom-Mom and Pop-Pop. Thanks for being there for me and having my back. As far as the rest of my so-called "family", those of y'all who are grown, I ain't got no rap!!! Kick rocks!!! We ain't family, we just related. How is it that I get more support from people that I don't even know! SHMFH!!!! I wish y'all the best, though.

Shout outs to my boys: Sham, Has, Biggie, Uncle Reese Hold ya head, Unc., Cousin Beast, Horsey and Boo Boo Hold ya head lil' bro, Peedi Crakk I love you, cousin. Get wit' me, Indy 500, Omillio Sparks, Cousin Flaco, Tali Da Don Hold ya head, brozay, Nips, Shokka Bop, D Nyce, and Marlo "Rasul" Clark. Congratulations, Sul. You're more than needed in the community, my brother. I have no doubts that you'll be a positive influence on our youth. Stay true and stay focused.

Last but not least, it's imperative that I give a very special shout out to Team LDP, and to all of my fans and supporters. Y'all make writing worthwhile, and I always keep you guys in mind whenever I pick up a pen. Thanks for supporting my literary career, and I appreciate all of the feedback in y'all book reviews. It took me a while to finish this part four, but with you all in mind, I wanted to take my time and make sure I brought the heat. I hope you enjoy.

Rayshon "Askari" Farmer

Askari

Previously in Blood of a Boss...

December 12th 2014
2:18 a.m.

Sonny was all alone in the Block Boy Room. A burning Dutch Master was nestled between his left thumb and index finger, and he was standing in front of the picturesque glass front window, looking down at the empty dance floor. Nipsy and The Reaper were headed toward The Swamp to get ready for what he had planned for Daphney, and the headless bodies of the twins were downstairs in the basement wrapped in old blankets.

"Talk about the worst day ever," Sonny said to himself and then took a pull on his Dutch Master.

As he exhaled the smoke, his iPhone vibrated in his pants pocket. He pulled it out and saw he had an incoming text message from his private investigator, Arnold Troutman.

Troutman: 2:17 a.m.:*How much longer do you want me to watch the house? The bedroom lights were just turned off, so I'm assuming she's done for the night.*

Sonny read the massage, then hit him right back.

Sontino: 2:18 a.m.: *I already got the information I needed, so you can go. I can handle the rest.*

Troutman: 2:19 a.m.: *Alright, buddy, you take it easy.*

After reading the last message, Sonny noticed he had a missed call from Gangsta. He clicked on his voicemail app and pressed *play.*

"Sonny, it's Gangsta. Whatever you do, you can't trust Grip. Him and Muhammad are planning to kill you. I've been calling you for the last half an hour, but you're not answering. Hopefully, you'll get this message before it's too late."

Sonny couldn't believe what he was hearing. He looked down at the diamond ring his grandfather gave him and anxiously bit down on his bottom lip. "This grimy-ass nigga," he snarled through clenched teeth. "He was setting me up the whole time."

He began to move away from the window, but stopped in his tracks when he noticed a slight movement in the corner of his left eye. Looking down at the dance floor, he spotted three muthafuckas dressed in all-black. They were strapped with M-16s and creeping toward the back staircase. *Yo, this nigga's really try'na park me!* He tossed the Dutchie and ran over to the mini bar in the back corner. Reaching under the bottom shelf, he pulled out a Thompson M-1 that was equipped with a 150-round drum. He cocked a bullet up into the chamber and then ran back over to the window.

"Hey, yo, dickheads, look up here!"

Bddddddddddoc!

A loud burst of gunfire shattered the window and torrentially rained down, killing two of the would-be assassins almost immediately. The third assassin was still alive. He was bleeding from his neck and shoulder, and tucked between the bodies of his dead cohorts. His M-16 was spraying wildly, breaking up the black marble that lined the roof of the bar and tearing up the liquor shelf behind it.

Sonny looked at him and gritted his teeth. Showing no remorse, he aimed the Thompson at the man's forehead and pulled back on the trigger.

Bddddddddddoc!

The blazing hollows ripped through the man's face, quickly turning his head into a gooey lump of flesh.

"Nigga, that's the best you got?" Sonny shouted, pestered that his grandfather would send something so weak. "You know what it is. You know what the fuck I do! And these the muthafuckas you sent?"

No sooner than he said it, a flash bang hand-grenade exploded on the dance floor, catching him by surprise.

Partially dazed, he swung the Thompson at the bright white flash.

Boom!

Another blast blew the front door clean off of the hinges. Shooters in all-black spilled in from everywhere. Their M-16s were

12

barking up at the window, knocking out the shards of glass that dangled in the frame and tearing through the walls all around it.

Outnumbered and clearly outgunned, Sonny crouched down low and dipped behind the wall to his right. He thought about creeping down the staircase and slipping out the back door, but fuck that! He was as a gangsta to the core, a true Block Boy, and Block Boys don't fold. They soldier the fuck up and get it down like G's—ten toes down with the cannon banging!

"What, y'all niggas thought it was sweet?" Sonny shouted over the gangsta music. "Thought y'all was just gon' come for a nigga, and dat be dat? Like I ain't gon' cock back and bang this muthafucka? You right!"

He popped back up in front of the window and continued squeezing, taking out as many as he possibly could. Unfortunately, his adversaries were just as determined as he was and for every one of them he chopped down, it seemed as though five more invaded the nightclub—weapons blazing!

***

At Sonny's Upper Dublin Estate

"I knew this motherfucker wasn't dead!" Daphney snapped out. She was sitting in the back seat of Troutman's Impala. His blood-covered cell phone was clutched in her right hand, and his dead body was stinking the front seat. "I knew that pussy-ass Egypt wasn't man enough to handle his business. Now, I've gotta kill this motherfucker myself."

Looking at Troutman, Daphney realized it wasn't a good idea to leave a dead body in front of her house, even though the large estate was the only house on the entire block. "Fuck it," she shrugged her shoulders, "I'ma just push his ass over to the passenger's side and then drive him up to the garage. I'll figure the rest of this shit out later."

As Daphney reached for the door handle, the door was forcefully snatched open and a pair of hands ripped her from the car. Initially, she thought it was Sonny. But when she looked up and saw the tatted-up face, the three-dimensional devil horns and the razor-sharp teeth, she screamed at the top of her lungs. "Nigga, who the fuck is you?" She was laying on the frost-covered ground looking up at the man in sheer horror. He was crouched down on the roof of the Impala with his tatted-up face freakishly leaned to the side.

"Me?" the Mexican smiled at her, showing off his one inched fangs. "I'm Diablo, the one who God sent to punish the world." He stuck out his tongue and flicked it up and down, taking in the scent of his prey. The bloody-red organ was skinny and long and slitted at the tip like a serpent's.

When Daphney saw it, she screamed even louder. "Oh, hell *naw!*"

She whipped out her .380 and quickly sprang to her feet. Gripping the pistol with both hands, she aimed it at the roof of the car, but Diablo was gone. It was almost like he vanished into thin air.

Utterly confused and stricken with fear, Daphney backed away from the car and hauled ass back to the house. She shot through the security gate and tore up the horseshoe driveway, all the while twisting her head from left to right looking for any signs of the Mexican monster.

Her intuition was screaming at her essence, telling her the monster was close behind. She could literally feel his fingertips nipping at the back of her neck. The phantasmal feeling made her scream even more.

Finally, Daphney reached the front door. Her thumping heart was beating out of her chest, and she was struggling to catch her breath.

She gripped the door knob and gave it a turn, but the solid gold handle refused to budge. "Goddamnit!" she cursed Sonny for his paranoia.

A few days ago, after hearing the news about Breeze and his family, Sonny installed a new security system that required a retina scan from either him or Daphney. There was simply no other way to gain entrance to the house. Unfortunately for Daphney, despite Sonny's urging her to do so, she never took the time out to master the high-tech device.

"Come on, man, damn!" Daphney complained, as she punched in the password for the second time.

The red light at the top of the box turned green, and an automated voice commanded her to look directly into the screen. Daphney did exactly that, and a few seconds later, the automated voice confirmed her identity.

"Daphney Moreno. Access granted."

The door mechanically eased open and Daphney barged inside of the house. She slammed the door behind her and rested her forehead against the oak wood frame.

What the hell was that thing? She thought to herself as she glanced out the peephole. *And where the fuck did it go?* No sooner than the thought crossed her mind, a loud squeal echoed throughout the foyer.

Eeeeeeiiiiii!

The animalistic wail was high pitched and guttural, reminding Daphney of a wild hog. She spun around with the .380 ready to spit, but everything appeared to be normal. She looked down the main hallway. Nothing. She looked up and down the grand dual staircase and then settled her gaze on the balcony. Nothing.

"What the hell is wrong with me?" Daphney stated aloud, uncertain as to whether or not her mind was playing tricks on her. "Come on, Daph, get it together. You're really starting to fucking lose it."

"Ju and me both," a voice spoke out from above.

"What the fuck?" Daphney cried out when she looked up at the ceiling. Diablo was directly above her, butt ass naked and dangling from the chandelier upside down. She attempted to run, but it was no use. He dug his fingers deep in her eye sockets and pushed her peepers into the pit of her brain. Gripping her face like a bowling ball, he grabbed the back of her head with his free hand and twisted until her neck popped.

Pop!

Daphney twitched and convulsed and then finally simmered to a deathly freeze. Her dead body was still standing erect, as Diablo's fingers were still jammed back in the depths of her brain. The gooey tightness reminded him of a soupy, wet pussy. Completely aroused, he extracted his fingers and Daphney hit the floor hard.

His slitted tongue sprang from his mouth and slid across the tips of his blood-covered fingers. Still dangling upside down, he coated his member with the sticky, wet blood and stroked himself to a climax.

Eeeeeiiiiiii!

***

On Route 309

"You're going the wrong way," Nipsy pointed out when The Reaper missed his turn and continued driving westbound. "Yo, you heard me, fam? I said you're going the wrong way. We was supposed to had turned off on Easton Road and took it all the way out until we hit Doylestown."

The Reaper didn't say a word. He just continued driving, moving the black utilities van at a calm 45 miles per hour. His right hand was gripping the steering wheel, and his left hand was gently caressing the shotgun that was laying across his lap. The sawed-off barrel was slightly arched, propped up on his right knee and aimed at Nipsy who was leaning forward in the passenger's seat. But Nipsy didn't even dig it, he was too busy looking out the window and shaking his head, as they proceeded in the wrong direction.

"Yo, my man!" Nipsy continued with heavy bass in his voice, mistakenly believing he was the one calling the shots. "You ain't heard what the fuck I said? Sonny gave us strict orders to drive out to The Swamp and get ready for what he's got planned for that bitch. Now, turn this muthafucka around and bang a left on Easton Road."

The Reaper looked at him and laughed. Not only was he seconds away from claiming another victim, he was envisioning the look on Sonny's face when he realized he sent the wrong muthafucka to kidnap and torture his wife. Had the young hustla done his homework, he would have learned that "Double R" didn't stand for Rayon the Reaper. Rather, the Double R was an acronym for *Rayon*

Rines. He was Daphney's uncle and the younger brother of Alvin Rines, the incarcerated boss of the Young Black Mafia.

In the late eighties and early nineties, acting on the orders of his older brother, Rayon was the one who made the competition *lay down* when they didn't want to *get down.*

The two-man tandem was simple: Alvin was the businessman and Rayon was the killer. But in 1994, when Alvin went to prison, Rayon was reduced to being a contract killer, freelancing his murder game to different upstarts throughout the city, Mook being one of them.

For twenty years, he was forced to lay dormant, just waiting for Alvin to give him the green light to resurrect the YBM. And now that Sonny was waging war on their family by commissioning the murder of Daphney, Rayon knew that would be enough to persuade Alvin to take him off the bench and put him back in the game.

"Fuck is you laughing at?" Nipsy lashed out, screwing his face at the old school gangsta. "What'chu think this shit a game, nigga? Sonny said—"

Boom!

An atomic blast from the shotty flipped Nipsy out of his seat and left him dangling through the busted-out window. The front of his face was somewhere across the street, and the top of his dome was rolling down the highway like a spent hubcap.

"That's what the fuck I'm laughing at," The Reaper replied in a cold, sinister voice.

His eardrums were ringing from the blast and he was covered in Nipsy's blood, but he didn't give a fuck. To him, it was just another day at the office.

He used the tip of the shotty to push Nipsy's body out the window and then settled back in his seat and continued driving westbound. The plan was to scoop up Daphney, then report back to Alvin.

But little did he know, things had just become more complicated than he could have ever imagined.

***

Back at Club Infamous

The entire dance floor was covered in smoke and the only thing Sonny could see were the fifteen or so fireballs that erupted from the M-16s below.

He was doing his best to hold it down, but the incoming gunfire was just too much. A blistering hot slug ripped through his left arm, forcing him to drop the Thompson. He reached down to scoop it up, and another bullet crashed into his chest and left him stretched out on the floor, spread eagle.

"Umm, fuck!" Sonny groaned from the pain.

He rolled over on his side and coughed up a snot-laced clump of burgundy goop. His insides were on fire—it felt like a hot knife had been jammed in his rib cage and twisted around every time he attempted to breathe. The malignancy of the pain was so intense, that although he was wearing a bulletproof vest, he didn't doubt for a second the bullet had gone through. He coughed up another wad of blood and shook away the dizziness that was quickly overwhelming him.

"I gotta—bust back," Sonny coached himself, refusing to die like a bitch-nigga. His left arm was mangled and twisted, so he rummaged around with his right hand desperately searching for the Thompson. When he couldn't find it, he attempted to look around, but the smoke from the dance floor had seeped in through the window, turning the room into a thick, hazy fog and he could barely see.

He tried to sit up, but a daggering pain shot through his chest and had him screaming like a banshee.

Suddenly, the gunfire stopped and the sound of footsteps running up the back staircase brought tears to his eyes.

Growing up in the game, he knew the day would come when he was forced to taste death. He just never imagined that day would come so soon.

Images of his mother and daughter flooded his mind, as his entire life flashed before his eyes. He could see himself at the age of three sitting in the back seat of his father's Benz. He could also see himself at the age of sixteen, dressed in all black, gun in hand, ready to catch his first body.

The life of a G, Sonny smiled and then coughed up another wad of blood. The hot fire scorching his insides simmered to an icy chill, and he could feel himself slipping away.

The eerie sound of footsteps running up the staircase grew louder and louder and off in the distance, he heard the blaring of a two-way radio. He also heard the voice of a white man calling out for help, alerting his dispatch that four officers were dead and that six more needed medical attention.

"Four officers dead?" Sonny questioned his hearing. *"And six more need medical attention? Yo, this rat-ass nigga put the boys on me?"*

The door to the Block Boy Room flew open and one of the shooters stepped inside. His M-16 was aimed at Sonny's face, and a black ski-mask covered his. A silver badge hung from his neck, and the word *SWAT* was written across the front of his vest in big bold letters. Seeing that Sonny was no longer a threat, he lowered his weapon and activated his two-way.

"This is Sergeant Lorenzo from Unit One. The suspect is in custody. I repeat, the suspect is in custody. He appears to be suffering from multiple gunshot wounds, so send up an E.M.T. We need to keep this one alive."

Still coughing and struggling to breathe, Sonny looked up at the officer and shook his head in disbelief. Instead of Grip and his goons, he now realized he'd been banging it out with the PPD.

The thought alone made him sick to his stomach. Aside from the headless bodies of the twins and the three hundred keys that were stashed downstairs in the basement, he knew that the killing of four police officers was more than enough to get him the death penalty.

It didn't even matter he was sitting on millions, as no amount of money could make a case of this magnitude go away. So, whether it be the gunshot wound to his chest or the needle the judge would surely stick in his arm, the life he knew was essentially over.

"Sontino Moreno," Sergeant Lorenzo addressed him, as he whipped out a pair of handcuffs. "On behalf of the citizens of Philadelphia and the Commonwealth of Pennsylvania, I am hereby placing you under arrest. Your black ass belongs to us now."

Welcome to Blood of a Boss IV: Rahmello's Betrayal

Prologue
The Conglomerate

The grand ballroom in The Waldorf Astoria was the personification of opulence. Priceless arts and Italian sculptures decorated the walls. Silk drapes with cashmere linings covered the windows and glistening chandeliers with crystals and platinum hung low from the ceiling, illuminating the room with a sparkling glow.

In the center of the room, spread across a long, oval mahogany table, were the remnants of a delicious feast. The waiters and hostesses were long gone. The security cameras had been deactivated two hours earlier. And it was now time to get down to business.

"Alright, ladies and gentleman, let's get this thing over with," Big Angolo spoke from the 42" television that had been placed at the head of the table.

Skinny, sick and looking more fragile than ever before, the old mafia don was present via Skype. He appeared on the screen just a few seconds earlier, and every eye in the room was fixed on him. Any and all conversations came to an abrupt halt, as the entire room became dead silent, so quiet that the only sound was the soft whoosh of warm air blowing out the ventilation system.

Slowly, yet brief and precise, the old man glanced around the room, taking inventory of the ten bosses in attendance. From right to left, he studied them closely, already knowing that at least one of them had played a role in the demise of his first-born son, and that a few others had already taken sides with Grip.

Seated to his right, was Vladimir Pulvochick from Russia. He was big and burly, with stout shoulders and a broad neck. His curly locks and cleaned shaved face gave him a look of civility, but Big Angolo knew better. The bear-like Russian was brutal and fierce. A master in the art of torture, he was more than capable of picking out the strongest man and breaking his will before he, himself, broke into a sweat. His services were much needed and appreciated, and depending on the outcome of this sit down, a few people seated around the table could very well be the next to unfortunately experience his wrath.

Seated to Vladimir's right, was *The Madam*, Geraldine François from Haiti. She was more beautiful than Big Angolo remembered, but just as deadly as the day he met her.

Seated beside Geraldine, was Sergio Victoro from Sicily. He was dressed in a cranberry smoking jacket, taking long pulls on a skinny brown cigarette. His criminal borgata was responsible for 40% of the heroin coming into the states, and had been that way since the French Connection of the 70's.

The next one down the line was Joaquin Alverez, the jeffe of the Sinaloa Cartel. His escape from a Mexican prison camp was a smooth one, courtesy of Gangsta and the fraudulent documents that were signed and stamped by Judge Johnson. However, despite being free, he was bubbling with anger. His son, Roberto, had been snuffed out in cold blood, and the jeffe wanted answers.

Seated to his right, was Su Kasaki from Japan. The beautiful Asian was the sole heir to the infamous Black Dragon Dynasty. Her diamond white Kimono was covered in black dragons, and her slanted black eyes were locked on Big Angolo's. She greeted the don with a slight bow of the head, and Big Angolo returned the gesture. Her late father, Su Jing Kasaki, had been his closest ally for nearly forty years. So, naturally, the bond between the two families was still intact.

Still looking around the table, Big Angolo settled his gaze on Kim Lee from China. The little man was quiet, yet calculated and ferocious. He was situated in the heart of Beijing, but his criminal enterprise stretched all the way over to San Francisco. He was arguably the wealthiest man seated at the table.

Directly to his right, was Mumar Khalifi from Saudi Arabia. His turban and sunglasses were jet-black, the same as his cold, cruel heart. Influenced by the C.I.A., his religious sect was responsible for many atrocities all throughout the middle east. These mayhems, though disturbing and inhumane, had been perpetrated by the U.S. government solely for the sake of stepping in and regulating the oil rich peninsula. Big Angolo couldn't stand Mumar, and the cocky

Arab knew it. But because he'd been handpicked by the C.I.A. to do their dirty work, there was nothing Big Angolo could do to have him removed from the roundtable. It was better to remain silent and roll with the punches, knowing the day would eventually come when Mumar's treachery against his own people would come back to haunt him. The C.I.A. would use him up and then throw him away like yesterday's trash, the same as they had done to Saddam. Big Angolo looked at Mumar and smiled. He was thinking about his late boss, Lucky Luciano. Specifically, the statement Lucky made on the night he was exiled and sent back to Italy. *"The cat's gonna always eat the mouse that it plays with, Angie. Always. And don't you ever forget that."*

Shaking his head at Mumar's stupidity, Big Angolo looked down at the dark skinned African, who was seated at the far end of the table. The son of a Yoruba chief, Abidemi Odeniyi was a consulate to the president of Nigeria. At the young age of thirty-six, his oil fields and diamond mines made him a billionaire three times over. Equipped with an army of five thousand, he was hands down the most powerful man seated at the table.

The man to his right, was Juan Nunes, the boss of the Medellin Cartel. His dark Versace frames were aimed at Big Angolo, but his beady black eyes were fixed on Joaquin. He was wondering if the Mexican drug lord knew about his involvement in his son's murder. But the more Juan thought about it, the more he realized that Joaquin was none the wiser. Because had he known, surely Joaquin would have made a move right then and there. The Sinaloa boss looked over at Juan, and Juan tightened his grasp around the handle of his compact 9mm. It was tucked under the table and aimed at Joaquin's stomach. One move and the Mexican was dead.

Felix Dubois, the last of the ten bosses, was seated right beside him. The billionaire playboy from France was a tech tycoon, who had a fetish for fine arts and beautiful women. His lineage was royal, dating all the way back to King Louis XIV. He noticed the gun under the table, but he didn't say a word. So long as the barrel wasn't aimed at him, he couldn't have cared less. He was more concerned about the state of The Conglomerate and the impending shift of power.

Only few people at the table were privy to his intentions, as they too had already taken sides with Grip.

A hand appeared on the screen, handing him a cup of cold water. Big Angolo knocked it down in one big gulp.

"Thanks, Mitchie," he said to the U.S. Marshal, who was standing outside the realm of the camera.

"Alright," the old man continued, returning his gaze to the table of bosses. "As you can see, I'm not doing too well, so I wanna make this quick. There's been a lot of turmoil going on these past couple of days, but from here on out, any friction between the families seated at this table must stop. And I understand that blood has been spilt, trust me, I do. But as the boss of all bosses, it is up to me to assure that all moves made by the men and women at this table are made in the furtherance of this organization. Señor Alvarez," he looked at Joaquin, "you have my deepest sympathy for what has happened to your son, Roberto. Yesterday, I, too, lost a son and a grandson. Both of which I have reason to believe were murdered by members of your organization. Was I angry and revengeful?" He squinted his eyes. "Absolutely. But did I act on those feelings? No. Instead, I arranged to have you released from custody. Why? Because it was best for business. My revenge would have only made things worse." He took a deep breath and coughed some more. "So, from here on out, I'm issuing a peace treaty, and anyone in violation shall face the cumulative wrath of everyone else seated around this table. If everyone is in agreement, say I."

"I," the bosses stated in unison, already knowing that their votes didn't matter either way. They were more or less going through the motions. Because once Big Angolo said something, it was already considered law.

"Good," Big Angolo said with a nod of the head. He coughed a little more and then gestured for Mitchell to give him a refill.

He handed over the empty cup and few seconds later, he was handed back a fresh cup of cold water. He sucked down a couple of sips and then placed the cup on table.

"Alright, now the next order of business is what you all already know. My cancer has been upgraded to a stage four, so obviously my reign as the head of this conglomerate is coming to an end. However, in accordance to the tradition that was set by Mr. Luciano, as the boss of all bosses, it is solely up to me to select the next boss. A few of you have already gone behind my back and declared your support for Gervin. I won't mention any names, but I already know who you are. And quite frankly, I don't blame you. At one point in time, I was also in favor of Gervin. Not only him, but Little Angolo as well. Together, my two sons were destined to rule with equal power. But because of their hate for one another and their discontent to carry out my wishes, all of that has changed. Little Angolo is gone," he cut his eye at Joaquin, "and Gervin is no longer in good standings with this conglomerate. So, because of this, I am now considering a new appointment. A few of you have aspirations to obtain this position. But it is only right that I inform you, that although your aspirations are being taken into consideration, I am strongly leaning toward my great-grandson, Sontino Moreno, as the next boss of this conglomerate."

The entire room erupted in chatter, as many of the bosses had never heard of Sonny. And those who did, were already aware of his latest arrest.

"Quiet!" Big Angolo raised his voice. "Goddamnit! I want quiet! Now!"

The chattering ceased to low whispers, then ultimately settled to an eerie silence.

Big Angolo took another sip of water followed by a blast of fresh air from his oxygen tank. Looking around the table, he studied the faces of the bosses, checking for any signs of dissension. Right away, he noticed that Juan Nunes had his lip curled. "Is there anything you would like to say, Mr. Nunes? Because it seems as though you have a problem with my line of thinking."

"Actually, I do," Juan replied, refusing to hold his tongue. "Notwithstanding Sontino may never again see de streets, he is only a kid, not even thirty years of age. How can we expect for somebody so young and inexperienced to handle such a responsibility?"

"The inexperience that you speak of, Mr. Nunes, could very well be attributed to every one seated around this table," Big Angolo replied, glancing around the room. "None of you could ever say that you're capable of, or even strong enough to carry a crown so heavy, because this is a burden that has never been bestowed upon you."

"Excuse me, Don Angolo," Madam François interjected, raising her hand. "With all due respect, the consequences of carrying such weight is a responsibility like no other? How can you, or we" she pointed around the table, "be so sure that Sontino is strong enough to carry such weight? As you already know, I have strong ties with the Moreno Family, and although I do not know Sontino personally, I have more than enough information to assume that he could very well work out, with the proper guidance and assistance of course. But in the wake of his latest legal woes, who's to say how all of this will even turn out?"

"I agree," said Felix Debois. He was leaned forward and looking around the table. "Like The Madam, here, I've also been made aware of Sontino Moreno. And while I must admit that I'm very impressed with the young man, I do, however, harbor a number of concerns. Especially in regards to his legal trouble. Who's to say that he won't expose any of us in order to save himself? Namely, Mr. Nunes to my left. According to my sources, for the past year or so, Mr. Nunes has been supplying Sontino with mass quantities of cocaine. Surely, in the face of such weary, with a death sentence looming above his head, Mr. Nunes could very well be the bargaining chip the government throws his way. Who's to say Sontino won't take it? Who's to say he won't reveal to the government whatever it is that he already knows about us? Who's to say?"

"I agree," Abidemi cosigned, in his thick Nigerian accent.

"Me, too," added Sergio and a few others. They were looking around the table at one another and nodding their heads in agreement.

But little did they know, they were playing right into Big Angolo's hand. He knew that in order for the bosses to take Sonny seriously, he would first have to prove his loyalty. He would also need to prove that his character was iron clad and that in the face of adversity, he was willing to stand tall without compromising his principles and morals.

So, in order to put his great-grandson to the test, Big Angolo set the wheels into motion to have Sonny arrested. He just never imagined that Sonny would shoot it out and murder a bunch of cops in the process. But even still, all of this played into Sonny's favor. All he had to do was hold his water and stand firm. Because then and only then, would the bosses respect his newly appointed position.

"I understand exactly where some of you's are coming from," Big Angolo spoke in a strained, raspy voice. "But once again, let me state for the record that my decision is not yet final. As far as Sontino's legal issues, the way I see it, they can cut one of two ways. On the one hand, we could easily arrange to have him released from custody. But on the other hand, what better way to test a man's integrity than to leave him assed out in a desperate situation, only to see whether or not he would give up someone else in order to save himself. It's sorta like the Prophet Job. The devil told God that Job was only faithful and true because of the hedge that had been placed over him, and that if God removed that hedge, then surly Job would curse Him. Well, in this case, when it pertains to Sontino, that hedge has already been removed. So, depending on how he conducts himself moving forward, that will determine the outcome of what we all know is sure to take place. If he stands firm, he's appointed as the new boss of this roundtable."

"And if he doesn't?" Felix questioned, speaking on behalf of the remaining bosses.

"Then he dies," Big Angolo replied with a straight face. He coughed long and hard, then he snatched up his oxygen mask and placed it against his face. He breathed in and out, in and out, and then shook away the dizzy spell that was beginning to overwhelm him. "That's it, I need to lay down and get some rest," he announced with another cough. "All in agreement, say I."

"I," they replied in unison.

"Good." Big Angolo coughed some more. "Meeting's adjourned."

Askari

Chapter One
A year and a half later…
June 1, 2016

La Casa Moreno's home theater was the epitome of lavishness. The fifteen-foot-high walls were deliciously painted the same color as eggnog: chocolate marble, octagon tiles decorated the floor and in the back-right corner, spiraling up the wall and connecting to a balcony overlooking the entire room, was a curving staircase with crystal balusters and sycamore stairs. Directly under the balcony, perched up on an angle, were three elevated rows of Cappuccino-colored, ostrich skin theater seats. Each row consisted of five seats, and the seats were separated by a three-foot platform and a two-step drop.

Comfortably attired in a Balenciaga short set, Rahmello was stretched out on the third seat in the front row. His crispy white Dior Homme sneakers were propped up on an ostrich skin ottoman, and his blue eyes were glued to the projection screen on the front wall. He was watching the Five O'clock News, and like always, the local media was fixated on what was sure to be the trial of the century— *The Commonwealth of Pennsylvania -vs- Sontino Moreno.* Listening to the information he already knew, Rahmello fired up a Backwood and took a slow, deep pull.

"It was right here, at the Criminal Justice Center in downtown Philadelphia, where district judge, The Honorable Paul Rogers, dismissed fifteen of the twenty-two charges against Black Mafia don, Sontino 'Sonny' Moreno," stated Roland Rushin, the lead correspondent for Fox News. He was standing on the corner of 13th and Filbert, right outside of the double doors that led to the courtroom.

"According to Judge Rogers, in his controversial decision, there was no legal justification for the raid on Mr. Moreno's nightclub. There was no probable cause and no search warrant, and as a result, fifteen of the twenty-two charges against Mr. Moreno were dismissed without prejudice. These charges include," he looked down at the piece of paper in his hand and then brought his gaze

back to the camera, *"six counts of murder, six counts of attempted murder, one count of reckless endangerment, one count for the possession of a stolen firearm, and the last count being the possession of a cocaine with the intent to deliver.*

"Wait a second, folks," he spun around to face the double doors, where Savino was emerging from the courthouse, *"here he is now, the defense team's lead attorney, Mr. Mario Savino."*

The dapper attorney was dipped fresh in a navy-blue Versace suit. A black briefcase was clutched in his right hand and a satisfying smile was plastered across his olive-complexioned face. He was accompanied by two paralegals and three attorneys from his defense team.

"Mr. Savino," the reporter jammed his microphone directly in front of Savino's face, *"the defense struck a heck of a blow in the courtroom today. Is there anything you would like to convey to the public?"*

"Absolutely," Savino confirmed, as he smiled for the cameras. *"First and foremost, not only is my client not guilty, he's the scapegoat of a biased and overzealous police department, simply because his last name is Moreno."* He took a deep breath and shook his head, putting on a show for the cameras. *"You know, it's really a shame when you think about it. In this great nation of ours, the United States of America, the land of the free and the home of the brave, and a young man is being persecuted, based solely on the premise of his last name? My client, Sontino Moreno, is a staple in the community. He's a loving father, an entrepreneur, and his ongoing charity to the disenfranchised cannot be overlooked, nor denied. Mr. Moreno is an innocent man, and we will not stop fighting until the bells of justice ring loud and clear."*

"Well, I certainly agree with one thing you just stated," Roland Rushin acknowledged, bringing the microphone back to his face, *"and that's Mr. Moreno's ongoing philanthropy. I've personally covered a number of his charity events and without a doubt, he's proven to be a champion in that regard. Now, with that being said, it is only right that I mention the remaining seven charges against your client. At least one of them involving the shooting death of*

Philadelphia Police Officer, Jason Clifford back in December of two-thousand and twelve."

"Once again, Sontino Moreno is an innocent man. And I can personally guarantee, that if this case should so happen to make it to trial, Mr. Moreno will without a doubt be acquitted on all charges."

Roland Rushin perked up and quickly pounced on the opportunity to stir up some drama. Bringing the microphone back to his face, he said, *"If? What exactly do you mean when you say the word 'if'? The Moreno Crime Family is notoriously known for making evidence and witnesses disappear before they ever reach a courtroom. So, is this something we should all look forward to, as this case proceeds to trial?"*

In the back of Savino's mind, he could literally see himself slapping the shit out of Roland Rushin. But for the sake of the cameras, he laughed it off and shook his head dismissively. *"You media guys,"* he wagged his index finger directly in front of Roland's face, *"you guys are truly something else, always looking to start a firestorm. Now, in regards to the accusation you just made against me and my client, not only was it unacceptable and slanderous, it was facially unfounded and could not have been further from the truth."* He looked directly into the Fox News camera and adjusted his necktie. *"Sontino Moreno is an innocent man and you can take that to the bank."*

As Savino moved away from the crowd and climbed in the back of his waiting Escalade, Rahmello blew out a thick cloud of smoke and stared up at the ceiling. He was thinking back to the night that changed everything, the same night Sonny was arrested.

December 12, 2014

"What the fuck is this?" Grip blurted out loud, as he and Rahmello found themselves in a traffic jam on Broad and Tioga.

Up ahead, he could clearly see the cop cars, paddy-wagons, and mobile units that were stationed outside of Infamous. The PPD were everywhere!

In addition to the twenty or so Swat Team members, there were dozens of uniformed and plainclothes officers, all of them standing around and mean-mugging the growing crowd of spectators. They even had police officers on horseback, who were trotting up and down Broad Street ordering the spectators to either keep it moving or return to their vehicles.

Another officer was standing in the middle of the street with a bright green, fluorescent vest. He had a glowing wand in each hand, and was desperately trying to make a lane for the three ambulances that were also wedged in the thick of traffic.

Ironically, the Temple University Hospital was just two blocks away from the deadliest crime that had ever been committed against Philadelphia's finest.

"Damnit, Sontino!" Grip banged his hand against the steering wheel. Being in the game for over fifty years, it didn't take long for him to figure out exactly what was going on.

"Was it the Mexicans?" Rahmello asked in a cracked voice. He was frantically looking around and trying to make sense of what happened. "They killed him, didn't they? They got to Sonny before we did."

Grip took a deep breath and sighed. "I wish it were that simple."

"Fuck you mean, you wish it was that simple?" Rahmello snarled at him. "That's my muthafuckin' brother."

"That's not what I was trying to say," Grip calmly replied. He was looking straight ahead and thinking of a way to ameliorate the danger that was surely coming his way. "Sontino's not dead, he's in jail."

"Jail?" Rahmello raised his voice. "And how the fuck you figure that? You don't see all these muthafuckin' cops out here? This ain't no ordinary drug bust, it's a muthafuckin' murder scene. Look!" He pointed up the street where a paramedic was pushing a sheet-covered stretcher. "That's Sontino, I know it is! Them pussy-ass Mexicans killed my fuckin' brother!" He pulled a Glock 40 from his waistband and cocked a bullet up into the chamber. "I don't give a fuck about nothing no more! Poncho and dem killed my pops, the Mexicans killed Sonny, and that rat-ass nigga, Bobby, was

fucking my bitch! Man, fuck that! I'm killing all these niggas!" He reached for the door handle, but Grip snatched him by the arm and slammed him back against the seat.

"*Goddamnit! Boy, calm your stupid ass down! Now, I done already told you Sontino's not dead, he's in jail.*"

"*Get'cha fuckin' hands off me!*" *Rahmello shouted, as he yanked his arm away. He anxiously bit down on his bottom lip and tightened his grasp on the Glock 40.* "*You got me twisted, Ol' Head, straight the fuck up.*"

"*Just calm down and hear me out,*" *Grip said in a much calmer voice, especially when he noticed that Rahmello had the .40 aimed at his stomach.* "*Sontino's not dead. If he were, then all of these cops wouldn't be cops out here. Why make such a fuss over another dead nigger? Right?*"

"*Right,*" *Rahmello was forced to agree.*

"*Right. So, the only reason they're out here throwing their weight around and showing unity is because one of their own must've got killed, and nine times out of ten, Sontino was the one who killed him. Now, how it came to that, I can't say. There's been a lot of shit going on these past few days. So, for all we know, somebody could have contacted the police and claimed to have seen something. Either way, the situation can't be good, especially for me.*"

"*Especially for you?*" *Rahmello scowled at him.* "*Nigga, ya ass ain't in no trouble, you sittin' here talking to me. Sonny's the one we need to be worried about, and ya ass got the nerve to be thinking about ya'self? Yo, that's crazy, Grip. Straight up, you'sa selfish muthafucka.*"

Grip closed his eyes and massaged his temples. He chose his next words carefully. "*They're gonna try to use Sontino to come and get me. The same way they tried to use Alvin. I wasn't worried about Alvin, because Alvin was my protégé, I raised him. But Sontino...*"

"*Hold up. What'chu try'na say. Sontino's a rat? My brother ain't no fuckin' rat.*"

Grip took a deep breath and opened his eyes. "In this life, grandson, you can never underestimate another man's will to survive, especially when it comes down to him or you. The muthafuckas who you think are gonna stand tall, have a tendency to fold. Then, in some cases, the muthafuckas who you think are gonna fold, are the ones who stand tall. It's a tricky game, and don't you never forget that. The more a man has, the more he has to lose, and when you consider everything that he has to lose, you can assess his potential danger."

Both, grandfather and grandson, sat there in total silence. Neither one saying a word, just sifting through their own individual thoughts.

Outside of the Maybach, the red and blue lights from the cop cars and ambulances were flashing and beaming, with their sirens were blaring nonstop. But inside of the Maybach, Grip and Rahmello were zoned out, totally ignoring the pandemonium.

"Can you still drive with your leg all banged up?" Grip broke the silence.

"Yeah." Rahmello nodded his head and looked at him skeptically. "Why?"

"Because I need you to drive back to La Casa Moreno and lay low until the morning. Then after that, I need you to gather up the family and bring them back to the house."

"But I'm saying, though. What'chu going somewhere?"

"I need to get away for a while and think things through," Grip told him, unapologetically. "I'm assuming you'll be hearing from Gangsta any minute now, and when you do, tell him I returned to the source, and that I'm leaving you in charge for the time being."

"But what about Sonny? What about Oli and the meeting with The Conglomerate? What the fuck am I supposed to do?"

"As far as Sontino, he's is not in the position to do anything. And as far as your old lady and the situation with The Conglomerate, all of that is irrelevant now. The only thing I'm worried about is strategizing our next move." He placed his hand on Rahmello's shoulder and looked him square in the eyes. "The weight of our family is all on you now. Our enemies may or may not come after

you, but either way I need you to be strong. Now, can I trust you to hold things down in my absence?"

Rahmello didn't say a word, he just took a deep breath and slowly nodded his head.

"Good," Grip said as he patted Rahmello on the shoulder. He flipped the hood on his sweat shirt and climbed out of the Maybach. "And one more thing," he knelt down and popped his head back inside of the car, "bosses only sit at the table with reflections of themselves, and don't you ever forget that."

With that being said, the old man closed the door and then disappeared into the thick of the crowd.

Back to June 1, 2016

A total of seventeen months and nineteen days had passed and still no word from Grip. The same could be said about Gangsta, The Sinaloas, and the remaining bosses who represented The Conglomerate.

Rahmello's transition to power was an easy one, but to him, the concept of being the boss was way overrated.

Nipsy was found dead on the side of the road and it was basically just Rahmello and Heemy, and the little niggas Heemy had working the streets.

Aziz and Shabazz were still around, but mainly for security purposes. And at the end of the day, Sonny was the big homie still calling the shots, even from his jail cell. But Sonny was so paranoid and worried about the feds stepping in and claiming jurisdiction over his case, that he wouldn't even talk to Rahmello. All messages were sent through Savino, and even then, Sonny made it pellucid that Rahmello was not to engage in any criminal activity, nor anything else that could possibly be linked back to him.

Initially, Rahmello fell in line and did exactly as Sonny directed. But after a year or so, when his stash got low and the hunger pangs began to kick in, Rahmello was right back at it.

He reached out to Heemy and just like that, the grind was back on. Together, they quickly reclaimed ownership of their four most lucrative drug corners, linked up with a new connect, and it was back to business as usual. Only this time around, Heemy was the one running the show, and Rahmello played the background, coaching him from a distance.

Rahmello exhaled a thick cloud of Loud smoke and then grabbed the iPad that was laying on the theater seat beside him.

The customized device controlled everything in La Casa Moreno from the security cameras to the room temperatures.

So, after turning off the news, he switched over to the security camera in the nursery on the second floor. The first thing he saw was his beautiful fiancé, Olivia Nunez.

She was sitting in the rocking chair beside the crib, slowly rocking back and forth, tapping her foot against the carpet. Their eleventh month old son, Omelly Ervin Moreno, was carefully nestled in her loving arms and from the sounds of it, she appeared to be singing him a lullaby in Spanish.

Rahmello took another pull on his Backwood and cracked a smile. For six months he had to walk around uncertain as to whether or not him or Mexican Bobby fathered Olivia's child. It wasn't until Omelly was born and Rahmello saw his blue eyes that he knew they baby was his. It was then Rahmello made a vow to protect his baby's mother and future wife at all cost. So if Sonny or anyone else wanted to harm Olivia, they would certainly have to kill him first.

"Damn, I hope this nigga don't be on that bullshit when he comes home," Rahmello said to himself.

He was thinking about Sonny and the latest developments in his case. "Oli's family now, so that's something he's just gonna have to accept."

He started to hit the intercom button and pop in on Oli and Omelly, but decided he didn't want to disturb their mother and son moment.

So, instead, he pulled up the security cameras at the front gate, where a cocaine-white, 2015 Ford F-250 was waiting to gain entrance into the estate.

Aziz approached the driver's side window and then looked back at the security booth and motioned for Shabazz to open the gate.

The pickup truck eased through the open iron gate, cruised up the cobblestoned driveway, dipped around the water fountain and parked beside Rahmello's Lamborghini.

Rahmello glanced at his iced-out Patek Philippe and gritted his teeth. The platinum shorthand was resting on the quarter cut diamond that represented a five, and the platinum longhand was slowly itching across the third baguette from the red ruby that symbolized a twelve. It was a little past 5:00 p.m., and for the third time that week, Heemy was running late.

"Time is money," Rahmello mumbled under his breath. He took another pull on his Backwood and then stubbed it out in the ashtray.

He then pulled up the security cameras in the main hallway and cracked up laughing. "Fuck is these lil' bad asses doing now?" Keyonti and Imani were racing down the hallway with Rocko a few steps behind. They were quickly approaching the theater room and before Rahmello could take his eyes off the screen, they were already barging inside.

The two girls hopped on his lap and Rocko laid down on the floor beside the ottoman.

"Uncle Mello," Imani addressed him in a voice so innocent and sweet that it reeked of manipulation. "Can you get us some ice cream?"

"Yeah, Uncle Melly," Keyonti second her motion, "we want cream-cream."

Rahmello looked back and forth between his two nieces and shook his head in astonishment. The two girls were beyond beautiful.

Imani was the spitting image of Nahfisah. She had a buttery tan complexion and silky black hair that flowed down the length of her back. Keyonti, on the other hand, had a rich chocolate complexion, chubby cheeks, and curly black hair that was twisted into four pigtails.

Umm mmm mmm! The day I see a titty or a hip, I'm getting me a house full of shotguns! Rahmello thought to himself, as he admired their natural beauty.

Their thick African lips, European noses, and aqua-blue eyes gave them an exotic appearance, and Rahmello dreaded the day his little princesses would grow into the beautiful, black queens they were destined to be.

"Come on, Uncle Mello. Please?"

"Yeah, Uncle Melly. Pweeeeaaaase?"

"Not at all." Rahmello shook his head *no*. "It's almost dinner time, and y'all ain't gon' do nothing but spoil y'all appetites."

Both girls folded their arms across their chest and stuck out their bottom lip. Their beautiful blue eyes were locked on Rahmello's.

"Pwease," Keyonti whispered, as Imani nodded her head up and down and pressed her palms together as if she was praying.

"A'ight, man, damn," Rahmello caved in. His nieces had already experienced so much pain in their young lives that he refused to disappoint them, let alone deprive them of anything their hearts desired. "Come on y'all, let's go find Heldga," Rahmello said as he wrapped them in his arms and stood to his feet. "See if we can get her to fix us some ice cream."

Satisfied with their teamwork, the two little con artists looked at one another and smiled. Mission accomplished.

Chapter Two

Nahfisah was sitting in the passenger's side of Heemy's F-250, looking and feeling like her old self. Her French-vanilla skin was flawlessly smooth, and her silky black hair was glistening like the purest Nigerian oil. It was pulled back into a single braid and flowing down the front of her right shoulder. Her slender, but curvaceous frame was tightly wrapped in a cream, mid-thigh Mason Martin Margiela sundress, and her cinnamon Giuseppe pumps were a couple of shades darker than her crocodile Gucci clutch.

Me and lil' bro need to sit down and have us a muthafuckin discussion, Nahfisah thought to herself as she dug down in her Gucci clutch and extracted a zebra striped MacBook. *'Cause a bitch ain't feeling the fact she can't touch her own money. Then, on top of that, he's got his lil' puppy dog sniffing up my goddamned ass and following me around everywhere I go? I'm a grown-ass woman, I don't need no chaperone.*

After checking her reflection in the compact mirror, she looked over at Heemy and scoffed. The young hustla was sitting behind the steering wheel, texting back and forth with one of his street captains. A perplexed expression was plastered across his brown skinned face, and he was steadily flexing his jaw muscles.

"Little boy!" Nahfisah addressed him in a spicy voice. "Now is *not* the time for you to be texting one of your little thots. So, put'cha lil' phone away, grab my bags out the back and carry 'em up to the house. Chop! Chop!" She rudely clapped her hands in front of his face. "Let's get it."

Heemy didn't reply. He just looked at her like she was crazy, then he went right back to texting. He loved Sonny and Rahmello to death, but hated the details of his job.

Ever since Nahfisah was released from the rehabilitation center, Heemy was given the task of being her personal bodyguard. It wasn't an everyday, twenty-four-hour thing. And whenever Nahfisah needed to go somewhere, Heemy was the one responsible for taking her.

"My sister's fragile," Rahmello told him on the morning Nahfisah graduated from her drug program. *"And I know you got mad shit on ya plate, but out of everybody I fuck wit', you're the only one I trust. So, I'ma need you to keep an eye on her for me, and make sure she ain't out here chasing that shit. It's only for a couple of months, or until I'm confident she can stand on her own two feet."*

That was six months ago, and every day since, Heemy regretted the fact he told Rahmello *yes.*

Nahfisah was a tough cookie, a diva's diva, and Heemy couldn't stand her. All they ever did was argue and for the past three hours, he had to follow her around the King of Prussia Mall, carrying her shopping bags and putting up with her stank-ass attitude.

Heemy flat out despised the broad, and let *him* tell it, Nahfisah was a spoiled brat who walked around like her dookie was rose pedal fresh.

"Little boy!" Nahfisah continued to pester. "Did you hear what I just said?"

Silence.

Irritated by Heemy's nonchalant demeanor, Nahfisah sat there scowling at him. Truth be told, the butterfly lips on her throbbing pussy were slippery and wet and her almond-sized clitoris was beginning to pulsate. She was secretly sizing Heemy up from his V-neck tee, to his Gucci cargos and high-top Gucci Pythons. His neatly trimmed, wavy hair was connected to a razor sharp five o'clock shadow, and the fragrance of his Amber White body oil was doing something strange to her senses.

"So, you're just gonna sit there ignoring me, huh?"

Silence.

"Oh, is that right?" Nahfisah rolled her tongue and flirted with her eyes. She reached across the leather console and snatched away his iPhone. "I'll bet that ass won't ignore me now."

Yo, I know this bitch ain't just snatch away my muthafuckin' phone! Heemy fumed, as he sat there staring at his empty hands. He took a deep breath and counted backwards from ten to one, doing everything he possibly could to keep from smacking the shit out of her.

"Nigga, I don't care if you get mad," Nahfisah said with a smile. She started to say something else, but was cut short when Heemy reached over the console and gripped the front of her face with his left hand, not too rough, but strong enough to let her know he wasn't fucking around.

Nahfisah wanted to buck back and put up a protest, but the feeling of a man's touch was just oh so good! It had been nearly a year and a half since the last time she had her pussy stroked.

"From now on," Heemy snarled at her through clenched teeth, "whenever you're around me, ya silly ass better be on chills. Now, I don't know what'cha problem is, and truthfully, I don't give a fuck. But whatever it is, you better check that shit. You understand?"

"Umm-hmm!" Nahfisah spoke in a muffled voice.

"Good. Now, gimmie back my fucking phone."

Nahfisah handed Heemy the phone, and he stuffed it down in his front pocket. He released her face, then he reached in the back seat and grabbed the Gucci duffle that was laying on the floor.

Settling back in his seat, he flipped the lid on the leather console and removed the false bottom. Inside of his secret stash was stacks upon stacks of rubber banded bricks of money. He placed each of the stacks safely inside of the Gucci duffle and then hopped out the truck without saying another word.

"Well, zamn, zaddy, it's about time you checked a bitch," Nahfisah called out behind him, but not loud enough for Heemy to hear. She seductively bit down on her bottom lip and then spread her legs to give her kitty kat some much needed air. "But let's see how you act when I break ya lil' fine ass off with some of this snappa!"

***

When Heemy entered the house through the side door and stepped into the kitchen, he was immediately greeted by Imani and Keyonti.

"Hey, Heemy!" The little girls smiled at him. They loved themselves some Heemy.

"What's up, y'all?" Heemy returned their smiles, then he embraced them with warm hugs and kisses on their foreheads. "What's up, Ms. Heldga?" He smiled and waved at the old housekeeper. Heldga smiled back, but didn't say a word, as she was too busy preparing her homemade biscuits. Heemy laughed it off and shrugged his shoulders. "Hey, yo, Melloooo!" he called out to his big homie. "Yo, where you at, bro?"

"Hey, yo, Melloooo!" Nahfisah mocked, as she stepped into the kitchen behind him. Her Prada shades were propped up on her forehead, and her shopping bags from Niemen Marcus and the Polo Store were clutched in both hands. "Yo, Melloooo!" she called out once again. "Where you at, bro? I need to holla at'chu about ya nut-ass young bul!" She playfully scowled at Heemy and stuck her tongue out.

"Ugh!" Heemy shuddered, looking at her like she was the ugliest thing he had ever seen in his entire life.

"Hey, Mommy," Imani greeted her with a mouth full of Butter Pecan. She was seated at the marble island, right beside Keyonti, who was standing up in her highchair doing a happy dance.

"Well, hey to you, too, Puddin' Pop!" Nahfisah walked over and kissed her daughter on the cheek. Looking at Keyonti, she burst out laughing. The little girl was on a sugar high, bouncing up and down and singing a made-up song about her undying love for ice cream.

"Cream-cream so sweet to me! Yah! Yah! So sweet, sweet, sweet, sweet!"

"Fat-Fat? Girl, if you don't sit ya'self down in that highchair," Nahfisah chuckled, as she sat her bags down on the floor.

"Hey Auntie Nah-Nah." Keyonti smiled, inadvertently showing off the dimple in her left cheek. She plopped down in the highchair and held her spoon out to Nahfisah. "We got cream-cream, want some?"

"No, baby, that's okay." Nahfisah sighed. "All I wanna do is hop in the shower and take me a nice long nap. Speaking of which, Mani, when you're done eating your ice cream, can you take Mommy's bags upstairs to her room, please?"

"Umm-hmm." Imani nodded her head up and down. "I'ma do it right now." She knocked off the last scoop of ice cream, then she grabbed the bags off of the floor and headed down the hallway toward the elevator.

"Dang, Ms. Heldga, what'chu over there cooking?" Nahfisah asked. She inhaled deeply, taking in the savory aroma. "Whatever it is, it sure smells good."

"I'm fixing up the rice fried and the lamb stewed," the old woman replied in her broken English.

"Well, if you want me to, I can help."

"No, no, no!" Heldga shut her down with the quickness. "No more food you cook. It forever be bad. It taste to Heldga like lumpy water and Heldga no like waste food."

Heemy burst out laughing and Nahfisah shot him the ice-grill. "First of all," she stated with the snap of her neck, "you ain't gotta be laughing like that, 'cause it wasn't the fuck funny!" She grabbed one of Heldga's biscuits and cocked it back like a major league pitcher. "Now, keep laughing and I'ma bust you in ya shit!"

Heemy laughed even harder and Keyonti joined in on the fun. "Heemy bad, Auntie Nah-Nah. Get him!"

Nahfisah launched the biscuit, but Heemy ducked out of the way. The balled-up piece of dough tumbled through the air and clonked Rahmello on the nose when he stepped into the kitchen.

Nahfisah shrieked and covered her mouth with both hands, while Heemy looked away as if he didn't know what was going on. Heldga was standing there looking at Rahmello with a blank expression and Keyonti was leaned over the highchair laughing her ass off.

"Uncle Melly got powder on him face!" the little girl shouted and pointed at Rahmello's nose. "Auntie Nah-Nah, look! Him got a powder face!"

"Yo, what the fuck is y'all in here doing?" Rahmello lashed out, looking back and forth between Heemy and Nahfisah. "Y'all always got some bullshit going!"

"Boy, you better calm down. It ain't even that serious," Nahfisah chuckled. She grabbed a towel from the closet, then she meticulously wiped the residue away from his face.

Rahmello looked at her and smiled. "You're lucky it's your birthday next week."

"Umm-hmm, whatever." Nahfisah smiled back. "Instead of checking me, you need to be checking ya nut-ass homie, 'fore I *fuck* his lil' young ass up."

Rahmello looked at her with a raised brow and then fixed his sights on Heemy. "Well, goddamn, is it sum'n one of y'all wanna tell me?"

"Nizzaw," Heemy quickly denied. He knew exactly what Rahmello was insinuating. "Not at all, bro. Nothing even close."

Nahfisah scoffed, then walked over and grabbed Keyonti out of her highchair. "Come on, Fat-Fat, let's go try on the new clothes that Auntie Nah-Nah bought you?" Turning back around to face Rahmello, she asked, "Did you hear anything from S-o-n-n-y? You know, since the court hearing earlier today?" She knew better than to say Sonny's name out loud, because had she done so, Keyonti would have went into a frenzy.

"Nah, not yet." Rahmello shook his head. "But I'm linking up with Savino in a couple of hours and nine times out of ten, he's gonna have a message for me. Why, what's up?"

"Him," Nahfisah nodded at Heemy, "that's what's up. I'm tired of y'all having y'all lil' puppy dog following me around. So, I'ma need y'all to handle that."

"We'll talk about it later," Rahmello said, as she carried Keyonti out of the kitchen.

"So, what's up, bro? We gon' handle this or what?" Heemy patted the Gucci duffle that was still draped over his shoulder.

Rahmello looked at Heldga, who was standing in front of the stove and then gestured for Heemy to follow him outside to the back patio. "Come on, my nigga. Come holla at'cha boy-boy."

When they stepped outside and closed the door behind, Heemy handed Rahmello the duffle bag. "That's an M right there, exactly. I stayed up all night counting that shit. I've got the other six-hunnid and twenty-five-bands at the spot out Jersey. The plan was to scoop it up first thing this morning, but fucking wit' Nahfisah, I didn't get a chance to grab it yet. But that's the first thing I'm doing as soon as I leave here. I also gotta make my rounds and collect all the money from the traps. So, by the time we holla at the connect, everything should be straight."

Rahmello sat down on the porch chair at the edge of the patio and laid the Gucci duffle across his lap. He pulled the zipper back and extracted one of the rubber banded stacks. Things were slowly but surely getting back to normal.

At the beginning of each month, Rahmello would link up with his new connect and receive 50 keys on consignment at $30,000 per key. It was nothing even close to the 100 keys of raw he and Sonny used to purchase from Poncho, but the work was 100% pure, so he was still able to make shit pop.

Using the same manufacturing process that Sonny taught him when he first stepped in the game, Rahmello stretched the 50 keys into 62½, and stashed away the ½ of a key for a rainy day. He then gave Heemy 50 of the 62 keys on consignment, charging him $32,500 per key.

Heemy moved the keys at $35,000 a piece, generating a total of $1,750,000. He kept $125,000 for himself, then he turned the remaining $1,625,000 over to Rahmello, who also pocketed $125,000. The remaining 1.5 million was handed over to the connect, who in turn, hit Rahmello off with another shipment of 50 keys.

In true Block Boy fashion, the remaining 12 keys were divided amongst the four trap corners they still controlled. They had Fairhill & York, Franklin & Diamond, Delhi & Dauphin, and Delhi & Cumberland. The four corners were ran by a street captain, a caseworker, and two runners, all of them receiving $1,000 per week. So, after paying off their foot soldiers, Rahmello and Heemy each received an additional $44,920.

"A'ight." Rahmello nodded his head and tossed the stack of money back inside of the bag. "But other than that, what's poppin'?"

"That Almighty Five, you already know."

"More or less," Rahmello smiled. He grabbed the Backwood that was nestled above his left ear and then dug down in his pocket and pulled out a solid-gold, flameless lighter. With the Wood in his left hand and the lighter in his right, he placed them together and like magic, the tip of the Wood began to burn like a smoldering red ember. He took a couple of pulls and then passed the Wood to Heemy. "So, what's up wit'chu and my sister?"

Heemy looked at him skeptically. "What'chu mean what's up?"

"You and Nah-Nah? Yo, you know she's feeling you, right?"

"Nahfisah? *Feeling me?*" Heemy was taken aback. "Man, that girl can't stand me. She hates my fuckin' guts. And that mouth of hers—little boy this and little boy that, man that shit be getting on my muthafuckin' nerves. Then, on top of that, she be acting all bougie, talking like she a muthafuckin' queen, and I ain't nothing but a peasant."

"She is a queen."

"Oh, she's a'ight—*The Queen of the Damned!*" Heemy shot back, causing Rahmello to laugh. He took a pull on the Wood and inhaled deeply. "That shit ain't funny, bro. Like, she really be getting on my fuckin' nerves."

"You just gotta be patient wit' her, my nigga. She's been through a lot," Rahmello reminded him. "My entire family for that mattter. But she *is* beautiful, she's strong as hell and I love her to death. And the only reason I'm bringing this up is because it's obvious that Nah-Nah's feeling you, and because I wanted you to know this ain't no Scarface, Tony and Manolo type shit. I ain't asking you to fuck wit' my sister or no shit like that, I'm just letting you know that if it came down to it, I'm giving you the green light. You'sa real nigga and I respect ya hand. I'd rather it be you, than a lame-ass nigga I don't know and can't trust."

Heemy thought it over and quickly shook his head *no*. Nahfisah was without a doubt a bad bitch, one of the baddest that Heemy had ever been around, but her arrogant ways and stank attitude were two things he considered a turnoff. And above all else, he knew better than to mix business with pleasure. There was simply nothing to be gained by dealing with the boss' sister.

"I appreciate ya faith in me and all, but I would rather keep me and Nahfisah's relationship strictly business. And speaking of business, her calling me every five minutes and telling me to come pick her up is really starting to interfere with this money. For example, she just had me in the mall for like three hours walking around on some bullshit. I coulda used that time to pick up all the money from the traps and then shot out Trenton to pick up the rest." He looked at his iced-out Rollie and saw that the time was 5:31 p.m. "And I *still* gotta run around and collect that shit. So, basically, her little fake-ass shopping spree ate up the majority of my day." He hit the Backwood once more, then he passed it back to Rahmello.

"I was thinking the same exact thing," Rahmello said as he hit the Wood. The Loud smoke seeped from his mouth, shot up his nose and then came back out in a hazy, thick cloud. "Nah-Nah doesn't know it yet, but I'm finally ready to take her off the leash. So, for her birthday next week, I'ma bless her wit' a new car and the house I just bought her out in Willow Grove. After everything she's been through, she deserves it. She could have easily let her addiction get the best of her, but she didn't. She bounced back like a champ, and I'm proud of her. So, little by little, I'ma start breaking her off wit' the money my pops left her and give her some room so she can spread her wings."

"But, what about me?" Heemy asked. "Does that take me off the hook, or do I still gotta babysit her?"

Rahmello cracked up laughing, knowing Nahfisah had his boy burned out to the max. "Just one more week, my nigga, one more week. Then, after that, you can get back on ya grind full time wit' no distractions. I'm also thinking about upping our monthly shipment, and breaking off the street captains wit' some of these birds. I ain't decided yet, but I'm thinking about it. We've been flying under the radar long enough now. I'm ready to turn this shit back up and let these muthafuckas know the city is still ours."

Vrrrrm! Vrrrrrm! Vrrrrrm!

Heemy's iPhone began vibrating in his pants pocket. He pulled it out and saw he had another text message from his street captain, Keeno. He pressed down on the messenger bubble and began reading.

Keeno: 5:32 p.m.: *Damn, Heem, where the fuck is you at? She's still out here drawnin', talking all this dumb shit about calling the cops if don't nobody break her off wit' a couple of yams. I ain't try'na disrespect ya mom, bro, but she out here bugging. You need to hurry up and get here.*

Heemy: 5:33 p.m.: *I'm on my way.*

"What's up, Heem, you good?" Rahmello asked when he noticed the look on Heemy's face.

"Everything's straight, I just gotta shoot past my block real quick." He stuffed his iPhone back in his pocket, then he embraced Rahmello with their Block Boy handshake. "Eight-thirty, right? Donkees?"

"Yeah," Rahmello nodded his head, "and don't bring that big ass truck. Bring the SS."

"Say no more, brozay. Big business."

"Business as usual."

Chapter Three
At the County Jail

"Ninety-eight. Ninety-nine. A hunnid," Sonny grimaced, as he finished his tenth set of one hundred push-ups.

Dressed in nothing but his Polo boxers, he hopped up on his feet with beads of sweat trickling down his chiseled chest and rock-hard abs.

Instinctively, he looked at the bullet wound on his left arm and traced his fingertips along the zipper that lined the front of his torso. A similar scar was sliced across the right side of his back, trailing from his inner shoulder to the bottom of his ribcage. It was there, in a shrewd attempt to save his life, the doctors had to cut him open and remove his right lung. It had taken nearly a year for Sonny to recover. But after six months of eating right, no alcohol and no Loud, and working out three times a day, he was back better than ever.

His five-foot-eleven-inched frame was bulky and ripped and packed with an additional twenty pounds of muscle. His light beige complexion had a vibrant glow, and his silky black hair was still wavy and sharp. The only noticeable difference was that his once smooth baby face was now covered with a thick, curly beard.

I know them pussies mad as hell that arrest warrant came up missing, Sonny thought to himself, reflecting back on the court hearing earlier that day. *"But I wonder who took it. I know it wasn't Savino 'cause if it was, he woulda told me. It was prob'bly that crafty-ass Grip. Knowing him, he's gonna spin it around like he did it to save me. When in all actuality, he only did it to save himself, assuming that if he didn't, I'ma turn around and rat him out. Ol' grimy-ass nigga.*

Sonny walked over to the sink at the front of his cell and splashed his face with two scoops of cold water. He would never admit it, but being in jail was beginning to take its toll.

The glitz and glam of being a boss was more like a dream, rather than the lifestyle he left behind. Now, it was just cold hard penitentiary steel and every element that came along with it—fake niggas telling fake-ass stories, ten-minute phone calls twice a day, commissary once a week and tiny little food trays covered in slop. And because every inmate basically had the same exact shit, a crackhead could get his weight up, perform his little crackhead hustles, stack his commissary and then walk around the jail like he owned the place.

The shit was bonkers and without a doubt, Sonny was running out of patience. To make matters worse, not a day went by where his face wasn't on the news and due to his hood star status, he instantly became a target when he first stepped in the building.

Seeing that Sonny was wounded and what appeared to be vulnerability, a couple of young niggas from South Philly tried to press him for $100K a piece. Big mistake.

The two men were bailed out of county that very same night and were never seen or heard from again. Their final destination was The Swamp.

From that day forward, Sonny's time in the county was smooth and at his own pace, as every soul in the building quickly realized the Moreno Family was real.

"Sontino," a feminine voice called his name. He looked to his left and saw the block officer, Alexis Jones a/k/a *Miss Jonesey*.

The brown skinned beauty was staring at him through the cell door window. Her hungry eyes feasting on his body with a famishing lust.

Sonny peeped game and spoke with a slight chuckle. "Damn, Lexi, what's up? You looking at a nigga like I did something wrong."

"Nah, you didn't do anything wrong," she calmly replied, looking at the front of his boxers where his massive print was threatening to spill out from behind the slit. "I was just checking to make sure you didn't have any contraband. You don't have any contraband, do you?"

"Contraband?" Sonny licked his lips. "This look like contraband to you?" He pulled his dick out and let it dangle between his legs. "Oops, my bad. So, I guess I'm in trouble now, huh?"

"You most definitely are, sir." She looked up at the bubble to make sure her partner was watching her back and then popped his cell door and slipped inside. The entire housing unit was down at the gym, so the last thing she was worried about was any of the inmates seeing her.

Gripping his wood with his left hand, Sonny backed up and gave her some room.

At five-foot-four, one hundred and thirty-five pounds, the cinnamon beauty was thick and juicy, just the way he liked it. She was just as beautiful as the day he first met her back in the tenth grade, back when they were two teenagers pissy drunk from their first taste of puppy love.

That was ten years ago, 2005, the same year Sonny got locked up and sent to juvie. But even at the age of sixteen, Alexis was the true definition of a ryder.

For his first year, not a day went by where Alexis didn't send him at least one letter. And every Friday, she sent him a couple of dollars so he could purchase a few items from the canteen. But by the time Sonny came home from serving his two-year bit, Alexis was gone. She and her family had moved back to New Orleans, where they were forced to evacuate in the wake of Hurricane Katrina.

Ironically, about five months ago, Alexis returned to Philly and linked up with Nahfisah. When Nahfisah told her about Sonny and what he was locked up for, Alexis, using her family's connections, got a job in the county as a c/o. Her only intention was to have Sonny's back, and if possible, find a way to get her baby out of there.

"So, what's up, Daddy? You miss me?"

"Hell yeah, I missed you. You know a nigga be stressing when I can't see you. If it was up to me, ya sexy ass wouldn't never have no days off."

"Is that right?" Alexis asked, slowly closing the distance between them. She wrapped her arms around his waist and kissed the scar on his chest, loving the taste of his sweat. "So, if you miss me the way you say you do, then why is it that you haven't kissed me yet?"

Sonny gripped her by the ass and pulled her in close. Slowly and lovingly, he placed soft kisses on the tip of her nose and then leaned his head to the side and pressed lips against hers.

"These lips of yours," Alexis moaned in between kisses, "damnit they're so soft." She nibbled on his juicy lips and then tongued him down like her life depended on it. Her tender kisses traveled from his neck, to his shoulders, to his chest and abs and then finally settled on his plum-sized head. She twisted her tongue all around it, then opened up wide and brought his every inch to the back of her throat. "Mmmmmm!" Alexis moaned with a mouthful of dick. She squeezed his ass and mouth-fucked him with no hands.

"Goddamn," Sonny groaned. He closed his eyes and leaned his head back. Her mouth was so warm and wet that it felt like a pussy.

Alexis was giving him the business. She popped his dick of out of her mouth, spat on it and stroked him with both hands. Still stroking, she slurped on his head and gunned him at a nice steady pace. She was humming and moaning, slurping and sopping, sucking him so good that his legs began to buckle.

"Yo.Yo! How much time we got?" Sonny panted. He knew by the tingling of his toes and the throbbing in his balls that if he didn't stop her, he would bust a nut and miss his opportunity to play up in the pussy.

She kissed his dick once more and then glanced at her watch. "Shelly's in the bubble watching out for Sarge and L.T.. They went on break about ten minutes ago, so we got about twenty minutes left." She slipped out of her pants and thongs and then sashayed over to the desk in the back of his cell. "So, how you want it, Daddy? You want it like this?" She leaned over the desk and arched her back. The sight of her super phat ass and thick thighs made his mouth water.

"Nizzaw. I got something else in mind," Sonny replied, looking down at her fat, fuzzy peach. It was sprouting out from between her thighs, begging him to stretch and stroke it. He grabbed her by the waist and sat her on the top bunk.

52

"Damn, Daddy, that's how you feel?" Alexis smiled at him. She spread her legs and seductively licked her lips. "Well, come get it, then."

With no time to waste, Sonny dipped his tongue deep inside of her pussy. He sucked and nibbled, finger-fucked and sucked on her pussy some more. He wrapped his lips around her clitoris and sucked it nice and slow, all the while massaging her with the tip of his tongue. His cream-coated fingers were steadily jabbing her walls, twisting all around and massaging her G-spot. She grabbed the back of his head and thrust her pussy against his face.

"Damn, I love the way you suck my pussy."

Fully aroused, Sonny snatched her off of the bunk and carried her around the cell, tonguing her down something vicious. Her legs were cradled in his arms and her phat ass was clutched in his hands. He pushed himself inside of her, and Alexis gasped.

"Oh, my God, you feel so fucking good." She bit into left side of his neck, as he lifted her body up and down on his dick. "Fuck me, Daddy. Fuck me."

Sonny obliged. He stretched her so deep and wide that her entire body began to shake. A creamy gush of hot cum covered his dick and balls, but Sonny wasn't finished.

Still long-stroking the pussy, he carried Alexis over to the sink and sat her down on the edge. Grinding his hips at a nice, slow pace, he stood up on his tippy-toes and stroked her from another angle.

"Umm. *Fuck!*" Sonny moaned, desperately fighting to keep his composure. Her pussy was so creamy and moist, that it began talking—sopping, popping and gasping for air. "Goddamn, you got some good-ass pussy, girl! Shit!" His balls began to tingle and before he knew it, he closed his eyes and released his seeds deep in her womb.

The feeling of his hot cum splashing her insides drove Alexis over the edge. She gripped his ass and pulled him closer. "Give it to me, Daddy! Gimmie that shit!" She cried out, cumming on his dick for the second time.

After holding one another for the next few minutes, Sonny kissed her on the forehead, then he released a long, heavy sigh.

"Damn, I wish I could hold you like this forever, twenty-four-seven, without ever having to worry about a muthafucka catching us." He kissed her passionately and then stepped back and helped her down from the sink.

"Our time is gonna come, bae. You just wait and see." She grabbed her pants off of the floor and then looked around the cell, searching for her panties. "Where you put my thongs at, bae?"

"They're over there on the floor," Sonny spoke in a dry voice, slipping his boxers back on.

He was already feeling stressed out and overwhelmed. Being with Alexis had that effect on him. Her beautiful face alone was a sure reminder that if he didn't beat his case, he would eventually lose everything he loved. That was the reason he placed a distance between him and his family, mentally preparing himself for the day he would never see them again. Every now and then he would write a couple of letters and make a few phone calls, but that was it. He wouldn't even accept visitation, not even from his mother.

So when Alexis came back in his life and the two of them picked up where they left off, it was always in the back of his mind that she too could one day be nothing more than a memory. That was the downside of facing serious jail time. He knew that if he blew trial and had to spend the rest of his life in prison, life on the outside would continue moving forward.

The love and support from his family and friends would eventually wither away, and in the end, the only thing he would have to look forward to was another day in a cold, hard cell.

"Come on, bae. I know you're not over there stressing," Alexis said as she slipped her pants back on and fastened the buckle on her belt. "Didn't I tell you I got this, and that I won't stop until I get'chu outta here?" She walked up on him and gently caressed his abs. "You seriously need to relax, bae. I got this. Now, gimmie a kiss."

Sonny wrapped his arms around her and did as she demanded. They had only been back together for the past three months, and it still amazed him how much Alexis was down for him.

Aside from blessing him with all the loving she could possibly give without being caught, she brought him home cooked meals every day she came to work. And if he asked her to, she would smuggle in whatever else he needed.

"Oh, yeah," Alexis sighed as she reached down in her back pocket, "I almost forgot."

"Almost forgot what?" Sonny asked, wondering why she was looking so sad all of a sudden.

"This." She pulled out a white envelope and passed it to him. "I was passing the mail out before I came over here, and I set yours aside. But the question is, who the hell is *from a friend?*"

"From a friend?" Sonny looked at her skeptically, then he read the front of the envelope. It was clearly addressed to him, but in the top left corner instead of a return address, it only said *From a Friend.*

He looked at Alexis and noticed she was scowling at him with her arms folded across her chest. She was waiting for an answer.

"So, who is this so-called friend?" she asked with a slight attitude. Her intention was to ask Sonny about it when she first approached his cell, but seeing him standing there in nothing but his Polo boxers had her thinking about one thing, and one thing only. "Are you gonna answer me or not? Because I'm telling you now, Sontino, if you're dealing with another chick, then let her ass be the one that's out there riding for you. Or better yet, the bitch can put her life on hold, the same as I have and get a job in this cruddy-ass jail, just to be closer to you. Let her ass bring you food every day, keep tabs on your mother and daughter, and sex you up and down the way I be doing. 'Cause if you think for one second that I'ma stand by and play the flunky bitch, while your black ass is creeping around with the next, you got another thing coming. It's probably one of these bumb-ass c/o bitches. I'm not blind, I see the way they be looking at you."

"Goddamn, Lexi, chill. I don't even know what this is, let alone who sent it to me. I'm just as confused as you are."

"Oh, I doubt that." Alexis scoffed. "For all I know, the second I leave, you got the next bitch sliding her little skank-ass up in here."

"Yo, is you serious?" Sonny looked at her sideways.

"I'm dead serious."

"You know what?" Sonny said as he tore open the envelope. "I'ma open this muthafucka right in front of you, because it's not like I'm hiding anything. I honestly don't know who the fuck this is."

After opening the envelope, he pulled out a folded-up piece of paper. He showed the paper to Alexis, then he flipped it open and began reading. "The Honorable Judge, Donate Hill," he read the words out loud and then noticed the Commonwealth's seal at the bottom of the page. He couldn't believe it, he was looking at the arrest warrant in his case. The same missing document that Savino used to suppress his charges.

"Oh, shit. Yo, Lexi, you know what this is?" Sonny said with a smile. "It's the arrest warrant in my case, the same one they used to come and get me that night. Look." He handed the paper to Alexis and she took her time reading it.

"But who sent it to you? And how did they manage to get it?" Alexis asked, handing the warrant back to Sonny.

"I'm not sure, but I think it was my grandfather. Either way," he tore the paper to shreds and flushed it down the toilet, "it was a boss-ass power move. My lawyer was able to use it to get the most serious charges against me thrown out. So now all I gotta do is beat these last two bodies, and I'm outta here. And for the record, Alexis, stop doubting me," Sonny said as he wrapped his arms around her and gave her a soft kiss on the lips. "I never had a woman love me and hold me down the way you do, and I appreciate that shit, Ma, straight up. I would never do anything to hurt you. My love and loyalty is bulletproof, Lex, and don't you ever forget that."

"Umm-hmm." Alexis smiled, loving the way Sonny was talking that shit to her. "I hear you, Mr. Moreno. And just so you know, when we do eventually get you out of here, I'm holding you to everything you just said."

"You do that." Sonny gazed into her beautiful brown eyes. "Now, gimmie another kiss."

Alexis stood up on her tippy-toes and pecked him on the lips. "Alright, bae, I need to get back to work before the Sarge and L.T. return from their lunch break." She turned around and headed toward the door, but Sonny grabbed her the arm and turned her back around to face him.

"I love you, Lexi."

"I know you do, bae. You always did. And stop all of that daggone stressing." She reached out and caressed the side of his face. I told you—we got this."

***

It was a quarter past six when Heemy pulled up on the corner of Delhi and Boston. Looking up the block, it was just like Keeno said in his text messages: his mother and her crack-headed girlfriend, Elisha, was out there running amuck. Treesha was backing Keeno down with a bat in her hand, threatening to bust him upside the head, and his two runners, ShortyRock and Yahyo, were standing on the sidewalk pointing and laughing.

"If it ain't one thing, it's a muthafucking 'nother," Heemy sighed, shaking his head in frustration. He grabbed his Tech-9 from the glove compartment, pulled the lever back and hopped out of his truck.

"Muthafucka, you done lost yo' goddamned mind!" Treesha shouted. She swung the baseball bat, missing Keeno's head by inches. "Selling that shit in front of my fuckin' house and can't even gimmie a goddamned blast! Ol' stingy muthafucka!"

"That's right, Treesha, girl. You tell him," Elisha instigated. She was standing in the middle of the street smoking a Newport and nursing a half empty can of Olde E.

Treesha swung the bat once more and cracked Keeno on the left side of his head. "Ahn-ahn, don't run muthafucka. I'ma teach ya stingy-ass 'bout holding out on Treesha. I'll call the cops and shut this shit the down. Now, fuck around if you want to."

"Fuck is y'all niggas just standing around laughing for?" Keeno shouted at ShortyRock and Yahyo. "This shit ain't funny, this crazy-ass bitch try'na kill me."

Whoosh!

Another swing from the bat almost sat Keeno down for the count, and he was sick of playing games. He threw his dukes up and bobbed his head from side to side, ready to take a swing. "I'm telling you, Treesha, you better go 'head somewhere."

Bitch! I wish the fuck you would!" Treesha shouted back. She was just about to take another swing, but pumped her brakes when Elisha told her that Heemy was walking up the street.

An eerie feeling spread throughout the block, as everybody got quiet. ShortyRock and Yahyo stopped laughing, and Elisha sat her smoking ass down on the curb. She knew better than to fuck with Heemy. His crazy ass killed his own father right in front of his mother, and Elisha knew it. She also realized she was standing in the very same spot where he did it.

Treesha was shook. She noticed the look in Heemy's eyes and then looked down and saw the Tech in his hand. She tried to explain what was going on, but Heemy pushed her out the way and got up in Keeno's grill.

"Nigga, what the fuck I told you?" Heemy snarled at him. He was referring to text message he sent out before leaving La Casa Moreno. "Didn't I tell you to give her the work, so she could take her stupid ass back in the house?"

"I know that's what you said," Keeno cowered. "But, but I'm saying, though..."

"*Saying what?*" Heemy lashed out. "Fuck is you saying?"

Keeno was shaking like a bitch. His droopy eyes was locked on the Tech-9, and he was desperately thinking of the right thing to say. "Come on, Heemy, man, just calm down."

"*Calm down?* Nigga, calm me the fuck down!" He smacked Keeno across the face with the Tech, and Keeno crashed to the ground. He popped back up, but another blow from the Tech dropped him to his knees.

"Agh, shit! Yo, Heemy, chill!" Keeno cried out. A gaping lash was sliced down the middle of his forehead, and a steam of blood was seeping into his left eye. "I ain't even do nothing. Ya mom was the one that started this shit."

"Muthafucka, I started shit?" Treesha shouted.

"Yes, you *did*!" Keeno shouted back. He rubbed the gash on his forehead and then looked at his blood-covered fingers. "Damn, dawg, you got my shit all fucked up. I thought we was squad."

"Bitch, don't nobody care about that shit you talking." Treesha smirked at him. "You shoulda done like he told you and gave me my shit, dickhead. Had you known how to listen and pay attention, ya stupid-ass wouldn't be out here bleeding."

Heemy shot her the look of death and then fixed his gaze on ShortyRock and Yahyo. "Come get this nigga and take him around the corner. I'll be around there in a minute." Looking at Treesha, he shook his head and gritted his teeth. He never forgave her for the situation with Pookie and Mar-Mar, where she ratted him out to the cops but at the end of the day, she was still his mom and the only family he had left. "Go down in the basement and look behind the washing machine. It's an eight-ball back there. You can have it, but don't be asking me for shit else."

"Thank you, baby," Treesha said with a smile. She kissed him on the cheek and then looked over at Elisha. "Come on, bitch, bring ya ass. We 'bout to parrrrtay!"

Heemy took a deep breath and sighed. He knew he was dead wrong for supporting his mother's habit and for taking her side when she was clearly the one out of pocket. But the heavy guilt of killing his own father was something he couldn't escape. The only thing that made him feel better was catering to the one parent he had left, even if she was a crack-headed piece of shit, who only cared about herself.

Still shaking his head, Heemy walked away feeling like a nut. *"I can't keep moving like this,"* he said to himself. *"The only reason she be pulling this shit is because she knows I'ma let it ride. And fa'real, fa'real that shit between me and Pookie was all on her. She knew that nigga was my fucking pop. Had she told me, I woulda never downed him."* He wiped the tear that was sliding down his face and then looked up at the sky. "I'm sorry, Pop. I'm sorry."

***

A tinted-out, pearl-white, Cadillac DTS was on the next block over, parked up with the engine running. The Reaper was sitting in the passenger's seat and Alvin's one time underboss was sitting behind the steering wheel. They were watching Heemy through a vacant lot, but the young hustla was too zoned out to notice.

"And you're sure that's him?" The Reaper asked. He was watching Heemy as he walked away.

"Yeah, that's him. I used to see his little bad ass all the time. But that was back when he was just a snot-nosed punk. His little ass got heart, though. I'll give him that. Shot up his own goddamned daddy."

"And what about the two smoka bitches? You said one of them bitches his mom, right?"

"Umm-hmm. Treesha. She's the one that was swinging the bat. She good peoples. We used to kick it back when I was dibbling and dabbling."

"Dibbling and dabbling?" The Reaper looked at him like he was crazy. "Nigga, ya ass wasn't dibbling and dabbing, you was out here smoking. And stop fronting like you talking about something from back in the day, talking 'bout *back when I was dibbling and dabbling*. Nigga, that shit wasn't even two years ago."

"Come on, baby, you know the streets can't hold me," the man said in a nervous voice, looking down at the sawed-off shotgun that was laying across The Reaper's lap. "Playas fuck up every now and then. But it's all about the get back, you dig? Look at me now. I got the baddest bitches in the city, the best dope and more money than I can muthafuckin' count. We legends, baby. You know the game don't stop. It's twenty-five years later and we still out here rocking and rolling. It's YBM 'til the sun burn out, you know that shit. Now, gawn and gimmie some." He smiled and held his fist out waiting for The Reaper to give him a pound.

The Reaper looked at his fist and got a weird feeling. He didn't know if it was the man's history or the fact he always had something up his sleeve. Either way, The Reaper didn't trust him and the only reason he was fucking with him was because Alvin said so.

"Come on, baby, don't leave a playa hanging. Gawn and gimmie some."

Reluctantly, The Reaper reached out and pounded fists. Speaking in a sarcastic voice, he said, "My man, Bushnut."

"The one and muthafuckin' only." Bushnut smiled. "Now, let's head on down to South Philly, so I can scoop up one of my gals." He threw the car in gear but before he could pull off, a triple black minivan pulled up beside his Caddy with the side door wide open. A man dressed in all-black with a ski mask covering his face was sitting in the back seat. A black, stockless AK-47 was clutched in his hands and the barrel was aimed at Bushnut.

"Boom!" the man shouted, causing Bushnut to scream out for help and scramble around the front seat.

"Nigga, stop bitching," The Reaper admonished. He was looking at Bushnut, shaking his head. "You was talking all that gangsta shit a couple of minutes ago but the second a muthafucka stick a gun in ya face, you screaming like a bitch. Now, back to the young bul. Is he really making money the way you said or is ya silly-ass exaggerating?"

Regaining his composure, Bushnut played it off, like he wasn't fazed, even though the choppa was still being aimed at his grill. Talking in a fly voice, he said, "Humph, do a bear take a shit in the woods and wipe his ass with a white fluffy bunny? Well, I guess not, but yeah. The lil' nigga definitely got the bag right now. He's moving about four keys a week."

"About four keys a week?" The Reaper looked at him skeptically. "On this rinky-dink ass block?"

"Nah. That's including the other three blocks I showed you. So, if Alvin wanna branch out and take over North Philly, then Heemy's the one we need to go at first. Because as far as I can tell, he's the one making the most money. So, if we make his ass get down, then the rest of these niggas gon' do the same. And if he doesn't? Well shit, that's even better. He'll be the perfect example. I'm telling you, Ray, the young bul is the key. So, what'chu wanna do?"

The Reaper rubbed his chin and gazed through the vacant lot looking over at Delhi Street. "But who the fuck is he working for?"

The Reaper asked, turning his head back around. "'Cause I know his lil' ass ain't the one running the show. He's got a boss and that's the muthafucka we need to be going at." He opened the passenger's side door and climbed out the Caddy. "So, the second you find out who it is, let me know so I can report back to Alvin. But in the meantime, I'ma need you to hit me off wit' a couple of keys. My dawgs is hungry. It's time to start feeding 'em.

Chapter Four
At the District Attorney's Office

"Where the hell is he?" The Police Commissioner, Monroe Jackson, shouted when he stormed inside of the D.A.'s office. He was visibly drunk and raging mad. His salt-and-pepper, George Jefferson baldie was glistening with sweat and his bulging eyeballs were damn near popping out of his head. A dark, wet circle soiled the front of his trousers and his powder-blue dress shirt was flapping wide open, showing off his nappy chest. "Goddamnit!" He pounded his fist against his palm and then knocked over the computer at the front desk. "I said where the hell is he?"

The receptionist jumped out of her seat and backed pedaled toward the wall. Her small hands were raised high above her head and she was shaking so har that her over-sized glasses were drooping down the front of her face. She thought about calling security, but what were they going to do? Not only was Commissioner Jackson, the top dawg of the Philadelphia Police Department, he was accompanied by ten of his most trustworthy officers. Every last one of them appeared to be just as angry as he was.

Commissioner Jackson grabbed the telephone from her desk and handed it to her. "You call that bastard and tell him bring his ass down here. Matter of fact, to hell with that. Come on, fellas." He stormed off toward the elevator, motioning for his officers to follow. "We'll go to him. That stupid sonofabitch!"

It had taken nearly thirty seconds for the Commish and his goons to reach the tenth floor. The elevator's double doors eased open and the first thing they saw was District Attorney Seth Willis. The middle aged black man was standing on the other side of the threshold slowly shaking his head. He attempted to plead his case, but a sloppy left hook from Commissioner Jackson sat him flat on his ass.

"You stupid sonofabitch!" The Commissioner bellowed. He kicked Seth in the ribs and then dove on top of him. The two men rolled around wrestling for position, and The Commissioner landed on top. "We had him, you stupid bastard. We had his ass dead to right and you fucking blew it." He wrapped his hands around the District Attorney's throat and squeezed as hard as he possibly could. "I'm gonna fucking kill you!"

"Some—body get him off of me!" The District Attorney groaned. He was gasping for air and desperately fighting to peel the Commissioner's hands away from his neck. "Goddamnit!" He looked up at Sgt. Lorenzo, who was clearly on the side of his boss. "Lorenzo, get him off of me, *please!*"

Two security guards ran into the lobby and attempted to pull the Commissioner away from Seth, but Sgt. Lorenzo and two of his officers, whipped their guns out and stuck them in the two men's faces. "Go mind your fucking business," Lorenzo snarled, tightening his grip on his Glock .19. "Final warning." The two men looked at one another and slowly backed out of the lobby.

The Commissioner banged Seth's head against the floor and then fell out beside him and broke down crying. "Those bastards murdered my daughter and granddaughter. We fucking had him and you let him off the hook, Seth. You let him off the goddamned hook. Goddamn you!"

"Monroe, please. I fucked up and I'm sorry," the District Attorney lamented. He caught his breath and looked over at his best friend. The two men had grown up together in the Germantown section of the city and had been fighting crime, side by side, for the past thirty years. "I can still make this right, Monroe. Trust me, my brother, I can still make things right. I loved Rebecca and Chelsey, too. I will not stop until the people responsible get their just due."

"Their just due?" The Commissioner shouted and pushed Seth away when he tried to console him. "Out of all cases, you lose the file to *this one?* I personally handed you that goddamned warrant. Me, not one of my officers, not one of my detectives, *me!* And now it's just gone, vanished into thin fucking air? You've gotta be shitting me! For all I know, you're working for the other side!"

"Monroe, please? I would never—"

"You shut the fuck up! You shut the fuck up right now!" The Commissioner cut him off. "There's more to this goddamned story, and I want to know what it is. Now, you tell me," he looked Seth dead in the eyes, "how in the hell did he get that warrant?"

"I—I—I don't know, honestly. All I know is that I received a copy of the motion that was filed by his attorney, alleging an illegal search and seizure. The motion was predicated on the fact that we didn't have a warrant. But I knew that was bullshit. It's just like you said, you personally handed me the warrant and I put it away in a safe place."

"Where, Seth? A safe place where?"

"My personal safe. It was tucked inside of my case file, and the file was stashed away in my safe. So, obviously I didn't pay the motion any mind. I assumed it was nothing more than a stall tactic, a futile attempt by the defense to have the trial pushed back for few more months. But when I returned home from the office, I went upstairs into the attic, looked inside of my safe and discovered the document was gone. I can't explain how," he shook his head in disappointment, "but someone must've taken it."

"Someone must've taken it?" The Commissioner screwed his face up. He knew that Seth was recently widowed and his only son, Rafiq, was living in Seattle, Washington with his wife and two children. So, obviously, no one else had access to his house, let alone the safe in his attic. His explanation was weak at best. "That's bullshit and you fucking know it," The Commissioner snarled at him. "Now, you tell me what really happened or I swear to God, I'll..."

"I'm telling you the truth, Monroe. I really can't explain how this happened," Seth stated, knowing he was lying. He knew exactly how the warrant went missing but in order to save himself, his freedom and his reputation, he would never tell his best friend about his secret lifestyle. That was between him, the little boys he encountered on his monthly visits to Thailand and the mystery woman who had it all on tape.

The Commissioner wiped his eyes and staggered back to his feet. "I tried to be diplomatic and handle things the right way," he spoke in a slow, slurred voice, "but not anymore. From here on out, I'm taking matters into my own hands. And I'm telling you now, Seth, if I were you, I'd keep clear out of my goddamned way. Come on, guys," he looked at Lorenzo and his men, "let's get out of here. We've got work to do."

As they piled back inside of the elevator, Seth hopped up from the floor and looked at his best friend with pleading eyes. "It's not over, Monroe. I just need you to trust that I can still make things right."

The Commissioner didn't respond, he just stood there shaking his head. Seth started to say something else, but the elevator doors closed in his face and he slouched down to the floor crying like a baby.

He'd bitten off more than he could chew, and he knew it. It was only a matter of time before The Commissioner's investigation exposed him and his dirty little secrets. And to make matters worse, by sabotaging his own case, he reneged on the deal that he made with Juan Nunez, the head honcho of the Medellin Cartel.

About a year ago, the Columbian drug lord reached out to Seth and offered him a million dollars in exchange for a conviction in Sonny's case, specifically the charges stemming from the nightclub massacre.

The two men had been doing business behind the scene since the late eighties. So, when Juan reached out and made Seth the offer of a lifetime, the shady district attorney didn't hesitate to accept.

In his twisted mind, he was killing two birds with one stone. Not only would he avenge the murders of Rebecca, Ronald and Chelsey, he would also make a cool million in the process. It was a win-win situation, or at least he thought it was. That was, until a few days ago, when his freaky demons came back to haunt him.

May 26, 2016

It was 11:47 p.m. and Seth was dead tired from spending the past twelve hours working on the case against Sonny. His assistants and paralegals were long gone. The security guards who patrolled the building had finished their shifts a little over an hour ago, and it was just him.

But he wasn't alone, he had a bottle of wine and six boxes worth of evidence to keep him company. The trial date was set for October 5ᵗʰ and like the seasoned attorney he was, he was hell-bent on preparing an open statement so strong that if Sonny's mother was sitting in the jury's booth, she would convict her own son before the defense had the chance to say a single word.

"Ladies and gentlemen of the jury," Seth stated in a clear, authoritative voice. He was gracefully moving back and forth through the makeshift courtroom on the third floor, acting as though he were talking to a real-life jury. "As some of you may or may not know, my name is Seth Willis, and I'm the district attorney for Philadelphia County. I absolutely hate the fact that we were forced to meet under such circumstances, but make no mistakes about it, these circumstances are very much necessary.

"Today, in the very place where our forefathers drafted the constitution and declared our independence, you too shall have the opportunity to make history and assure that the bells of justice ring loud and clear. We have a hardened criminal in our midst, ladies and gentlemen. A brutal, calculated, murderous cocaine kingpin, who on the night of December 12ᵗʰ, 2014, not only murdered and decapitated two young men, but used a high-powered assault rifle, yes, ladies and gentlemen, a Thompson M-1, a machine gun reminiscent of the infamous Al Capone, and brutally chopped down and fatally wounded ten of Philadelphia's finest.

"I submit to you, ladies and gentlemen of the jury, that this man," he pointed at the makeshift defense table where Sonny would have been sitting had this been an actual trial, *"Sontino 'Sonny' Moreno, the reputed crime boss of the Moreno Crime Family, is the one responsible for more tears and toe tags that you or I, could ever imagine, let alone count. This defendant,"* he calmly approached the makeshift jury box, *"is the bogeyman hiding beneath your beds at night. He's the monster lurking in the shadows just waiting to pounce. He's the murderous, bloodly, devilish demon, who threatens the well-being of society as whole.*

"The drug corners and drug wars that plague our communities, that's him. The bullets, the pipe bombs, the crime scene tape and

the mothers crying their eyes out because their child never made it home that night, that's him, ladies and gentlemen, I assure you. And now that we've finally got him, the rest is up to you. The safety of our city and society as a whole, is all on you now. You guys hold the key.

"So, on behalf of the law-abiding citizens of the Commonwealth, you have the duty, ladies and gentlemen, the duty, and rightfully so, to listen to and ingest the mountain of evidence that I am prepared to present against Sontino Moreno and in the end, I'm one hundred percent certain that you will come back with the correct verdict. Guilty. Guilty. Guilty.

"It's all up to you ladies and gentlemen." He shook his head and looked each of the make-believe jurors square in the eyes. "Let's do the right thing, ladies and gentlemen. Let's put this mad dog out of his misery once and for all."

"Bravo," a sarcastic, feminine voice spoke out from behind him. "So precise and to the point. I'm impressed."

Completely caught off guard, Seth spun around and looked in the direction of the voice. The room was a tad bit darker than he remembered. He was so caught up in perfecting his opening statement that he failed to notice someone had dimmed the lights down.

He leaned forward and squinted his eyes and immediately spotted the three shadowy figures that were standing in the rear of the makeshift courtroom. A curvy, hourglass figure was positioned between two bulky figures that he estimated to be about 6'5" and 275 pounds apiece.

The curvy, hourglass figure stepped forward and into the light, allowing Seth to get a good look at her. She was dressed in a burgundy, skin-tight, silk gown with matching gloves that rode up to her elbows. A pair of jet-black, oversized Chloe shades disguised her mocha-complexioned face and her thick, neatly groomed dreads were wrapped up in an elegant crown. Her thin waist was accentuated by thick hips and a juicy bosom and the slit running down her inner thigh was showing enough flesh to make a gay man take a second look.

"Excuse, Miss, but is there something I can help you with?" *Seth asked. "Or better yet, how in the hell did you people make it inside of this building? You know this is trespassing, right? Which is a serious offense, considering this is a government building. But ah, depending on why you're here, I can possibly be persuaded to let it slide." He rubbed his hands together and licked his lips.*

"Don't flatter yourself," the woman replied. "I'm here on business, and my time is of the utmost importance."

"The utmost importance, huh? And you are?"

"Madam François," the woman stated with a regal authority. "And as I previously stated, my time is of the utmost importance. I'm here to speak with you about the Sontino Moreno case. My associates and I would like for this case to go away and in return, we promise not to leak the information we've gathered concerning your monthly trips to Thailand."

Excuse me?" Seth replied. "Do you have any idea who the fuck I am?"

"No," Madam François stated, signaling for her bodyguards to stop when they took a step forward. Both men were strapped with shiny, long machetes and had the look of death in their eyes. "Simmer down, now. That is not why we are here," Madam François said as she brought her gaze back to Seth. She held her hand out to him and said, "Come now."

"Come where? I'm not coming over there," Seth replied. He was looking at the two bodyguards when he said it. "Look, Miss, I don't know who the hell you people are or what you call yourselves doing here, but I'm sick of this shit. I'm calling the police." He pulled his cell phone from his pants pocket and dialed 911.

"Before you press down on the call button, I strongly suggest you listen to what it is that I have to say. Because I'm almost certain the last thing you'd ever want is for the police to find out about you and your dirty secrets. That's right, Mr. District Attorney, my associates and I know all about you and your freaky little getaways to Thailand.

From the underage male prostitutes that you love so much, to the lady-boys in Bangkok that you seemingly cannot get enough of.

You've been a naughty, naughty boy, Mr. District Attorney, and my associates and I have the video recordings to prove it. I've personally watched every last one of them, and I must say, I was disgusted and appalled."

Listening to everything she said, Seth slowly put his phone away. "And how am I supposed to know that you're telling the truth? For all I know, you could be bluffing."

"I figured you'd say something like that." Madam François smiled. "Pierre," she called on the Haitian giant that was standing a couple of feet behind her. "Bam mwen telephone nan," she spoke in her native Creole tongue, telling Pierre to hand over his cell phone. When he gave her the phone, she pulled up the video clips and held the phone out to Seth. "Come. See for yourself."

Seth thought it over for a few seconds, then he slowly approached her with his eyes glued on the two bodyguards. He could literally see the shimmering of their machetes. The lights from the ceiling were beaming down, reflecting off the blades and shifting around with their each and every move.

He grabbed the cell phone from Madam François and looked at the screen. Flexing his jaw muscles, he watched scene after scene of himself and different little boys engaging in the most unholiest of acts.

"I assume that video is enough to persuade you to deal?"

Swallowing the lump in his throat, Seth took a deep breath and released a long, stress-filled sigh. There was no getting around the video. The freaky prosecutor had been caught with his hands, among other body parts, in the cookie jar. "What exactly is it that you people want?" he asked in a defeated tone.

Whack!

Madam François back handed him across the face. "I already told you what we want!" she raised her voice a few octaves. "Sontino Moreno is to be released from custody within the next twenty-four hours or this video will be released to every news station in the country. The choice is yours."

"But you can't expect me to blow the entire case," Seth replied, holding his face where she smacked him. "This case has already

garnered national attention. There's simply no way he can just, just walk out of jail without at least going to trial. That's simply not possible. I don't even have the type of juice and assuming I did, the Attorney General would surely step in and take over the case."

Madam François thought about what he said, and realized he was right. Having Sonny walk away Scott-free, without so much as going through the process of a trial, would certainly raise all type of red flags. In addition to that, she knew The Conglomerate would never approve of the unwanted attention that could possibly come their way, as a result. Thinking fast, she came up with another solution.

"Okay." She nodded her head. "He'll have his day in court, but not for the charges stemming from the nightclub incident. Those charges need to go away and as for the rest of his charges, my associates and I will assure that he's acquitted."

"But, but I can't just make those charges disappear. He's already been arraigned. The legal system doesn't work that way."

"The original arrest warrant will suffice," Madam François stated. "Without an arrest warrant and no probable cause, any evidence that was gathered during the raid on his nightclub, and everything else that took place thereafter, will legally be deemed Fruit of a Poisonous Tree. So, the arrest warrant is what we want. It's either that or have fun watching yourself on 60 Minutes."

With no other feasible options left on the table, Seth was forced to hand over the original arrest warrant in Sonny's case. He didn't even care that he was going against the deal he made with the Columbians. His main interest was not being exposed for his freaky, despicable trips to Thailand.

Back to June 1, 2016

"It's over, it's all over!" Seth cried out, banging the back of his head against the elevator doors. "My life, my career, my reputation, it's all over. I'm fucking finished."

After a few more minutes of sitting there crying, he calmed himself down and got up from the floor. He took a few steps in the direction his office, but froze in place when his cell phone began to ring. The sound of the ringtone had him shaking in his Stacy Adams. He pulled his Samsung from his coat pocket and looked at the screen. His worst fear was confirmed. The caller was the very last person he wanted to hear from, Juan Nunez.

"Now, before you say anything, just let me explain," Seth said when he accepted the call.

"Dere is nothing left to for ju to explain," Juan replied in his thick, Spanish accent. He was flaming mad that Seth dropped the ball. "I trusted ju to take care of business, and ju fucked up."

"Señor Nunez, please. Just give me some time, I can still fix this," Seth cried out.

"Dere is nothing for ju to fix!" Juan shouted through the phone. "I told ju from de beginning, ju black fucking monkey—*Never fail me!*"

"But I didn't. All I need is a little more time. His trial date is right around the corner. At the very least, I can guarantee a life sentence."

"A life sentence?" Juan snarled. "I told ju to stick him in de fucking chamber wit' de gas. Ju failed me, ju stupid fuck. But ju will never fail me again."

The line went dead and the beeping sound of the elevator caused Seth to spin around quickly. As the double doors opened up wide, he was staring at a small Columbian man dressed in all-black with black sunglasses covering his eyes. His black leather gloves were tightly clutched around a black, sawed-off, double-barreled shotgun and the chopped off barrel was aimed at Seth's chest. Seth turned around to run.

Boom!

A thunderous blast lifted him off of his feet and sent him flailing across the lobby.

"Agh! Aggghhhhhh!" Seth screamed when he crashed to the floor. He rolled over on his back and looked down at the bloody honeycomb bursting out the front of his shirt. He felt the wound and then stared at his bloody red palms. In a matter of seconds, his entire body grew rigid and cold. Gasping for air, he looked toward the elevator and saw the Columbian hitman slowly walking toward him. "Pa—Please," Seth gasped and then coughed up a coppery-tasting chunk of blood.

The small Columbian towered over Seth and then leaned forward and shoved the smoking double-barrels deep down into the base of his throat.

Without the slightest bit of hesitation, he pulled back on the trigger and blew brains and teeth flying out of Seth's face.

A warm gush of blood shot up in his, but the trained killer didn't even flinch. He just reached down and grabbed Seth's cell phone from his warm, dead hand.

After pressing down on the last incoming call, he held the sticky wet phone against his left ear.

"Don Nunez, he finished."

"Dat's good, Chee-Chee, real good. Ju always come through. Now, don't forget, ju are not to leave de states until de Moreno brothers are dead. Dey are de only ones still breathing dat can link us to what we had done to dat piece of shit, Bobby. Do not fail me, Chee-Chee."

Click!

Down the hall, the two security guards that Sgt. Lorenzo sent away, heard the loud blasts of the shotgun. Throwing caution to the wind, they hauled ass back to the lobby, only to find Seth stretched out on the floor in a puddle of his own blood.

"Look," one of the men said, pointing at the elevator.

His partner turned his head, but the only thing he saw was a quick glimpse of a small Spanish man dressed in all-black.

Chee-Chee gave them the finger, then he disappeared behind the closing double doors.

Askari

Chapter Five
ADX Florence Correctional Facility
Florence, Colorado

"I'm here to see Angolo Gervino," Gangsta said to the U.S. Marshal at the front desk of the prison's all-white lobby. He was dressed in a cinnamon and cream, Dennis Basso, fox fur coat, a pair of dark blue Balenciaga jeans and cinnamon Mauri's. A thick, 35", iced-out Cuban link was blinging between the open flaps of his fur and huge solitaire white diamonds were dangling from his earlobes.

The U.S. Marshal gave him the once over and scoffed. "And who the hell are you?"

Gangsta reached into his back pocket and removed his wallet. He flipped it open, showing off his federal identification and white-gold shield. "Terrance Long. DEA."

"DEA?" The Marshall looked at Gangsta's badge and I.D. card. "Is that so?"

Gangsta nodded his head, looking at the white man with a straight face. There was nothing else to say, his credentials said it all.

"And what exactly do you want with Mr. Gervino?"

"Not that it's any of your business, but I'm here to conduct an official interview. I have a case that I'm working on, and I suspect that Mr. Gervino has some information that could possibly assist me in my investigation. My flight back to Quantico is scheduled to take off two hours from now, so I'd appreciate it if we could speed things up."

The U.S. Marshall gritted his teeth and looked Gangsta up and down for the second time. He wanted to ask a few more questions, but decided not to. The last thing he needed was being accused of impeding a federal investigation. So, against his personal apprehensions, he activated his two-way radio and ordered the Marshal in the center control station to open the door leading inside of the prison.

He then reached under his desk and pulled out a visitation blotter. He flipped it open and handed Gangsta a pen. "I just need you to sign right here." He pointed at the bottom of a long list of names.

Each name was connected to the federal inmate they came to visit. Gangsta examined the list and flexed his jaw muscles, as eight of the names flew off the page and smacked him in the face. For the past month and a half, every representative of The Conglomerate, except for Joaquin Alverez and Juan Nunez, had flown out the prison to visit Big Angolo.

He saw Felix Dubois from France, Abidemi Odeniyi from Nigeria, Mumar Khalifi from Saudi Arabia, Kim Lee from China, Su Kasaki from Japan, Serga Victoro from Sicily, Geraldine François from Haiti and Vladimir Pulvochik from Russia.

"Tell me about it," the Marshal said, noticing that Gangsta was evaluating the names on the list. "These recent visits wouldn't have anything to do with your investigation, now would it?" he asked in a sarcastic tone.

Gangsta didn't respond. He just added his name to the list and then walked through the open glass door. He checked his weapon at the officer's station on the other side, then he was led to an elevator that took him forty feet underground.

He was then escorted to a small room at the end of a long hallway. The cramped room couldn't have been any smaller. It was eight feet long and for feet wide, and was separated by a glass partition, a medal desk and wooden chair. A small hole was embedded in the middle of a glass, and a foot long metal slot occupied the bottom.

After fifteen minutes of sitting in the small cramped room, Gangsta couldn't believe his eyes when he laid them on Big Angolo. The old mafia don was feeble and bony, about thirty pounds lighter than the last time Gangsta saw him. An oxygen mask was draped across the front of his face and his sunken, poppy eyes had dark rings around them.

He was moving slower than Gangsta remembered and was hunched forward so far that it seemed as though his next step would leave him lying flat on his face.

The U.S. Marshal that was escorting him down the hallway appeared to have a deep care and concern for the old man, and Gangsta knew right away that the Marshal was Big Angolo's inside man, U.S. Marshal, Wayne Mitchell.

The Marshal unlocked the door, and Big Angolo stepped inside of the visiting booth with his oxygen tank in tow. He sat down across from Gangsta on the other side of the glass. The first thing he noticed was the way Gangsta was looking at him.

"Well, hello to you too," Big Angolo spoke in a raspy, sarcastic voice. "What am I, a friggin' alien ova here? You're looking at me like I've got a pair of tits growing out of my forehead."

"My bad. I'm just not used to seeing you like this."

"You and me, both, kid. You and me, both," Big Angolo said and then coughed loud and hard. "This friggin' cancer, it's kickin' me up the ass something special."

"So, what? Another round of chemo?" Gangsta asked, already knowing about his grandfather's pancreatic cancer.

"Nah, not this time." Big Angolo shrugged his shoulders. "It's no use. Stage four and the friggin' thing's spreading like wildfire. They're telling me I've got another three months, tops. And that's one of the reason I called you out here. I wanna know how the brothers are doing."

"The brothers?" Gangsta leaned his head in confusion. "You mean Sontino and Rahmello?"

"No, you moron, I'm talking about Tito and Jermaine. Of course, I'm talking about Sontino and Rahmello. What are you a friggin' idiot?"

Gangsta smiled, getting a kick out of the old man's Italian wit. He was a hundred years old and three months away from death, but still had the aura of a boss.

"As far as I know, Sonny's still holding his water. I saw on social media that he just beat the charges from the nightclub, so that's a good thing. And as far as Rahmello, I stayed away like you told me, so we never officially met. He's laying low for the most part, but he's still in the streets. From what I'm hearing, Sonny told him not to, but he's doing it anyway."

"And Gervin?" Big Angolo asked. "You saw him lately?"

"About a month ago," Gangsta replied. "I flew out to Cuba to see him."

"And how'd that turn out?"

Gangsta took a deep breath and sighed. "It was one of the hardest things I ever had to do, being cordial with this muthafucka, knowing he killed my peeps. I played it cool, though. I didn't want to let on that I knew about what he done, not yet anyway."

Big Angolo coughed, then he placed his oxygen tank up to his face and inhaled deeply. "I've been receiving a lot of visits lately, mostly from some of the bosses at the roundtable."

"I know." Gangsta nodded his head. "I saw the names in the visitation book. What's that about?"

"Vultures being vultures," the old man replied and coughed some more. "They smell death, so they're swooping down. Some were more discreet than others but in the end it's all the same, everybody's looking to take a bigger chunk of the power pie. That's the reason I was so upset with Little Angie and Gervin.

"The two of them together would have been a powerhouse, a sure way to keep my legacy alive. But their greed and disdain for another was too great. I shoulda seen it coming, but I didn't." He coughed so hard that his pale, yellowish face turned beet red.

Gangsta wanted to help him, but the thick glass window wouldn't allow it. He looked past his grandfather and caught the attention of Mitchell. "Get him some water," Gangsta said. He pointed at Big Angolo, then he made a motion like he was taking a sip of water.

The Marshal nodded his head, then he hurried over to the water fountain down the hall.

"Goddamnit. Now, what the hell was I saying?" Big Angolo continued after catching his breath.

"You were telling me about Grip and Little Angolo, and how you wanted them to team up and continue your legacy."

"Right." Big Angolo cracked a smile. "You're a good listener, kid, not as stupid as you look."

Gangsta smiled back and shook his head. "So, what's the next move? What exactly do you want me to do?"

Before Big Angolo could answer, the door cracked open and Mitchell handed him a plastic cup of cold water. "Thanks, Mitchie," the mafia don said with a smile. Then he nodded his head, signaling for Mitchell to take a hike. After the door closed behind him, Big Angolo knocked down the water in one big gulp. "Alright, now back to business. I've been meeting with different bosses from the roundtable, and they're split down the middle when it comes to Gervin. He's somehow managed to sway a few of them, but left a bad taste in the mouths of the rest. His slippery ass is up to something, I know it. I need you to get back in close with him and find out exactly what it is. He's too smart for his own good, but never will he ever be as smart as me. The teacher knows what he knows, but the student only knows what the teacher taught him."

Big Angolo coughed some more and then reapplied his oxygen mask. "I'm tired, kid. I think I'm gonna head back and get a little rest." He slowly stood up from the table and pulled his oxygen tank toward the door. "Oh, and before I go," he turned back around to face Gangsta, "there's one more thing."

"And what's that?"

"Sontino. I want him out there. He's held his water long enough. I don't care how you do it, just get it done. That kid is the future of this family."

"Consider it done," Gangsta confirmed. He looked at his grandfather one last time and then walked away without saying another word. It was time to put his plan in action.

Back in Philly

"Fuck is this nigga at?" Rahmello said, glancing at his watch. It was 9:17 p.m. and the connect was running late. He and Heemy were sitting in Heemy's tinted-out, 1996 SS Impala. The glossy black paint was the same color as the 22" rims and the 5% tint made it impossible to see inside. They were parked in front of Geno's Steakhouse in South Philly.

Across the way, directly in front of Pat's, was Heemy's first cousin and street captain, Squeeze. He was sitting behind the tinted windows of a black-on-black Ram truck, looking out for anything suspicious.

Heavy guns were on deck in both vehicles, so God bless the muthafucka who tried to flex.

"Now, you're sure this the whole one-point-five?" Rahmello asked. He was sifting through the bricks of money in the duffle bag that was laying across his lap.

Normally, he would have taken the time out to count each and every dollar himself, but Nahfisah and Olivia wasted about an hour of his time that he didn't expect.

The two women cornered him the second he stepped out of the shower and didn't let him get dressed until he promised to stop being so over protective. He didn't want to do it, but against his better judgement and for the sake of time, he agreed.

"One-point-five on the dot," Heemy spoke with confidence. "Not a dollar more, and not a penny less."

"Say that." Rahmello nodded his head. He glanced at his Patek once more and gritted his teeth. He was thinking about the five and a half hours Him, Heemy and Squeeze still needed to breakdown and whip up the work.

It was already 9:20 and by the time they reached the stash house in Norristown and spent another five to six hours preparing the work, they wouldn't get any rest until somewhere around four in the morning.

"So, what's poppin', bro? You good?" Heemy asked.

"Am I good?" Rahmello gave him a quizzical look. "Of course, I'm good. Why wouldn't I be?"

"I don't know. You just seem a little stressed, that's all. You ain't said nothing the entire ride over here."

"I just got mad shit on my mind, Heem. Besides all the shit that I'm going through with wifey and my sister bitching and complaining about not having any freedom, plus I still gotta worry about my brother."

"But Sonny's straight, though," Heemy replied. "You see he just spanked all them cases from the nightclub shit, and knowing him, he fuck around and touch down before the summer's over."

"And that's what I'm worried about," Rahmello sighed.

"You're worried about *that?*" Heemy squinted his eyes. "I don't understand."

"Me and Sonny ain't really seeing eye to eye right now," Rahmello confessed. He kept Heemy abreast on most issues but some things he chose to keep to himself, and the circumstances surrounding Easy's murder was one of them.

"But I'm saying...it ain't nothing that you and Sonny can't get past though, right?"

"Shit, for his sake, I hope so."

Heemy was floored. That was the last thing he expected Rahmello to say. He had crazy love for Rahmello and looked at him like an older brother. But Sonny was his guy, the nigga he grew up idolizing and the one who gave him a cup of water when he was thirsty. So he decided right then and there that if worst came to worst, his loyalty was to Sonny.

His brain began to race as he sat there taking it all in. He wondered what it was that had Rahmello so uptight about Sonny coming home and on top of that, he was thinking, *Why was this nigga so eager to play the background and put me in the forefront?* A lot of things just didn't make sense. He looked across the leather console and saw Rahmello sitting there with his eyes closed. He was massaging his temples and flexing his jaw muscles.

A pair of flashing high beams flickered in the corner of Heemy's left eye. He looked through the windshield and saw a silver Range Rover pulling into the parking lot. "Hey, yo, Mello, ya man just rolled up."

Rahmello opened his eyes and looked down at his watch. "It's 9:25. Disrespectful-ass nigga." He fastened the zipper on the duffle bag and then popped the passenger's side door. Looking back at Heemy, he said, "If shit get crazy, you know the drill: no questions, just hop out and blast."

Heemy nodded his understanding, and Rahmello climbed out the SS. He looked across the way at Squeeze, and Squeeze cut on the dome light inside of the truck, signaling that everything was kosher.

Satisfied, Rahmello strapped the duffle bag across his shoulder and casually made his way toward the Range Rover.

"Damn, man, what the fuck took you so long?" Rahmello asked when he climbed inside of the SUV. He closed the passenger's side door and sat the duffle bag on his lap. He looked around the parking lot once again for safe measures and then settled his gaze on Savino. "You're damn near thirty minutes late, dawg. What's up wit' that?"

"You seen the news?" Savino asked in a calm, low voice. He was leaned back in the butter leather seat smoking a Cohiba cigar.

The windows were rolled down about one inch from the top, and the air conditioner was on blast. It was cold as hell inside of the truck, but Savino's white ass was dressed like he'd just finished playing basketball, in pair of Nike ball shorts and a V-neck tee. The only thing about his appearance that screamed money was the iced-out big face Rollie that decorated his left wrist and the diamond studded wedding band that adorned his ring finger.

"Of course, I seen the news. I was watching the shit earlier today. Sonny beat most of his charges like you told me he would."

"No. I'm talking about the Six O'clock News. Not only that, but the shit is all over Twitter and Facebook. Somebody whacked the district attorney and that goddamned Roland Rushin is already stirring up his bullshit, reporting that the murder may somehow be linked back to Sontino."

Rahmello shrugged his shoulders. "A'ight, and what the fuck that gotta do wit' me?"

"Are you shitting me right now?" Savino looked at him sideways. "Do you have any idea of the type of heat that's about to come down? This isn't just another dead nigger in the streets, no pun intended. But this is the goddamned district attorney we're talking about. Somebody had the balls, some big fucking cahunas, to slip inside of the DA's office and kill the prosecutor in your brother's case, and you's got the nerve to ask me what does it have to do with you? You've gotta be shittin' me right now." Rahmello's demeanor was so unexpected that Savino's words came out in a confused chuckle. He simply could not believe that Rahmello was so naive about something so serious.

"I mean, that's my brother and all, but Sonny's his own man. We ain't the same. That nigga's sitting in jail, and I'm sitting right here. Now, let's talk about this muthafuckin' money."

Savino just sat there shaking his head. *Stupid motherfucker,* he thought to himself, but knew better than to say it out loud. He took another pull on his cigar and then sat it in the ashtray. "Back seat," Savino said, looking out the driver's side window. He was so disgusted with Rahmello that he couldn't bear to look at him.

Rahmello tossed his duffle bag in the back seat, then he reached back and grabbed the two gym bags that were laying on the floor. "And just so you know," Rahmello said, settling back in his seat, "starting next month, I wanna up the shipment to seventy-five. I got a team of young niggas that's ready to move it and on top of that, I'm 'bout to take back all of our Camden spots. I know it's not gonna be easy, but it is what it is. Niggas gon' have to respect it or check it."

Savino didn't reply. He was silently regretting the decision he made to fuck with Rahmello when Sonny specifically told him not to.

"Yo, you heard me, fam? I'm try'na up my shipment to seventy-five."

"Yeah, Rahmello I heard you. But I'm telling you now, with all of the heat that's about to come down, if shit gets crazy for you, you keep me out of it, you understand?"

Rahmello frowned at him. "Damn, fam, why you coming at my neck like I'm a muthafuckin' rat or something?"

"I'm just sayin'," Savino replied, then he pulled down on the gearshift and put the transmission in drive. He was staring straight ahead, still incapable of looking Rahmello in the eyes.

"Man, whatever," Rahmello said as he opened the door and climbed out the Range with the gym bags clutched in both hands. He closed the door with his back side and began to walk away.

"And Rahmello," Savino called out behind him.

"What, man, what's up?" Rahmello spoke with an attitude, turning back around to face him.

"Don't let this shit get back to Sontino."

"Hey, yo, Savino, what'chu threatening me, dawg?"

"No, I'm not threatening you," Savino said in a calm voice. "I'm just sayin'." He pulled out of the parking lot, leaving Rahmello standing there caught up in his feelings.

"Bitch-ass nigga," Rahmello said as he tightened his grasp on the gym bags.

He looked around the parking lot to make sure nobody was watching, then he nodded his head at Squeeze, signaling that everything was straight and that it was time to move out. After that, he walked back over to the SS and motioned for Heemy to pop the trunk.

"Talking 'bout don't let this shit get back to Sonny, like I'm a muthafuckin' pussy or something," he said to himself as he leaned forward and stashed the fifty keys in the secret compartment that was built into the walls of the trunk. "Man, fuck Sonny. His ass just mad 'cause he fucked that paper up and now he want a nigga to just sit back and starve? Not at all, especially when it's up to me to feed the whole family. Shit don't stop just because his stupid-ass got booked. And at the end of the day, Grip left the whole shit to me, so fuck what Sonny talking 'bout. From here on out, I'm doing this shit my way and if his ass don't like it, then it is what it is. I'm ready for whatever."

He hopped back in the SS and Heemy pulled off with Squeeze right behind them. Their destination was the stash house in Norristown. It was time to get money.

Chapter Six
Back at the County Jail

Sonny was all alone in his jail cell, laying on the top bunk and staring up at the ceiling. He was thinking about what he saw on the news a couple of hours ago regarding the murder of District Attorney Seth Willis.

On the surface, it appeared as though someone was behind the scenes pulling the strings in his favor, but Sonny was smarter than that. He knew better than to trust the obvious.

"You gotta lean on the jab and watch for the hook," he could hear Easy's voice in the back of his mind. *"That hook will hurt you, son. It's always the punch you don't see coming that'll hurt you the worst."*

The statement was made in reference to boxing but growing up in the game, Sonny applied it to his everyday life, especially after dealing with Grip and all of his shifty ways. So, if there *was* someone behind the scenes going out of their way to help him, then why wouldn't this person, at the very least, give him a heads up and make themselves known?

There had to be more to the story, and Sonny was determined to figure out exactly what it was. For all he knew, the person behind the scenes was doing the exact opposite, going out of their way to make sure he never saw the streets again. He had no involvement whatsoever with the district attorney's death, but didn't doubt for a second that the heat would surely fall back on him. It was just another hurdle between him and his freedom.

Vrrrrrm! Vrrrrrm! Vrrrrrm!

His iPhone vibrated inside of his pillow, snapping him out of his thoughts. He hopped down from the top bunk and placed a towel over his cell door window, assuring that nobody walking past could look inside and see what he was doing.

Then after that, he returned to the bunk and carefully removed his cell phone from the pillow. Looking at the screen, he noticed the incoming call was from a blocked number. He usually didn't accept such calls, but after everything that had taken place, from the missing warrant popping up to the situation with the district attorney, his curiosity got the best of him. Maybe the caller was this so-called *friend*.

"Who the fuck is this?" Sonny spoke in a low voice when he accepted the call.

"You still got that mouth of yours, I see."

"Grip?" Sonny questioned the deep voice on the other end of the phone. He hadn't heard a peep out of his grandfather since the night he was arrested and couldn't understand why now, after all of this time, he chose to reach out. "Fuck is you calling me for? Or better yet, how the fuck you get this number?"

"I've got my ways," Grip replied in a calm voice. "I thought you knew that by now?"

"Man, fuck all the fly shit," Sonny shot back. "I know you ain't calling to see how I'm doing, so what's ya whole thing? I know you ain't doing nothing but working angles, so what's up?"

Grip chuckled. He always got a kick out of dealing with Sonny. In many ways, it was like dealing with himself. "I've got some information pertaining to your well-being."

"My well-being? Fuck is that supposed to mean?"

"I just left a meeting with some of the bosses from The Conglomerate, and I finally made them see things my way. We're now at the head of the table, officially. A few of the bosses were against it, but I managed to sway the majority."

"And what the fuck that gotta do wit' me?" Sonny snapped out, speaking louder than he intended. "These crackas try'na bury me under the fuckin' jail, and you got the nerve to be calling me about some muthafuckin' Conglomerate? Nigga, fuck The Conglomerate!"

"What? You ungrateful, little bastard. Can't you see that I'm doing this shit for you and your brother? Our entire family for that matter? This isn't about me."

"Nigga, it's always about you," Sonny hissed at him. "And for the record, I ain't never asked ya muthufuckin' ass for nothing, not a goddamned thing. So, I'd appreciate it if you kept ya nose out of my fuckin' business!"

"Excuse me. You wanna run that by me again?"

"Nigga, you heard what the fuck I said. Keep ya nose out of my goddamned business. I know you're the one that's behind the scene, manipulating my fuckin' case. The missing warrant was one thing, *but killing the district attorney?* What the fuck was you thinking? That shit don't help, it only makes things worse. It's all gonna fall back on me now!"

"The missing warrant?" Grip asked in a confused voice. "Killing the district attorney? What the hell are you talking about?"

"Nigga, you know *exactly* what I'm talking about. At first, I thought you was doing this shit to help me. But naw, nigga, ya ass ain't try'na help, you try'na hurt me. You try'na line me up for the feds!"

"Line you up for the feds?" Grip shouted through the phone. He was so angry that his hands began to quiver. "Why the fuck would I do something like that? That doesn't even make sense."

"It does to me," Sonny replied. "It makes all the sense in the muthafuckin' world. Because why else would you do a bunch of crazy shit, knowing it's gonna come right back to me? And now that I think about it, who's to say you're not this secret witness they keep telling me about? The one that's supposed to be testifying against me?"

"A secret witness?" Grip screamed at him. "Boy, are you fucking crazy? Did you really just accuse me of being a goddamned government informant?"

"Nigga, I said what the fuck I said," Sonny shot back. "Ya ass is looking real suspect right about now."

The line went quiet, as both men calmed down and thought about everything that was just said.

Sonny had every reason to believe Grip was the person behind the scenes, but now, after hearing what his grandfather had to say, he wasn't so sure.

Grip was flabbergasted. He'd been accused of many things in his life, but never had anyone accused him of being a rat. He had no involvement whatsoever in the outcome of Sonny's case. In fact, the case against Sonny was the last thing on his mind. Because whether or not Sonny was convicted, it really didn't matter. Grip had already taken the necessary steps to have him smuggled out of the country and brought to Cuba, where he could operate as the boss of The Conglomerate without the C.I.A. controlling his every move. That was Big Angolo's mistake, and the main reason Grip was no longer on American soil. He knew better than to trust the government.

"Sontino, I need you to listen to me and listen clear," Grip spoke in a calm, steady voice. "Everything that I'm doing is for you and Rahmello. Now, I know we've been through a lot over the past few years, and you have every reason not to trust me. But at the end of the day, you're my grandson and I love you. I've worked my ass off my entire life, just to put my family in position and now that we're finally here, the only thing I wanna do is kick back and enjoy my great-grandbabies and whatever time I've got left on this God-forsaken earth. There's a lot of things in the works that I can't tell you about right now because I don't wanna jeopardize anything. But trust me, when it's all said and done, you're gonna be exactly where you're destined to be. That's something you can bet on."

Sonny was at a complete loss for words. That was a side of his grandfather he'd never seen before. He didn't quite know how to take him. "But I'm saying, though, if you ain't the one meddling in my case, then who is?"

"I was just thinking the same exact thing," Grip replied. "Because it's definitely not me. I'm ten steps ahead of that shit, I assure you. So, the only other option is one of our enemies."

"But, who? The Mexicans?" Sonny asked.

"No, I highly doubt it. That's not Joaquin's style. And besides, Big Angolo settled the score between us and them. Jaoquin's a man of his word, so if he agreed to a truce, then a truce it is." Grip thought about it for a few more seconds, then hequickly put two and two together. "That's it! I know exactly who it is. It's that god-damned Juan Nunez. I know it is."

"That sounds about right. Him and Poncho must know that I found out about what they did to Pops. They're prob'bly try'na get me out of the way before I get a chance to retaliate."

"Him and Poncho?" Grip asked. "What do you mean him and Poncho? Poncho's dead. Him, his wife and their son. They're all dead. I thought you knew this already."

"Nah, I never heard that before. When the fuck did all of this happen?"

"The same night you were arrested," Grip told him. "You mean to tell me you're not aware of what's going on around you?"

"Nah, it ain't that. It's just the only thing on my radar for the past year and a half was getting my health back. That, and try'na find a way to get the fuck out of jail. But, back to this bitch-ass nigga, Poncho. That was us who did him in? For what he did to Pops?"

Grip took a deep breath and sighed. "No. It wasn't us. The plan was to strike back, but we never had the chance."

"Well, if it wasn't us, then who?"

"The word going around is that Juan done it."

"Juan? But why the fuck would he kill his own brother?"

"The same reason he's behind everything that's going on with you and your case. You're a link between him and Roberto, and he knows that if you expose him to Joaquin and Chatchi, his ass is finished. He more than likely had plans to hit you on the outside, but now that you're in jail, he's doing everything he can to keep you quiet. And what better way than to have you convicted of a capital crime? So, it really doesn't matter whether it's a shank to the neck or the death penalty, either way he has you exactly where he wants you. I'm telling you, Sontino, it's gotta be him. That sonofabitch is going out of his way to keep you quiet."

Everything that Grip said was beginning to make sense. It didn't account for the missing warrant, but it damn sure accounted for the murder of Seth Willis. By killing the district attorney, who was prosecuting Sonny's case, he without a doubt made an acquittal nearly impossible.

"A'ight, well if that's the case, then the same thing applies to Rahmello," Sonny said with a sense of urgency. "Mello was there when Juan and Poncho paid me the hunnid bricks to kill Mexican Bobby. So if Juan's coming after me, then he's coming after

Rahmello, too. We need to get to Mello and let him know what's going on before it's too late."

"Don't worry about Rahmello, I'll do everything in my power to make sure that he's fine. I just need you to sit tight and watch your body while in you're in there. If you want me to, I can send in some reinforcements. A couple of guys to keep an eye on you and watch your back."

"Nah, I'm good," Sonny declined. "I just need you to hold down Mello, and make sure my lil' nigga's straight. He be moving too fast for his own good and if something was to go down, I'm afraid he won't see it coming. So, don't worry about me, just focus on Mello. I can handle mines."

Vrrrrrm!

The cell phone vibrated, alerting Sonny of another incoming call. He looked at the screen and saw that the caller was Alexis. She was calling from an emergency number. "Hey, yo, Grip, I gotta take this other call," Sonny cut the conversation short. "But hit me back in another hour and lemme know what's good wit' Mello."

"That's a plan," Grip replied. "And Sontino."

"Yeah, man, what's up?"

"Be safe in there."

"You already know." He disconnected the call and then switched over to Alexis, who he knew was in the bubble working a double-shift. "What's up, Ma? What's wrong? Why you calling me from this number?"

"Get rid of that phone and whatever else you got stashed in there. They're coming to get you!"

"They're coming to get me?" Sonny said, snatching his shank from his hip. "Who?"

"The motherfucking cops! They just came on the unit. They're running up the steps as we speak. Whatever you got, get rid of it!"

"Fuck!" Sonny shouted in frustration. He hopped off the top bunk and tossed the cell phone in the toilet. He almost forgot about the shank in his hand, but tossed it in the toilet bowl at the same time he hit the flush button.

Zzzzz!

The cell door buzzed open and Sgt. Lorenzo and three of his officers bum rushed the cell. Sonny was standing there with his dick in his hand, acting like he was taking a piss.

"Get on the goddamned floor!" Lorenzo shouted, tightening his grip on the stun-gun he was aiming at Sonny. "Do it now!"

Sonny smiled at him and shook his meat. "Damn, Lorenzo, I ain't see you in the courtroom today. What's up wit' that? I thought you was my biggest fan."

Tttttttat! Tttttttat!

Lorenzo squeezed the trigger on his stun-gun and Sonny went down hard. He struggled against the high-power voltage, but to no avail. In no time at all, he was shaking and convulsing, pissing on himself and foaming at the mouth.

"That's enough! Y'all ain't gotta do him like that!" Alexis shouted from the doorway. After alerting Sonny to their presence, she shot out the bubble and ran up the steps behind them.

Sgt. Lorenzo looked at her and scoffed. "This is *official* police business, so I'd suggest you keep it moving and let us do our goddamned job."

Alexis didn't move an inch. She just folded her arms across her chest and rolled her eyes at the Puerto Rican Swat Team leader.

Sgt. Lorenzo turned back around and looked down at Sonny, who was laying on the floor shivering and shaking. With a satisfying smile, he whipped out a pair of handcuffs, then knelt down and locked them around Sonny's wrist. He then looked up and addressed the officer that was standing right beside him. "Tear this goddamned cell apart and don't stop until you find that warrant. I want every piece of mail, every goddamned picture and whatever else you can find. Everything is to be tagged and bagged and brought back to the precinct. You got that?"

"Yes, sir. That's a ten-four." The officer nodded his head. "Come on, guys, let's get to work."

As the three officers ransacked the cell, Sgt. Lorenzo yanked Sonny back on his feet. He attempted to push him out of the cell, but Sonny staggered to his knees, still groggy from the effects of being tazed.

"Damn, Lorenzo, you ain't figured it out yet?" Sonny chuckled, as the Sargent snatched him back to his feet. He was slobbering out the side of his mouth and struggling to catch his breath. "You—You playing for the wrong team," Sonny gasped. "But I'll tell you what. When I spank this case—and get back to doing my thing, I got a job for you. Ya bumb-ass can come down North and work for me."

"You drug dealing, cop killing son-of-a-bitch!" Sgt. Lorenzo snarled at him. "I'd rather die than work for you."

"Well, you know—that's always an option."

Raging mad, Sgt. Lorenzo roughed him up and speed-balled him down the tier. Their destination was the 26th District, a place that Sonny knew all too well.

***

"Mamacita, lemme get another double shot of Remy," Keeno said to the bartender.

He was all alone sitting at the bar in La Presiosa, a small Spanish bar off the corner of Germantown and Norris. His head was still pounding from the pistol-whipping he received from Heemy and the twenty-two stitches above his left eyebrow were beginning to itch. He reached up to give it a scratch, but quickly pulled his hand away when he felt the pain.

The Perc 30's he received from the emergency room were beginning to wear off, and the blistering pain that was previously shooting through his dome was coming back even stronger. The more it hurt, the more he thought about Heemy and how he wanted to kill him for what he'd done.

Not only Heemy, but Shorty Rock and Yahyo, as well. They were supposed to be his best friends, his right hand mans. But instead of helping, they just stood around laughing while Heemy molly whopped him with the pistol.

Then, to make matters worse, when Keeno went to the hospital to get stitches, Shorty Rock and Yahyo were right back on Delhi Street hustling for Heemy.

"Nut-ass niggas," Keeno seethed, *looking at his reflection in the mirror behind the bar. "If it wasn't for me, them nigga would still be in the projects, robbing the pizza man. And now they wanna act like they riding wit' Heemy, when I'm the one who brought 'em around there in the first place. Them pussies coulda helped or at the very least rolled out to the hospital wit' me. But naw, they'd rather dick ride Heemy, talking 'bout Heemy said he got some paper for me and that he was sorry. Fuck that! A couple of dollars ain't gon' put no muthafuckin' blood back in my body or take away this muthafuckin' headache. They think this shit a game, but I got 'em. First chance I get, I'm going dead at them niggas, all of 'em! Shorty Rock, Yahyo, Heemy and his stupid-ass mom. Ol' smoking-ass bitch!"* he thought.

"Papi, you want some ice for that?" Mamacita asked, as she placed Keeno's drink down in front of him. "Some ice?"

"Nah, Ma, I like my Remy warm."

"No, Papi, I'm not talking about your drink," she replied in a compassionate voice. "I'm talking about your eye. It's swollen." She pointed at Keeno's sunglasses. The dark tinted Gucci's were blocking his eyes from the front, but from the side, she could clearly see that his left peeper was swollen shut. Not only that, but she also noticed the stitches that were trailing along the length of his eyebrow.

Keeno gritted his teeth and shook his head slowly. He was just about to tell Mamacita to mind her business, but was interrupted when someone slid up beside him and placed their hand on his shoulder.

He looked back and spotted the old head that stepped into the bar a few minutes after he did. The last time he noticed the man, he was shooting pool in the back of the bar, but somehow, he managed to creep up without Keeno noticing. He smiled at Keeno and gave his shoulder a light squeeze.

"Don't even sweat that shit, young soldier. Everybody takes a beating every now and then. That's just a part of the game, baby."

"Old head, if you don't back the fuck up." Keeno reached for the Nine Millie that was tucked in his waistband.

"Whoa now. Easy, young soldier, easy," Bushnut said as he took a step back, palms out in a defenseless posture. "Ya name's Keeno, right? Miss Darla's ya grandmom?"

"Nigga, how the fuck you know my name?" Keeno snarled at him. He snatched the gun off of his waist and hopped up from the bar stool.

"I'm a friend of the family, young soldier. I knew ya daddy, too. His name was Kenyon. We used to run together back in the day."

"A friend of the family?" Keeno cocked the hammer back. "I don't know you, nigga."

"I don't know what's going on, but y'all need to leave," Mamacita warned. She pulled out her cell phone and called the police on speed dial. The bar was already on the brink of being shut down as a result of too much violence, and the owner had given her strict orders to call the police whenever she'd seen a gun or had a reason to believe that somebody was packing. "The cops are already on the way, so I'd suggest y'all leave."

"Come on now, put the gun away, baby boy," Bushnut replied in a calm voice, still holding his hands in the air. "I got my Caddy parked outside. Just take a ride wit' me and hear me out. And if you want, we can get ya granny on the phone so I can talk to her. I swear to you, young buck, I don't mean you no harm. All I'm try'na do is give you some game and put some money in ya pocket. And don't even worry about them bitch-ass niggas from Delhi Street. 'Cause we gon' fix that shit and make it right, you dig?"

Keeno thought it over for a minute and then slowly put the gun down. He figured that at the very least he could listen to what the old head had to say. Especially since he mentioned knowing his late father, who was murdered back when Keeno was only nine years old.

"A'ight, man, but first I'ma call my granny," Keeno said as he tucked the Glock .19 back his waistband. "And I'm telling you now, if she say anything other than what'chu told me, I'ma park you."

"Shit, I ain't got no problem with that," Bushnut replied, bringing his arms back down. He hadn't seen or talked to Miss Darla in nearly ten years, around the same time Kenyon was kidnapped and murdered, but he didn't doubt for a second that his tight man's mother would remember him. He reached down in his pocket and pulled out a thick wad of fifties and twenties. He peeled away a couple of fifties and sat them down on the counter. "For your trouble," he said to Mamacita. He then motioned for Keeno to follow him outside to his car. "Now, let's get up here, young soldier, 'fore the po-po come. We got a lot of shit to talk about."

Askari

Chapter Seven
In South West Philly

Ever since linking up with The Reaper a few months back, Doo Dirty, Killah Kye and Murda Mont had been shaking down nearly every drug dealer in the city. Their mission was simple–*Get Down or Lay Down!* Whoever got down with the movement and accepted the dope being supplied by Bushnut, they were given a pass and allowed to operate as a YBM affiliate. But on the flip side, any and all who refused, they were forced to lay down and when they laid down they stayed down.

Uptown Samir was one of the few who refused, so now he had to pay. He had no idea that The Reaper was parked outside of his house and that Doo Dirty, Killah Kye and Murda Mont were creeping through the dark in his second-floor hallway.

The three men were strapped and moments away from bringing the pain.

They approached his bedroom door and stopped. The only thing they heard were the sounds of Uptown Samir getting his freak on.

"Goddamnit, Samir! Shit!" His new chick, Kia, cried out.

She was leaned over the bed with her ass in the air and Samir was right behind her, long-dicking her from the back. Samir was going ham in the pussy, stroking so hard that the headboard was banging against the wall with a loud, thunderous clap.

Whop! Whop! Whop!

He smacked Kia on the ass and pulled her hair with both hands, all the while digging her guts out like a seasoned porn star.

Kia was doing her thing, as well—winding her hips and popping her ass, matching Samir stroke for stroke. He was so deep in her essence that Kia could feel him pressing against her stomach.

"Fuck this pussy, Baby! Just like that. Fuck me, Samir! Fuck me! Aaaggghhhnn!"

Her pussy was so tight and juicy that every time Samir plunged inside of her and pulled back out, the Magnum on his ten-inch pole became whiter and whiter, covered in her creamy warm nectar. He looked down and bit his bottom lip, loving the sight of her fat pussy swallowing his dick.

"Pop that pussy, babe. Pop that shit."

"Like this?" Kia replied. She rolled her hips and bucked even harder.

"Yeah, Mommy, just like that. Now, tell Daddy how much you love this dick."

"I love it, Daddy. I fucking love it!" Kia shuddered and moaned. "You feel so good I wanna fucking bite you! *Shit!*"

Samir leaned forward and grabbed her around the shoulders. Stuffing his hamma deep inside of her, he gyrated his hips and mashed his meat against the bottom of her pocket.

"You like it when Daddy hit that spot?"

"Yes, Daddy, right there! Keep it right there!" She squeezed her walls around him and popped her ass a few more times. Her body began to shiver and her eyes rolled into the back of her head. "Oh, my God, baby, shit! I'm cumming! I'm cumming, Baby! Uggghhhhnnnnn!"

A watery stream of hot cum squirted from her pussy and splashed Samir on the stomach. Completely aroused, he stroked even faster. The headboard was thumping, his chest was heaving and the toes on his right foot curled into a ball. He struggled like hell to keep his composure, but his testies had a mind of their own. Before he knew it, he was hunched over grunting and groaning and filling up the tip of the condom. "Aaagggggggrrrrrrr! Fuck!"

Exhausted, the two lovers, sticky and wet, collapsed on top of the bed. The euphoric sensation of busting a nut had Samir going through the motions, unaware that death was right around the corner, literally!

"I see you, my nigga. I couldn't have hit the pussy better myself," Doo Dirty snickered as he slipped inside of the room with Killah Kye and Murda Mont right behind him.

"Huh? What? Yo, what the fuck is this?" Samir shouted. He hopped off the bed with his semi-erect dick flopping all around. The cum-filled Magnum slipped from his shaft and landed on the floor in front of him.

Doo Dirty aimed his choppa at the condom, then brought it back to Samir's face. "Yo, that's some nasty-ass shit, dawg. Like, real shit."

Samir looked at the three intruders and shook his head, realizing he made a big mistake. He should have never underestimated them. The situation was bad and he knew it. By running up in his spot bare faced, he knew the three men had come with the intention to kill.

"A'ight, man, just chill," Samir spoke in a calm voice. He was looking at Doo Dirty when he said it. "I'ma get down wit' the program, I swear. Whatever y'all want me to move, I'ma move it. Just don't kill me, dawg, I'm begging you."

"That ship done sailed, homie," Doo Dirty replied with a twisted smirk. He looked at Kia and shook his head. "Well, damn, Keys, for a dyke bitch you was sure 'nough taking the dick like a mu'fuckin' champ. I'm surprised."

Kia glared at him and gave him the finger. "Fuck outta here, Dirt. You nut-ass nigga."

"Key"?" Samir scowled at her. "Hold the fuck up. Bitch, you know these niggas?"

Kia smiled at him. "YBM all muthafuckin' day, baby," she stated in a voice much deeper than what he recognized. She got up from the bed butt-ass naked and slipped her thongs back on, showing no embarrassment whatsoever. She normally lived her life as a man, and had tag-teamed so many bitches with the crew that she was used to them seeing her naked. Her only gripe was that her sexy, butterscotch body had a perky pair of titties and a fat, shaved pussy, rather than a muscular chest and a big hairy dick. "Had you been thinking wit'cha big head instead of ya little one, ya stupid-ass wouldn't have been caught slippin'. I gave you the pussy on the first night, then the next day, you got me up in ya spot like I live in this muthafucka. Stupid-ass nigga."

Samir couldn't believe it. The beautiful woman he met just a few days earlier was talking and moving around like a dude. After slipping her clothes back on, she reached inside of her purse and pulled out a chrome 9 Millie. "I would tell ya stupid-ass to strip, but'chu already naked," Kia said, cocking a bullet up into the chamber. She walked up on him and pressed the cold steel to the side of his dome. "Now, where the fuck is the paper at?"

Samir was shaking like a stripper. He returned his gaze to the three men standing by the door and threw his hands up in a defenseless posture. "Look, fam, I fucked up. I should'a took y'all niggas serious, but I didn't. Whatever y'all want me to move, I'ma move it. Or better yet, it's just like Kia said, I got money. I got a hunnid racks in the closet and another two hunnid at my baby mom's house. Let me go and it's yours. I'll hustle for ya'll and ya'll can still keep the money. Just don't kill me, dawg, I'm begging you."

"You got a hunnid racks?" Doo Dirty asked, looking at him sideways. "In that closet right there?"

"Yeah." Samir nodded his head feverishly. "It's in the Louie bag on the top shelf."

"Kye, go over there and check it out."

Killah Kye made his way to the closet, not once taking his eyes off of Samir. He reached up on the top shelf and grabbed the brown Louie sack. He unbuckled the flap and looked inside. "Yeah, Dirt, it's definitely in here."

Doo Dirty nodded his approval, then he tightened his grip on the choppa. "A'ight, now what about the rest of the shit?" He looked at Samir. "Where the fuck ya baby mama live?"

"On 7ᵗʰ and…"

Boca!

"Cambria," Samir finished his sentence with a penny-sized hole on his forehead. His steamy hot brains were splattered on the wall behind him, trickling down like a spilt jar of Ragù. He dropped to his knees with his mouth wide open and then tumbled over dead before he hit the floor.

"Damn, Keys, what the fuck?" Doo Dirty shouted with his eardrums ringing. "Fuck you shoot him for? He was just about to tell us where the rest of the money was at!"

"But—but it wasn't me," Kia replied in a shaky voice. She was looking at The Reaper, who was standing behind Doo Dirty with a black .45 in his hand.

Thin strands of smoke were rolling out the mouth of the barrel, which was now aimed at the back of Doo Dirty's wig. Unbeknownst to everybody in the room, the old school gangsta crept up just a few seconds earlier. He gestured for Murda Mont to head outside to the car and then took matters into his own hands, tired of all the talking and politicking.

"Fuck you mean it wasn't you? You the only one that was standing there!" Doo Dirty continued shouting. The gunshot was so loud and had taken place so fast and unexpected, that he didn't realize it was fired from behind.

"Nigga, I shot him," The Reaper snarled in a cold, murderous tone.

"Huh?" Doo Dirty uttered, as he spun around just in time to see the bright flash of the flaming fo' pound.

Boca!

The blazing hollow zipped past his face and crashed into the wall, sending chunks of plaster flying through the air. He dropped his choppa and placed his hands over his ears.

"Damn, Double R, what the fuck I do?" Doo questioned.

"Ya stupid ass was talking too much," The Reaper said, looking him square in the eyes. He glanced around the room at Killah Kye and Kia, then he brought his gaze back to Doo Dirty, who he selected as the captain of the crew. "The next time I tell you to do sum'n, do it. Get in and get the fuck out, and don't be fucking around. Now, come the fuck on. We still got work to do."

***

At the 26th District

"Damn, man, the least y'all can do is gimmie a fuckin' blanket!" Sonny shouted at the two-way mirror in the interrogation room. He was handcuffed to a stainless-steel table in the center of the room, dressed in nothing but a pair of sweat pants and a wife-beater. The central air was on full blast, and the room was so cold that his fingertips and toes were beginning to go numb.

"Fuck is my lawyer at?" Sonny continued snapping at the mirror. He knew someone was on the other side looking at him. "Y'all violating my rights! I wanna talk to my fucking lawyer!"

Police Commissioner, Monroe Jackson was seething on the other side of the two-way mirror. His initial plan was to have Sonny taken from the county and brought down to the precinct, where he would mysteriously hang himself in one of the holding cells. But things didn't turn out the way he anticipated.

For starters, Roland Rushin was somehow tipped off about the raid at the county jail and by the time Sonny was brought down to the precinct, he and his camera crew were camped outside of the building thirsty for a news break. In addition to that, Savino popped up a few minutes later, ranting and raving about his client's constitutional rights and now the Attorney General, William Gleason, was downstairs in the lobby demanding to speak to Monroe.

"You lucky son-of-a-bitch," Monroe mumbled under his breath, still peering at Sonny through the two-way mirror. He looked back at Sgt. Lorenzo, who was standing in the doorway. "Let 'em up."

"Which one?" Sgt. Lorenzo asked. "The Attorney General or fuck boy's attorney?"

"Goddamnit! I said the both of 'em!" Monroe raised his voice. He was frustrated and pissed off to the max.

The word around the Criminal Justice Center was that the feds were on the brink of taking over Sonny's case. And now, after the murder of Seth Willis, it seemed as though the feds were going to step in sooner rather than later. This was bad news for The Commissioner. He knew that the second the feds took over, his opportunity to get even with The Moreno Family would be lost forever.

He opened the door to the interrogation room and stepped inside. He was just about to tear into Sonny and give him a piece of his mind, but was interrupted when the Attorney General called his name from behind.

"Yeah, Bill. I was just about to begin the interrogation," Monroe said as he spun around to face him. He noticed right away that the Attorney General was accompanied by two Pennsylvania State Troopers. Both men were scowling at Monroe with guns in their hands, just daring him to make a move. Confused, Monroe locked eyes with the Attorney General. "Hey, ah, Bill, what's going on? What the hell is this about?"

"Monroe, I'm going to need you to turn around and place your hands behind your back."

"Excuse me?" Monroe replied, looking at the skinny white man as though he'd heard him wrong. "You wanna run that by me again?"

"Cuff him," the A.G. ordered his men. He was looking at Monroe when he said it.

The two Troopers stepped forward and pinned Monroe against the wall. "Wait a minute, goddamnit! You can't arrest me, I'm the goddamned Commissioner!"

"Not anymore," General Gleason stated. He stepped forward and snatched away Monroe's Commissioner's badge. "You're under arrest for the murders of District Attorney, Seth Willis and Michelle Drayton."

"This is ludicrous!" Monroe protested. "I didn't murder anyone, let alone the goddamned district attorney! Are you out of your fucking mind?"

The State Troopers snatched Monroe off the wall and pushed him toward the door.

"Get your goddamned hands off of me, you sons-a-bitches!" He was so furious, that he was foaming at the mouth. "I swear to God, I'm gonna have your asses for this! Do you have any idea who the fuck I am? I'm Monroe Jackson, goddamnit!" He bucked and yanked, twisted and pulled, but was forced out into the hallway nonetheless. Once in the hallway, he immediately noticed that Sgt. Lorenzo and three of his officers were being placed under arrest as well. They looked at Monroe with pleading eyes, but there was absolutely nothing he could do. He couldn't even help himself. Exasperated, he looked at Gleason and attempted to reason with him. "This is bullshit, Bill, and you know it. You *know* me. You know that I would never do anything like this."

General Gleason gritted his teeth. He looked Monroe in the eyes and thought about everything he just said. He knew that nine times out of ten Monroe was speaking the truth but at this point, it really didn't matter.

There were two security guards swearing up and down that Monroe and his men stormed inside of the D.A.'s office and attacked Seth moments before he was gunned down. They also indicted they were threatened at gun point and ordered to leave and that a few minutes later, after hearing what they assumed to be gunfire, they discovered the mutilated bodies of Seth and Michelle Drayton, the young receptionist who worked downstairs on the ground floor.

The security cameras had been wiped clean, except for the footage of Monroe and his men storming into the building moments before everything went down.

In addition to that, Gleason had his own personal reasons for taking down the commissioner. The situation was out of his hands, much bigger than him and his office. The only thing he could do was follow orders.

"Get him out of here," Gleason ordered his men. He stood there watching as the State Troopers escorted Monroe and his officers down the hallway. When they were out of his sight, he stepped into the interrogation room where Sonny was handcuffed to the table. He started to say something, but Sonny spit on the floor and told him to fuck off.

"I don't know who the fuck you think you dealing wit'. But if you think for one second that I'm giving up any tapes, you can kiss my ass. I rather die than be labeled a snitch," Sonny spoke with a menacing scowl. "And on top of that, where the fuck is my lawyer? I know he's around here somewhere. He was pulling up when they snatched me out the paddy-wagon."

Gleason popped his head out the door to make sure nobody was listening and then turned back around to face Sonny. "Now, you listen, kid, and you listen close," he spoke in a low voice, barely above a whisper. "There's some very important people, who want you out of here. Some very, *very* important people."

Right away, Sonny knew he was referring to The Conglomerate. He didn't know how connected General Gleason was, or why he was saying the things he was saying, but he knew better than to say another word. He just sat there quietly.

"Does the name Madam François mean anything to you?"

Sonny didn't flinch. He'd never heard the name before, but even if he did, he would have never revealed it.

"No?" Gleason frowned, showing his confusion. He popped his head out the door once more and then brought his gaze back to Sonny. "Well, here's a name you should know—Big Angolo Gervino." Sonny squinted his eyes, and Gleason cracked a smile. "That's right, you know exactly who I'm talking about. I mean, after all, he's your great-grand father. He told me to tell you to sit tight, and that your days behind the wall are numbered."

Sonny scoffed. "Oh, yeah? And what the fuck is that supposed to mean?"

"It means that The Conglomerate is arranging to have you released from custody. I can't exactly say how or when but I do know the day is coming, and that it's coming soon. So just sit tight and keep quiet. Not a goddamned word, especially about this conversation that never happened. You got that, kid?"

Sonny looked at him and nodded at the camera hanging from the ceiling in the back-right corner.

"It's already been deactivated," Gleason told him.

Sonny bit down on his bottom lip, internalizing everything that General Gleason just told him. Some of what he said made sense, but the part about Big Angolo threw him through a loop. As far as he knew, the old mafia don was murdered back in the 60's when Grip was establishing The Moreno Family, or at least that's what his grandfather led him to believe, even though he never came right out and said it.

Gleason turned around to leave, and Sonny called out behind him. "Hey, yo, my man, hold up."

Gleason looked at his watch, then he peeked out the door. "Hurry up, kid. What is it?"

"This secret witness in my case, who is it?"

The General took a deep breath and sighed. He was clearly uncomfortable with the entire situation. "I'm not at liberty to say. I do exactly as I'm told, nothing more, nothing less. It's safer that way. But I will say this, the person who's scheduled to testify against you, is someone close. I wish I could tell you more, but I can't. But at the end of the day, it really doesn't matter. The Conglomerate wants you out of here, and that's exactly what's going to happen. So, if I were you, I'd just sit tight and wait for my moment. It's as simple as that."

With that being said, he headed out the door and left Sonny sitting there sifting through his thoughts. *"It's someone close,"* the General's words burned in his brain. He suspected Grip, but that was too obvious, too easy. Maybe it was Gangsta? He'd been fooled by his cousin once before. But what would Gangsta have to gain by throwing him under the bus? Rahmello? Highly doubtful, but at the same time, Sonny knew better than to rule him out. The last time they saw one another, he was seconds away from killing Olivia for the role she played in Easy's murder. And now that her and Rahmello had a baby together, who's to say that Rahmello wouldn't do whatever necessary to keep Olivia safe. Aside from that, Sonny knew Rahmello was going behind his back, moving weight and using Heemy to do it. For the past two months, he'd been using Alexis to keep tabs on him, and didn't doubt for a second that Rahmello was still in the game. The only thing he couldn't figure out was the identity of the person supplying him. *"It's someone close."* The words played over and over in his mind. *"It's someone close."*

"Whoever it is, they better strap the fuck up and get ready for war," Sonny mumbled under his breath. "'Cause I ain't doing no muthafuckin' talking.

106

Chapter Eight
A Week Later

It was a little past 4:30 p.m. when Nahfisah pulled up in front of Annie's hair salon on Broad and Nedro. She had spent the better part of the day shopping and cruising around in her brand-new Maserati, top down, hair blowing in the wind and loving the attention she was receiving.

Rahmello had been true to his word about giving her more freedom.

A few days ago, he blessed her with a new Maserati and the keys to the new house he bought her in Willow Grove. He also agreed to hit her off with the money Easy left her when he died. Not the entire $600,000, but increments of $5,000 a month.

Nahfisah was ecstatic. Being the ghetto girl she was, a steady flow of five racks a month was more money than she could have ever asked for.

So now that her money was right and her living situation was straight, her main focus was to do right by Imani. The plan was to attend college in the fall, earn a degree in business and learn how to make her money grow. So that way her and Imani would never again have to experience the harsh reality of living in the hood.

After looking at her beautiful face in the rearview mirror, Nahfisah threw the transmission in park and killed the engine. She was feeling good and looking even better.

Her birthday party was the following night, so after having her hair shampooed and styled, her next destination was the Koreans up the block to get her nails done.

Then after that, it was back to La Casa Moreno to pick up Imani. The day before they moved into their new house, which just so happened to be right up the block from Miss Mary's house, the nurse and mother figure Nahfisah met while doing her time in the rehab, she grabbed her Gucci tote from the passenger's seat and then climbed out the coupe.

She didn't make it three steps before the sound of a familiar voice made her freeze mid stride.

"Well, damn, butterfly, where you been at? I've been looking all over for you."

"What the hell?" Nahfisah said to herself as she spun around slow, not really knowing what to say.

Standing before her was Beaver Bushnut, looking and smelling like a million bucks. She could tell right away that he was playing with major paper.

The white diamonds dripping from his necklace were shining so brightly they should have come with a light bill, and the same could be said about the bling in his Rolex and his iced-out pinky ring.

His slender, six-foot frame was covered in a soft-yellow, D&G short set, topped off with a Gucci straw hat and a pair of yellow gators. His salt-and-pepper hair was barbered to perfection, and his light complexioned face was chiseled and handsome, reminding Nahfisah why she fell for him in the first place.

Damn, this muthafucka fine as hell, Nahfisah thought to herself as she stood there staring at him.

The last time she'd seen him, he was cracked out of his mind, dingy, dirty and laying on the ground with Sonny stomping on the back of his head. Since then, she hadn't given him much thought. But now that he was standing there smiling and rubbing his hands together and looking at her like he wanted to eat her, she didn't know what to do. After all, this was the man who stole her heart after Tommy was murdered and Imani was taken away. He was also the man who had her turned out on crack and selling her body, just for the sake of supporting his habit.

He was no good and she knew it. But there was something about him that she just could not shake, no matter how hard she tried. He was more addictive than any drug known to man, and Nahfisah fell for him every time. So instead of throwing shade and calling him out for the bastard he was, she batted her eyes and cracked a smile.

"That's right." Bushnut smiled at her, knowing she was still under his spell. "Come on over here to Daddy and gimmie some sugar." He opened his arms and she embraced him with a warm hug. He kissed on the forehead, then he took a step back and admired her body from head to toe. "Damn, butterfly, you looking real good, baby. Done gained a little weight and everything."

"Thank you." Nahfisah smiled. "You ain't looking too bad yourself."

"So, what'chu been up to?" Bushnut asked. He was looking at the Maserati she just stepped out of. "I see you out here riding clean."

"I'm just chilling," Nahfisah replied. "Focused on taking care of me and my daughter."

"Just chilling?" He nodded at the champagne coupe. "It looks to me you're doing better than just chilling. So, what's up wit' that? You done found ya'self a new sponsor or sum'n?"

"Nah, it's nothing like that. My brother's been holding me down until I get back on my feet."

Bushnut looked at her with a raised brow. "Who? Sonny? That nigga locked up."

"Nah, not Sontino. I'm talking about our younger brother, Rahmello."

"Oh, yeah?" Bushnut rubbed his goatee, automatically thinking of a new way to make a come up. He should have known better than to think the Moreno's would fall back just because Sonny was locked up in the county. "I don't think I know Rahmello. But what's up wit' the nigga? What, he took over for Sonny? It's too much fetty out here for a muthafucka to sit back, so I know they still doing they thing. What they fucking wit, the coke or the dope?"

"Excuse me?" Nahfisah screwed her face up. She could see the jealousy in his eyes, and knew right away that she was talking too much. This was one of the things Rahmello made her promise not to do when she came home from the rehab.

She knew from watching the news that her family was on a whole new level, but it wasn't until she saw La Casa Moreno and the way Rahmello was living that she began to ask questions. He told her all about the status of their family, and that she needed to conduct herself accordingly.

He also made it clear that family business was just that: *family business* and that no outsider should ever know the inner workings of the family business. He never told her he was still hustling but Nahfisah wasn't stupid, she knew the deal. She also knew that Sonny was against it, and that Rahmello was using Heemy to run the streets while he managed him from the background.

"You know what?" Nahfisah glanced at her Cartier watch. "I think I better get going. My hair appointment was at 4:30 and after that, I still gotta get my nails done. It was good seeing you, though." She turned to walk away, but Bushnut grabbed her by the arm and turned her back around to face him.

"Come on now, butterfly, don't just walk away from me like that. I didn't mean to pry, I just wanted to know how you was doing. I ain't seen you in a while, and I wanted to make sure you were properly being taken care of."

"Taken care of?" Nahfisah shot back. "Since when you cared about somebody taking care of me? You sure as hell didn't."

"Now, why you bringing up old shit?" he asked in a low voice, twisting his face like she stabbed him in the heart. "Butterfly, I was at my worst back then, but it's different now. I finally got my shit together. I've been clean for over a year and half, and done scraped some money together to make some new investments. I'm a new man, butterfly. You gotta believe me. Matter fact, don't even take my word for it, just gimmie the opportunity to show you."

"I don't know." Nahfisah sulked.

Bushnut gently caressed her chin and gazed into her blue eyes. "Come on, butterfly, gimmie the chance to show you. I love you."

Nahfisah smiled. That was the first time in almost two years that someone other than her daughter professed their love for her. The look in his eyes seemed sincere, and the softness of his voice made her heart melt.

Holding her hand out, she said, "Lemme see your phone." He handed over his Samsung, and Nahfisah punched in her phone number. "My birthday is tomorrow and my brother's throwing me an all-white party. I want you to come through and depending on what you bring me, maybe we can talk about it."

"Now, that's what I'm talking about," Bushnut said with a smile. "So, where's the party at, and what time you want me to come through?"

"The party's on the waterfront, down Penn's Landing. He rented me a big ol' yacht, so it's basically a boat party."

"That's what's up." Bushnut nodded his head. "You mind if I bring a few friends wit' me?"

"Yeah, that's cool. Everybody's gonna be there anyway. I heard on the radio that Yo Gotti's performing, so you *know* it's going down. Philly love 'em some Yo Gotti!"

"No doubt," Bushnut replied, looking at his Rollie. "Lil' bro must be really doing his thing. I mean, since you telling me he's got Yo Gotti coming through and all."

"I know, right. And he never even told me. I'm just now hearing about it on the radio."

The door to the salon swung open and Annie stepped outside with a suspicious look on her face. She knew Bushnut from back in the day and was well aware of his get down. There was something about him that she never liked. She used to always tell Easy not to trust him, but Easy never listened. He was blinded by the duffle bags of money Bushnut was spending on the regular. It wasn't until the day he went down Richard Allen to serve him a brick, and was kidnapped by the YBM that he finally listened, even though Bushnut swore up and down that he didn't have anything to do with it.

He was nothing but trouble, and Annie knew it. She was oblivious to the history between him and Nahfisah, she just knew her stepdaughter was fragile, and that the likes of Beaver Bushnut was something that could possibly make her slip back into her old ways.

"Ah, em!" Annie cleared her throat, making her presence known. Bushnut attempted to speak, but Annie gritted on him. "Humph." She folded her arms across her chest and looked at Nahfisah. "Girl, if you don't get'cho ass in here, so I can do your hair. Your appointment was over ten minutes ago."

"Alright, Mama Annie, I'm coming right now," Nahfisah replied. "Just gimmie a couple of minutes."

"Humph," Annie scoffed, refusing to move an inch. She stood right there on the stoop ice-grilling Bushnut and watching his every move.

A cherry-red, CLS 500 pulled up and parked behind Nahfisah's Maserati. Alexis hopped out with three packs of hair in her hand, ready to have her hair done as well. The first thing she noticed was Nahfisah standing there hugging on Bushnut. She looked at Annie and saw the way she was scowling at the man and then looked back at Nahfisah, who was walking toward her with a bashful grin on her face.

"Well, damn, bitch, who the hell was that?" Alexis asked, as Bushnut hopped back in his Caddy.

"Nobody," Nahfisah answered. "Just an old friend."

"An old friend?" Alexis smiled back. "Well, damn, bitch, you sure as hell coulda fooled me. 'Cause the way y'all was hugging on one another, I woulda thought that was your man. Look at'chu, all giddy and smiling and whatnot, don't make no sense."

She looked at Annie, waiting for her to say something, but the only thing Annie said was, "Humph." She looked at Nahfisah and rolled her eyes, then she turned around and dipped back inside of the salon.

"Dang, Nah, why Mama Annie look at'chu like that?"

"I 'on't know." Nahfisah shrugged her shoulders. "You know Mama Annie crazy as hell."

The two women cracked up laughing as they stepped inside of the salon. Nahfisah didn't pay it any mind, but Alexis did. She didn't understand why Annie was throwing shade, but she made a mental note to ask her about it when Nahfisah wasn't around.

She knew that Annie loved Nahfisah like the daughter she never had, so her stank attitude must have had something to do with the guy she was seeing. Alexis had never seen him before, but he appeared to be touching some nice paper. Surely this was something she would speak to Sonny about.

112

Chapter Nine
At Sci Graterford

The Reaper was sitting in the lobby of the state prison, waiting for the officer at the front desk to call his name. He was there to visit Alvin and like always, the situation was bittersweet. He hated that his brother had been locked up for the past twenty-four years but after everything the two had been through, at least they were still alive.

The majority of the gangsters from their generation had died off decades ago, victims of a cold Philadelphia, that during the late eighties and early nineties, amassed a body count that was north of three thousand. The YBM could account for many of those murders, whether directly or indirectly, but the two brothers were still alive to talk about it.

So, if nothing else, The Reaper had to respect it, especially when it came to himself. He could have easily been sitting in a cell right next to his brother, or even worse, he could have been six-feet-deep, dead and gone and long forgotten about.

The Reaper had many thoughts running through his mind as he sat there quietly. But the main thought was something that always seemed to pop up whenever he went to visit Alvin, and that was the night he found the mutilated body of his only niece.

December 12, 2014

It was twenty-two minutes past three when The Reaper cruised down the two-way street that led to the front gate of Sonny's mansion. The front of his van was covered in Nipsy's blood, with yellowish plasma and small chunks of brain smeared across the windshield.

The chilly December wind was blending with the heavy snowfall, turning everything into a frosty white blur, and the barren branches on the English Sycamores that lined the street on both sides were swaying back and forth, causing The Reaper to twist his head from left to right.

He could barely see ahead of him, let alone the large estate to his left. It was tucked behind an eight-foot-high, Greco Roman style wall that ran up and down the street and around the block, reminiscent of an old army fort.

Suddenly, a dashing movement in the corner of his left eye made him mash down on the brake pad, causing the van to fishtail out of control. It skidded about five feet and then crashed into the back of a snow-covered car that he didn't even see coming.

Wham!

"What the fuck was that?" The Reaper said to himself, frantically looking around the stone wall and in between the sycamores. He could have sworn he'd seen a man with no clothes on scouring around on all fours. But now the only thing he saw were the sporadic shadows from the swaying branches dangling down from up above.

"Man, I know I'm not trippin'," he mumbled under his breath, still looking all around the front gate.

Looking up the block, he spotted a white-tailed deer and a young calf trotting across the street. Assuming that was the movement he saw, he threw the utilities van in reverse, tearing the rear bumper from the snow-covered Impala.

"Sum'n ain't right," he mumbled some more. He'd been calling Daphney back-to-back for the last ten minutes, but every call went straight to voicemail. And now this mysterious car was parked outside of her house.

The dome light was still on and the back-passenger's side door was wide open. He grabbed his shotty off of the passenger's seat and slowly exited the van.

Glancing up and down the block, he approached the vehicle with the sawed-off shotty leading the way. The first thing he noticed was the pink snow on the ground beside the passenger's side door. A thick, syrup-like stream of blood was trickling from the crack at the base of the front door accumulating on top, and the dead body of a white man was slumped in the front, hunched over the center counsel. The only thing he saw in the back seat was a blood-covered cell phone.

"Eeeeeeiiiiiiiii!"

A shrilling cry caught The Reaper by surprise, causing him to spin around with the shotgun flaming.

Boom!

The bright burst lit up the entire block, but nothing was there. Instinctively, he looked down at the snow searching for any traces of footprints. He spotted two pairs, one being smaller than the other. They trailed from the back of the car all the way up to and straight through the open front gate. He didn't know what was going on, but his cold heart was telling him that Daphney was in trouble.

"Eeeeeeiiiiiii!"

The piercing sound of another wail grabbed his attention. It appeared to be coming from the house. He darted through the open gate and ran up the horseshoe driveway. Approaching the front of the house, he noticed the front door was slightly ajar. He pushed it open and stepped inside.

"Hey, yo, Daph? You in here?" he called out, his deep voice echoing throughout the foyer. His shotty was tightly clutched in both hands and beads of sweat were trickling down his dark-skinned face. The house was so dark, he could barely see. He did, however, notice a foul stench. It was fecal and coppery, reminiscent of a fresh kill. "Hey, yo, Daph? Where the fuck is you at? It's ya Uncle Rayon."

Silence.

"Come on, Daph, if you in here, say say sum'n."

Suddenly, someone cut on the lights and The Reaper took a step back. Nothing could have prepared him for something so cruel. A skinless Daphney was high in the air, dangling from the balcony by her large intestines. The slimy, gray rope snaked out of her stomach, twirled around her neck and looped around the bars of the banister. Her skinless flesh was a reddish-pink, similar to raw chicken dipped in hot sauce, and the twisted bones of her ribcage were spiky and long, bursting out of her torso like a bloody bagpipe. Her severed left arm was grotesquely sticking out of her pussy from the elbow down, and her mouth was ripped wide open, pushed back so far it appeared as though the front of her face had been torn in half.

"Damn, Daph! What the fuck?"

"*What's de matter, chico? Ju no like?*" *Diablo asked, looking down at The Reaper with bloodshot eyes. He was dressed in a brown leather cape and leaning over the balcony. It's a work of art, no?*"

"*Muthafucka, I'ma kill you!*" *The Reaper shouted. He leveled the shotty at the top of the balcony and let off a shot just as Diablo was leaping over the banister.*

Boom!

"*Eeeeeiiiiiii!*"

The flaming buckshot whizzed past Diablo and blew a chunk out of Daphney's face. The little Mexican came down hard, causing both men to fall to the floor. They rolled around punching and scratching, struggling to gain the upper hand. Diablo was fast. He scratched The Reaper across the face and kneed him in the nuts before biting down on his left shoulder.

"*Agh, shit!*" *The Reaper cried out.*

"*Eeeeeiiiiiii!*" *The Mexican shrieked.*

The Reaper caught him with a headbutt and a short right hook to the ribs. "*Pussy, get'cha ass up off me!*" *He landed another blow to the left side of his neck and Diablo grunted like a pig.* "*Yeah, nigga. That ass gon' die today!*"

They rolled around some more, with Diablo somehow managing to land on top. He was much stronger than The Reaper anticipated. He released another wail and then dished out a headbutt of his own.

Wham!

He hit The Reaper with another headbutt.

Whm!

Then another headbutt.

Wham!

The Reaper was dazed and disoriented, quickly running out of steam. A hammer-punch to his forehead split his dome down the middle, and he could feel the blood seeping into his eyes. He struggled some more and then screamed in pain when Diablo sank his fangs into the base of his throat.

116

"Agh, fuck!" The Reaper grimaced. He was gasping for air and punching as hard as he could, doing everything possible to push Diablo away from his neck. "Get—the fuck—off me!"

Diablo was in a frenzy. The taste of fresh blood had him grunting and groaning and shaking his body like a Pitbull in a death match. His animal-like fangs were seconds away from rupturing The Reaper's windpipe, and it seemed as though there was nothing The Reaper could do to stop it. He scratched Diablo on the side of his face, hoping to break free, but Diablo just clamped down harder.

The Reaper gasped. His time was running out and he knew it. In a desperate attempt to break free, he clawed at Diablo's face, scratching out one of his eyeballs.

Diablo shrieked like a banshee. As he stumbled backwards and reached for his dangling eye, The Reaper rolled over and spat out a mouthful of blood. Struggling to catch his breath, he looked to his right and saw his shotgun laying on the floor. He crawled toward it and scooped it up quick. But when he turned around to let off a shot, Diablo was gone. His brown leather cape was laying on the floor and a trail of his blood leading out the front door. The Reaper stumbled over to the door and spotted the Mexican running across the snow-covered lawn. He aimed the shotty and let off a shot.

Boom!

"Eeeeeiiiiii!"

A bloody-red mist burst out of Diablo's left shoulder, but it didn't stop him from running. The Reaper squeezed off another round, but he missed. And before he knew it, Diablo hopped over the stone wall and disappeared into the dark of the night.

Exhausted and still struggling to breathe, The Reaper spun back around and looked up at Daphney's mutilated corpse.

Trembling with rage, he looked down at the brown leather cape. He saw a belly button with a diamond stud and two chocolate nipples with Sonny's name tatted above the left areola. It was then that he realized the brown leather cape belonged to Daphney. It was her peeled away skin.

***

Back to 2016

Vrrrrrm! Vrrrrrm!

The vibrating of his cell phone snapped The Reaper out of his nightmarish day dream. He rubbed the front of his neck where four scars reminded him of unfinished business, then he looked down at his cell phone. The caller was Bushnut. He accepted the call and placed the phone against his ear. "What?"

"Well, damn, playa, it's about time you answered," Bushnut replied. "I got some information for you."

"Oh yeah?" The Reaper retorted, still rubbing the scars on his neck. "Well, spit it the fuck out. I ain't got all day."

"You ever heard of Sonny having a little brother? Some lil' nigga named Rahmello?"

"Yeah, I heard the name before, but I ain't never had no dealings wit' him. Why, what's up?"

"I was kickin' it wit' one of my lil' tenderonies and according to ol' girl, the lil' nigga, Rahmello, got the bag right now. Ummhmm, he been out here getting money the whole time, right up under our goddamn nose. I'm assuming he musta stepped his weight up and took over for Sonny."

"Is that right?" The Reaper replied, gritting his teeth.

He was trying to make sense of what Bushnut was telling him. The last he heard was that Grip and Rahmello were on the run ducking a federal indictment. As the YBM's second in command, The Reaper had been dealing with the Moreno Family for well over twenty years. They were usually out and about, flaunting their wealth and making noise around the city. But for the past year and a half, he hadn't heard a thing, not a peep. Their nightclub and sports bar had been shut down and boarded up ever since Sonny went to jail. There were no annual turkey giveaways on Thanksgiving and so far, every time Sonny went to court, his only supporter was his mother.

The Reaper was planning to kill her, solely for the sake of sending a message to Sonny, but Alvin wouldn't allow it. Annie was the only one looking after his grandbabies, and the last thing he needed was for Dayshon and Keyonti to be separated and shipped off to different foster homes.

"But I'm saying, though, the bitch that told you this? Is she reliable? 'Cause according to the streets, Grip and the young bul, Rahmello, supposed to had left the country when the cops ran down on fuck boy."

"I heard the same thing," Bushnut replied. "But I'm telling you, Ray, this is coming straight from the horse's mouth."

"The horse's mouth? What the fuck is that supposed to mean?"

"It means that the bitch I'm talking about is a Moreno. Her name's Nahfisah, and she's Sonny and Rahmello's sister. So, if anybody knows what's going on, it's her."

"A'ight, just keep tabs on the bitch and see what'chu can find out. Hopefully, we can get a line on this nigga."

"Shit, nigga, I can do you one better than that. He's throwing a boat party for her tomorrow night down Penn's Landing. So, what's the deal? Is we down there or what?"

"I don't know. Lemme see what's up wit' Alvin first," The Reaper replied, looking at the corrections officer at the front desk. She was calling his name and waving him over to be searched before going into the visiting house. "In the meantime, I want y'all to go around Delhi Street and see what's up wit' the young bul, Heemy. If he gets down wit' the program, good. But if he doesn't, then y'all make sure his lil' ass wish that he did."

The Reaper disconnected the call and then strolled over to the front desk. As he checked in with the corrections officer, he noticed that a cinnamon complexioned black woman was sitting in the corner of the crowded lobby watching his every move. She was sitting there with two towering black dudes with thick, bushy dreads. Both men were giving him the ice grill. He started to say something, but the woman cracked up laughing and her two companions did the same.

He wasn't sure whether or not they were laughing at him but either way, he had more important things to worry about. Namely, Alvin and the urgent phone call he received earlier that day telling him to come up to the jail.

So, while the woman and her two flunkies sat there staring at him, he stepped inside of the search room and prepared himself for the sit down with Alvin. There was absolutely no telling what his older brother was up to.

Chapter Ten
N Jardines De la Reina, Cuba

Grip was finally home, settled, relaxed and enjoying his native Cuba. The moist, Caribbean weather was a breezy 81° and for the first time in nearly sixty years, he could finally sit back and enjoy the fruits of his labor.

The $300,000,000 that he used to establish an agreement with the Castros not only provided him and his family with political asylum, it awarded them with their own private island. It was one of many that made up the Jardines De La Reina Islands off the western coast of Cuba.

At first glance, the small, unpopulated island was nothing more than seventy-two acres of palm trees, green pastures and sugarcane fields. But after spending close to $10,000,000., in less than a year, the island was transformed into what Grip liked to call his tiny little slice of heaven on earth.

On the northern coast of the island, calmly swaying to the rhythm of the soft tides rolling in from the ocean, was *La Gabriella* the double-deck yacht that he named after his mother.

Docked and anchored, the fifty-foot yacht was where he entertained most of his guests. It was also his means of transportation whenever he had to travel back and forth to the mainland.

About a mile from the northern coast was a large hangar and a gaping runway for the two private jets that he used to travel the world. The spacious runway spilled into a two-way lane that eventually split into three separate cobble-stoned roads. The main road went straight, right up a grassy hill that led to a plush 30,000 square-foot mansion. The subsequent roads traveling east and west dipped down into the southern tip of the island where two mansions sat on both sides of a five-acre, man-made lake.

The mansion on the right was designated for Sonny, and the mansion on the left was designated for Rahmello. Both mansions were a tad bit smaller, but just as opulent as the big house on the hill. Grip was doing the damn thing, and he knew it. He couldn't wait to show his grandsons what he'd been working on.

"I'm telling you, nephew, if this isn't the epitome of blood, sweat and tears, then I don't know what is," Grip said with a satisfying smile.

He was talking to Gangsta.

The two men were standing on his back patio looking down on the two mansions at the bottom of the hill and the Caribbean Sea that stretched across the horizon. It was a little past eight-thirty and the passion-red, yellowish sun was slowly descending, looking as though the Atlantic Ocean to their left was swallowing the ball of fire, whole.

"This Family came a long way," Grip continued, taking soft totes on his burning Cohiba. "I started out as a snot-nosed, just ten years old, every day, in the presence of bosses. I used to park their Cadillacs and Lincolns, light their cigars in the middle of poker games, and bring them sandwiches and drinks. But even as a snot-nose, I was smart enough to pay attention. I studied their every move and digested their every word. I'm telling you, nephew, I was a goddamned sponge, just sitting back and taking it all in, knowing that if I played my cards right, I would one day grow to be more powerful than every last one of 'em put together. And look at me now, I got enough money and juice to make the Pope get touched, if I wanted to," he clarified with a chuckle and a devious grin. "I mean, who would've imagined? Me, the little Spanish talking mulatto from South Philly, who the niggers used to bully and laugh at? The bastard son of a mafia boss who was rejected by his own kind, based solely on the African blood running through my veins? But look at me now, over fifty years in the game, using everything those muthafuckas taught me, and I'm two moves away from being a goddamned billionaire. I've got silver in Nevada, copper in Montana, natural gas in Texas and crude oil in Indonesia. I've got coffee in Jamaica, gold in Mali and rubber plantations in the Congo. The next move is linking up with Joaquin and the Sinaloas to garner a percentage of their pipeline. Then after that, strike a deal with Madam François that will enable the family to tap into the international sex trade. Speaking of which," he bit down on his cigar and lifted his

Rolex, "Where the hell is Joaquin and Chatchi? They should've been here over a half an hour ago."

Gangsta didn't say a word. He was sick to his stomach, grinding his teeth and looking straight ahead. It was killing him inside to be standing next to the man who murdered his mother and father. He wanted so bad to snuff out the old man and settle the score, but now was not the time. There was bigger fish to fry and a meticulous plan in action that needed to be drawn out to a tee. So, for now, the old man was afforded the luxury of having a heartbeat. But when the time *did* come for Grip to get his just due, Gangsta vowed that nothing would stop him from avenging the double-cross that had been perpetrated against his parents.

Grip looked to his left and shot his nephew a funny look. His body language was off and the old man could sense it, the same way a great white shark could zero in on a single drop of blood in the vast, infinite depths of the largest body of water.

It all started on the night Grip left for Cuba and later learned that Gregory and his wife had been tortured and murdered.

In addition to that, he heard about Ahmed and Mustafa. They were found dead in Gregory's kitchen with gunshot wounds to the back of their domes. The two men were supposed to had been with Gangsta, Shabazz and Aziz. So, when he realized the three men were still alive, and Ahmed and Mustafa weren't, he reasonably grew suspicious. He confronted Gangsta about it a few months later, but Gangsta claimed that he sent Ahmed and Mustafa to check in with Gregory when he didn't accept his phone calls.

According to Gangsta, they must've stumbled on the person or persons who killed Gregory and his wife and were caught slipping. The story didn't sit too well with Grip, but he had no other choice than to believe what Gangsta told him. There was nothing to contradict what he said, and as far as he knew, his nephew didn't have any reason that would justify killing his own men.

Even still, there was something about his demeanor that Grip wasn't feeling. He began to inquire, but was cut short when Gangsta pointed up at the sky and said, "There they go."

Grip looked up and calmly removed the cigar from his mouth. Up in the sky, about thirty feet from the ground, was a white helicopter with dark tinted windows. It was slowly descending, seconds away from landing on the helipad in the middle of his back yard.

His pilot, Fernando, had left over an hour ago to pick up Joaquin and Chatchi from the airport in Havana. And now that the Sinaloa bosses had finally arrived, Grip was all smiles, ready to talk business.

The gusting wind from the chopping blades grew stronger and stronger as the helicopter safely touched ground.

The side door slid open and Chatchi appeared in the threshold. He was dressed in a pair of gray slacks and a white dress shirt. He nodded his head at Grip and Gangsta, who were now off the patio and walking toward the chopper, then he carefully made his way down the three-step ladder.

Another man appeared in the threshold. He was small in stature, but bulky in width. His black, short sleeved dress shirt was decorated with solid-gold Versace buttons. The same Versace emblems appeared on his black suede shoes and his black and gold sunglasses. His long, slicked back hair was tied into a Samurai pony-tail and his smooth bronze complexion had a rich tan, courtesy of the Amazon sun that he'd grown accustomed to over the past year and a half.

After stepping down from the helicopter, he removed his sunglasses and scoped out the back yard before settling his gaze on Grip. "Don Moreno." The little Mexican nodded his head, showing his respect.

Grip was taken aback. He knew that Joaquin had undergone a procedure to reconstruct his face, he just never imagined it would be so drastic. His flat, round face was much different than Grip remembered. His brown eyes appeared to be closer together and more slanted than they used to be. His once wide nose was now skinny and short with a beak-like tip and his lips were so slim they appeared to be half their normal size.

Still looking at Joaquin, Grip took a pull on his cigar and exhaled the smoke. "A little Michael Jacksonish, but it served its purpose nonetheless," he said with a smile. He gestured toward

Gangsta, completely unaware that the two men were already acquainted. "This is my nephew, Terrance. He's my head of security, and I called him out here to attend our meeting. I hope you don't mind."

"I no mind, not at all," Joaquin replied, staring at Gangsta. He had much love and respect for the young Moreno. Had it not been for him and Big Angolo, Joaquin would still be rotting away in a Mexican prison camp. "Please to meet you, Señor."

"Likewise," Gangsta replied with a straight face. He extended his right hand and embraced Joaquin with a firm handshake.

"Alright, well I'm sure you two gentlemen had a long flight from Brazil. What do you say, we relax and little and then get down to business?" Grip asked, looking back and forth between the two Sinaloa bosses.

Joaquin looked at Chatchi, who shrugged his shoulders, then he looked back at Grip. "I no have any problems wit' dat."

"Sure shit," Grip replied. He flicked his cigar in the grass and then pulled out his Samsung and called up to the house. "Madam François," he spoke into the phone, "our guests have arrived and would like to spend a little down time before attending the meeting." He paused for a moment and listening to what Madam François was telling him. "Absolutely. Just send 'em down and we'll take it from there."

A couple of minutes later, dressed in nothing but lingerie and high-heeled pumps, ten of Cuba's most beautiful women emerged from the house. They sexily made their way down the patio steps and formed a line at the bottom. Flirting with their eyes, they stood there quietly, patiently waiting to be chosen.

Grip's blue eyes feasted on each of the ten beauties. He had already sampled their various flavors and had no doubts whatsoever that his guests would be satisfied.

"The choice is yours, gentlemen," he said as he turned back around to face Joaquin and Chatchi. "Do as you like and take as much time as you need. Whichever room you choose is equipped with its own shower and sauna. Just leave your clothes at the door and one of my housekeepers will tend to 'em. So relax, enjoy yourselves, then freshen up and get ready for the meeting. The Madam and I will be waiting in the dining room in the east wing. If you can't find it, just hit one of the intercoms in the hallway and one of my staff members will come and show you the way."

With that being said, the Black Mafia don headed toward the house with Gangsta right behind him. The Alvarez brothers looked at one another and then fixed their sights on the ten beauties, quietly selecting three women apiece.

It was time to get down and dirty, Mexican style!

***

About two hours later, Grip and Madam François were sitting at the chess table in the far corner of his dining room. The large ivory table was trimmed in platinum and topped off with red coral and white marble. The life-like, four-inch chess pieces were carved out of red-ruby and white crystal, and from the looks of it, Grip's red army was two moves away from tasting defeat.

Gangsta was standing behind right behind Grip with both hands behind his back. He appeared to be studying the chess board waiting for the Madam to make her next move. But in all actuality, he was caressing the handle on the Glock .9 that was sticking out the small of his back and contemplating on whether or not he should blow Grip's brains out the front of his face. The feeling was so intense, his balls were tingling.

The Madam looked up and saw the look in Gangsta's eyes. She was well aware of Gangsta grievance, but just like Gangsta, she too had strict orders from Big Angolo and killing Grip right then and there was not a part of his plan.

She looked at Grip, who was still hunched forward studying the board, none the wiser, and then brought her gaze back to Gangsta. "Terrance," she lifted her empty flute glass, "would you be a dear and bring an old woman another glass of champagne?"

Gangsta looked at her and bit down on his bottom lip, still caressing his burner. When he didn't reply right away, Grip turned around to look at him. "Well, damn, boy, don't tell me you done gawn and went deaf. It's bad enough you've been slacking and dragging ass lately. Don't stand there looking stupid, go fetch the Madam another glass of bubbly. And bring me another stogie while you're at it."

Grip didn't notice, but Madam François was looking at Gangsta behind his back, pleading with her eyes for him to calm down and stick to the plan.

With flaring nostrils, Gangsta released his hold on the nine millie, then he spun around and headed toward the kitchen.

"That goddamned boy's been losing his mind lately," Grip stated as he turned back around to face the chess board. "Now, where were we?"

"It's my move, but there's no sense in playing the rest of the game," Madam François spoke in a soft, silky voice. "I already won."

"And you're sure about that?"

"I am," she replied with certainty. "Because my next move is this." She snatched his Rook and replaced it with her Bishop. "Then after that, you're gonna do this." She snatched her own Bishop and replaced it with his Queen. "And then, I'm going to do this." She pushed her Pawn forward, trapping his King. "See? Checkmate."

Grip looked at the board and scratched his head. "Ain't that a bitch! I sho'nuff would have snatched that goddamned Bishop, not even realizing I would have exposed my King to your Knight and Pawn. Damnit."

Madam François smiled at him. The two had known one another for years and had played too many chess games to count. "Patterns, my old friend. Patterns."

Grip laughed it off, but inwardly he was full of rage. *Am I really that predictable?* He questioned himself, still looking at the board wondering how he allowed himself to be two steps behind. It was usually the other way around.

"So, now, before we began this meeting, how much longer do we wait until it's time to get Sontino out of there?" Madam François asked. "He's suffered long enough now, don't you think?"

"I mean—yeah, he's been there longer than I would like. But now that we know the identity of this secret witness, I think it's imperative to let things play out. At least until after his trial. And speaking of which, why are you so hell-bent on getting him out of there? You've been bugging me about it for months now."

"Let's just say I have my own personal reasons," the Madam replied.

"You're own personal reasons?"

"Certainly." The Madam nodded her head. "Sontino and his— *affiliations,* shall I say, from Philadelphia to Los Angeles, will be the key to our distribution network. Similar to Joaquin's connections with the Chicanos in Chicago and all throughout the Midwest. That was the main reason I agreed to let you in on the international sex trade. I break bread with you and you break bread with me. But without Sontino, none of this would make sense. I have no faith in your other grandson, Rahmello. No offense."

"None taken."

As the two continued going back and forth about Sonny and his case, Joaquin and Chatchi stepped into the dining room. They appeared to be somewhat disturbed, and Grip took notice right away. "What's the matter, gentlemen? Is everything okay?"

"No, Señor. Everything is not okay," Joaquin replied with in his Mexican accent. "I just receive a phone call from my top man back in Sinaloa. We have a major problem."

"A problem?" Grip asked, cutting his eye at Madam François, who had just as much to gain from their meeting as he did. "What type of problem? Is it something that we can help you with?"

"I do not think so. It's Diablo. My Roberto was his best friend."

"And what does that have to do with anything?" asked Madam François.

"Yeah," Grip added on. "And who the hell is Diablo?"

Joaquin whispered something in Chatchi's ear, then Chatchi stepped forward and began to break things down.

"Diablo is a very dangerous man, Señor, very dangerous." He shook his head for emphasis. "My brother and me created this monster, but lately—it's like we can't even handle him. Especially since we pick up and move down to Brazil. I left my top man, Jorge, in charge back in Sinaloa. Right now, he is de one making all de moves.

So for safe measures, I give him Diablo to make sure things go smooth and to assure dat nobody steps out of line. I give Diablo strict orders to stay away from de states and explained to him dat all debts between us and ju family have been settled, but Diablo no listen."

"He doesn't listen?" Grip retorted with a creased brow. "My partner and me have invested hundreds of millions of dollars in your operation. We called you guys out here to talk business, and now you're telling me we have a problem? Because you can't control one of your men? Are you shitting me right now?"

"Ju no understand," Chatchi spoke humbly. "If Diablo is back in de states, dat means he's coming for ju family. Dey are not safe, Señor, trust me. If I was ju, I'd send for dem immediately."

Askari

Chapter Eleven
Back at La Casa Moreno
8:47 p.m.

Sonny's trial was only three weeks away, and Rahmello's anxiety was at an all-time high. The threat against everything he loved was inescapable, as he didn't doubt for a second that Sonny would come home seeking revenge for what happened to Easy. He also knew that Sonny's aggressions would eventually come knocking at his front door, and that a war between them was inevitable.

Not only did he disregard his older brother's orders to stay away from the coke game but a little over a week ago, he reached out to Juan Nunez and squashed the beef between them. He also made it clear that he and Sonny were no longer playing for the same team. It took a little persuading, but by the end of their meeting, he and Juan struck a deal that would finally allow Rahmello to step out of his brother's shadow. At the beginning of each month, Juan would hit him off with 300 keys on consignment for the low price of $25,000 apiece. In Rahmello's eyes, it was all about the money. Sonny was locked up and Grip was missing in action. It was up to him to keep the family afloat and that's exactly what he planned on doing. Especially since Savino cut him off, claiming that the streets were too hot to be doing business.

"Fuck it, man, it is what is," Rahmello said as he stuffed a brick of money in his money-counter.

He was sitting behind the desk in his home office counting the money he received a few hours earlier from his playa down in South Carolina. The money-counter went to work, swiftly sifting through the bills.

Fluddddddddddd. Beep!

He looked at the digital screen and read the figures out loud. "That's twenty bands plus the four hunnid and eighty thousand I just counted. Damn, this was a crazy-ass week, and it ain't even over yet. I still gotta shoot up-top to holla at Ra and all the Bishops out Brooklyn. Then after that, I got the homies flying in from out Cali. It's like the good ol' days all over again, only this time I ain't gotta worry about Sonny and all the politics and bullshit. 'Cause at the end of the day, if it don't make money, it don't make sense. Fuck politics. It's a new day and a new time, and I'm doing this shit my way. Ain't that right, little man," he said to Omelly, who was sitting on the floor playing with a brick of money.

The little boy looked up at his daddy and smiled. Rahmello smiled back, then he reached down and gently caressed his soft curly hair.

"Come on, Mello, I know you're not down here still counting that goddamned money," Olivia whined when she stepped inside of his office.

She was butt-ass naked, except for the colorful socks she was wearing. The chocolate nipples on her juicy C-cups were standing at attention and the neatly-trimmed fuzz box between her thighs was begging to be sucked and stroked.

"You told me you were coming to bed over an hour ago." Olivia placed her hands on her hips. "What's up with that?"

"I'ma be up there in a minute," Rahmello replied. He removed the $20,000 from the money tray and wrapped a rubber band around it. "I still need to go downstairs and stash this shit in the vault."

"Well, you seriously need to hurry up, 'cause I'm horny as hell and I'm supposed to be on my second nut by now."

"Damn," Rahmello licked his lips and leaned back in his high-back chair, "it's like that?"

"It's just like that," Olivia replied. She came a little closer, then she looked down and noticed Omelly was sitting on the floor, gumming on the brick of money in his hand. "Omelly, no! Don't be putting that in your mouth, it's dirty." She confiscated the brick of money, then she tossed it in the duffle bag sitting on top of the desk.

Omelly looked at her like she was crazy and then stuck out his bottom lip. When she didn't give him the money back, he burst into a temper tantrum. He was wailing at the top of his lungs and rolling around on the carpet, kicking and swinging at the air.

"Damn, Oli, why you gotta come in here wit' the nut shit?" Rahmello said as he reached down and scooped Omelly off of the floor.

He sat him on his lap and gave him another brick of money. Omelly stopped crying and began playing with the money like nothing had ever happened.

"Don't make no dag-gone sense." Olivia shook her head and smiled. "I can't tell who loves the money more, you or him."

"This my youngin' right here, he's supposed to be in love with the money," Rahmello shot back, bouncing Omelly on his lap. "It's in his blood."

Still shaking her head, Olivia grabbed the little boy from his lap. "Come on, little man, it's time for bed. You should've been asleep hours ago. Now, tell Daddy night-night."

"Nigh-nigh, Dada," Omelly mumbled, never taking his eyes off the money in his hands.

"Damn, Oli, leave us alone, we chilling."

"Yeah, y'all chilling alright. His little ass is about to go chill in his bed until he falls asleep, and his daddy better wrap this shit up so he get in his own bed and give his mommy what she needs." She turned to walk away, and Rahmello called out behind her.

"Hold up, his little ass still got my money in his hands."

"What money?" She turned back around to face him.

"Yo, stop playing, you know what I'm talking about."

"Oh, you mean *my* money that I'm using to go shopping in the morning for Nahfisha's party. It looks to be about eighteen or twenty thousand. So, that's a brand-new bag, a pair of red bottoms, a sexy little Coogie dress and the weekly allowance that you still ain't gave me yet."

Rahmello cracked up laughing. "So, what, you shaking me down now?"

"Yup."

"Just like that?"

"Umm-hmm." She nodded her head and smiled at him. "Just like that. Now, wrap this up so you can come upstairs and play in this pussy."

When Olivia left the office, Rahmello tossed the last brick of money in the duffle bag and zipped it up. He backed away from the desk prepared to leave, but was caught by surprise when the phone on the desk began to ring.

This was the first time since he'd been staying at La Casa Moreno that someone called the number to Grip's office, so he knew right away that the caller was his grandfather.

He looked down at the phone as it continued ringing. "After all this time, why the fuck is he calling me now?" Rahmello mumbled to himself. "I ain't heard nothing from this nigga in over a year and a half. Then as soon as I reach out to Juan and establish a deal, he's calling the house all of a sudden? Sum'n ain't right. This nigga must know what I'm up to."

The phone stopped ringing and the only thing Rahmello heard was thumping sound of his heart beat. He was feeling guilty and somewhat afraid, uncertain as to whether or not Grip was calling because he learned about the side deal he cut with the Columbians.

And to make matters worse, if Grip knew about it, then nine times out of ten, Sonny knew about it as well. Rahmello wasn't prepared for such a thing. His decision to do business with Juan was based on the assumption that Grip would continue keeping his distance, and that if Sonny somehow managed to wiggle out of his case, Rahmello would kill him within the first twenty-four hours he hit the streets.

It was a hard stance to take, but in Rahmello's mind, he had no other choice. He knew Sonny would kill him the second he discovered his younger brother had taken sides with the people who murdered their father and attempted to take out their entire family. The element of surprise was a muthafucka, and without it, Rahmello was vulnerable. The only thing he had going for him was his ability to flood the entire Block Boy Family with cocaine from the east coast to the west, which was something he assumed would garner their support if a war broke out between him and his brother.

But if Sonny came home and had enough time to rally the troops, that, and in addition to his inevitable position in The Conglomerate, Rahmello knew he didn't stand a chance. It was imperative he remained two steps ahead. Not only for his sake, but for Olivia's sake as well.

Somewhat shaken, Rahmello strapped the duffle bag over his shoulder and proceeded to leave the office. He made it halfway toward the door, but stopped abruptly when Heldga popped on the other side. She was dressed in a nightgown, a silky pink head scarf and a fluffy pair of house shoes.

"Damn, Heldga, what's up?" Rahmello frowned as she stepped inside the office and approached him with a cell phone clutched in her hand.

"No, you say to me, what's up Heldga," she vehemently stated. "Heldga very, very mad. No more Heldga wake up from the sleep. Now, here." She held out the cell phone. "You grandpapa call. He wanna talka to you right away."

Damnit! Rahmello sighed as he accepted the phone. He waited until Heldga left the office and then placed the phone against his ear. "Yeah, man, what's up?" he spoke in a calm voice, trying to play it off like everything was cool.

"Heldga said that you're in my office. I just called, why didn't you answer?"

"I didn't make it to the phone in time. You musta hung up."

"Alright, well check out the security monitors and look at the cameras covering the front gate," Grip spoke in an urgent voice. "Do it now."

"For what?" Rahmello asked. He was paranoid and suspicious, assuming his grandfather was seconds away from pulling his card. "I ain't heard nothing from you in the longest, and now you're calling me outta nowhere talking about check the security monitors? Fuck is that about?"

"Goddamnit!" Grip snapped at him. "There's no time to be fucking around. Now, stop asking so many goddamned questions, and do as you're told."

Shaking his head, Rahmello walked back over to the desk where ten security monitors were built into the far-left wall. He looked at the monitor covering the front gate and saw that everything was normal. Shabazz was posted in front of the gate standing at attention, and Aziz was sitting in the security booth, feet up, watching TV.

"What exactly am I supposed to be looking for? Because right now, I don't see shit."

"Who's out there securing the gate?"

"Shabazz and Aziz," Rahmello replied. "But you still ain't said nothin'. What the fuck is going on?"

"Hit the intercom and get 'em both on the line," Grip commanded, totally ignoring Rahmello's inquiry.

"Nigga, I ain't doing shit until you tell me what's going on. Fuck I look like?" Rahmello snapped at him.

"There's a possibility that you and the family may be in danger," Grip revealed.

"In danger?" Rahmello gritted his teeth. "It's Sonny, ain't it? What, that nigga sent somebody to kill me?"

"What? Sontino? No. What the hell are you talking about? This doesn't have anything to do with Sontino. It's the Sinaloas. Well, not the Sinaloas, but some motherfucker they call Diablo. From what I'm hearing, he's supposed to be feeling some type of way about what happened to Roberto, and there's a strong possibility that he's coming for you."

"Well, let his ass come, then," Rahmello shot back, growing more amped up by the second. "I ain't no muthafuckin' bitch. I'm wit' whatever!"

"You seriously need to calm down," Grip spoke in a settled voice. "I'm more than confident you can hold your own, but we still need to take precautions. Now, hit the intercom and make sure Shabazz and Aziz are on high alert. For all we know that motherfucker could be somewhere in vicinity, just waiting to pounce. I don't wanna take any chances."

Rahmello removed the duffle bag from his shoulder, then he reached inside of the desk and pulled out his 1911, .45 Kimber. He cocked a bullet into the chamber and then looked at the monitors on the wall, studying the screens one at a time. Again, everything appeared to be normal.

"Rahmello, you still there?" Grip asked when the line went silent. "Say something."

"Yeah, I'm here. Just hold up a second, so I can hit this intercom button." He laid the cell phone on top of the desk and then activated the intercom. "Yo, Aziz?"

"Yeah, Rahmello, I'm here." Aziz replied, looking up at the camera that was right above his station.

"I got the old man on the phone. He's talking about some Mexican nigga named Diablo might be coming this way. He's supposed to be looking for some type of drama."

"Is that right?" Aziz perked up, thirsty for action. "Brother Shabazz." He motioned for his partner to come over to the booth. "I got Rahmello on the line. He's saying that he just received word from Grip, and that we possibly have a situation on our hands. Go around back and grab the big boys from the pool house."

"I'm all over it." Shabazz nodded his head. He opened the front gate and trotted off toward the pool house where a cache of weapons were stashed.

"Alright, now let me get this straight," Aziz spoke into the intercom. "When you say this cat is looking for some drama, what exactly do you mean? Are you certain he's making his way toward the house, or is this a situation where the sucka might try to run up on you in the streets?"

"I'm not sure. But the way Grip's kicking it, I'm assuming the nigga must be coming this way, or could possibly already be here, laying in the cut some-muthafuckin-where. So, just check it out and lemme know what's good."

"Say no more. A sucka come through here, his muthafuckin' ass gon' feel it."

"You already know," Rahmello agreed. "Now, hold on for a second and lemme holla at Grip. I wanna know exactly what we're looking for." He picked the phone back up and placed it against his ear. "I just hollad at Aziz. Him and Shabazz are on point, so if anything pops off, we're ready. All I need you to do is tell me what this nigga look like, so that way I can be on point when I'm out and about."

"Out and about?" Grip retorted. "The only out and about you're doing is gathering up the rest of the family the second we end this call. I'm gonna need you need to get 'em all together: your sister, her daughter, Sontino's kids and his mother and then bring 'em back to the house. Then first thing in the morning, I'll be sending a Sprinter van to transport you all down to the airport. My private jet will be on standby, waiting to fly you guys straight down here to me."

"Nah, that's not gonna work," Rahmello declined.

"What do you mean it's not gonna work?"

"Ain't that what I just said? I can't just pick up and leave, I got too much shit going on. And on top of that, I don't even know where the fuck you at."

"I could care less about whatever it is you claim to have going on. I'm more concerned about your safety and well-being."

"My safety and well-being?" Rahmello shot back. "You don't give a fuck about me. The only one you care about is Sonny. I know you're the one busting all them muthafuckin' moves, try'na to make sure his ass get out of jail. But what about me and everything that I was going through? Ya ass didn't care, you just turned ya back and left me for dead!"

"Left for you for dead?" Grip raised his voice, matching Rahmello's intensity. "How? By keeping you comfortable in that big ass mansion, driving my cars and eating the food that I paid for? Not only you, but that goddamned girl. I've made life easier than you could have ever imagined, and this is the thanks I get? I even went out on a limb and made you the acting boss of this family. You've got a lot of goddamned nerve."

"Nigga, I ain't never care nothing about being the boss of this family, you got me mixed up wit' Sonny. For the past year and half, I been sitting on my ass without a dollar to my fucking name, and not once did you reach out and send sum'n my way. So, now that I'm finally back on my feet and doing my own thing, you wanna pop up outta nowhere and try to play hero? Nah, nigga, fuck that! I can handle my own. So if a nigga wanna get froggy, all he gotta do is leap. And that go for you, Sonny, and whoever the fuck else. Niggas gon' respect this shit here! And as for me and mines staying at'cha crib, driving ya cars and eating the food that you paid for, that's a muthafuckin' dub! I hold my own and get it how the fuck I live!"

Grip was astounded. The last thing he expected when he made the call was that he and Rahmello would end up in a pissing match. He tried to calm things down and explain to Rahmello how severe the situation was, or may possibly become, but the only thing he heard was a dial tone.

"Goddamnit!" The old man slammed the phone down and swiped all the chess pieces off the board in a fit of rage.

"Well, what did he say Gervin?" Madam François asked, sipping on the champagne that Gangsta just poured in her flute glass.

"His stupid ass won't listen. He thinks he's fuckin' invincible."

"Sound familiar?" She smirked at him, and Grip scowled.

"Don Moreno, ju need to call him back," Chatchi insisted. "He has no idea what he's up against. Joaquin, tell him."

"My brother is right, Señor," Joaquin stepped forward with a look of concern. "Diablo is a nightmare walking. I shoulda put him down years ago, but my Roberto would have never forgiven me. Ju need to call ju grandson back right away, and get him to see things clearly. 'Cause if you don't, Señor, dere is a good chance he won't live to see tomorrow."

Grip took a pull on his Cohiba and slouched back in his chair. He rubbed the stubble on his chin and then blew out a thick cloud of smoke. "Gangsta," he looked over his shoulder, "I need you to head back to the states and keep an eye on Rahmello. Chances are, you won't be able to persuade him to fly down here, but in the meantime just keep him safe. And the same goes for everyone else who has my blood running through their veins."

"Can't do it," Gangsta replied. "I've got federal business that I need to tend to, mandatory field training. Actually," he looked at his watch, "I should've taken off about an hour ago."

"Don't worry about it, Gervin," Madam François stated, reaching across the table to pat him on the hand. "I've got a few of my people stationed in Philadelphia. I can have them keep tabs on Rahmello and the rest of your family. My people are well trained and will guard them with their lives, trust me."

Thumbing his cigar, Grip looked the Madam square in the eyes. "And you're sure about that?"

"Absolutely." She nodded her head. "I mean, after all, we're partners now. One hand washes the other."

Grip didn't reply. He just took another pull on his cigar and looked up at the white diamonds glistening off the chandelier that was hanging from the ceiling. He couldn't quite put his finger on it, but something wasn't right.

After fifty plus years in the game, his instincts had never failed him. They were the reason he made it as far as he had, and now they were telling him that something was weighing against him. The feeling was somewhat eerie.

Gangsta's demeanor was nothing short of hostile, the Madam's eagerness to assist him was somewhat uncharacteristic and the apparent rift between Rahmello and Sonny was something he didn't see coming.

Is Rahmello hiding something? he thought to himself as he sat there quietly. "*And what exactly does he have going on that he can't just pick up and leave?*"

"You know what, I think I'm going to retire for the night," Grip said as he got up from his chair. "You're all welcome to stay. But if you choose to leave, just send word to Fernando and he'll fly you back to Havana. Now, please, excuse me. I have a few things I need to think about."

Chapter Twelve
At Nahfisah's House in Willow Grove

"Baby, that's just—why I love you so muuuch. Baby, that's just—why I can't get enouuugh. Baby, that's just—why I love you so muuuch. I love only youuu!" Nahfisah crooned along with Monica as the warm water from the shower spigot splashed her in the face and trickled down her entire body.

There were so many things running through her mind, but mostly the fact that she ran into Bushnut and couldn't believe how good he was looking.

She'd been floating on Cloud Nine ever since, so much so that when she barged inside of La Casa Moreno a few hours ago to pick up Imani, Rahmello and Olivia were giving her the third degree, wondering why she was so upbeat, blushing and smiling.

They would never understand, so she didn't bother spilling the goods. At best, they would only judge her, and who were they to do so? They didn't know the pain she felt, growing up with a crack addicted mother and a father who wouldn't even look in her direction. All she ever wanted was the love and affection of her daddy, but because Easy would never give it to her, she fell head over heels for just about any man who did.

That was one of the issues she was forced to address during her stay in rehab.

But the second she ran into Bushnut, the man who had her strung out on crack and selling her body to keep the two of them afloat, everything she learned working with Nurse Mary went smooth out the window. She didn't necessarily love him, but to feel adored and wanted by a man was something she couldn't resist. So if Bushnut was willing to give her the love and affection she needed, no matter how corrupt and twisted, Nahfisah was willing to accept it.

What other choice do I have? Nahfisah thought to herself as she turned the water off and stepped out of the shower. *Nobody else is willing to love me, so I guess I've gotta take what I can get.*

The spacious bathroom was steamy and hot, so foggy that Nahfisah could hardly see. Her lecherous craving for something juicy and long had her gumdrop nipples stiff and erect, and her neatly-trimmed honey pot creamy and moist.

Between Heemy and his sexual chocolateness and now Bushnut and his fine, smooth talking ass, the only thing she wanted to do was puff on a Dutch and then pull out her Bedroom Kandi and stroke herself until she begged for mercy.

Dripping wet, she carefully removed her shower cap and draped it over the shower's glass door. She then grabbed a towel from the towel rack and wiped herself dry.

Feeling relaxed, yet burnt out from a long day, she threw on her Chanel bathrobe and fastened the belt around her waist. The terry cloth fabric was like heaven against her soft, tender skin.

As she moved toward the door, the bathroom lights began to flicker.

"What the hell?" She looked up at the ceiling, trying to figure out why the lights were going in and out. "I know good and damned well these motherfuckers is not turning off my goddamned electricity. They better go 'head with that bullshit. My bills is paid!" The lights were extinguished no sooner than the words left her mouth. "Damnit!"

Nahfisah stormed out of the bathroom and grabbed a flashlight from the hallway closet. She cut it on and damn near suffered a heart attack when she spun around and noticed that Imani was standing right behind her. "Damnit, Imani! Don't be creeping up on me like that. Shit!"

"Mommy, I'm scared," the little girl spoke in a soft voice. She was fiddling with her fingers and looking at Nahfisah like she was ready to cry.

"What? Girl, you better go on somewhere. Ya little ass is too old to be scared of some dag-gone dark."

"But, it's not the dark that I'm afraid of," Imani replied, pushing out tears. "There's a monster in my closet."

"Really, Imani? A monster?" Nahfisah scoffed. She placed the light on Imani's pajamas pants and saw the wet ring around her crotch. "And I'm assuming that's the reason you wet the bed again, huh? You were too scared to get up and go the bathroom? Girl, I ought to whip yo' ass! Eight years old and still pissing in the goddamned bed. Don't make no dag-gone sense."

"But I'm telling you the truth," Imani insisted. "There's really a monster in my closet. He was smiling at me."

"Oh, yeah." Nahfisah scowled at her. "And what exactly did this so-called monster look like?"

"He was really, really skinny—like a skeleton. He had a whole bunch of writing on his face and some big ol' teeth like a werewolf. He's got big bumps on his forehead like something was try'na bust out and a long skinny tongue like a lizard's. I'm telling you, Mommy, he's in there. He's hiding in my closet."

"Girl, if you don't get out of my face with that mess."

"I'm telling you the truth, Mommy, I swear. If you don't believe me, then come on, I'll show you."

Nahfisah wanted to lash out and give the little girl a spanking. But at the same time, she also realized her previous lifestyle was the main reason Imani was having so many problems. Aside from the death of her father and the trauma she experienced when Sheed invaded their home and tried to drown her in the toilet, she was taken away from everything she knew and loved and had to spend nearly two years in a foster home. So instead of chastising, Nahfisah calmed herself down, knowing it was best to remain patient and do whatever necessary to support her daughter.

"Alright." Nahfisah sighed. "Come on, let's go see what you're talking about."

"Okay." The little girl sniffled.

They slowly made their way through the dark with Nafisah's flashlight leading the way. Imani was right behind her tugging on her bathrobe.

Damn. This little girl is really afraid, Nahfisah thought to herself. She could literally feel the soft trembles of Imani shivering. *"Did she really see something, or is this one of those PTS symptoms that Nurse Mary was telling me about?"*

When they reached the bedroom, Nahfisah stepped inside, but stopped walking when she noticed Imani was no longer holding onto her bathrobe. She looked back and peeped the little girl was still standing in the hallway.

Nahfisah motioned for her to come inside, but Imani shook her head *no*. "He's in there." Imani pointed at the closet.

Nahfisah took a deep breath and swallowed the lump in her throat. She, too, was now beginning to feel afraid. Not because she actually believed there was a monster in the closet. But because her daughter was so shaken and terrified, the dreadful feeling appeared to be somewhat contagious.

She turned back around and shined the flashlight on the closet door. It was slightly ajar, cracked open about three inches wide. Nahfisah approached it slowly. She grabbed the door handle and pulled it open.

Wham!

Out came Mr. Snuffles, the bunny rabbit Rahmello bought Imani for her birthday a few months back hopped up from the closet floor and knocked the flashlight out of Nahfisah's hand as she stood there screaming.

"Goddamnit, Imani! Didn't I tell you to put Mr. Snuffles back in his cage before you went to bed?" Nahfisah shouted as Mr. Snuffles darted out of the room. "Now, we're gonna have them lil' Coco Puff shit balls all over the house! I told Rahmello not to get'chu that stupid-ass rabbit!" She scooped up the flashlight and stormed out the room mad as hell.

"But, Mommy, where you going?" Imani called out, trailing down the hallway behind her.

"Downstairs to the garage," she shot back. "I need to see if I can turn these lights back on."

Nahfisah trotted down the stairs and marched through the dining room and kitchen. The darkness was just as thick as the rooms upstairs, but that didn't stop her from moving like she had a purpose. Mainly, to show Imani that there was nothing to be afraid of. She approached the door in the kitchen that led to the garage and then grabbed the door knob.

"Mommy, wait!" Imani cried out. "If you open that door, the monster's gonna get'chu."

"What?" Nahfisah looked over her shoulder. "Mani, I'm getting sick of this shit. There's no such thing as monsters."

"Yah-huhn." Imani nodded her head defiantly. "There *is* a monster. And he's in there. I can hear him."

Nahfisah squinted her eyes. She held her finger in front of her lips, signaling for Imani to be quiet, then she turned back around and placed her ear against the door. Imani was right. There *was* something on the other side of the door moving around. She didn't know what it was, but something was definitely in there. It was knocking things over and making eerie high-pitched scratching noises.

"Mani," Nahfisah whispered, looking over her right shoulder. "Go over to the counter and grab me one of those knives from the knife rack. Grab me the biggest one."

"Okay." Imani nodded her head. She darted over to the counter and did exactly as Nahfisah told her. "Here, Mommy." She handed Nahfisah a nine-inch steak knife.

"Alright, now go back into the living room and stand by the front door. If there's somebody in here, I'm gonna scream for you to run and get help. Just run down the block to Miss Mary's house as fast as you can, and tell her to call the cops. Do you understand?"

"Ahn-huhn." Imani began to sob. "But I don't wanna leave you. If anybody tries to hurt you, they have to hurt me too." She ran back over to the knife rack and grabbed another knife for herself.

Nahfisah wanted to cry. After everything she did to hurt and disappoint Imani, it touched her heart to know that no matter what, her daughter still had her back. "Ughn-ughn." Nahfisah shook her head, desperately fighting to keep herself from crying. "Just go in the living room and do like Mommy told you."

"You sure?"

"Yes, baby, I'm sure. Now, go on. Mommy's gonna be just fine."

Gripping the steak knife with her right hand, Nahfisah turned back around to face the door. She took a deep breath and then turned the knob and opened it slowly. The flashlight illuminated the darkness as she swept it all around the garage.

"I don't know who's in here, but whoever you are, you better make ya'self known before I start shooting," Nahfisah bluffed. "I'm not playing. I got a gun and I'll use it."
Silence.
"Alright," she tried to play it off like was she was hard. "Fuck around if you want to. Get'cha goddamned nuts blown off."
The movement stopped the second she opened the door, so it was hard to tell exactly where the noise was coming from. She shined the light on the grill of her Maserati, then she traced it along the walls and ceiling. The only thing out of place was a knocked over trashcan. She flashed the light on the trashcan and cautiously made her way toward it. She was just about to flip it over, but quickly spun around when she heard a noise coming from the back of her car.

Still holding the knife, she moved toward the car with the flashlight beaming on the back right fender. Her heart began to thump, as the noise grew louder.
Glowing red eyes. Razor-sharp teeth.
Nahfisah shrieked.
The animal lunged.
"Eeeeeeeiiiiii!"

Chapter Thirteen
Back in North Philly

The Doo Drop Inn was a small, rinky dink bar on the corner of 11th and Cumberland, right across the street from the Fairhill Projects. The owner of the bar was an old head named Smitty, who was known throughout the city as a quiet millionaire.

At best, one would see Smitty in a throwback Lincoln, wearing nothing but a pair of a slacks and a white dress shirt. But that was only when one saw him in the hood.

Now, outside of the hood was a different story. It was nothing to see the old man cruising around the 'burbs in his brand-new Bentley, leaned back behind the steering wheel in a chinchilla fur with a beautiful, young chick so exotic, he would give a person a hundred dollars if they could guess her nationality.

Smitty was the man, and had been so since the late seventies. Whether it was loan sharking, gambling, real estate or drug money, Smitty had his hands in it.

Everybody in North Philly loved him, especially Heemy, who Smitty treated like the son he never had. Even as a little kid, Heemy used to pop in and hang out at the Doo Drop. In many ways, the bar was the only place that felt like home.

Smitty, like everyone else in the neighborhood, knew that Treesha was so strung out that Heemy was basically left to fend for himself. So, whenever Heemy needed something to eat, a couple of dollars for his pocket, new clothes, a pair of sneakers or a coat, he would swing past the Doo Drop and holla at Smitty, knowing his old head was there to hold him down.

So now that Heemy was all grown up, doing his thing and making major moves in the city, it was only right he showed love to the man who had his back when no one else did. Not only did he break bread, giving Smitty five percent of everything he made, whenever the old man needed something or someone taken care of, Heemy was there to handle business. No questions asked.

It was a little past 10:00 p.m. when Heemy pulled up in front of the Doo Drop. The weather outside was a warm 88°, so he looked somewhat out of place when he hopped out his F-250 in a black hoody, a pair of jeans and a fresh pair of black Chukkas.

The hoody was flipped up, pulled down low over the front of his Eagles fitted and his bulky wide chest was courtesy of the Teflon vest that was strapped to his torso. His Glock .40 was locked and loaded, tucked down in the small of his back with a thirty-shot clip sticking out the side and his two extra clips were stuffed down in both of his back pockets.

After scoping out the corner, he grabbed his book bag from the passenger's seat, locked the doors and then strolled inside of the bar.

It was a Friday night, so the Doo Drop was lit, packed to capacity with a rowdy bunch of young niggas and neighborhood thots tipping off the Molly. The jukebox was bumping Young Jeezy and everybody was on the dance floor, dabbing and bucking with the lights turned down low. The ghetto aroma of fried chicken, Loud smoke and cheap liquor permeated the air, making the small dance floor funky and humid, but nobody seemed to care.

Glancing around the bar, Heemy recognized just about every face in the building but at the same time, he knew better than to be caught slipping.

The neighborhood bars in North Philly were nothing short of a death trap, one way in and one way out, and the Doo Drop was no different.

So, instead of making his way through the crowd, he leaned against the cigarette machine by the door and placed his hand behind his back, looking for any signs of drama.

The word going around was that a crew of young wolves calling themselves the YBM had been asking questions about him and Rahmello. They'd been running down on all the brick layers in the city and taxing all the drug corners, forcing them to get down or lay down. They even killed a couple of Heemy's weight customers, fucking up his weekly quota.

He told Rahmello everything he heard, but Rahmello just shrugged it off, claiming that the YBM was outdated and overrated, nothing that they needed to be worried about.

"Come on, Heem," Rahmello downplayed the situation. *"Them niggas know what it is. They know what the fuck we do. Out of all the blocks they hit, you see they ain't touch none of ours. So, don't even sweat that shit, bro. All you gotta do is keep ya eyes on the money."*

"Yeah, that's easy for you to say," Heemy mumbled to himself, still looking around the bar. *"'Cause while you sitting up in that big ass mansion, I'm the muthafucka that's out here in the trenches."*

A couple of females walked up on him trying to holla, but Heemy shooed them away. He scoped out the bar for a few more minutes and then casually made his way toward the bar, where the bartender Miss Darla was bopping to the music and smoking on a Newport. She noticed Heemy right away and flashed him a big bright smile.

"Well, damn, baby, if I didn't know any better I woulda thought you was coming up in here to rob me." She chuckled. "Wearing all them dag-gone clothes and whatnot. Come on over here and gimmie some sugar." She turned her face sideways and Heemy pecked her on the cheek.

"Smitty around?" Heemy asked, cutting all the small talk. He had crazy love for Miss Darla, but tonight was all about business.

A little over an hour ago, he received a call from Smitty telling him to stop by the bar. That usually meant was something was wrong. The old man never called unless there was an issue that needed to be taken care of.

"Yeah, baby, he's upstairs in his office. He told me you was stopping by. You hungry? Want sum'n to drink? I got summa that Tee Peezy to get'chu off the heezy." She cracked up laughing. She grabbed a bottle of Taylors Port from the liquor shelf and held it in front of his face. "I know that's ya favorite."

"Nah, I'm good, Miss Darla. I just stopped by to holla at Smitty. Can you call upstairs and let him know that I'm here?"

"I sure 'nough will." She nodded her head, then she reached under the bar and pulled out a cordless phone. "But before you leave, make sure come on back down here and get'chu one of these chicken wing platters."

"Yes, ma'am," Heemy replied. Like Smitty, Miss Darla had been feeding him and looking out for him since he was a kid. He walked over to the kitchen area where a steel door led to the small apartment on the second floor. He looked into the camera at the top of the door frame and pulled his hoody back so Smitty could see his face.

Bzzzzzzz!

The door buzzed open and Heemy stepped inside of the stairway. He closed the door behind him and then jogged up the stairs to the second floor. When he stepped inside of the apartment, the first thing he noticed was Smitty sitting on the couch. He was wearing a pair of leather gloves and had a blue surgeon's mask strapped across the front of his face. On the coffee table in front of him was a digital scale and a whacked-up brick of dope.

"Say now, young blood, what'chu doing walking around like you ready for World War Three?" Smitty asked, giving Heemy the once over. He could clearly see the outline of Heemy's bulletproof vest and the extended clip that was bulging out the back of his hoody. "Now, how many times I gotta tell you, you can't make money and go to war at the same time. The shit don't mix."

"Come on, Smitty, you know how it is around here," Heemy said, still looking at the dope on the table. "Here." He pulled off his book bag and tried to hand it to Smitty. "I brought you something."

"And what the hell is that?" Smitty looked at it with a raised brow.

"You know what it is, it's my way of showing appreciation for everything you done for me over the years."

"Now, that's another thing I done told you about, young blood. Don't make sense to be out here risking ya life for the almighty dollar, just to turn around and give it to the next muthafucka. That's hustling backwards, young blood. And we both know I done taught you better than that."

"But I'm saying, though," Heemy countered, "you ain't just another muthafucka, you Smitty. You was down for a nigga when nobody else was. So it's only right that I look out and show love whenever I can. So, here." He held the bag out a little further. "I want you to take it. It's yours."

Smitty pulled off his rubber gloves and lifted the mask over his face. He then reached out and grabbed the book bag from Heemy. "The only reason I'm taking this money is because I don't wanna offend you. But from here on out, young blood, you better start stacking that shit. You understand?"

Heemy just stood there with a blank face. Because no matter how many times Smitty chastised him for kicking up money, he was determined to do it anyway. So, instead of saying anything to the contrary, he just stood there and remained silent.

"Sure, you don't." Smitty chuckled. He sat the book bag under the coffee table and then leaned back on the couch. "So, what's going on wit' that bulletproof vest and that big-ass gun behind ya back? You got some type of drama going on?"

"Nah, not exactly." Heemy shook his head. "I just been hearing a bunch of shit about some niggas calling they'self the YBM. Supposedly, they been going around jackin' niggas for they shit. So, the second they try to run up on me, I got sum'n for 'em. A thirty-shot clip and two more for extra measures. I ain't playing with these niggas. Talking 'bout *get down or lay down*? I ain't playing that shit. The first nigga that try me, I'ma blow his fuckin' head off."

Smitty took a deep breath and sighed. "I can't even front, young blood, you got the heart of a lion and that's one of the reasons I love you the way I do. But I seriously need you to think things through before you do anything stupid. 'Cause at the end of the day it's all about the money. The money comes first, and that's sum'n you need to keep in mind."

Heemy looked at him skeptically. "I'm not sure I'm following you, Smitty."

"In this game, young blood, the key to survival is being diplomatic," the old man spoke in a calm voice, looking Heemy square in the eyes. "Now, I done dealt with Alvin Rines and his brother, Rayon, in the past, and they was always good to me."

"Who the fuck is Alvin Rines?" Heemy asked.

"A legend," the old man stated matter of factly. "You can always tell a legend by his name, his first name and his last. Most niggas is only known by a nickname. But the legends, young blood, the Gervin Morenos, the Sam Christians and the Aaron Joneses, you always hear the streets call 'em by their first and last name, and Alvin Rines is one of 'em."

Heemy shrugged his shoulders. "A'ight, and all of this is relevant because..."

"It's relevant because Alvin Rines is the boss of the YBM. Even after spending the last twenty-five years behind bars, his ass is still a giant out here in these streets. And trust me, young blood, when niggas like the YBM come calling, you better answer, you dig?"

"Hell naw, I don't dig," Heemy quickly shot back. "Especially if they thinking they can just run up on me and put they thing down. I ain't no muthafuckin' pussy. I'm wit' whatever they wit', me and every nigga that's out here riding wit' me. These streets will get real bloody real muthafuckin' fast, and that's a fact."

The old man released a long sigh and then rubbed the front of his face. He was thinking of a way to talk some sense into Heemy. "Dig this here, young blood, the situation ain't as bad as you think. I just need you to put ya pride to the side and hear me out. Only for a minute," he added when he noticed that Heemy was beginning to lose patience. "You gotta believe me, young blood, the only thing they doing is cornering the market, with the best product and the cheapest price, nonetheless. You see this shit right here." He gestured toward the dope on the table. "This the best shit I seen since I was stationed over in 'Nam, at the very least it's a nine. And these muthafuckas is fronting it to me for ten grand less than the number I was paying my connect down in B-More. The only catch is that I gotta bring 'em they money by the first of every month. But with a product so pure and a price so cheap? Sheiiiit, a muthafucka ain't never gotta twist ol' Smitty's arm for Smitty to make himself some money. That's the kicker to the twist."

Heemy shook his head and cracked his knuckles one at a time. It was killing him to know that his old head had been taken advantage of. "Damn, Smitty, man, why you ain't just call me? I woulda came through and bodied them niggas."

"Come on now, young blood, you know me better than that. The only thing that woulda done was defeat the purpose. It's just like I told you, you can't go to war and make money at the same time. I'ma hustla, young blood. I'll take the money over the gun smoke any day of the week. And besides," he pulled his mask back over his face and slipped his gloves back on, "at the end of the day I made out. At least I ain't gotta take them trips down to Maryland no more and run the risk of getting pulled over by the state troopers. Trust me, young blood, it's better this way."

Heemy could see through the bullshit. Smitty's mouth was saying one thing, but his body language was saying another. For as long as Heemy could think back, his old head was independent, doing his own thing and standing on his own two feet. But now he was under the thumb of The YBM.

"Lemme see one of them bags." Heemy pointed at the dope on the table. Smitty grabbed one and tossed it to him. Heemy held it in front of his face and looked at it closely. The stamp on both sides of the bag was a Mr. Peanut with the words *NUT SHIT* printed at the bottom. "So, this is the reason you called me over here? To talk me into riding these niggas' wave?"

"That's the best thing for you, young blood," Smitty spoke in a defeated voice. "It's only a matter of time before Rayon and his boys come looking for you. I figured I could talk some sense into you before you jumped out the jet and bit off more than you could chew."

Vrrrrrm! Vrrrrrm! Vrrrrrm!

Heemy's iPhone vibrated in his hoody pocket. He pulled it out and saw that the caller was Nahfisah. Flexing his jaw muscles, he sent her straight to voicemail. But before he could stuff the phone back in his pocket, she was already blowing him up all over again.

"Hold on, Smitty, lemme take this call right quick." He accepted the call and then placed the phone against his ear. "Fuck is you blowing up my phone like that for?" he hissed at her. "A'ight, so what'chu calling me for? Why you ain't call Rahmello?" He listened to what she was saying and shook his head in frustration. "A'ight, man, I'm on my way—Didn't I just tell you I'm on my way!" he snapped at her. "Damn!"

He disconnected the call and then stuffed the phone back in his pocket. "Yo, Smitty I gotta bounce," Heemy said as headed toward the door. "And as far as the YBM go, tell them niggas I said suck a dick and get a Glock. I'm wit' whatever they wit'."

Chapter Fourteen

Nahfisah could not believe an opossum was trapped inside of her garage. After discovering what the noise was, she hauled ass out of the garage and slammed the door behind her. She thought about going outside to open the garage to let him out, but quickly dismissed the notion. She was way too freaked out and afraid, still thinking about his beady little red eyes and spiky, pin-like teeth.

"Man, I wish the hell I would," Nahfisah mumbled as she ran upstairs to her bedroom with Imani close behind.

She grabbed her cell phone from the nightstand and called Rahmello, hoping she could persuade him to drive out to the house.

When Rahmello didn't answer, she scrolled down her list of contacts and pressed down on the number that Bushnut locked inside of her phone. He answered on the third ring, and right away Nahfisah noticed she caught him in the middle of a sexual encounter. He was grunting and groaning, breathing heavy and panting. She also heard the sounds of a female moaning, emphatically begging Bushnut to fuck her deeper.

"You know what? Fuck you, Bushnut! You fucking bastard!" Nahfisah shouted into the phone.

After seething for a couple of minutes, she called Heemy and told him what was going on. She asked him to drive out to the house, and surprisingly he agreed.

That was a little over a half an hour ago.

The house was still pitch-black dark, so she lit up a bunch of candles and spread them all around. She then made Imani hop in the shower and throw on a fresh pair of pajamas, before making her lay down in the guest room. Her own bed was still wet from when she pissed in it.

Finally, Nahfisah could sit back and relax. She was chilling in the living room, sitting Indian style on her leather sectional. A Dutch Master filled with Grand Daddy Kush was smoldering in the ashtray beside her, and her iPhone was clutched in her left hand. She was scrolling down the news feed on her Instagram. It seemed as though everybody was talking about her party, some of them she didn't even know. They were posting videos of their new clothes, designer shoes and hairstyles, and bragging about how they were going to shut down the party down. She even had a message in her DM from Yo Gotti wishing her a happy birthday.

Nahfisah was hype.

"Man, this party is gonna be lit!" She cracked up laughing. She grabbed the Dutchie from the ashtray and hit it real hard. As she exhaled the smoke, a pair of headlights pulling into the driveway sliced through the window blinds and illuminated the candle-lit room. The lights cut off and Nahfisah got up from the sectional. She walked over to the window and peeked through the blinds just as Heemy was hopping out of his F-250. *"This lil' young bul is so goddamned fine,"* she mumbled to herself. "Wit' his thug ass." She tightened the belt on her bathrobe and opened the front door.

"Well, damn, nigga, it took you long enough," Nahfisah said when she stepped onto the front porch.

"What?" Heemy shot her the ice-grill. "Fuck you mean *it took me long enough?*"

"Ain't that what I just said? I called ya ass almost forty-five minutes ago."

"Yo, I'm out." Heemy shook his head. "Ain't nobody got time to this shit.

He turned around to leave and Nahfisah ran down the steps and wrapped her arms around his waist. "Don't go," she spoke in a soft voice. She squeezed him tightly and pressed her face against his back, taking in the scent of his cologne. "I was only playing wit'chu, dang. Why you gotta be so sensitive all the time?"

Heemy stopped walking and flexed his jaw muscles. He couldn't explain the feeling, but for some reason, Nahfisah wrapping her arms around him made him feel safe and secure. They made him feel wanted and needed, something that he never experienced before.

He wiggled himself free and turned back around to face her. She was looking up at him with her bottom lip poked out like a big baby. Her silky black hair was pulled back into a thick long braid and her edges looked so soft, that Heemy was tempted to touch them.

"You's an ungrateful mu'fucka, Nah, I dropped everything I was doing to come out here and check on you and Mani and before I even had the chance to ask if y'all was okay, you already coming at my neck. For all that, I coulda just brushed you off and continued doing what I was doing."

"I said I was sorry." Nahfisah pouted. Her long eye lashes, aqua-blue eyes, butter soft skin and thick juicy lips were making him hot around the collar. She wrapped her arms around him once more, and for the first time noticed the bulletproof vest that was tucked under his hoody. She started to ask him about it, but decided not to.

"Yo, what's up wit' all this touchy-feely shit?" Heemy asked, even though he was secretly loving every second of it.

"I 'on't know. I guess I just miss you," Nahfisah confessed. "I'm used to having you around every day. But now that Rahmello trusts me enough to be on my own and doesn't have you following me around everywhere, I guess I kinda miss it. Imani does too. When I told her you was coming, she was happy as hell, talking 'bout *I want my Heemy!*" Nahfisah chuckled, imitating the way Imani said it. "I think my baby has a crush on you."

Heemy smiled for a brief moment, then he quickly regained control of his emotions. He wiggled himself free for the second time and then made his way over to the garage. "Yo, how I open this jawn?"

"I gotta go back in the house and grab my keys. It's an automated system but since the power's off, it might not work. You're prob'bly gonna have to use the key." She ran inside of the house and came back out a few minutes later, holding her keyring. "Here." She handed the keys to Heemy. "And be careful. That motherfucker's big as hell!"

"Is that right?" Heemy replied, clearly unmoved. "I got sum'n for his ass." He walked back over to his truck and opened the driver's side door. He reached inside and pulled out his Glock .40 with the extended clip.

Nahfisah's eyes grew bigger than golf balls. "Boy, you can't use that!" She looked up and down the block, hoping none of her neighbors were watching. "You'll wake up my neighbors."

"What? Man, fuck ya neighbors."

"Ahn-ahn, Heemy, no! They'll call the cops out here." She folded her arms across her chest, daring him to put an argument. "Ya ass know good and damned well the last thing you need are some county cops rolling up. Especially with that bulletproof vest you're wearing," she slid in. She couldn't resist mentioning it.

"Well, how the fuck I'm 'posed to get his ass, then?"

"I 'on't know. Just open the door and let him run out."

Heemy looked down at his Glock and then looked over at the garage. He looked at his Glock once again and then settled his eyes on Nahfisah.

"I'm not playing with you, Raheem. You better not shoot that gun. Matter of fact," she held her hand out, "give it to me."

Reluctantly, he handed over the Glock and Nahfisah darted up the porch steps. "Damn, you just gon' leave a nigga hanging?" He laughed at her.

"Yup. I ain't playing wit' that big ass 'possum. He almost bit me the last time."

"Ain't that a bitch?" Heemy mumbled under his breath. He slowly approached the garage and placed his ear against the door. When he didn't hear anything, he pushed the key inside of the lock and reached down for the door handle. He didn't even raise it past his shin bone when the opossum burst out of the darkness and scampered toward the flowerbed on his right-hand side.

"Oh, shit!" Heemy shouted. He dropped the garage door and fell flat on his ass before popping up and making a dash for the porch. Nahfisah was cracking up. "Fuck is you laughing for?" Heemy snapped at her. "Gimmie my fucking burner!" He snatched the Glock from her hands and spun back around to shoot up the flowerbed.

"Heemy, no!" Nahfisah laughed even harder.

"Fuck you mean *no*? That muthafucka almost killed me!"

"Boy, hush." Nahfisah laughed at him some more. She tugged on his arm and led him inside of the house. "You shoulda kept that dag-gone door open. I still need you to check the fuse box and see if you can turn these lights back on."

"Not at all." Heemy shook his head *no*. "For all I know, it's a whole family full of them muthafuckas in there. You better wait until the morning and call the exterminator, the critter catchers or whoever the fuck else. 'Cause my black ass is on chills. I wish the hell I would go in that garage."

"Ol' scary ass." Nahfisah hit him on the shoulder. She was getting a kick out of seeing a gangster scared to death of a tiny little animal. "I'll tell you what, how about we go in there together. I won't let the bogeyman get'chu."

"A'ight, but as soon as we're done, you better hit a nigga off wit' somma that Loud I'm smelling." He leaned his head back and inhaled deeply. "Damn, Nah, you was in here blowing on that Kush, wasn't you?"

"What? Boy, come on."

She tightened her bathrobe, then she led him through the kitchen and over to the door that led into the garage. After tricking him to go in first, she posted up in the doorway and watched as he opened the fuse box and reset the power. The light above the stove turned on immediately, but the rest of the house was still dark, illuminated only by the candles she lit earlier.

"Well, thank you very much, Mr. Raheem."

"Yo, stop try'na play me." He looked at her with a raised brow.

"I was only thanking you, dang." Nahfisah shot back as they made their way back into the living room. "I'm saying, though, you might as well just chill over here until the morning because it really doesn't make any sense to be driving around this late."

"Shit, I ain't got no problem wit' that. I ain't feel like driving back to the city no way."

He looked around the candle-lit living room and then looked at Nahfisah, who was standing a few feet away. Feeling somewhat uncomfortable, he looked away and fixed his eyes on the front door.

"Yo, why don't you go put some clothes on. Ya nipples all poking through ya bathrobe and shit." He wanted to take a second look, but he didn't. He knew that a second look would only cause trouble.

"Raheem, look at me." Nahfisah said as she approached him slowly. When he didn't respond, she reached up and grabbed his face with both hands. "Look at me, I said."

Heemy flexed his jaw muscles, then he turned his head back around to face her. She was so beautiful standing there. The energy between them was so crazy that the only thing he wanted to do was wrap his arms around her and never let go. "A'ight, man, I'm looking at'chu. What's up?"

"Kiss me," Nahfisah demanded. Her voice was soft, yet stern and passionate at the same time.

"Yo, you trippin' right now."

"No, I'm not. I want you to kiss me."

"I mean, don't get it twisted, I want to. But on some G shit, I ain't the type to mix business wit' pleasure. 'Cause at the end of the day, you're Sonny and Rahmello's sister. I don't wanna do nothing that'll fuck up my business wit' 'em."

"My brothers ain't got nothing to do with this. I'ma grown ass woman. And speaking of business, I'm waiting on you to boss up and make me yours."

"Make you my what?" Heemy licked his lips. "My girl or my business?"

"That, and whatever else you wanna make me," Nahfisah replied, seductively biting down on her bottom lip. "Hopefully, you can make me cum." She stood up on her tippy-toes and pecked him on the lips before sliding her tongue in his mouth.

Initially, Heemy resisted. But when the tip of her tongue found his and slid all around it, he couldn't hold back any longer. He gently palmed her ass and pulled her in closer.

After kissing for a few more seconds, he grabbed her by the pony tail and titled her head back. Taking his time, he twirled his tongue up and down the front of her neck. His soft, tender kisses traveled from her neck to her chin and then finally back to her lips, where he kissed her hungrily.

"Damnit, you feel so good." Nahfisah shuttered when she pulled her lips away from his.

"You sure this is what you wanna do?" Heemy asked, gazing into her beautiful blue eyes. He pecked her on the lips and waited for an answer.

"Umm-hmm." Nahfisah nodded her head. "I've wanted you ever since the day I laid eyes on you."

"Is that right?"

"Umm-hmm. Why do you think I used to go out of my way to get on your nerves? I was try'na get you to notice me. To see me as more than just Sonny and Rahmello's sister."

"Yo, I'ma ask you this one more time. You sure this is what'chu wanna do? 'Cause once I put my stamp on sum'n, it's mines. I don't do no sharing. And I damn sure don't be puttin' up wit' no stank-ass attitude. So, if you really try'na rock wit' a nigga, you better check that shit at the door."

"I got'chu." Nahfisah kissed him some more. "I'ma play my part, baby, I swear." She clapped her hands and the sounds of *Anywhere* by 112 erupted from the sound system.

Here we are all alone, you and meeee, privacy. And we can do anything. Your fantasy? I wanna make your dreams come truuueeee. Candy lips she's calling me between your legs, loud and clear. I wanna talk back to her, make love to herrrr. I wanna hear you scream my name...

Looking up in Heemy's eyes, Nahfisah slowly removed her bathrobe and let it spill down to the floor. The burning glow from the candles had her entire body looking as though she'd been dipped in honey.

Heemy was on stuck. Her perky titties, feminine abs, shapely thighs and three-inch gap had him open off the rip, and Nahfisah knew it.

Winding her hips to the music, she placed her finger inside of her mouth and then pulled it back out glistening wet. Still looking at him, she traced her finger around the rim of her left areola, then she motioned for Heemy to come closer. He licked his lips and

161

nodded his head. Closing the distance between them, he slipped out of his hoody and removed the straps on his bulletproof vest, one at a time. All the while, Nahfisah was still winding her hips to the music.

I can love you in the shower both of our bodies dripping wet. On the patio we can make a night you won't forget. On the kitchen floor as I softly pull your hair. We can do it anywhere.

Completely naked, Heemy stood before her harder than steel. His ten inches was thick and veiny and topped off with a big, strawberry head, just the way Nahfisah liked it.

After admiring his body from head to toe, she reached out and traced her fingers along the rippled creases of his chest and abs. His skin was a little sweaty from the vest he was wearing, but that didn't stop Nahfisah from kissing and licking on his chest. She bit into his left pec and then slid her tongue down the middle of his eight-pack.

"Ummmm!" Nahfisah moaned, loving the salty taste of his skin. She trailed her hands down the front of his body as she dropped down to her knees. Looking up in his eyes, she mouthed the words, "I wanna suck this dick so bad."

Using no hands, she moved her face up and down and all around his shaft. Heemy bit into his bottom lip and stared up at the ceiling. He grabbed the back of her neck and Nahfisah went straight to work—slurping and sopping, humming and moaning. Heemy could have sworn she was jerking him off with both hands. But when he looked down and saw she was only using her tongue, he damn near buckled. Her tongue was so long, she had it wrapped around his girth, slowly stroking him back and forth. Still using no hands, she spat on his helmet and then swallowed him up in one big gulp.

"Damn, Nah. Shit!" Heemy moaned. He grabbed the back of her head and thrust his hips until he hit the back of her throat.

"Umm-mmm!" Nahfisah mumbled in protest, smacking him on the leg. She slurped him out of her mouth, looked up at him and scowled. "Boy, is you crazy? You better stop messing in my daggone hair. I just had it done for the party tomorrow."

"I ain't try'na hear that shit," Heemy panted. "I'll take you to get it done again in the morning." He gripped the back of her head with both hands and pushed himself deeper into the depths of her throat.

Nahfisah's gobble game was so vicious, that if he didn't know any better, he would have sworn he was swimming up in some pussy.

After sucking him off until he begged her to stop, she looked up at him and smiled. "Talking all that fly shit about putting ya stamp on sum'n, and look at'chu now, crying like a bitch and begging me to stop. I shoulda knew dat ass wasn't fit."

"Oh, yeah?" Heemy chuckled. "Crying like a bitch, though?"

"Umm-hmm." Nahfisah nodded her head. She licked his sack, then she kissed him on the tip of his helmet. "Ain't that what I just said?"

"Get'cha lil' ass up on that couch." Heemy pointed at the sectional. "I'ma show you how I put my stamp on sum'n."

"Ut'oh. I'm in trouble now," Nahfisah giggled as she crawled over to the sectional.

She climbed up on the cushion and spread her legs wide open, giving Heemy a clear view of her neatly-trimmed box. Her rose pedal lips were sprouted back on both sides, exposing the pinkness in between and her chocolate clitoris was swollen and fat, reminding Heemy of a Hershey's Kiss. Right above it was a silky tuft of curly black hair.

Damn, this a bad muthafucka, Heemy thought to himself, as he stood there stroking his dick nice and slow. Eating pussy wasn't really his thing, but she was looking so good, he decided to get him a taste.

"So, what'chu waiting on?" Nahfisah purred. She was sucking her fingers and touching herself all over. "You gon' put'cha stamp on this pussy or what?" She spread her rose pedals and blew him a kiss. "Come suck this pussy, Daddy. Come sop it up for Mommy."

Licking his lips, Heemy made his way over to the sectional. As he got down in between her thighs, the sounds of 112 faded away and then on came the heavy bass line of Janet Jackson's *Any Time, Anywhere.*

In the thundering raaaain you stare into my hearrrrt. I can feel your haaand moving up my bodyyyy. Skirt around my waaaaist. Wall against my faaaace. I can feel your liiiips. Oooohhh...

Taking his time, Heemy kissed each one of her nipples. He kissed her all the way down to the crack of her ass and buried his nose dead smack in the center of her rose bush, taking in the sweet scent of her nectar. He dipped his tongue inside of her and twirled it around, smiling when he heard her gasping for air. "Oh, you like that, huh?"

"Uhn-hun," Nahfisah cried out, grinding her pussy to the rhythm of his tongue. "Sop it up, Daddy. Sop it up for Mommy."

Heemy slid his fingers inside of her and stirred them around slowly. He then wrapped his lips around her Hershey's Kiss and caressed it with the tip of his tongue.

"Damn, Daddy, just like that," Nahfisah moaned, as her eyes rolled into the back of her head. She reached out and softly raked her fingernails along the back of his shoulders. "Damnit, you sucking this pussy so good."

The sounds of her soft moans, coupled with the sweet taste of her pussy, had Heemy harder than a muthafucka. He sped up the flick of his tongue and finger-fucked her so good that Nahfisah tried to wiggle away. She pushed down on his shoulders and tried to back herself into the corner, but Heemy wasn't having it. He grabbed her by the waist and pulled her back down to his mouth and fingers.

"See, I wasn't even gon' do you like this," he licked the hood of her Hershey's Kiss and pounded her pussy with his fingers, "but it's ya mouth. You don't never know when to shut the fuck up, so now you gotta learn." He slipped in a third finger and pounded her pussy even faster.

"Baby, please!" Nahfisah shuddered. She arched her back and gyrated her hips. "Get up in this pussy, Daddy, please! I need you inside of me so fucking bad."

Obeying her demands, Heemy moved his lips from her pussy to her abs and then up to her chocolate nipples where he kissed them one at a time. Still stroking her with his fingers, he moved his kisses up to her lips and dipped his tongue inside of her mouth. "I can't even front, Nah, ya pussy taste gooder than a muthafucka." He breathed heavily. "You wanna taste it?" When she nodded her head *yes*, he slipped his fingers out her pussy and placed them in between their lips. As their tongues began to wrestle and lick away the cum from his fingers, Heemy reached down with his left hand and grabbed the base of his hamma. Stroking himself nice and slow, he parted her lips with the tip his helmet, slowly caressing the crease of her pinkness.

"You sure this what'chu want?" He pushed the head inside of her, then he quickly pulled it back out.

"Ummmmmm!" Nahfisah purred. "I want all of it, Daddy. Gimmie every last inch."

Heemy dipped it in a little further and then pulled it back out. "You sure?"

"Yes, Raheem, I'm sure!" Nahfisah snapped at him. "Now, stop teasing me, dang." She shifted her hips doing her best to find it, but Heemy pulled himself away. "Oh, my God!" Nahfisah whined like a baby. "Why you teasing me like this? Stop playing and stick it in!" She reached down to do it herself, but Heemy grabbed both of her hands and pinned them against the cushion. "What? Oh, hell nawl. I know the fuck you didn't!" She bucked and twisted, kicked out her legs and tried to bite him, but Heemy refused to let go.

"You better calm dat ass down," he checked her in no nonsense tone. "See, that's another problem," he shook his head in disappointment, "you always want what you want, when you want it. Ya ass ain't running' nothing. I'm the muthafuckin' lion up in this piece!" Nahfisah calmed down, and Heemy smiled at her. "Good. Now, relax and lemme do what I do."

Any time and any place. I don't care whose around.

As the music continued to play, Heemy nibbled on her earlobe. He moved in a little closer and softly sank his teeth into the left side of her neck, causing her body to tense up.

"Ughn," Nahfisah gasped, loving the feeling of being manhandled. Her hands were still pinned against the cushion, and Heemy's rock hard body was pressed down against hers, slowly moving to the sound of the music.

I don't wanna stop just because you feel so good inside of my love. I'm not gonna stop, no, no, no. I want you. All I wanna say is...
Down below, pressing against her ass and thighs, Nahfisah could feel the warmth of his juicy bulb. It was poking all around, feverishly searching for the softest place on earth. She shifted her hips, doing her best to find it. But every time she did, Heemy pulled himself away and chastised her for being so thirsty. He placed his mouth on top of hers and kissed her passionately. All the while, his throbbing thickness seemed to have a mind of its own, still searching all around, pressing against her ass and thighs.

Suddenly, it moved a little higher. It swept across her clitoris and lips and then buried itself deep inside the core of her essence.

"Uggghhhnn!" Nahfisah moaned from the pleasure, finally feeling what she'd been yearning for. "Put'cha stamp on this pussy, Daddy. Stamp that shit. Ugghhnn!" He was so long and thick that she could feel him pressing against the bottom of her pocket. "Right there, Daddy. Keep it right there. Eeeouugh!"

Taking his time and moving his body to the beat of the groove, Heemy interlaced his fingers with hers and made love to her slowly. The threat of the YBM was the last thing on his mind. The only thing he was thinking about was Nahfisah. She told him to put his stamp on it, and that's exactly what he did.

***

As Heemy and Nahfisah made love for the very first time, they had no idea that the bringer of death was just a few feet away, tucked behind the cracked door of the living room closet.

Diablo was watching their every move. His initial plan was to bend Nahfisah over his lap and fuck her in the ass with a hot curling iron. Then as soon as she was *nice and hot*, skin her alive and toss her body in a bathtub full of bleach. But when he slipped inside of the house and discovered Imani, his icy black heart grew warm and soft, as the sight of the little girl tossing and turning in her sleep reminded him of the cruel nightmare that he called his childhood.

At the tender age of twelve, Diablo, who was then known as Diego Ramirez, was left for dead after witnessing the murders of his pregnant mother and his father.

They were gutted out right before his eyes, then savagely burnt alive and chopped into tiny little pieces by the Mexican Mafia. That was the same night he ended up on the doorstep of Joaquin Alverez, the jeffe of the Sinaloa Cartel.

Not only was Joaquin the number one rival of the infamous *Eme*, he was also the father of Diego's best friend, Roberto.

At first glance, it appeared as though Joaquin had taken in Diego as a second son. His wife and mother adored him, and there was nothing Roberto had access to that Diego didn't.

In all aspects, despite seeing the fetus of his unborn sister ripped from his mother's womb and stomped to a pulp, Diego appeared to be normal. But Joaquin was too sharp to not know any better. The little boy had a certain look in his eyes, one that he was all too familiar with, and he didn't doubt for a second that beneath the surface was something vicious, something evil and sinister.

So, on the night of Diego's thirteenth birthday, Joaquin put him to the test. He handed the young man two machetes and a scalpel and then drove him out to his horse stable on the edge of town.

Inside of the stable, hanging upside down from a beam in the ceiling, were the three men responsible for murdering Diego's parents. They were bloodied and bruised, sliced up and bashed in and teetering on the brink between life and death. Their bodies were still one piece, but surely that would soon change. It was then and there, on that fateful night, where Diablo was born and Diego was lost forever.

He'd been murdering at the behest of Joaquin ever since.

Looking at the two of them rolling around on the sectional, Diablo shook his head slowly. He wanted so bad to attack, but the demons from his past would never allow it. There was simply no way he could ever do to a child what the Eme had done to him. So, instead of releasing his fury and bringing down a reign of terror, he crept out of the closet and silently slipped out the front door.

"Next time, mija. Next time."

Askari

Chapter Fifteen
The Following Morning

It was 7:38 a.m., and Keeno was sitting behind the tinted windows of his smoke-gray, Dodge Challenger. He was parked in the middle of Delhi Street, two doors up the block from Treesha's house. The A/C was on full blast and the Loud smoke inside of the car was heavy and thick. A small mountain of fives, tens and twenties were piled up on the passenger's seat, and laying on his lap was a Ziploc bag full of bundles. Each bundle was consisted of fifteen bags. They were bound together by a rubber band, and ¾'s of the way filled with the finest Chyna White heroin. Keeno reached inside of the Ziploc and removed one of the bundles. He peeled away one of the bags and held it up to his face. "Nut Shit," he read the stamp out loud. *"This nigga, Bushnut, crazier than a muthafucka,"* he mumbled to himself. He was twisting the bag with his fingers and looking at the stamp of Mr. Peanut on both sides. It was somewhat similar to the Mr. Peanut on the Planter's logo, only this Mr. Peanut was much more gangsta. Instead of leaning on his walking cane with a big, welcoming smile, the Mr. Peanut on the dope stamp was leaning on an AK-47 and had a twisted, devilish grin plastered across his peanut face. His top-hat and everything else appeared to be the same.

"Yeah, this nigga definitely shot the fuck out," Keeno said as he placed the bag with the rest of the bundle.

He tossed the bundle inside of the Ziploc, then leaned over the console and stashed it in his glove compartment.

Settling back in his seat, he looked into the rearview mirror and saw Shorty Rock and Yahyo walking up the street. He also caught a glimpse of the two-inch gash that Heemy left above his eyebrow. It was gray and ashy, and stitched together by a navy-blue thread.

"Bitch-ass nigga," Keeno said as he picked at the scab. "Gon' bust me in my shit and then hit me off wit' a punk-ass 4½, like everything sweet, like I'm 'posed to just fall back and let that shit ride. This nigga got me fucked up. His ass ain't invincible. He can get touched just like anybody else."

Tap! Tap!

"Yo, Keeno, man, roll down the window," Shorty Rock said. Not only was it the first Saturday of the month, it was Fourth of July weekend, and the two youngins were expecting to make some nice dough, most of which they were planning to use to cop some new clothes for Nahfisah's party.

Tap! Tap!

"Aye, yo, Keeno, man, stop bullshitting," Shorty Rock persisted. He was looking at his G-Shock when he said it. "It's going on a quarter to seven. The smokas 'bout to start coming through any minute now."

Keeno rolled down the window and blew a cloud of smoke in his face. At one point in time, he considered Shorty Rock and Yahyo as his best friends. They'd been thicker than thieves ever since their school days at Ferguson. But in Keeno's mind, ever since Heemy pistol-whipped him in the middle of the street, Shorty Rock and Yahyo didn't respect him anymore. In addition to that, they didn't do anything to help him.

"Damn, dawg, what the fuck is you just sitting there lookin' stupid for?" Yahyo chimed in, with a silly-looking grin on his face. "You better pass them bundles off, 'fore I call Heemy around here. And you *knoowww* what happened the last time he came through the block. That nigga whupped—yo—ass!"

As the two of them stood there laughing and popping off at the mouth, Keeno reached under the driver's seat and gripped up the handle on his .38 snub. He was thinking about busting some heads. But instead, he let it go of the burner, then he reached back and grabbed the paper bag full of bundles that was right behind it.

"Here." He handed Shorty Rock the paper bag through the window. "That's sixty bundles. Thirty for you, and thirty for him."

Shorty Rock snatched the bag from his hands, then he began walking toward the vacant lot across the street. He didn't even make it two steps before Treesha came running out of the house, hooting and hollering.

"Ahn-ahn, muthafuckas! Y'all better hand over my goddamned shit! Y'all know the drill. Raheem said I'm supposed to get one bundle a day."

She ran up on Shorty Rock, who stuck his hand out like the Hiesman trophy to keep her at bay. "Damn, Treesha, calm the fuck down."

"Calm down, shit! I want my muthafuckin' bundle!"

As always, Treesha was looking like a hot damned mess. A burning Newport was dangling out the corner of her mouth, and he could tell from the smoke that it was laced with cocaine. Her dingy, white T-shirt was crusty and yellow, and a bloody red tampon string was hanging out the bottom of her lime-green biker shorts.

"Don't be lookin' at me like that," Treesha wolfed at him, giving him the same stank-ass look he was giving her. She took a pull on her Newport and inhaled deeply. "I know one thing," she blew the coke-laced smoke in his face, "you muthafuckas better come up off my shit, 'fore I call the po-po out this muthafucka."

"Yo, here you go wit' this po-po shit again." Shorty Rock scowled at her. He reached down in the bag and pulled out one of the bundles. "This what the fuck you want? Well, go fetch it, then!" He threw the bundle across the street, and Treesha damn near had a heart attack.

She clutched her chest and looked up at the bundle as it flew through the air. It seemed as though it was moving in slow motion. It bounced off of the curb and then hit the ground, before rolling toward the sewer hole in the middle of the block. Moving at top speed, she ran over and scooped it up just in time.

"Stupid ol' bitch-made bitch!" she shouted at Shorty Rock, who was already in the vacant lot stashing the rest of the bundles. "Made me drop my goddamned cigarette. Fuck is you looking at?" she snapped at Keeno. She kicked the back his car and then ran up the steps to her house. "I'll call the po-po and clear all this shit the fuck out."

Yahyo cracked up laughing when she stormed inside of the house and slammed the door. He looked at Keeno and smiled, but

Keeno just shook his head and shot him the ice-grill. He then rolled up the window and slowly pulled away from the curb.

"Fuck this nigga always leaving for?" Shorty Rock asked when he returned from the lot with a handful of bundles.

"I don't know?" Yahyo shrugged his shoulders. "You know he been on some fuck shit ever since that situation between him and Heemy. Now, he acting all super distant and shit, acting all secretive and whatnot. I might be wrong for this, Rock, but I'm really starting to think this nigga's up to sum'n."

"Oh, yeah?" Shorty Rock stared him down. "Sum'n like what?"

"Like some crazy shit, bro. Some Tupac, Bishop in Juice, throw a nigga off the roof type of shit."

"Man, that nigga ain't doin' nuffin." Shorty Rock laughed at him. He handed Yahyo three of the bundles and then plopped down on the stoop next doors to Treesha's. He pulled out a box of Dutchies and got his roll on. "Ain't nobody thinking about no mu'fuckin' Keeno. The only thing I'm thinking about is this muthafuckin' party tonight. You know it's an *all-white* jawn, so I prob'ly just fuck around and Balenciaga my whole situation. You smell me? And then crush 'em wit' the white-on-white, high-top Louie Spikes. Whatever the case, I already know I'ma end up spending a couple racks. What about you, though? What'chu wearing to the party?"

Yahyo didn't respond. He was too busy looking up the block at Keeno's Dodge Challenger. It was sitting in the middle of Cumberland Street with the engine running. The tail lights were flaming red, so he knew right away that Keeno was pressing down on the brake.

"See what I'm talking about?" Yahyo pointed up the block. "Why the fuck is he sitting in the middle of the street for?"

"Who gives a fuck?" Shorty Rock waved him off. "He prob'bly just texting on his phone or sum'n."

As they continued looking up the street, a black minivan spun the corner at the bottom of the block and cruised up slowly. Shorty Rock peeped it and tapped Yahyo on the leg. "First trap of the day, dawg. You want it, or you want me to get it?"

"Nigga, you know damn well ya fat ass ain't climbing off that muthafuckin' stoop," Yahyo said with a smile. He looked down the block and nodded his head at the oncoming van, alerting the driver that he was open for business.

As the van came closer, he saw that the passenger's side was empty, and that a pretty red-bone chick was sitting behind the steering wheel. She pulled up in front of him and rolled down the driver's side window.

"What's up, boo? Y'all got summa that Nut Shit out here?" Kia asked in a sweet, innocent voice. She licked her lips and then looked on the stoop where Shorty Rock was puffing on his Dutchie.

"Nut Shit? What the fuck is that?" Yahyo frowned at her. He glanced up the block and scratched his head when he noticed that Keeno was still sitting there. *Fuck is this nigga doing?*

"Come on, boo. How y'all niggas ain't out here hustling, and y'all ain't got no Nut Shit? It's the best dope in the city."

"Listen, shorty, I'ma tell you this one more time," Yahyo spoke slowly. "I don't know nothin' about no Nut Shit. But if you want some raw," he held up one of his baggies, "we got grams of blow for thirty dollars. No change and no shorts."

"Grams of blow for thirty dollars, huh?" Kia's demeanor changed. "So basically, what'chu telling me is that y'all niggas ain't try'na get down?"

"Get down?" Yahyo looked at her like she was crazy. "Get down wit' what?"

"This!" She stuck a .45 out the window, and pressed the lips of the barrel dead smack against the center of his forehead.

Boca!

"Oh, shit! What the fuck?" Shorty Rock shouted as a warm spray of blood splashed against the front of his. He hopped off the stoop just as Yahyo was crumbling to the ground. The gunshot was so sudden and unexpected that it left him in a state of shock. Shivering and shaking and frantically trying to make sense of what happened, he looked down at Yahyo and broke down crying. His best friend was stretched out on the sidewalk with a quarter-sized hole in his forehead. A pool of blood was forming around the back of his dome and his glassy eyes were wide open, peering off into the distance. "Naw, man. Yahyo get up, dawg. Get up!" Shorty Rock cried even harder. He was too zoned out to remember how his best friend ended up dead in the first place. But all of that changed when Kia tagged him with the pound.

Boca!

A burning sensation spread throughout Shorty Rock's neck as he spun around and crashed into the stoop. He popped back up and staggered backwards when another bullet crashed into his shoulder. The side door of the minivan slid open, and a shooter dressed in all black hopped out with a choppa in his hands. Shorty Rock pushed him out the way and ran up the street. He noticed that Keeno was still parked at the top of block, so he ran toward the Challenger.

"Yo, Keeno, help man! Help! These niggas try'na kill me!" He was running as fast as he could, but not fast enough to outrun the rapid fire that Doo Dirty let off behind him.

Bdddddddddddoc!

His fat body crashed against the Challenger, causing Keeno to bang his face on the steering wheel. Raging mad, he pulled down his ski mask and climbed out the car with his .38 snub. He looked at Doo Dirty, who was jogging up the block, and waved him off. "Go 'head, Dirt. I can take it from here."

"You sure?" Doo Dirty gave him a funny look. He'd only been around Keeno for the past two weeks and didn't see him as a killer. Keeno was more of the hustling type.

"Ain't that what the fuck I just said?" Keeno snapped at him, tightening his grip on the tre-eight.

As Doo Dirty backed away with the smoking choppa clutched in his hands, Keeno looked down at Shorty Rock and gritted his teeth. His one-time best friend was hunched on his knees, coughing and crying and doing his best to keep his intestines from touching the ground. They were dangling out the bottom of shirt, bloody, funky and steaming from his body heat.

"Pussy, turn ya bitch-ass around," Keeno snarled at him. He kicked him in the ass and Shorty Rock toppled over on his side, still holding his intestines with both hands. He was shivering so bad that his teeth began to chatter.

"Ke-Ke-Keeno—I'm—c—c—c—cold!" Shorty Rock gasped. "Don't—let—let them niggas kill me."

Keeno's eyes became glossy and wet. The two of them used to play in the sandbox together, and now he was seconds away from taking Shorty Rock's life. His thumping heart was telling him to help his friend. But his ego and pride, coupled with the fact that he had already taken sides with the YBM, was telling him that he needed to boss up and handle his business.

He looked over his shoulder and saw that Doo Dirty and Kia were still parked in the middle of the block, watching his every move. So, he knew if he backed out and didn't finish the job, they would surely finish him.

Keeno took a deep breath and wiped away his tears with the same hand he was using to hold the pistol. Biting down on his bottom lip, he aimed the .38 at Shorty Rock's left eye.

"Come—Come on, man. Please."

"I'm sorry, Rock. But I done already took my stance."

Boca!

Askari

Chapter Sixteen
A Few Hours Later

"Damn, man, why the fuck I ain't just listen when she told me not to mess up her goddamned hair?" Heemy sighed, looking at the time on his iced-out Rollie. It was a quarter past twelve, and he was sitting in his F-250 parked outside of Annie's hair salon on Broad Street.

Nahfisah was inside getting her hair fixed from when he messed it up the night before and so far, she'd been in there for the past three hours.

Initially, Heemy was chilling inside sitting in the waiting area. But after forty minutes of being bored out of his mind, he hopped back in his truck and got his blaze on while watching *New Jack City*. The only thing he needed was a tub of popcorn. New Jack City was his favorite movie, and he was loving every second of it.

"This isn't about me," Heemy blurted out, mimicking Nino Brown word for word. "This is about—all you politicians who lobby against making drugs legal. I mean, let's kick the ballistics. Ain't no Uzis made in Harlem. I bet not one of us in here owns a poppy field. This thing is bigger than Nino Brown. This is big business. It's the American way."

Vrrrrrm! Vrrrrrm! Vrrrrrm!

Heemy's iPhone vibrated in his lap. He picked it up and saw the caller was Treesha. She'd been blowing up his jack since earlier that morning. But every time she called, Heemy ignored it and sent her straight to voice mail. This time was no different. He sent the call to voice mail and continued watching the movie on his dashboard.

A cocky Nino was just about to tell on his man, and as always, Heemy was shaking his head and calling him every rat in the book. "You ol' T.I., Alpo, Frank Lucas, Sammy The Bull ass nigga! Done fucked up the whole movie wit' this rat-ass shit!"

Vrrrrrm! Vrrrrrm! Vrrrrrm!

"Fuck she keep calling me for?" Heemy flexed his jaw muscles, vexed that he was missing his favorite part of the movie, the final scene where the old man killed Nino.

"I know Shorty Rock done hit her off already, so why the fuck she keeps calling me?" He looked at the phone screen and then up at the dash. "I ain't giving her nothing else. She better take her ass around the corner and holla at one of them projects niggas."

After ignoring her call for the umpteenth time, he returned the phone to his lap and then lit the tip of the Backwood he twisted a few minutes earlier.

As the credits from the movie rolled up the screen, he took another pull on his Wood and thought about Nahfisah. After making love on the sectional the night before, they went upstairs to her bed room and put it down all over again. Laying in the bed with Nahfisah cradled in his arms, they spent the rest of the night talking about any and everything.

Nahfisah told him all about her past, and Heemy told her all about his. He even told her about the beef between him and Pooky, how he never knew that Pooky was his father and how Treesha tried to set him up the day after he killed him.

Nahfisah never judged him because Heemy never judged her. Not even when he revealed that he remembered Nahfisah from when she used to come over his house and smoke crack with his mother.

Nahfisah cried when he told her, and Heemy kissed away the tears. He never imagined that *Little Miss Attitude* was so fragile and insecure. She was usually on her bullshit, acting all stuck-up and stank. But the more she opened up to him, the more he realized how delicate she actually was and that her stank attitude and smart-ass mouth was only a façade, a way to make herself feel like she was more than what her broken heart told her she was. Through all of her hardships and pains, and the feelings she harbored of being unwanted and neglected, deep down, the only thing Nahfisah ever wanted was to be loved and cherished, and Heemy decided he would be the man to do it. To him, Nahfisah was a beautiful diamond, and that's exactly how he planned to treat her. Not only her, but Imani as well.

Exhaling a thick puff of Loud smoke, he looked through the windshield and spotted Nahfisah stepping out the salon. Her best friend, Alexis, was right behind her.

As the two women hugged one another and promised to meet up at La Casa Moreno before leaving for the party, Annie appeared in the salon's doorway. She looked over at Heemy and smiled. He smiled back and waved at her, completely unaware that Nahfisah had been bragging about him for the past two hours.

She told Annie all about their relationship and how they were taking things to the next level. Annie was happy, she was a big fan of Heemy's. She knew from talking to Sonny that Heemy was a stand-up guy, someone she could trust and rely on if she ever needed help. She didn't know the full extent of his and Sonny's relationship, but what she did know was that for the past six months, Heemy was more of a son to her than Rahmello was.

Every first of the month, he would break her off with a bag full of money, half of which he told her to keep for herself and the other half, he told her to put away for Sonny. So, when it came to Nahfisah, Heemy was definitely Annie's the number one choice. She would much rather see her stepdaughter with Heemy than the likes of that crab-ass Bushnut.

"Alright, girl, I gotta make a few runs and check on a few things," Alexis said as she opened the door to her Benz. She climbed inside and looked up at Nahfisah. "Nine o'clock, right?"

"Yup." Nahfisah nodded her head. "I spoke to Rahmello this morning, and he said that we gotta leave the house around a quarter after. He flew in a bunch of niggas from Cali and Georgia, and another bunch of niggas from Brooklyn and Pittsburgh. So, when we leave La Casa Moreno, we gotta swing past the neighborhood and scoop 'em all up. He swears up and down that the party's for me. But the way this nigga's been acting, you woulda swore it was his birthday instead of mines."

"Tell me about it." Alexis sighed. "That Rahmello sure is something else. I just wish Sonny was out here to celebrate with us."

"I know, right?" Nahfishah shook her head, thinking about her brother. "I miss him so much. I wish he wasn't so hellbent on not letting none of us go see him. Especially Keyonti, that little girl is so in love with her daddy. You can't even say his name without her throwing a fit. I hope everything works out for him, and he beats his case. These cracker-ass crackas always fuckin' wit' somebody, jealous 'cause we living' better than they is."

"You can say that again," Alexis concurred. She turned on the engine and threw the Benz in gear. "Well, listen, girl, I gotta go. But I'ma see you later on tonight."

"Alright, Lexi. Be careful out here, and I love you."

"I love you, too, Nah."

As Alexis closed the door and pulled off, Annie waved Nahfisah over to the door. She whispered something in her ear, then the two of them looked at Heemy and smiled. Nahfisah gave her a hug and then walked over to the truck and climbed inside.

"Yo, what's up with all this mu'fuckin'' smiling?" Heemy asked when Nahfisah settled back in the passenger's seat. "Y'all was in there talking about me?"

"Wouldn't you like to know?" Nahfisah replied with a mischievous smirk. She leaned over the console and kissed him on the lips. "Had you kept ya chocolate self in the waiting area, you woulda known what we were talking about."

Heemy looked at her with a raised brow. He could only imagine the things they'd been saying about him. He started to pry, but decided not to. Instead, he examined Nahfisah's new haircut and nodded his head in approval. Her silky black hair was flowing down the right side of her face, and the edges on the left side were faded down and lined up nicely.

"I like the way she did ya hair," Heemy complimented, loving the way her new hair style showed off her beautiful face and the three-carat diamond in her left ear. "You lookin' sexier than a mu'fucka right about now."

Nahfisah blushed. "Miss Annie did her thing, right? I told her that I wanted something different, and this is what she came up wit'."

180

"Yeah, she definitely did her thing," Heemy said as he started the engine.

He looked in the rearview mirror, sizing up the oncoming traffic. As soon as the lane was clear, he banged a U-turn in the middle of the street and headed southbound to North Philly.

"Now, where in the world is you takin' me to?" Nahfisah purred in his ear. She was leaned over the leather console nibbling on his earlobe. "You supposed to be takin' me back to the house, so I can get my car. You know I still got a bunch of shit to do. I gotta pick up Imani from Miss Mary's house and then drive out to the La Casa Moreno to pick up Fat-Fat, so I can drop 'em off at Miss Annie's. Then after that, I *still* need to take a shower and get dressed. Not to mention, Flo. I gotta wait for her to get off work, so she can come through and beat my face before we head out to the party. In the meantime, I was planning to catch up on my beauty sleep being as though *somebody*," she gently bit down on his earlobe, "thought it was a good idea to keep me up all night. So, once again, just where in the world do you think you're takin' me to?"

"Yo, chill, shorty, I got this," Heemy smoothly replied. He was leaned back in the driver's seat, pushing the truck at a calm 35 mph. "I'ma shoot over to Max's real quick to grab us some cheese steaks. I know you gotta be hungry. It's going on twelve-thirty, and we ain't ate shit all morning."

"Max's?" Nahfisah shot back. "I don't need no cheese steak from Max's, I got my cheese steak right here." She moved in a little closer and unbuckled his jeans. When she noticed his soldier was already standing at attention, she looked at him and licked her lips. "Well, zamn, zaddy, I guess somebody's been missing me already, huh?" She kissed the tip of his hamma and then slowly made it disappear. "And don't be touching on my goddamned hair," she mumbled with a mouth full of dick.

"Yo, chill!" Hemmy calmly replied, looking at her face going up and down on his monster. "Do what'chu do, and lemme do what I do."

With that being said, he placed his hand on the back of her neck and continued driving. He was so caught up on Nahfisah that he momentarily forgot about the drama with the YBM.

But little did he know, the YBM had already made the first move. The next move was his and Rahmello's. Or was it?

***

About Thirty Minutes Later

Vrrrrrm! Vrrrrrm! Vrrrrrm!

Heemy's cell phone had been going off nonstop for the past ten minutes. He left it on the center console when he hopped out of the truck and strolled into Max's.

Nahfisah looked at the phone and then looked through the front door of Max's, where Heemy was standing at the counter. He was waiting for his order of two chicken cheese steaks with mayonnaise, salt, pepper and ketchup.

Vrrrrrm! Vrrrrrm! Vrrrrrm!

Nahfisah knew better than to be nosey, but the sound of his phone was driving her crazy with each and every *Vrrrrrm!* In addition to that, being as though she'd been around Heemy every day for the past six months, she knew he had three apartments and a cache of young thots all throughout the city.

Damn all that! Nahfisah's curiosity got the best of her. *That's my muthafuckin' man now. So, all these lil' skally-wags of his gon' have to step the fuck off. 'Cause I ain't going for it.*

She glanced out of the window to make sure Heemy was still inside of Max's. When she saw he was, she picked up the phone and accepted the call. "And your business is..." she rudely spoke into the phone.

"Ahn-ahn. Where Heemy at? Who dis?" a female's voice came through the phone. The tone of her voice was just as feisty as Nahfisah's was.

"You ain't gotta worry about nunna dat, boo-boo. 'Cause whatever the two of y'all had going on, that shit is a wrap."

"Oh, yeah." The girl chuckled. "Is that right?"

"I don't remember stuttering."

"Yo, stop playing wit' me. Where Heemy at?"

"Bitch, you ain't heard what the fuck I just said?" Nahfisah raised her voice. "Whatever the fuck y'all had going on, that's a muthafuckin' wrap!"

The girl laughed at her. "Dang, you mad, huh? Talking all tough on the phone like you really about that life. I'ma let that slide. You just tell Heemy that Precious called."

Click!

Nahfisah slammed down the phone and balled up her fist. She knew she didn't have any right to be mad, but she was. They hadn't been together for longer than twenty-four hours, but she was already feeling territorial. She'd be damn if she sat back and let another chick from his past step in and take away what she had.

"What'chu lookin' all mad for?" Heemy asked when he climbed back in the truck. He reached between her legs and sat the grease-stained bag on the floor. "What's going on? What happened?"

"Who the fuck is Precious?" Nahfisah asked with her arms folded across her chest.

As soon as she said the name *Precious*, Heemy looked at his iPhone. "Yo, you was going through my phone?" He looked at her with a screwed up face. "What type of time is you on?"

"First of all," Nahfisah snapped her neck and rolled her eyes, "wasn't nobody going through ya phone. It was ringing back-to-back, nonstop, so I answered it."

Heemy took a deep breath and sighed. "Yo, I seriously hope you ain't the jealous type, Nah. Especially, when you already know what I do. I'm a hustla, and dealing with a bunch of bitches is the safest way for me to do business. But that doesn't mean that I'm fucking any of 'em. It only means that I need 'em for certain shit, so I keep 'em around strictly for that."

"Whatever, nigga. That's what'cha mouth say. Every last one of you niggas is the fuckin' same. Thinking that just because y'all making a little bit of money, y'all can do whatever the fuck y'all want, sticking y'all dick in every bitch that got a pussy. Then as soon as female do the same shit, we ain't nothing but a hoe-ass-thot!"

"You doing the most right now, Nah. Straight up. Me and Precious ain't even on that time. The only thing we do is get money together, and that's it. Ain't no fuckin', suckin' or nunna of that shit."

"Whatever, Raheem. Just take me home."

Heemy shook his head and sighed. Nahfisah didn't know it, but he was actually telling the truth. Precious was his number one runner down in Richmond, Virginia. It was the first Saturday of the month, and she was calling to make sure that everything was straight.

Another chick named, Monica, who also worked for Heemy, was supposed to had drove down to Richmond to drop off another brick and pick up the money that she owed Heemy for the last one, but she never arrived.

Tired and hungry and sick of going back and forth, Heemy started the engine and threw the transmission in gear. He was just about to pull away from the curb when his phone went off–vibrating and bouncing all around the console. He picked it up to see if it was Precious, but when he saw that the caller was Treesha, he laid it back down.

Nahfisah scoffed. "Oh, so now all of a sudden muthafuckkas don't wanna answer they phone? Un-fuckin-believable!"

"Yo, you know what? Just because you think I'm lying, I'ma answer the fuckin' phone." He snatched it back up and accepted the call. "What?" he shouted into the phone, after switching it over to speaker.

"Boy, don't be whattin' me! I'll break my foot off in ya goddamned ass! I'm still ya mother!" Treesha's voice bellowed through the speaker. "You need to get'cha lil' ass 'round here and see what the fuck is going on. They done killed them boys you had working the corner this morning."

"What boys? What corner?"

"Well, damn, boy, how many corners you got?"

"I'm serious, Mom. Who the fuck is you talking about?"

"Shorty Rock and Yahyo. They got they asses lit this morning. Right in front of the house. Well, not Shorty Rock, they shot his fat ass up the street. But that Yahyo, they killed him right in front of the stoop next door."

"Fuck!" Heemy shouted, banging his fist against the steering wheel. He had a feeling it was the YBM, but he couldn't say for sure. The hood was funny like that, anything could pop off at any given time for any given reason. "Do they know who did it?"

"They, who? The Po-po? I don't think so. They was out here all morning, deep as hell, about ten of 'em. Had they lil' yellow tape and them lil' triangle thingies they be using to count all the shell casings, musta been about forty of 'em."

Heemy licked his lips and flexed his jaw muscles. "I'm saying, though, what about you? You ain't seen nothing?"

"Hell nawl, I ain't seen nothing." Treesha shot back. "My black ass was on the floor hiding under the coffee-table. You know how it go when these muthafuckas get to shooting. But listen here," she spoke in a calm steady voice, "all this shit popped off 'fore I was able to get my bundle this morning. You think you could stop by and bring me one?"

"What? Man, get the fuck off my phone!" Heemy snapped at her and disconnected the call. He pounded his fist against the steering wheel and then leaned back on the headrest. Looking up at the ceiling, he shook his head slowly. "I knew it, man. I fuckin' knew it."

"I'm sorry, baby," Nahfisah said as she reached over and massaged his shoulder.

"Fuck off me." Heemy nudged her away. "Had I not been fucking wit'chu, but instead handling my business, nunna this woulda never happened. My niggas would be alive right now."

"But—But—"

"But nothing," Heemy cut her off. He shot her the ice-grill and then peeled away from the curb, leaving skid marks in the middle of the street.

Scurrrrrr!

Confused, hurt and disappointed all at the same, Nahfisah looked out of the window and cried.

Once again, it seemed as though love was kicking her in the ass. And for the first time in nearly nineteen months, she was craving the one thing that always seemed to take her pain away—the warm smoke seeping out the end of a crack pipe.

Chapter Seventeen
At the Food Court in The Willow Grove Mall

Olivia was devastated, and rightfully so. The night before, she was expecting Rahmello to come upstairs and make love to her but when he barged inside of their bedroom anxious and hype and blabbering about how he was too much of gangsta to bow down to the next nigga, she was instantly turned off.

Initially, she didn't pay him any mind. But when he mentioned that Diablo was back in the States and possibly coming to kill their family, Olivia freaked out. She didn't know Diablo personally, but had heard enough about him to know he was extremely dangerous, more so than Rahmello could ever imagine.

The Night Before

"Fuck that, nigga. We ain't going nowhere," Rahmello snapped out when Olivia suggested they pick up and leave.

"Baby, please, I'm telling you!" Olivia cried. "Diablo's crazy, he's not normal."

"Crazy?" Rahmello scowled at her. "Not normal? And how the fuck you know all that? From that nigga you was cheating on me with?"

"This isn't about that. This is about the safety of our family. If Diablo's coming after us, he's gonna kill us," her voice trailed off. "The same way he killed my mama and papa."

She broke down crying, and Rahmello went over to the bed to console her. He wrapped his arms around her and held her close.

"Damn, baby, stop crying. I got us, I swear," he spoke in a calm, soothing voice. "Nine times out of ten, these niggas is bluffing. I can't say how, but I'm assuming they know about the side deal that I cut with Juan, and now they're try'na scare me into coming clean. But it's not going down like that. I got the blood of a boss running through my veins, the same as they do. So, if they wanna go to war,

*I'ma take 'em to war. I just need you to have my back, and trust that
I can hold shit down. Can you do that for me?"*

*"Umm-hmm." Olivia sniffled and nodded her head. "But when
you say they, who exactly is it that you're talking about? You mean
Roberto's family?"*

*"Naw." Rahmello shook his head. "I'm talking my family.
Sonny and Grip."*

Olivia broke down crying all over again.

Back to the Present

"What did I do? What did I do? What did I do?" Olivia said to
herself. She was sitting at the third table in the first row right across
from the Wendy's.

Her flush, red face was covered in tears, and her puffy eyes were
bloodshot from crying all night. She never told Rahmello, but the
reason she believed Grip and Sonny were after them, had nothing
to do with the side deal that he cut with her uncle. Rather, it was all
about the false testimony she was scheduled to give at Sonny's trial.
The testimony that would surely get him the death penalty.

December 17, 2014

*A few days after the night Sonny was arrested, Olivia learned
the mutilated bodies of her mother and brother were discovered in
their Bucks County home. She was then contacted by Detective Se-
bastian Phoenix and informed that the body of a man he believed
was her father had washed up on the rocky shores of Cobb's Creek.*

*He suggested that Olivia meet him at the city morgue to see if
she could make a positive identification, and Olivia agreed.*

*She asked Rahmello to come with her, but he flat out refused.
He was still suffering from the gunshot wound he sustained the day
before and aside from that, he was uncertain as to whether or not
there was a warrant out for his arrest. He'd been watching the news
for the past four days, and it seemed as though the only thing they
were talking about was him and his family.*

According to the news, he was a "Person of Interest" in the murders of Pooky and Mar-Mar. They also mentioned that Sonny was being charged with everything from murder to drug trafficking and that Grip was on the run as a result of being charged in a forty-one count, federal indictment. So, when Olivia asked him to come with her to meet the detective at the city morgue, Rahmello wasn't having it. As substitute, he sent Aziz.

When Olivia and Aziz arrived at the morgue, they were immediately surrounded by twenty or so police officers. Aziz was apprehended and brought in for questioning and instead of identifying the body of her father, Olivia was whisked down to Police Headquarters, Homicide Division. She was escorted to an interrogation room on the Fifth Floor, where Detective Phoenix was already inside waiting for her.

"Have a seat," Detective Phoenix stated with a blank expression on his face. He was sitting on the left side of the small wooden table that was pressed against the back wall. A yellow legal pad was laying on the table in front of him, placed between a manila folder and a smoldering cup of black coffee.

Olivia looked at the officer who escorted her down to the station and then looked back at Detective Phoenix. She nervously bit down on her bottom lip and did exactly as the detective told her, slowly making her way toward the opposite end of the table. Her entire body was shaking from head to toe, and the only thing she could think about was Rahmello. She knew the authorities were looking for him, and assumed they were using her to get to him.

"Why am I here?" Olivia sobbed as she sat down in the wooden chair. "What is this about? I thought you wanted me to identify the body of the man you suspected was my papa?"

"There's no need for that." Detective Phoenix shook his head. "He was positively identified by his fingerprints a few hours earlier. I just used him as a means of peeling you away from Rahmello." Olivia's eyebrows shot up, and the detective flashed her a knowing smile. "That's right, Ms. Nunes. I know all about your boyfriend, as well as the boyfriend before him, but we'll get into that a little bit later." He opened the manila folder and pulled out a stack of

pictures. "For now, I just wanna tell you everything I know about you and your family. Hopefully, that'll deter you from insulting my intelligence by telling me a bunch of lies."

"But—But I don't know anything," Olivia propounded. Her voice was high pitched and squeaky.

"Well, I beg to differ, Ms. Nunes, because this is exactly what I know. Your father, Pedro Nunes, was the second in command of the Medellin Cartel. He entered the states in the summer of eighty-six and up until yesterday morning when his body washed up on the shores of Cobb's Creek, he's been responsible for nearly ninety percent of the cocaine coming into the country."

He picked up the first picture, which was a mugshot of Poncho, and slid it across the table to Olivia. When she looked at it and pushed it away, he laughed at her and took another swig from his coffee cup.

"Umm." He licked his lips and popped his tongue along the roof of his mouth. "Columbian roast!" He laughed at his own joke, but Olivia just scowled at him.

"Alright, now, where were we? That's right, your father. I know he owned a bodega on the corner of Marshal and Tioga. I also know a vast majority of the cocaine that's been plaguing our city for the past thirty years was sold from that exact location. His customers would visit the bodega between the first and the tenth of every month. During these monthly visits, they would either purchase, or receive on consignment, a large quantity of cocaine.

"Now, your mother," he slid a picture of Marisol across the table, "she was the bookkeeper. She would work the cash register and keep tabs on all of the dealers who came into the store. You know, the typical drug dealer bullshit—who came, who went, how much yahyo did they leave with, and whether or not it was a purchase or a consignment. But recently, on the rare occasions where she wasn't the one keeping the books, it was you who worked the register and kept tabs on all of the dealers."

He reached inside of the folder and removed an excerpt of the handwritten ledger that was discovered in their Bucks County estate.

He slid it across the table, then he leaned back in his chair and interlaced his fingers behind his head.

"Now, I'll be the first to tell you, Ms. Nunes, I'm far from being a handwriting expert. But at the same time, I'm almost a hundred percent certain that a number of these entries were personally handwritten by you. Especially when considering you left your initials at the conclusion of each and every last one of your entries."

Olivia looked down at the ledger and broke down crying. At the very least, she knew it was enough evidence to warrant a conspiracy charge, even though that was the only role she played in her family's operation.

"Now before you get yourself all bent out of shape, please allow me to make things clear. I handle strictly homicide cases, none of that drug dealing, corner boy shit. My only concern is gathering any and all information pertaining to the murders of your family. That, and in addition to a few other case's that I believe may possibly be connected. So, basically, that's the meat and potatoes of this interview. I could care less about whatever involvement you had in your family's operation. Do you understand?"

"Umm-hmm." Olivia sobbed. She slowly nodded her head and used the back of her sleeve to wipe away the snot that was threatening to spill from the tip of her nose.

"Good. Now, let's see if we can get things back on the right track. I've got another picture I would like for you to take a look at."
He removed a picture from the folder and slid it across the table. It was a picture from the crime scene in Easy's murder. He was burned to a crisp and blown to pieces in the trunk of his Jaguar. It appeared as though everything in the picture was charcoal-black, all except for his bone white teeth and the yellowish gleam of his solid gold Rolex. The second Olivia saw the picture, she looked away and covered her mouth with both hands.

"Too gruesome for you to look at, huh?"

She nodded her head and without looking, forcefully slid the photograph back across the table.

"As you should already know, the man in that picture was Ervin 'Easy Money' Moreno. In addition to being one of your father's

customers, he was also the father of your boyfriend, Rahmello. Now, I must inform you, Ms. Nunes, we have no doubts whatsoever that Mr. Moreno was murdered in your family's bodega. This assertion is based on the data we collected from the navigational system in Mr. Moreno's car. It clearly depicts his last stop, prior to being stuffed in his trunk and blown to pieces, was at your family's store. We also have evidence from your mother's ledger. Not only did she mark down that Mr. Moreno came into the store on the night he was murdered, in her very next entry she X'd his name out. It's almost as though he walked into the bodega, and never walked back out."

"But what does any of this have to do with me?" Olivia cried. "My mama and papa are dead! And instead of trying to find the person who killed them, you're wasting your time harassing me!"

"And who's to say we don't already have them? Well, at least one of them, anyway."

"You do?" Olivia gave him a quizzical look. "You really got him?" Up until then, she was under the assumption that Diablo was the one who murdered her family. But now, after listening to the detective, she wasn't so sure. He couldn't have been talking about Diablo, because if he was, then surely, she would have heard about it, or seen it on the news.

"Now, don't quote me on this, because I'm still building my case. But I've got a gut feeling that Sontino and his grandfather, Gervin Moreno, are the ones responsible for killing your family. I believe it was done in retaliation for what happened to Easy. I also believe there's a strong possibility that they're coming for you next."

"Coming for me?" Olivia sobbed. "But, why? I didn't do anything. Why would they be coming for me?"

"The Moreno Family is very dangerous, Ms. Nunes, very, very dangerous. So, the question is—why wouldn't they be coming for you?"

"But—But Sontino's locked up, and I heard on the news that their grandfather is on the run from the feds. So, if the two of them are out of the picture, then that should mean I'm safe, right?"

"Ummmm, not quite." Detective Phoenix grimaced? "As far as Gervin, you shouldn't be too concerned. But when it comes to Sontino, well, now that's a different story."

"A different story? How?"

"I mean, let's put this thing in its proper prospective. Let's say, for instance, you've got a store owner. He's working in his shop, minding his own business, when a bunch of guys dressed in all-black swarm the premises and began shooting at him. The store owner defends himself and he defends his store, and in the process, kills one of the intruders, only to later find out that the intruders weren't intruders at all. They were a bunch of police officers who stormed inside of his place of business, without identifying themselves and elicited a shootout. Now, you combine that theory with the expertise of a high-powered attorney, and what do you get? An Acquittal, Ms. Nunes!" He raised his voice and pounded his hand on the table. "You get an acquittal, which in this case, means that Sontino Moreno is back out on the streets!"

"But that's impossible," Olivia said, wiping her eyes. "There's no way he's coming home after killing those cops. Rahmello said that he's gonna get the death penalty."

"But what if he doesn't?" Detective Phoenix countered. "What if he somehow manages to wiggle himself out of his case? What if he comes home looking for revenge, looking to set the record straight for what happened to his father and then there you are," he paused for moment, leaving Olivia hanging on his every word, "fragile and all alone, with nobody to help you? What do you think is gonna happen, Ms. Nunes? Not only to you, but to Rahmello, as well? I'm pretty suret he loves you enough to try to save you. So, what happens, then? These people are extremely dangerous, Ms. Nunes, and I believe you already know that. You seen what they did to your mother and brother."

"But what am I supposed to do?" Olivia whined. "Everything I had is gone. My family is dead. I don't have any money, nowhere to go. What am I supposed to do?"

"Cooperate," Detective Phoenix suggested. "Help me put Sontino away for good."

"But I don't know anything. I only know Sontino from coming into the bodega to see my papa. And If I cooperate with that, it'll hurt Rahmello."

"I'm not interested anything pertaining to drugs." He reached back in his folder and pulled out a picture of Police Officer Jason Clifford. He held it in the air and shook it around like a Polaroid. "This man was a dear friend of mine," he stated in a calm voice. "He was murdered back in two thousand and twelve, and Sontino was the one who killed him. I've been trying to bring him to justice for over four years now, but so far, I didn't have enough evidence. The only thing I had was Sontino's Benz speeding away from the scene, it was captured on the dashcam in Jason's car. But if you agree to help me, Ms. Nunes, help me to get justice for my friend, I promise that I will do everything in my power to keep you and Rahmello safe. And as far as your mother's ledger, I can make it go away. I just need you to help me, Ms. Nunes. Please?"

"But how can I help you? I didn't even know Sontino back then."

"Sure you did," Detective Phoenix said as he got up from his chair. He approached Olivia on the other side of the table and placed his hand on her right shoulder. He gave it a firm squeeze and then leaned forward and ran down the story that he wanted her to tell. "You remember Sontino Moreno from two-thousand and twelve. Specifically, you remember a night, just a couple of weeks before Thanksgiving, when he came into the store and asked to talk to your father. You led him to your father's office. But instead of walking away, you stood there listening to their conversation through the slightly cracked door. It was then that you overheard Sontino taking credit for the police officer he killed in South Philly. According to him, he only did it to prove his loyalty to the cartel."

Olivia sniffled and wiped her eyes. "And you're sure that's what you want me to say?"

"That's exactly what I want you to say," Detective Phoenix confirmed. "With that testimony, in addition to the evidence I already have, it'll be more than enough to get a conviction."

"But—But wouldn't that be like, like giving false testimony?"
Olivia asked in a low voice. Still wiping her eyes, she turned her
head to look at him. "I thought you guys weren't allowed to do that."
"Are you kidding me?" Detective Phoenix smiled at her. "This
is Philadelphia. We do this shit all the time."

Back to the Present

Olivia agreed, and now there she was, in the middle of the food court, forehead pressed against the table and crying her eyes out. There were many times over the past year in the half that she wanted to come clean and confess to Rahmello what she'd done. But because she was afraid of what he might say or do, she kept it to herself.

She knew Rahmello loved her to death and would do anything for her, but she also knew he loved his brother. So, the only way to soften the blow of what she had to tell him, was to sow seeds of enmity between him and Sonny.

Hopefully, that way, at the very least, Rahmello would despise Sonny so much that when he found out Olivia was the secret witness in Sonny's case, he wouldn't even care.

About seven months ago, Olivia put her plan into action. It was right around the time Rahmello was running out of money. She knew he was still somewhat insecure about her past relationship with Roberto, so the first thing she did was play on his insecurities, constantly reminding him of the luxurious trips and expensive gifts that Roberto used to shower her with.

She then suggested he disobey Sonny's orders to stay away from the streets and get back on his grind, claiming that Sonny was only holding him back because he didn't want Rahmello to surpass him financially. So, in order to appease Olivia and prove he was more of a man than Roberto was, Rahmello went behind Sonny's back and linked up with Savino. But when Savino cut him off, claiming Rahmello was too hot, Olivia used it to her favor.

She reached out her uncle, Juan Nunes, and convinced him to cut a side deal with Rahmello. But only on the condition that

Rahmello had to turn his back on and sever his ties with Sonny and Grip. Rahmello accepted, and Olivia assumed she was in the clear. But the second she learned that Grip and Sonny had sent Diablo to kill their family, she did everything in her power to persuade Rahmello to pick up and leave, but he flat out refused. The money had gone to his head, and his lust for power was just too strong. He figured that an all-out war between him and his family was the only way to prove to Sonny and Grip that he was his own man, his own boss, capable of standing on his own two. So, instead of running from the beef, his mind state was to run toward it. But what Olivia knew and what Rahmello didn't was that death was right around the corner and that her only way to stop it was to not testify against Sonny.

That was the reason she was sitting in the food court. She had just finished talking to Detective Phoenix. She told him everything that Rahmello told her, but the detective didn't care. His reply was a simple one: *"Either testify or go to jail."*

Chapter Eighteen

After hanging up on Grip the night before, Rahmello was turned up to the max. He figured all of the talk about Diablo coming to kill him and his family was only a scare tactic. A frivolous ploy to manipulate him into confessing about his back-door deal with the Columbians. But in Rahmello's mind, what Grip didn't know was that Juan had already put him up on game.

According to Juan, Grip was making a brash power play to take over the head seat as the boss of The Conglomerate. He also revealed that Grip's number one ally was the Sinaloa Cartel. So, if Diablo was a Sinaloa hitman, and Grip had the Sinaloas in his back pocket, then how could the Sinaloas be coming to come kill him?

The situation, he reasoned, could only be one of two things: either the story about Diablo coming to kill him was a bunch of bullshit, or Diablo was in fact coming to kill him and he was commissioned to do so by Sonny and Grip.

In any event, Rahmello didn't give a fuck! Instead of running and hiding like a little bitch, he was dead smack in the middle of the hood, chilling in front of his trap house on Fairhill Street. So that way, if Grip, Sonny, the Sinaloas or anybody else was looking for him, he wanted to make sure he wasn't hard to find. Not only him, but the fifty or so shooters he flew in earlier that morning. They were scattered up and down Fairhill from York Street to Dauphin, strapped and ready to wet whatever Rahmello pointed at.

"It's going on one o'clock, dawg, where the fuck is you at?" Rahmello spoke into his iPhone. He was dipped in Gucci, smothered in diamonds, and leaning against the back of his snow-white Lambo. The customized sound system was thumping *War Pain* by Meek Mill, and Rahmello was loving every bar, feeling just as hostile as Meek.

Catch you out in Brooklyn, get'cha chain tookin'. My Philly boys will creep up on you when ain't lookin'. Wit'cha lil' memes, I be wit' the real Queen, screamin' free the real Preme. We be doin' real things. Pull up wit' a bad bitch, whippin' sum'n real mean. Marching, all these fuckin' drums on me like a drill team. I be wit' my young niggas, all they know is kill things...Don't make me make a real scene.

"But, I'm saying, though, Mikey, you were supposed to had been here over an hour ago," Rahmello continued talking to his jeweler, Mikey Millions.

He was waiting for Mikey to drop off the eleven iced-out Cubans he purchased for him and his street captains about two weeks earlier. Each necklace weighed a half of a kilo, and was accompanied by an iced-out BBB charm. The triple B's representing the Block Boy Bishops.

"I got'chu. I should be there in about thirty minutes," Mikey replied.

"A half an hour? Nigga that's the same thing you told me an hour ago. Come on wit' the bullshit, Mikey. I paid you ten jawns and two hunnid bands. That's damn near a half a mil."

"I know, and I appreciate it, my G. I'm just now hopping on ninety-five, so trust me, I'm on my way."

"A'ight, man, I'll see you when you get here. And don't be stopping for nobody either. Mu'fuckas in the hood see a young Jewish nigga pushin' a Ferrari? They'll jack his ass every time."

"Tell me about it." Mikey chuckled. He was a rich, young Jewish cat from Hamilton County, who swore he was hood. "Motherfuckers can try, but I've got two cars behind me. Not to mention, I've got an aim out of out of this world."

Rahmello laughed at him. "My fuckin' nigga." He disconnected the call and looked up and down the block. His shooters were everywhere. His Brooklyn boys were posted at the top of the block, his Georgia niggas were chilling down the street and his Cali thugs were positioned all around him, chilling in front of his trap house.

"Aye, yo, Snot Box, lemme get summa of that Kali Budd you smoking on," Rahmello said to his homie from the San Del Rio Projects.

"Fa'sho, my nigga. But you gotta be careful wit' it," Snot Box replied with droopy red eyes. "That muthafucka strong as hell." He hit the Dutchie and inhaled deeply. He coughed a couple of times and then passed it to Rahmello.

Rahmello grabbed it and looked at the burning cherry. "B.I.P., my nigga, Kali Budd," he sent a prayer up to his dead homie. He then placed the Dutchie between his lips and hit it real hard. "Umm." Rahmello tasted the sweet smoke. "Yeah, that's definitely that shit." He hit the Dutchie once more and passed it back to Snot Box. "And that's that same shit you can get me for the low?"

"Fa'sho, my nigga. All you gotta do is make that trip and come holla at'cha Bishop."

As the two of them went back and forth, discussing when, where and how Rahmello could get his hands on a tractor trailer full of Kush, Rahmello's iPhone vibrated in his pocket. He pulled it out and saw that the caller was Heemy. "Box, lemme take this call real quick. It's the lil' homie, Heemy, I was telling you about."

"Fa'sho, my nigga, handle ya biz."

Rahmello nodded his head and accepted the call. "Damn, nigga, I've been calling you since last night. Where you at?"

"I just dropped off Nahfisah. I'm on my way back to the city," Heemy replied in a salty voice.

"You just finished dropping off Nahfisah? What's that about?"

"That's irrelevant right now," Heemy sidestepped the question. "Niggas got drama right now. Them bitch-ass YBM niggas hit the block this morning. They smoked Shorty Rock and Yahyo, and I think they might've kidnapped Keeno. I've been calling this nigga back-to-back for the last hour, but he's not answering."

"Oh, yeah?" Rahmello replied nonchalantly. "So, what'chu gon' do about it?"

"What am I gon' do about It? You mean what is *we* gon' do about it?"

"Nah, nigga, what is *you* gon' do about it?"

"Huh?" Heemy replied, confused and completely caught off guard. He was expecting Rahmello to be just as mad as he was. "I ain't understanding you right now. Them niggas just hit our mutha-fuckin' block, and you making it sound like it's all on me."

"That's because it is all on you. Them niggas ain't hit my block, they hit yours. You gotta look at the bigger picture, Heem. When it comes to business, I'm just the nigga that's supplying you. Where and how you conduct business is all on you. The only thing I care about is my money. So, again, them niggas ain't hit my block, they hit yours. Now, what'chu gon' do about it?"

"Yo, is you serious right now?" Heemy raised his voice. As far as he was concerned, their entire team was family, one unit. At least that's the way it was when Sonny was at the helm. But, now, all of a sudden, Rahmello was on some bullshit.

"Nigga, I ain't playing, I'm dead-ass serious," Rahmello confirmed. "Ain't nobody got time for this petty-ass shit. It's bad enough I got Grip and Sonny coming at me. And now here you go, calling my phone wit' all this YBM shit. I told you once, and I'ma tell you again *fuck them niggas*, dawg! Its bigger fish to fry, and I'ma burn up every last one them muthafuckas. Speaking of which, as soon as you hit the city, shoot around Fairhill Street. I done flew in a bunch of Block Boys from around the country, and we out here strapped up and ready. Niggas ain't hiding. Whoever want it, can come get it. And on top of that, I'm still having the party tonight. Fuck these niggas. So, hurry up and get'cha ass around here. I wanna introduce you to some of the homies."

"I'ma be around there, but first I need to handle this situation wit' Shorty Rock and Yahyo. Them niggas was like family. So, it's only right I swing through and holla at they peoples. If for nothing else, I wanna let 'em know that if they need anything, I got 'em."

"A'ight, man, fuck it." Rahmello glanced at his watch. "Just make sure you meet us at La Casa Moreno around nine. I got sum'n I need to show you."

"Say that."

"And Heemy."

"Yeah, man, what's up?" Heemy sighed.

"Big business."

The nerve of this nigga, Heemy thought to himself. *How the fuck he talking about Bishop Love when not even two minutes ago, he was basically saying I'm out here fending for myself?* He considered hanging up without replying, but doing so would have only made things worse. So instead of revealing how he truly felt, he swallowed his pride and gritted his teeth. "Love, my Bishop."

"My mu'fuckin' nigga." Rahmello chuckled. As he disconnected the call, he noticed a black minivan with dark tinted windows was slowly creeping up the block. He didn't say a word. He just stuffed the phone in his pocket and calmly removed his .45 Kimber.

Cocking a bullet up into the chamber, he positioned himself in the middle of the street, forcing the minivan stop. His Cali homies followed suit. They whipped out the second they saw the look on his face, and quickly formed a circle around the minivan.

"Yo, roll this muthafuckin' window down," Rahmello said as he tapped the .45 against the driver's side door. The tinted window eased down slowly. "Damn, shorty, you pretty as shit." Rahmello smiled, surprised to see that a woman was pushing something so gangsta.

"What's the matter?" Kia asked, looking all sweet and innocent. She batted her eyes and returned his smile. "Did I do something wrong?"

"The windows."

"My windows?" Kia looked confused. "What's the matter wit' 'em?"

"The tint," Rahmello replied, unapologetically. "We got a *no tint rule* in affect."

"A *no tint rule*? What the hell is that supposed to mean."

"It means that any car coming through the block wit' tinted windows is getting aired the fuck out. So, if I was you, I'd tell that lil' boyfriend of yours to take the tint off his windows. That shit ain't safe."

"Well, excuse the hell out of me." Kia laughed. She looked at the pendent on his iced-out Cuban and read the word aloud. "Mello, huh? That's ya name?"

"Don't even worry about that, ma." He tucked the .45 in the small of his back and then motioned for his shooters to take a step back. "Just get the tint off these mu'fuckin' windows. First and last warning. Now, get this piece of shit outta here."

As the minivan cruised up the block and banged a left at the corner, Rahmello looked over at Snot Box. "A'ight, now, back to this Kush. How far a hunnid bands gon' take me?"

***

At ADX Florence

It was 10:35 a.m., Pacific time, and Gangsta was jet lagged and tired. His three-exchange, eleven hour flight from Havana was a gruesome one.

He attempted to get some rest, but every time he tried, the only thing he saw was Grip. He could literally see the old man lying on the ground choking on his own blood, suffering the same fate he dished out to his parents.

Gangsta could see himself towering over him, smoking gun in his right hand, with the barrel aimed down at the old man's mouth. It was there that he shot him, over and over again, for every lie the old man had ever told him, for every mind game he ever played, for manipulative antic, all of which were solely based on furthering his own interest.

These were the nightmares Gangsta had on the regular, ever since the night he stumbled upon the truth. For as long as he could remember, his Uncle Grip was the father he never had. He was his role model and mentor, a man he would have killed and died for, only to find out thirty years later that Grip was the same man who robbed him out of his mother and father.

There were numerous times he could have killed the old man after finding out what he'd done. But out of respect for Big Angolo and the vision he had for the family, Gangsta remained patient, knowing his day would eventually come. He just hated the fact he had to spend so much time around him without acting on what he truly felt, and that's the reason he flew out to the federal prison. He needed the OK from Big Angolo to take a step back until it was time to kill.

"Terrence Long. DEA," he announced his presence when approached the officer's station. He pulled out his badge and pressed it against the glass window. "I'm here to see federal prisoner, Angolo Gervino."

"Is that right?" The U.S. Marshal looked at him with a smug grin. He was the same chubby white man from the last time Gangsta visited the prison. "Well, I'm happy to be the one to tell you, sir. That's not gonna happen."

"That's not gonna happen?" Gangsta scowled him. "What do you mean, that's not gonna happen? I'm a federal agent. This prisoner is a person of interest in a federal investigation."

"Not anymore, he's not."

"Yo, my man, ain't nobody got time for this shit. Matter of fact, go get'cha supervising officer."

"For what?" The U.S. Marshal spoke in a low, raspy voice, doing his best rendition of Vito Corleone from The Godfather. "He's only gonna tell you the same thing I'm telling ya. The Don got whacked last night. Bodda-Boom! Bodda-Bing! His cancerillo got the best of him. So, if you wanna see him, you's gotta go back to Philadelphia. We shipped out his body about an hour ago."

Gangsta gave him a sharp look, squinting his eyes and flexing his jaw muscles. He had only known his grandfather for a little over nineteen months, but during that time, he developed a deep love and respect for the old man. He was the last of a dying breed. And now that he was gone, the same could be said about the peace treaty amongst The Conglomerate.

There was no one else around to keep the blood thirsty wolves in check. Their muzzles had been removed, Grip's in particular. It was only a matter of time before his hunger for power was met head on with the aggressions from the remaining bosses who weren't a part of his Super Pack.

These aggressions would not only be aimed at him, but his entire family as a whole. So instead of lashing out against the slick remarks that were made in reference to his grandfather's death,

Gangsta spun back around and headed out of the door. It was imperative that he make it back to Philly, and fast. A storm was brewing.

Chapter Nineteen
Two Hours Later

Rahmello was becoming too big for his britches, and Heemy was feeling some type of way. It was one thing to leave him hanging on the situation with the YBM, but to actually hear Rahmello say out of his mouth that he was taking Sonny to war, was something completely different.

So, after paying his respects to Yahyo's sister and dropping off some money to Shorty Rock's mom, he drove out to the county jail to visit his big homie. He knew Sonny forbade anyone from coming to see him because he didn't need the heat, but in this case, Heemy had no other choice.

So, for the past hour, he'd been sitting in the visiting room, anxiously scoping out the door that separated the visiting house from the inner workings of jail. He was hoping that Sonny would come through the door, but so far, he was 0 for 40.

"I hope this nigga come out here to see me," Heemy said as he looked at his watch and saw that the time was a quarter past six. "I'ma give him twenty more minutes. Then after that, I'm out."

As he leaned back in his chair, he looked around the visiting room. The large space was beginning to fill up.

When he first arrived, it was just him and six chicks and a rowdy bunch of bad-ass kids. But now, in addition to the forty inmates that came through the door, the crumb-snatchers multiplied to seventy, and the number of baby mamas grew to thirty.

Cracking his knuckles one at a time, Heemy looked to his left and saw a light skinned chick that reminded him of Nahfisah. She had the same body type and hair style.

She was hugged up and cuddling with one of the inmates. She was so beautiful that Heemy could not stop looking at her. She cracked up laughing, and the high-pitched snort was just another thing that reminded him of Nahfisah, not only her, but the foul way he treated her.

After accusing Nahfisah of being a deadly distraction, Heemy drove back to the county in total silence, showing no concern as she sat there crying. He should have apologized and did his best to console her, but he didn't. Instead, he kicked her out of his truck the second he pulled up in front of her house. He didn't even stick around to see if she made it safely inside. He just mashed down on the gas pedal and sped back to the city, too furious to realize he broke his promise to never hurt her.

So, now, as he sat back finally coming to terms with the harsh way he treated her, he took a deep breath and shook his head slowly. She was too precious to lose, and the thought alone, had him caught up in his feelings. He didn't even notice Sonny when he came through the door.

"Well, damn, lil' nigga, what's poppin'?" Sonny said as he slid up on him. His husky arms were folded across his chest and his hazel brown eyes were locked on Heemy's. "Out of all the brozays, I woulda bet a million dollars you'd be the last nigga to go against my orders. So, what's up wit' that?"

Heemy looked up at him and rubbed his eyes. It was almost as though he were looking at a ghost. Sonny's deep voice and wavy hair appeared to be the same, but everything else about him was different. He had more muscle weight than Heemy remembered and his smooth baby face was now covered in a thick bushy beard.

"Don't just sit there looking stupid." Sonny smiled at him. "Gimmie some." He held his hand out, and Heemy stood to his feet. After throwing up Four Hunnid, they embraced one another with their Block Boy handshake.

"Yo, it's good to see you, bro," Heemy said as he sat back down. "I know you ain't want nobody coming to see you, but I needed to holla at'chu. This nigga, Mello, been out here running around on some fuck shit."

"Is that right?" Sonny replied in a slow, skeptical voice. He sized Heemy up from his iced-out Cuban to his big face Rollie and then sat down in the empty seat beside him. "Because it seems to me that the same thing applies to you. Both of you niggas been on some fuck-boy shit. Not listening, just running wild and doing whatever the fuck y'all want. Hard headed shit."

206

"Huh?" Heemy looked at him with a creased brow. "I been playing my part the whole time. Whatever Mello asked me to do, I did. And on top of that, thirty-five percent of everything I made, I passed off to ya mom."

"See what I'm saying, that's the muthafuckin' problem right there." Sonny shook his head in disappointment. "Fuck is y'all niggas doing out there hustling? I gave Rahmello strict orders to fall back until I see what's going on wit' my case. Y'all know these crackas try'na stick a nigga under the fucking ground. So, whatever they can use against me, they gon' use it. Especially if they catch somebody close to me doing some dumb shit. They gon' attribute that shit right back to me."

"Yo, on some G shit, bro, this is my first-time hearing this," Heemy spoke the truth. "You gotta remember, when they released me from being questioned about that situation wit' Pooky and Mar-Mar, I came home to nothing. You was already locked up and Mello was missing in action. I ain't seen the nigga in damn near a whole year. Then one day, he popped back up and told me that everything was going back to normal. It took us a few days to clean house and reclaim all of our territories. But after that, it was right back to the money."

"And Mello told you that I cosigned this shit?"

"Nah, not exactly. But ya man was the one frontin' us all the work, so I assumed you knew."

"My man?" Sonny looked at him with squinted eyes. "My man, who?"

"The lawyer bul," Heemy quickly replied. "The Italian nigga you sent down to get me out the precinct. The same one that's always on the news talking about you. For some reason, I can't think of his name right now, but it's sum'n like Soprino."

"You mean *Savino?*" Sonny screwed his face.

"Yeah, that's it." Heemy nodded his head. "Savino."

"And you're sure about this?" Sonny asked in a calm voice. His brain was working in overdrive trying to make sense of what Heemy was saying. He would have never guessed in a million years that Savino was the one supplying Rahmello. Especially when Savino knew first hand that any mishaps could lead to him spending the rest of his life in jail.

"Of course, I'm sure. Me and Mello used to meet up wit' the nigga every first of the month."

"And what'chu mean by that?" Sonny flexed his jaw muscles. "You saying that Savino ain't the one supplying y'all no more?"

"Nah." Heemy shook his head *no*. "He cut us off about a week ago. He said that Mello was too hot, and he was falling back."

"So, who the fuck is y'all coppin' from now?"

"I 'on't know." Heemy shrugged his shoulders. "According to Mello, he linked up wit' a new connect. I asked him who it was was, but he wouldn't say. The only thing I know is that he hit Mello off wit' three hunnid bricks. Twenty-five bands a piece, on consignment."

Sonny gritted his teeth and stared up at the ceiling. He knew right away Rahmello was dealing with one of two people: either Grip or Juan Nunes.

Aside from the Sinaloa Cartel, his grandfather and Juan were the only two who had enough juice to make such a deal possible. He knew that it couldn't have been the Sinaloas, so he excluded them immediately. He also excluded Grip, knowing that his grandfather was laying low in Cuba, strategically planning his next move. So, the only one left on his list was Juan.

But why would he give Rahmello such a sweet deal, or even cut deal with him in the first place? Could it be that Grip was behind the scene, still playing Puppet Master? Or did Rahmello stab him in the back and take allegiance with the other side?

"And that's one of the reasons I came to see you," Heemy continued talking. "Them YBM niggas hit one of our blocks this morning and killed two of the homies. I told Rahmello, and this nigga talking 'bout…"

"The YBM?" Sonny cut him off mid-sentence. He peeled his gaze from the ceiling and placed it on Heemy. "When you say the YBM, you mean the *real* YBM, or some niggas calling themselves the YBM?"

"The *real* YBM," Heemy confirmed. "Alvin Rines. Get down or lay down. He's got a bunch of young niggas rydin' for him. Them niggas out here running down on everything moving, bro. The word on the streets is that they looking for me and Mello. I told Mello, but he think it's a game. Then, earlier today, them niggas killed two of the homies. I told Mello, but the only thing he was talking about was you and Grip."

"Me and Grip?" Sonny's eyes got low. "Talking about me and Grip, how?"

Heemy took a deep breath and sighed. "Man, this nigga on some other shit, bro. It's like, damn, man, I don't even wanna be the one to tell you this shit."

"Tell me what, Heem? Stop talking in circles and spit it the fuck out."

"The money, bro, he's letting this shit go to his head."

Sonny's face became red with anger. He turned around in his seat and faced Heemy straight on. "Aye, yo, dig right, you my mu'fuckin' young bul and I fucks what'chu. But if you keep playing these mu'fuckin' word games, I'ma *smack* the shit out you! Now spit it the fuck out!"

"A'ight, man, fuck it." Heemy shook his head. "Mello said he was taking you and Grip to war. For some reason, he got it in his head that y'all coming for him."

"What?" Sonny looked at him like he was crazy. "Taking us to war? Is this nigga serious?"

"Hell yeah, he's serious. When I told him about the shit wit' the YBM, he was like fuck them niggas. He said the only thing he was worried about was you and Grip. He flew in a bunch of homies from all around the country. So, I'm assuming they rydin' wit' him. Mello got the bag right now, bro. Them niggas following the money."

Sonny was so mad that his hands began to tremble. He didn't tell Heemy what he knew, but he didn't doubt for a second that Rahmello switched sides and was now claiming loyalty to Juan. This was the only way his little brother could ever assume he was strong enough to take on the family. It also explained why Juan agreed to give him so much work.

"So, what'chu wanna do, bro? Just gimme the word, and I'll blow his fuckin' brains out."

The statement was so blunt that it caught Sonny by surprise. His initial instinct was to pop off, solely on the fact that Heemy was talking about his brother. But because he knew his little homie was only being loyal, he calmed himself down and gave him a pass.

"Nah," Sonny said as he got up from his seat. He stretched out his arms and back, and rolled out the crook in his neck. "'Cause at the end of the day, that's still my brother. I can't just take what'chu said and run with it. At the very least, I still gotta investigate and make sure everything you told me was the truth."

"But it *is* the truth!" Heemy insisted. "I wouldn't lie to you, bro."

"I'm not saying you would." Sonny raised his hand to calm him down. "But until I know exactly what's going on, I can't just jump out the jet and give you the green light on my little brother. Just fall back and lemme see what's going on. If anything, just keep the nigga close. I'm assuming he doesn't know you came to see me, right?"

"Nah, he don't know," Heemy spoke in a somber voice. He was already kicking himself in the ass for sticking his nose in Moreno Family business.

"Good, and we gon' keep it that way," Sonny assured him. "And like I said, in the meantime, just keep tabs on the nigga. Especially the muthafuckas he flew out to the city. I need to know exactly who they is, and where the fuck them niggas came from. But other than that, just lay low and keep ya cool. The element of surprise is a muthafucka."

Heemy stood to his feet with his head held high. Despite the fact Sonny made it seem as though he was working angles, he was determined to let him know he had his back. He extended his right hand and looked Sonny square in the eyes. "I got'chu, big homie. Trust."

"Trust?" Sonny met his gaze with a cautionary stare. He accepted Heemy's hand and gave it a firm squeeze. "That's a hell of a word. So, I'ma trust that everything you told me was the truth. For now. But if I find you lied, or misrepresented anything you just told me, you know what I'ma do, right?" Heemy nodded his head, and Sonny released his hand. "Good. 'Cause you can trust that, too."

He turned to walk away and Heemy called out behind him. "But what about the YBM?"

"What about 'em?" Sonny spun back around to face him.

"Them niggas violated, bro. I'm try'na go dead at 'em."

"I feel you, my nigga. Trust me, I feel you. But that's the least of our concerns right now. My trial's less than three weeks away. You think you can hold tight until then?"

"Yeah, man, I can hold tight. But I'm telling you, bro, if they run up on me..."

"Then soldier the fuck up and get it down like a Block Boy!" Sonny snapped at him, talking louder than he intended to.

The anger inside of his chest was beginning to seep out, and everybody could see it. The inmates and visitors were looking at him and whispering. A few of the inmates he knew from being on the same side of the jail, so when he gave them the ice-grill, they bitched up and looked away. One of the inmates was so shook, he slapped his baby mama when her nosey ass continued looking.

Gritting his teeth, Sonny took a step closer. He was talking so low that Heemy could barely hear him. "I know the nigga, Alvin Rines, personally. So, let me reach out to him and see what's good. In the meantime, just do like I told you and stay close to Mello. If he's out there moving the way you said he was moving, then nine times out of ten, them niggas ain't gon' want no smoke. Niggas know who to fuck wit', and who not to fuck wit', you feel me? So, just fall back and play ya position."

With that being said, Sonny threw up his set, and Heemy threw it up back at him.

"Big business."

"Business as usual."

***

When Sonny returned to his housing unit, he knew right away something was wrong. For starters, the block was open, as opposed to being locked down. He knew from talking to Alexis the day before that she was calling out sick, and that her girlfriend, Michelle, would be the only officer working the unit. So, therefore, the block should have been locked down. The only inmates that should have been out on the tier was him and his boys. But as he looked around the day room, the only one he saw from his crew was his little homie, Smurf, from South Philly. Tall and lanky and looking more vicious than a Pit bull with a Rattlesnake tied around his neck, the young gangsta was standing in front of the mop closet. His skelly hat was cocked to the left, confirming everything that Sonny was assuming: drama was in the air and it was time to put on.

Smurf threw up the Four Hunnid, signaling for Sonny to come over, but Sonny gestured for him to wait a minute. Still looking around the day room, he approached Michelle at the officer's station.

"Yo, Shelly, what's poppin'?" Sonny said as he handed over his visitation pass. "Lexi came to work?"

"Uhn-uhn." The slender built, brown skinned woman shook her head *no*.

She grew up a few blocks away from the Bad Landz, so the two of them had known one another for years. They even fucked a few times in the past, but it was something they never talked about. Especially since her and Alexis were friends, and because Smurf was her new boo thang on the block.

"So, what'chu open the block for?" Sonny asked, still looking around the crowded day room.

"Ask ya man." She nodded at Smurf. "His crazy ass is the one who told me to do it, talking about he needed me to open the block so he can handle something. You *need* to go over there and see what's going on, 'fore them muthafuckas get me in trouble. You know the Sarge been on my ass since that nosey bitch on Pod Four said she seen me and Smurf creeping out the supplies room. Ol' nosey-ass bitch."

"More or less." Sonny dipped off without saying another word.

He was halfway across the day room when he heard someone calling his name. He looked to his left and saw his uncle, Sweet Pea, walking toward him. The husky old head was Annie's younger brother. But because he was always locked up, Sonny hardly knew him. He only remembered seeing Sweet Pea about ten times in his entire life, and two of those times were at his grandparents' funerals. And even then, Sweet Pea was locked up. He was shackled and chained, bigger than Debow, and crying louder than everybody else in the church. So, it wasn't until Sonny came to jail, that the two of them really got to know one another.

Sweet Pea reached out to pull him aside, but Sonny brushed him off. "Not now, Sweets. I'ma holla at'chu later."

"Later, shit. Ya little ass gon' holla at me now!" Sweet Pea replied in his raspy, deep voice. He grabbed Sonny by the arm and spun him back around to face him.

"Aye, yo, Sweets, if you don't get the fuck up off me!" Sonny looked at him like he was crazy.

"A'ight, neph. But hear me out." He released Sonny's arm and backed away a couple of steps. "Listen, man, you my mu'fuckin' nephew, and I love you. All I'm try'na do is give you the heads up, 'fore you do sum'n stupid."

"Before I do sum'n stupid? Fuck is you talking about, Sweets?"

"Them young buls of yours. They done fucked up and put they hands on the wrong mu'fucka. That ain't just anybody they got in that mu'fuckin' mop closet. That little nigga's a *somebody*."

"A *somebody*?" Sonny shot him a funny look. Sweet Pea had been locked down so long he didn't understand how bossed up his nephew truly was. Even when Sonny tried to tell him, Sweet Pea laughed it off, accusing his nephew of being a jailhouse megalomaniac. But only if he knew. "Hey, yo, Smurf." Sonny gave his little homie the nod. "Get over here."

Smurf stuck his head inside of the mop closet and told the homies, Muncie and Maniac, to come out and guard the door. The second they took over his post, he G-strolled over to Sonny and Sweet Pea.

Askari

"Wh—Wh—What's poppin', brozay?" he spoke in his perpetual stutter. The first word of everything that came out his mouth, came out in a stutter followed by a brief pause and then the rest of his sentence. It was never said to his face, but behind his back, everybody called him *Stuttering Smurf.*

"Who the fuck y'all niggas got in the mop closet?" Sonny asked with his arms folded across his chest.

"Th—Th—This fuck nigga that just came down came down from upstate. T—T—Talking all this YBM shit like, like them niggas running sum'n. N—N—Nigga even said ya name. T—T—Talking 'bout, 'bout you a bitch and that, that they better give you the death penalty before, before he do. S—S—Said sum'n 'bout, 'bout you killing his bitch-ass sister."

"Killing his sister?" Sonny frowned at him.

"And that's what I'm talking about," Sweet Pea interjected. "That's A.J. them niggas got hemmed up back there."

"A.J.?" Sonny shot him a quizzical look. "And who the fuck is A.J.?"

"See, man, I knew you was lying!" Sweet Pea perked up. "You young niggas always coming through the jail talking this boss shit, lying like a mu'fucka. How the fuck you don't know who A.J. is when you the same nigga that said you was married to his sister."

"Who, Daphney?"

"Yeah, nigga, *her!* Alvin Rines' daughter. The same bitch you told me they found dead in that big-ass mansion of yours. See, that's the nut shit I'm talking about. You ain't gotta lie to kick it, neph. I'm ya mu'fucka uncle."

Ignoring everything Sweet Pea just said, Sonny stood there shaking his head. As far as he knew, Daphney was an only child. Not once did she ever mention having a brother. So, what the fuck was Sweet Pea talking about? He looked at Smurf and then looked back at Sweet Pea.

"Yo, you sure about that, Sweets? 'Cause I ain't never heard nothing about Alvin having a son."

"Hell yeah, that nigga got a son. A.J., Alvin Junior. Ain't a nigga in the D.O.C. don't know about A.J. He's one of them

214

Juvenile Lifers. Little nigga caught a body back in ninety-eight when he was sixteen. They just now bringing him down, so they can modify his sentence. But the second he see the judge, he's outta here, right back out on the streets. So, you know what that means," he pointed at Smurf, "you little dick heads done fucked up. Fuck around and get'cha mother smothered. Especially, wit' Rayon out there."

"Rayon?" Sonny screwed up his face. "You mean, Rayon, as in Double R, Rayon the Southwest Reaper?"

"The Southwest, who?" Sweet Pea shook his head. "Nawl, I'm talking about Double R, as in *Rayon Rines*. Alvin's little brother, Mr. Get Down or Lay Down, aka, Mr. Blow Nigga's Head Off!" Sweet Pea turned up the volume. He was amped up, talking wit his hands and bouncing around like the YBM was the illest shit in the world. He was one of them jailhouse old heads that was still stuck in the past. Specifically, the early nineties, when EST was still the hottest in Philly, and the YBM had the city in a headlock.

Sonny didn't say a word. He was too busy contemplating his next move. It was all beginning to make sense, from everything Heemy told him about the YBM, to now hearing about A.J. accusing him of killing Daphney.

He hadn't spoken to Alvin since the night everything went down, but based on the way things were looking, the conclusion was inescapable: Alvin was declaring war.

However, the only piece of the puzzle that didn't fit was The Reaper. As far as Sonny knew, Rayon was the one killed Daphney. So, why would he kill his own niece, or at the very least go along with Sonny's plan, without ever mentioning that he and Daphney were related?

Luckily for Sonny, the answers to his questions were just a few feet away in the mop closet.

"S—S—So, what's poppin', brozay? W—W—We gon' finish getting at this nigga, or, or what?"

Sonny cracked his knuckles and nodded his head slow. "Let's get it."

215

As Sonny and Smurf walked away and disappeared inside of the mop closet, Sweet Pea just stood there shaking his head.

"Stupid-ass nigga. Crazy just like his goddamned daddy!"

Blood of a Boss 4

Chapter Twenty
Fifteen Minutes Later

Whack!

"Ummmm!"

"P—P—Pussy, shut the fuck up!" Smurf shouted after cracking A.J. upside the head with the wooden handle of a deck brush. *Whack!*

He cracked him once more and then looked over at Sonny, who was leaned against the wall, arms folded across his chest and watching his little niggas get busy. "W—W—Want me to crack his ass again, or, or what?"

"Nah, Smurf, fuck that!" shouted Sleepy Biz. He snatched away the wooden handle and sized up the left side of A.J.'s forehead. Gritting his teeth, he worked him over until Sonny told him to stop.

"That's enough, Sleep, chill," Sonny said as he moved away from the wall. He motioned for his youngins to take a step back and they posted up beside the door.

The two homies, Munchie and Lil, were standing on the other side, mean-mugging the entire day room. Their facial expressions said it all: *Play hero and get dat ass fucked up, too!*

Rubbing his hands together, Sonny circled the mop closet like a caged lion. The small, concrete room was a tad bit larger than two cells put together, equipped with a broom rack, a mop rack, three mop buckets, a water hose and a three-foot drain.

The ventilation system was nonexistent and the windows were glued shut. So, naturally, the raw stench of A.J.'s feces were nothing short of horrendous. He was butt-ass naked and hogtied on the concrete floor. His raw, bloody back was sliced open and torn to shreds, courtesy of the extension cord that was now roped around his ankles and wrists.

Poor A.J., he couldn't have weighed more than a buck-sixty, soaking wet in a sweat suit. But his pumpkin sized head was swollen and fat, that had he taken a selfie from the neck up, he would have appeared to be somewhere north of four hundred pounds. Poor A.J.

Still circling the mop closet, Sonny looked at him and shook his head. "Alvin Junior, huh? Prince of the YBM? Ya ass got a lot of explaining to do, dawg. A lot of explaining."

"Ummmm!" A.J. shouted through the bloody, soaked socks that were stuffed down inside of his mouth. "Ummmm! Ummmm!"

Sonny laughed at him and made the same exact noise. "Ummmm! Ummmm! Ummmm! Bitch-ass nigga." He got down on one knee and rubbed the top of A.J.'s swollen head. "Look at'chu, laying on the floor bleeding and shit. Well, daaamn, homie? Them niggas said you was the maaan, homie. What the fuck happened to you?" Sonny laughed at him some more and then placed his index finger in front of his lips.

After signaling for A.J. to be quiet, he removed the bloody pair of socks from his mouth. He didn't even get a chance to ask him any questions, as A.J. was already dishing out threats.

"Nigga, you's a muthafuckin' dead man!" A.J. laughed in his face. "You might as well kill me now. 'Cause if you don't, the second I hit the streets, it's a wrap. I'm killing you, and every muthafucka that look like you."

"Sounds like a plan," Sonny replied in a nonchalant voice, rubbing A.J.'s head like a good little boy. "I wouldn't have it any other way. A nigga like me ain't never been the type to turn down a muthafuckin' gangsta party. But for now, my only concern is all this YBM shit I've been hearing about. First, I get word from my young bul telling me that y'all hit one of my blocks and killed two of my soldiers. And now here you come wit' the fuck shit, talking all this nonsense about fuck Sonny."

"Nigga, you killed my sister!"

"Killed ya sister? Nah, homie, that wasn't me. That was ya uncle, Rayon. Now, pardon me if I'm wrong, but The Reaper is ya uncle, right?"

"Fuck you!" A.J. snapped at him. He gathered up a bloody clump of mucus and spat in Sonny's face.

Tfft!

The second he did it, Smurf ran over and kicked him in his ribs. A.J. grinded his teeth and endured the pain without giving them the

218

satisfaction of hearing him scream. After kicking A.J. about a dozen times in rapid succession, Smurf leaned over tired and sweaty. He spat a stray razor from his mouth and reached down to give him a buck-fifty, but Sonny waved him off.

"Chill, Smurf, I got him," Sonny said, wiping the spit from his face. He looked over at the broom rack and told Smurf to hand him one. Smurf did as he was told and grabbed the broom that was closest to him. He handed it Sonny, and Sonny looked down at A.J. "Yo, put them socks back in his fucking mouth."

As Smurf went to work, Sonny looked up at Sleepy Biz, who was still standing beside the door. "You got'cha jack on you?"

"Yup." Sleepy Biz nodded his head. "Never leave the cell without it." He reached in his back pocket and pulled out a Samsung Galaxy S6. "Can't do noting wit' it, though. Not in here, anyway. Ain't got no reception."

"Don't need no reception." Sonny hopped up on his feet. "Just turn the recorder on."

"Say no more," Sleepy Biz replied, clicking on his video app.

Using the spit that was cupped in his left hand, Sonny lubricated the broom stick. He added a little spit of his own to make sure it was nice and slippery. He then looked down at Smurf, who had just finished stuffing the socks back in A.J.'s mouth.

"A'ight, now spread his muthafuckin' legs apart. *Wider, Smurf!* I wanna make sure his daddy can see every inch of this muthafucka. Bitchin' about his muthafuckin' daughter. I'ma give his ass another one."

"Ummmmmmmmm!" A.J. shouted when Smurf grabbed around the knees. He was laying on his stomach with his arms and legs pulled back like the letter U, so far back that his lower torso was the only part of his body touching the floor. He was struggling and twisting and doing his best to break free, but all he managed to do was fall over on his side.

"Fuck is you doing, Smurf? Get his ass under control," Sonny barked at him.

"I—I—I got him," Smurf replied, flipping A.J. back on his stomach.

He stuck his foot in between A.J.'s arms and forcefully pressed down on the back of his shoulders. A.J. squeezed his ass cheeks together, but it was no use. Smurf grabbed him by the thighs and spread him wide open.

Sonny looked back at Sleepy Biz and flexed his jaw muscles. "You recording this shit?"

"Yeah, bro, we live. I'm looking at'chu on the screen."

"A'ight, now zoom in on my face." After waiting for Sleepy Biz to give him the nod, Sonny looked into the camera with a menacing glare. "Yo, Alvin. First of all, nigga, I ain't killed ya muthafuckin' daughter. That's sum'n you need to holla at'cha brother about. On another note, I've been hearing some fucked up shit, dawg. Like some really, really fucked up shit. Niggas running around the city on some YBM shit, flexing on niggas, talking 'bout get down or lay down. But the worst part is that they hit one of my blocks and killed two of my people. And then here comes this bitch-ass nigga, A.J...."

"Ummmm!" A.J. shouted as loud as he could, still struggling to break free. "Ummmm! Ummmm!"

"Oh, and just so you know, that's him in the background by the way. What'chu think I'm lying?" he stated with a raised brow. "Yo, put the camera on this bitch-ass nigga. Let his daddy see that I'm dead fuckin' serious." Sleepy Biz placed the camera on A.J. and then brought it back to Sonny. "That's some fucked shit, right? Got'cha lil' man roped up on the floor, laying on his stomach like a faggot-ass trick wit' his ass all out. Lil' Nigga brought it on himself, though, coming in the jail talking about fuck Sonny. You believe that shit?" His nostrils began to flare. "Fuck Sonny? Nah, nigga, fuck you!" He raised the broom stick high above his head and then broke it clean across the back of A.J.'s dome.

Crack!

"Now." Sonny looked back at the camera with fiery red eyes. "Since ya stupid-ass thought it was a game, I'ma show you how I get it the fuck poppin'!"

He jammed the splintered broom stick deep down in the crack of A.J.'s ass, and A.J. screamed out at the top of his lungs. *"Ummmmmmmmm!"*

He was shaking his head and looking up at the ceiling like he was calling on God. Unfortunately for him, it seemed as though God wasn't listening. The fifteen inches of broom stick was literally tearing him a new asshole, ripping through the lining of his stomach and pushing his guts all around.

Sonny pulled out the shitty, red broom stick and held it up to the camera for Alvin to see when he eventually received the video. It was covered in blood and had tiny little chunks of A.J.'s rectum stuck in between the fork-like splinters.

"And this is what the fuck you want?" Sonny screamed like a raving lunatic. He was looking at the camera and foaming at the mouth when he said it. "I'm a muthafuckin' monster, bitch! You ain't never in ya life seen a nigga like me! And this is what'chu want? This what the fuck you want? Well, come and get it, then!"

He buried the broom stick back inside of A.J., causing him to scream even louder. Showing no remorse and not a scintilla of concern for a human life, he plunged the broom stick in and out of A.J.'s rectum with a devastating force, not once taking his eyes off the camera.

"You see this shit, nigga?"

Wham!

"I will sever," *Wham!* "ya fucking," *Wham!* "head off!"

Wham!

"Now, turn that muthafuckin' recorder off!" he shouted at Sleepy Biz, who was holding the phone with one hand, and covering his nose and mouth with the other.

"Oh, shit. Yo, what the fuck is that?" Sleepy Biz blurted when Sonny yanked the broom stick out of A.J.'s ass. It slipped out with a loud *plop* and sloppy wet *brrrnnnnn!*

221

Sonny looked down and noticed that a burgundy bubble was growing out of A.J.'s elongated rectum. After swelling to the size of a basketball, it popped with a loud *whop,* and sent a bloody gush of diarrhea splashing against the concrete wall. A.J. toppled over with his eyes rolled into the back of his head. The pain was so intense he couldn't even scream. He just laid on the floor shivering and shaking and sobbing like a newborn baby.

Still holding the shitty, red broom stick, Sonny looked back and forth between Sleepy Biz and Smurf. The two youngins were scared to death. It was one thing to shoot and stab a muthafucka, but to violate another man with a broom stick? That was something completely different. They would have never imagined that Sonny could be so vicious.

"Which one of you muthafuckas made the decision to tie this nigga up in the first place?"

Sleepy Biz moved away from Smurf and left him standing there by his lonesome. Smurf was shaking like a stripper, not knowing what to say or do. He could see Sonny was mad at him, but he didn't know why.

It never dawned him that he made a mistake by moving on A.J., without first talking to Sonny. At the very least, he should have consulted with his big homie and given him the opportunity to properly think things through. But because he didn't, he dealt Sonny a fucked-up hand, where his only option was to take Alvin to war, which was the last thing he needed at the moment. Especially when considering all the fuck shit he'd just heard about Rahmello.

"T—T—The nigga was talking, talking crazy, bro," Smurf tried to explain when Sonny approached him with the broom stick clutched in his left hand. He sucked in a deep breath when Sonny laid the stick on his right shoulder.

"The next time you call ya'self playing shot caller, without first coming to me to get the green light, you and this broom stick gon' get real muthafuckin' acquainted. You understand?"

"Y—Y—Yeah," Smurf stuttered, struggling to hold his breath.

"Good." Sonny smeared the shitty broom stick up and down the right side of Smurf's face. "That's real good. Now, clean this shit the fuck up."

Askari

Chapter Twenty-One
Later That Night, in Southwest Philly

"Now, you listen here, bitch, and you listen good. Don't be touching my goddamned radio," Bushnut said to the sexy white chick that was sitting in the passenger's side of his brand-new Lexus.

It was a quarter to nine, and he was parked outside of a three-story row home on 54th Street. It was there that the YBM planned out most of their missions, and where Bushnut kept a portion of his money and dope.

He cracked open the driver's side door and stepped one foot outside of the car, leery about leaving the white girl unattended. He just met her the night before, and she was already turning tricks for him.

She didn't know it, but the radio was the trigger for the secret stash box that was built into the floor of the back seat. Had she turned the volume up to ten and pushed *play,* the carpet in the back seat would have mechanically slid back, revealing the customized box that was stash underneath.

Inside, she would have discovered a P89, $10,000, and a half a brick of dope, which in her case, was more than enough to skip town and never have to worry about fucking and sucking for a buck, just to turn around and hand the money over to a playa pimp like Bushnut.

"Bitch, you ain't heard nothing Daddy just told you? I said don't touch," he paused for a brief moment, "this muthafuckin radio."

"Yeah, yeah, yeah," she replied in a sing-song voice. She rolled her eyes and then snorted up the first of the three coke lines that were sprinkled across the length of her compact mirror.

"Yeah, yeah, yeah, my muthafuckin' ass. Play pussy and get'cha white ass fucked."

She laughed at him and flicked her tongue up and down, freakishly. "Whatever, Daddy. You was planning on fucking this pussy any ol' way, so don't even front. Huhn." She held out the compact mirror and the hundred-dollar-bill that was rolled up like a straw.

"Clean up this last line for me. This shit got me horny as hell. Where'd you get it from, anyway?"

"Stop asking so many goddamned questions," Bushnut replied, taking the mirror and straw. He placed the bill in his left nostril and inhaled deeply. *Smucckkk!* "Whoooh, goddamn!" He tilted his head back and popped his tongue against the roof of his mouth.

It was the best cocaine he tasted in years. He'd been snorting it nonstop since Doo Dirty gave it to him earlier that day. It was courtesy of the sixty bundles that were confiscated from Shorty Rock and Yahyo. And now that Bushnut got him a taste, he wanted some more. But unfortunately, Heemy was the one who had it, and he knew from talking to Smitty that Heemy had refused his proposal to get down with the program.

When Smitty told him, it didn't really matter too much. Because whether or not Heemy got down, Bushnut knew just the way to get the young hustla to see things his way.

Instead of going to Heemy, he would make Heemy come to him. Then as soon as he did, he would bring the young gangsta crumbling to his knees. Not only for the sake of taking over his drug territories, but for the sake of the ultimate prize. That ultimate prize being Rahmello, who he and The Reaper recently discovered was the man behind the scenes calling the shots.

He wasn't Sonny, but he was a Moreno nonetheless. And according to YBM protocol, in order to takeover and reclaim the streets of Philly, the Moreno Family was at the top of their shit list. They had to be dealt with.

"Daddy, you okay?" the white girl asked when she noticed the way Bushnut was staring out of the window, eyes wide open, almost as though he were looking at a ghost. "*Daddy?*" she raised her voice and nudged him on the shoulder. "What's wrong, baby, talk to me."

"Huhn, what?" Bushnut shook away the effects of the cocaine. He wiped the tip of his nose and then looked down at the girl's hand on his shoulder. "Aw, hell nawl!" He yanked away his arm and looked down to see if she left any smudges on his crushed linen Versace shirt. "You done lost yo' goddamned mind? I know you see this muthafucka all white!"

"But, Daddy, I thought—"

"Thought?" He looked at her with a creased brow. "Bitch, ya silly ass ain't thought nothing. See, that's the problem wit'chu new age hoes, always thinking y'all can think, wit'cha stupid asses. Don't think, bitch, listen." He pointed at his ears. "And watch." He pointed at his eyes. "Listen and watch, bitch. Listen and watch," he rambled on, pointing back and forth between his eyes and his ears. *"Bitch musta lost her rabbid-ass mind,"* he mumbled under his breath, still checking to see if she left any smudges on his shirt. "Touching on my muthafuckin' Versace shit." He handed back the compact mirror, but kept the girl's rolled up hundo.

"Now, I'm giving you fair warning, bitch. Don't be touching on that goddamned radio." He rubbed his nose once more and then climbed out the Lex, looking like new money.

He was dipped head to toe in a crushed white, Versace linen short set. The gold, Medusa head buttons on the front of his shirt were unfastened, showing off the iced-out necklace that was tucked underneath. The 30" chain was smothered in diamonds and topped off with an iced-out Mr. Peanut that was customized into the image of his dope stamp. The only thing missing were the words *NUT SHIT*.

A diamond studded bracelet was glistening on his wrist, pressed against the iced-out bezel on his big face Frankie, and the solitaire diamonds in his earlobes were shining even brighter.

The white girl would have never believed that less than two years ago, he was a full-fledged smokah, and that the only reason he made it up from the bottom was because he found the duffle bag of money that was stashed in the back seat of Pookie's Range Rover.

Closing the car door, Bushnut glanced around the intersection and then scoped out the front of the house. He received a call from The Reaper a little over an hour ago telling him to swing past before the party. But now that he was there, he was wondering why the house was so dark. All of the lights were turned off, and the only thing moving was the bear-like German Shepherd that was going crazy on the other side of the front gate. He was chained to a large spike sticking out the ground, running back and forth from one side of the yard to the other. He was growling at Bushnut and barking at the Lexus, where the white girl was egging him on through the partially rolled down window.

Bushnut hated the German Shepherd, but The Reaper loved him. The massive K9 was the only thing The Reaper trusted.

"Bitch, if you don't leave that dog alone, 'fore I feed you to him."

"What—ever." The white girl pouted. She rolled her eyes and slouched back in the seat, looking straight ahead. She mumbled something under her breath, but it was too low for Bushnut to hear.

"Stupid-ass snow bunny," Bushnut shot back, knowing the girl said something slick. He made his way up the steps to the front door, conscious of brushing up against the gate and fucking up his lay. He turned the door knob and was surprised to see that it was unlocked. *"These muthafuckas slippin' like shit,"* he said to himself.

He pushed open the door and stepped inside of the vestibule. The tiny space was warm and sticky and reeking of German Shepard. Holding his breath, he pushed open the second door and stepped inside of the living room. The lights were turned off and the room was empty. But off in the distance, he heard the sounds of Young Chris's new album *The Network 4* and could smell the Loud aroma of a smoke out session.

After locking the front door and turning on the lights in the living room, he followed the smell of the smoke and the baseline of the music, ultimately ending up in the kitchen. He approached the basement door and pulled it wide open.

"Yo, Rayon? Dirt? Kye? Y'all down there?"

"Yeah," Doo Dirty called out, recognizing Bushnut's voice. "Niggas down here getting ready. Come on down."

When Bushnut descended the stairs and stepped into the finished basement, he saw that the smoke-filled room was damn near just as dark as the living room on the first floor. The only sliver of light was the bluish hue from the wide screen television that was propped up on the front wall. It was playing *Scarface*, but nobody seemed to be watching.

Doo Dirty and Murda Mont were sitting on the leather couch passing a Backwood back and forth, and loading up banana clips. Kia was across the way, slouched back on the love seat. A nickel plated fo' pound was laying across her lap with an extended clip sticking out the bottom. She was dressed in a pair of black chukkas, black sweat pants and a bulletproof vest with a black T-shirt sticking out from underneath.

Bushnut scowled at her, and Kia scowled right back. The two of them couldn't stand one another. Kia hated Bushnut because she hated all pimps, and Bushnut hated Kia because he couldn't understand how a chick so beautiful could be so rugged and gangsta, yet sexy and sassy at the same time. To him, it was asshole backwards. Instead of acting like a man and stomping with the big dawgs, the pretty faced gangsta should have been out on the hoe stroll, rain, sleet or shine, rolling and turning tricks and giving him every dime.

"Don't make no goddamned sense," Bushnut mumbled under his breath, shaking his head and looking around the basement.

Keeno was sitting at the mini bar in the back corner, and Killah Kye was stretched out on the floor in front of the TV. He puffing on a sherm and blowing shotguns of smoke into the mouth of his red-nosed puppy Pit.

Still shaking his head and growing madder by the second, Bushnut locked eyes with The Reaper, who was taking a shit with the bathroom door wide open. The Reaper squeezed out a mondo dook and took a drag on his Newport, never taking his eyes of Bushnut. He was daring Bushnut to check him and tell him to close the door, but Bushnut looked away and fixed his eyes on Kia. He would much rather talk shit and take his frustrations out on her. Nahfisah's party was less than an hour away and instead of wearing white, everybody was dressed in all black.

"Why the fuck y'all ain't dressed yet?" Bushnut snapped at her.

"Nigga, we is dressed," Kia shot back. She slipped on a black hoody and pulled the hood up over her head. "See?"

"What'chu try'na be funny, bitch?"

Click! Clack!

"Nigga, call me a bitch again!" Kia hopped off the love seat with the fo' pound clutched in her right hand. "Go 'head, nigga, say it. I'ma bust ya fucking ass."

"Nah, Keys, chill," Doo Dirty said as he motioned for Kia to sit back down. He was the leader of the Goon Squad, so it was all on him to make sure everything went smooth.

"Nah, Dirt, I'm tired of this nigga. He always got some fuck shit coming out of his mouth. Irrelevant-ass nigga."

"Irrelevant?" Bushnut seethed. "Muthafucka, I'm the one feeding you."

"Not anymore, you're not." Kia smiled at him, knowingly. "You ain't heard?"

"Heard what?"

"That my baby's on his way home."

"Ya baby?" Bushnut frowned.

"Yup." Kia nodded her head. "A.J., he's coming home next week. So, your irrelevant ass is about to be on the bench, watching the game from the sidelines. You fucking nut!"

"Yo, Keys, what the fuck!" Doo Dirty shouted, giving her the look to be quiet. He was praying The Reaper hadn't heard what she'd just said. He was supposed to had been the only one other than The Reaper who knew about A.J. coming home. But because he and Kia were close, and because he knew that A.J. was Kia's first and only love, he slipped up and told her.

"Aye, yo, Rayon!" Bushnut blew up the spot, storming toward the bathroom. "What the fuck is this bitch talking about?" He posted up in front of the bathroom door, waiting for an answer.

"Hand me some of that toilet paper." The Reaper pointed at top shelf in the bathroom closet.

"A'ight, man, but what the fuck is this bitch talking about?" Bushnut replied, stepping into the bathroom holding his nose. He grabbed one of the toilet paper rolls and handed it to The Reaper. "A.J.'s coming home? And that I'm 'bout to be sitting on the bench watching the game from the sidelines? Fuck is that about? What, Alvin try'na push me out the way? After everything I did for his ass? Shit, I'm the main one that helped you put this muthafucka back together! And now I'm 'posed to just hand everything over to A.J. and step off to the muthafuckin' side? Man, that's some fucked up shit, Rayon! It's fucked up and you know it!"

"First of all," The Reaper said, wiping his ass, "you better take all that muthafuckin' bass out'cha voice." He wiped his ass some more and then got up from the toilet with his dick dangling down in between his legs.

"Come on, man. Don't nobody wanna see that shit," Bushnut said as he looked away.

"Well, don't be looking, then, muthafucka. Ain't nobody tell ya ass to come over here no way," The Reaper shot back. He flushed the toilet, then he pulled his pants back up around his waist. He was just about to wash his hands in the sink but instead, he reached out and rested his left hand on Bushnut's shoulder. Bushnut damn near had a heart attack. He was so mad that his entire body began to shake. He looked down at The Reaper's hand and gritted his teeth.

What'chu got a problem, nigga?" The Reaper challenged him with his eyes.

"Naw, man, I'm good," Bushnut replied. He took a step backwards and brushed his shoulder off, looking to see if The Reaper left any skid marks on his shirt.

"A'ight, well let's go upstairs, so we can talk. I don't want everybody in our muthafuckin' business."

The Reaper stepped out of the bathroom and scowled at Doo Dirty. He then looked over at Murda Mont, who was still seated on the couch loading up banana clips. "Yo, Mont, you just been promoted to the captain of the Goon Squad."

"Captain?" Doo Dirty looked at The Reaper with puppy dog eyes. "But I thought I was the captain?"

"Not with that big ass mouth of yours. You lucky I 'on't shoot you in that muthafucka."

Doo Dirty sulked, and Murder Mont smiled. He didn't say a word, he just grabbed another banana clip and commenced to stuffing bullets down inside of it.

"Come on, Nut," The Reaper said, motioning for Bushnut to follow him up the stairs.

When they reached the kitchen and moved over to the living room, Bushnut continued firing off questions.

"So, what the hell is going on with all this talk about A.J.?"

"He's coming home next week." The Reaper released a long sigh and plopped down on the leather sectional. "I talked to Alvin yesterday on a visit, and that's when he told me. He said that A.J.'s coming home in a few more days, and that he wants him to take over the business side of things."

"The business side?" Bushnut retorted. "That's my mutha-fuckin' role on the team. So, if A.J.'s taking over the business, then what the fuck I'm 'posed to do, be his muthafuckin' side kick?"

"Listen, man, I don't like the shit no more than you do. But Alvin's the boss, and that's the order he passed down. I'm just the messenger."

"I don't believe this shit." Bushnut fumed. He looked down on the coffee table and saw an empty wax bag with the Nut Shit stamp. "Look at this shit." He snatched up the wax bag and held it in the air for The Reaper to see. "I'm the muthafuckin' face of this mutha-fucka. You see the words on this goddamned bag? It says Nut. Shit. That's *my* muthafuckin' name on that dope stamp!"

"And that's another thing," The Reaper said as he fired up a Newport. "All that dope shit is over with. Alvin said that it's too hot. He wants us to go back to selling coke like we did back in the day."

"Coke?" Bushnut screwed his face up. "Is you shitting me, or is you kidding me? That coke shit don't make no muthafuckin' money, not like the dope. Last month, alone, we raked in a quarter mil. And this nigga's talking 'bout coke?"

"Yeah, man," The Reaper exhaled a cloud of smoke, "that's what he told me. He said that he reached out to the Columbian nigga we used to deal with back in the day. The nigga, Juan Nunes, down in Miami. He said that Juan's willing to give us a good deal, and that A.J.'s the only one he wants dealing with him."

"And who the fuck said that? Juan or Alvin? Because Juan knows me. I used to fly down to Miami with Alvin to go see him. So, I'm pretty sure that if he knew I was the one handling business, he'd be more comfortable dealing with me, than he would A.J."

232

"That's the same thing I said." The Reaper took another pull on his Newport. "But Alvin wasn't going for it. He said that his name was on the line, and the only one he trusted to do business with him was A.J."

Bushnut was heated.

For the past year or so, he'd been kicking up nothing less than five grand a week to Alvin faithfully. And now, just because his punk-ass son was coming home from jail, he wanted to act like none of that mattered. It was all about A.J., fuck everybody else.

"A'ight," Bushnut said after thinking it over for a bit, "what if we work it like this—I continue to hold down the business side, but only in regards to the dope. Then, on the other side of the coin, A.J. can come home and do his thing with the coke. That way it's all love, and everybody's doing they own thing. And at the end of the day, we can both come together and break bread as one big family."

"Nope." The Reaper shook his head. "Not gonna work."

"It's not gonna work? Why?"

"Because Alvin don't want us fucking with the dope, period. He said it's too hot with all this opioid crisis bullshit they keep showing on the news. All these muthafuckin' crackers overdosing and shit. These white folks ain't goin' for that. It was one thing to have the hood fucked up from the crack, but that's the hood, so them muthafuckas ain't care. But now that little Becky from Bucks County all strung the fuck out and stealing from mommy and daddy to get her hands on a needle, it's a muthafuckin' crisis. So, from here on out, as soon as we finish this last shipment, we fucking with the coke. And that's coming straight from Alvin. He said that it's only a matter of time 'fore the feds start cracking down, and that our best bet is to switch lanes before they do."

Damn! Bushnut thought to himself as he stood there shaking his head. All of this was coming out of left field, and the thought of not being able to do his thing with the dope was killing him inside. The Nut Shit stamp was the only thing he had going for himself and without it, he was back to being a nobody—just a regular, every day, has-been smokah. He *had* to come up with a way to make things work. Because with or without the YBM, giving up his position and handing everything over to another muthafucka was out of the question.

Beep! Beep! Beeeeeeeep!

"Goddamnit!" Bushnut snapped when heard the blaring of his car horn. "I told her cracker ass don't be touching shit."

"Fuck is you talking about?" The Reaper looked at him skeptically.

"My little snow bunny bitch that's outside in the car. Speaking of which, what's the deal with this party? It's less than an hour away, and everybody's dressed in all black. I thought y'all was rolling out wit' me?"

"We is," The Reaper replied. He stubbed out his cigarette and got up from the sectional. "But instead of us getting on the boat, we gon' stay outside and play the parking lot."

"The parking lot? For what? Everybody's gonna be on the boat."

"Everybody except us," The Reaper replied in a casual voice. "I didn't tell you yet, but aside from the situation with the dope, Alvin made another change."

"Another one?" Bushnut threw his hands up in defeat. "I'm still fucked up from the first one, and now you 'bout to hit me wit' another bag of bullshit? Un-fuckin-believable! How many goddamned changes Alvin gon' make?"

"As many as he want to, muthafucka. Fuck is you talking 'bout?" The Reaper's nostrils began to flare. "And if you feel some type of way about it," he reached under the sectional and snatched up his sawed-off shotty, "we can straighten that shit right on out."

"I didn't mean it like that, I'm just saying—"

"Saying what, nigga? What the fuck is you saying?"

"That—That I'm still trying to catch up from the first change," Bushnut spoke in a calm, clear voice, being careful not to come off in an aggressive manner. "I'm just try'na take it all in, man. That's it. That's all I'm try'na do."

The Reaper smiled at him, loving the sound of fear in his voice. "My man, Bushnut." He chambered a round into the barrel of the shotty and then laid it across his left shoulder. "So, this is the thing: initially, when I first talked to Alvin and told him everything you

234

told me about the young bul, Rahmello, he told us to run up in the muthafucka and smoke his stupid ass. But a few hours ago, he called me back and said that he talked to Juan. According to Juan, Rahmello's his go-to-man in the city, and he only has room for one. So, in order to get that number one spot, we need to get his ass out the way. But we can't just kill him. First, we gotta take back the three hunnid birds that Juan just hit him off wit' a few days ago. If we do, then that'll be our first shipment moving forward."

"And how the hell is we supposed to do that?"

"Kidnap him," The Reaper replied in a cold, menacing voice. "And this party's the best way to catch his ass slipping. I heard he's got a white Lamborghini, so that's what we looking for. All we gotta do is find the car, lay low in the parking lot and wait for the party to end. Then as soon as he hop his ass in that muthafuckin' ride, we follow him, hopefully back to his crib. We swoop in, handle our business, get the birds and then twist his muthafuckin' cap back. It's as simple as that. The nigga won't even know what hit him."

"But what about me, though?" Bushnut pointed at his clothes. "I can't be hiding out in the parking lot dressed in all white. I'll be sticking out like a white bitch in a bean pie factory."

"Nah, you good," The Reaper assured him. "'Cause I'ma need you on the inside to keep a line on this nigga. A lot of muthafuckas gon' be coming off that boat and being as though it's an all-white party, everybody's gonna basically be wearing the same shit. So, while you're in there, I'ma need to you to locate his ass and keep him close. That way, when everybody's coming off the boat, we don't lose him in the thick of the crowd. You feel me?"

Beep! Beep! Beep! Beeeeeeeeeeeep!

"Yeah, man, I feel you." Bushnut gritted his teeth, mad as hell that the snow bunny was still blowing up his car horn. "Don't even sweat it, baby, I'm on it. Now, let me get on outta here 'fore I end up choking this bitch."

As he turned around and headed toward the door, The Reaper called out behind him. "Yeah, man, what's up?" Bushnut said as he spun back around, only to be greeted with the black hole of the sawed-off shotty. A sprinkle of piss trickled down the front of his leg and his teeth began to chatter. "D—D—Damn, baby, what the business is?"

"Alvin," The Reaper spoke calmly. "Make sure this the last time you ever question his orders."

Swallowing the lump in his throat, Bushnut nodded up and down like a bobble head doll. The only thing on his mind was living to see another day.

"My man, Bushnut." The Reaper smiled at him. He lowered the shotgun and smacked him on the ass. "And don't forget what I told you. You keep his ass close."

Bushnut nodded his head some more, then he spun back around and reached for the door handle. He damn near broke it off trying to move so fast. He slammed the door behind him and sped walked back to his Lexus, where the white girl was still beeping the horn.

"Goddamnit! Now, I done told you, bitch!"

Chapter Twenty-Two
At La Casa Moreno

"What the fuck is going on out here?" Heemy said to himself as he cruised down the hilly lane that led to the front gate of La Casa Moreno. Down below, on the other side of the gate, was a group of men that he'd never seen before. They were dressed in all-white, with icy bright jewelry, standing around and talking shit for the cell phones that were aimed at them. "Fuck is these niggas doing? And who the fuck is they?" Heemy mumbled to himself, as he slowed down and killed the headlights. He pulled over on the side of the road and grabbed his Tech .9mm from the passenger's seat. Still looking at the crowd, he finally realized they were some of the men Rahmello flew in earlier that morning. They were showing off and putting on for Instagram, fronting like the mansion in the background belonged to them. "Weirdos." Heemy shook his head slowly. "Stone cold turkeys." He laid the Tech back down and scooped up his cell phone. After dialing Rahmello's number, he placed the phone against his ear.

"Yo, where you at? It's almost time to roll out," Rahmello said when he answered on the third ring. He could tell by the number that the caller was Heemy.

"I'm halfway up the hill, looking down at all these weirdos standing around the front gate. What's up with Shabazz and Aziz? I'm looking at the security booth, but I don't see 'em?"

"Oh, them niggas around. They hanging out back. But come on down, so I can holla at'chu before the party. I wanna show you sum'n."

"More or less. But call down to one of ya turkey burgers, and let 'em know that I'm pulling up at the gate. I'd hate for a nigga to get froggy and catch somma this hot shit."

"Say no more," Rahmello said as he grabbed his iPad and pushed the button to open the front gate. "I'ma call down to Snot right now. But hurry up, so I can holla at'chu. We rolling out in like fifteen minutes."

Heemy disconnected the call and continued cruising down the hill. When he approached the gate, it was already wide open with all eyes on him. He noticed one of the men was talking on his cell phone and nodding his head up and down. He motioned for Heemy to stop the truck and then he put away his phone.

"What's poppin', lil' homie?" Snot Box greeted when Heemy rolled down his window. "You Heemy, right?"

"Yeah," Heemy replied in a defensive voice, more so than he intended to. He knew the homies Rahmello flew in were riding with him against Sonny, so in Heemy's eyes, they were already his enemies. But at the same time, he knew that in order to find out exactly who they were and where they were from, he needed to blend in and not raise any flags. So instead of showing his true feelings, he twisted his grill into a fake smile and stuck his hand out the window. "Yeah, I'm the bul, Heemy. What's up wit' it?" he spoke in a voice that was friendlier. "Who you be, Blawd?"

"The name's Snot Box, Triple O.G., from that Almighty Pueblo," Snot Box replied, connecting his hand with Heemy's. "I heard you was a down ass nigga over this way."

"Oh yeah?" Heemy gave him a skeptical look. "And who told you that, Rahmello?"

"Nah." Snot Box shook his head. "I got that straight from Sonny."

"Sonny?"

"Yeah. Me and the fool go way back. The homie, Mookie, well y'all knew him as Mook, but that was my little cousin on my momma side. He used to bring Sonny out to Cali wit' him to kick it wit' the homies, but that's another story for another day. Anyhow, I just finished barkin' at the fool about an hour ago. Matter of fact, pop the do' so I can hop on up in the truck."

"More or less," Heemy replied. He popped the lock on the passenger's side door, then he leaned over and grabbed his Tech off of the seat.

He slipped his finger in the trigger guard and laid the burner across his lap, with the barrel aimed at the passenger's side door.

For all he knew, he was walking into a setup. He could tell by the look in Sonny's eyes that he didn't all the way trust him when he told him about Rahmello. So, being as though Sonny reached out to Snot Box and mentioned his name, who's to say he didn't also reach out to Rahmello? And if he did, who's to say he didn't tell Rahmello about Heemy going behind his back and driving out to the county jail to see him? The situation was dangerous, and Heemy knew it. He should have never stuck his nose in Moreno Family business.

Damn, Heemy thought to himself as he sat there weighing his options. *Fuck it. If worst come to worst, at least I got this nigga in the truck wit' me. So that way if shit get crazy, I can back out and mash. I doubt they'll shoot up the truck if they know the big homie's in here. At least, I hope they won't.*

He tightened his grasp on the Tech and flexed his jaw muscles as Snot Box climbed inside of the truck. The second he closed the door and settled back in his seat, Heemy activated the locks and began to interrogate.

"A'ight, now what'chu was saying about Sonny? You said you just finished talking to him? What's that about?"

Snot Box looked down at the Tech in Heemy's hand and cracked a smile. He could tell right away that the little homie was everything Sonny said he was.

"Yeah, man, I just got off the phone wit' him not too long ago," Snot Box replied in a calm voice. He grabbed the blunt that was resting in his right ear and pulled out a cherry red lighter. "You mind if I put somma this gas in the air?" He held up the blunt and lighter, waiting for Heemy to give him an answer.

"Go 'head and do ya thing," Heemy replied, glancing out the corner of his left eye.

He was scoping the homies as they stood around the front gate laughing and talking shit. It appeared as though they weren't paying attention, but Heemy was sure to keep them in sight. He threw the transmission in *reverse* and placed his foot over the gas pedal, preparing to mash out if he needed to.

Snot Box fired up his Philly and hit it real hard. He reached over the console to pass it to Heemy, but Heemy declined. "Nah, fam,

I'm good. I'm just waiting to hear about this conversation between you and Sonny? I wanna know what he said about me? Did he talk to Rahmello?"

"Well, shit, nigga, that's more for me." Snot Box shrugged his shoulders. He hit the Philly once more and then looked down at the Tech .9mm, seeing that the muzzle was aimed at his ribcage. He blew out a thick chain of smokey white O's and then nodded his head in approval. "That's a nice lil' burner you got, cute little airholes and extended clip."

"Man, fuck all that." Heemy bit into his bottom lip. "Fuck is up wit' this muthafuckin' phone call?"

"Gawn and calm down, lil' bruh, you good. Me and the homies gotcha back."

"Got my back?" Heemy aimed the Tech at his face. "Fuck is that supposed to mean? What'chu try'na play mind games, nigga?"

"Never that," Snot Box replied casually. "That's some hoe-ass shit, and I'm too much of a G. You feel me?" He looked Heemy square in the eyes, then he reached out and calmly pushed the Tech away from his face. "I'm hip to Rahmello and the fuck shit he tried to pull. Had me flying out this mu'fucka thinking it's all gravy, only to find out this nigga working angles, talking 'bout he fit'na lace a nigga wit' sum'n nice. Mu'fucka ain't said one word about no beef between him and Sonny. Said sum'n about some punk-ass S.A.'s, but never nothing about Sonny. I woulda checked that shit from the do', you feel me? So, I'm assuming he was planning to spring that shit later on tonight at the party. Nigga said he had the upper deck cleared out, so he could bring niggas up to speed on how we fit'na get this money. Ol' mark-ass nigga. Thinking he can dangle a few dollars and sway the homies to ride out on some bullshit. But nah, bruh, shit ain't going down like that. You feel me? That Be-Bop love sum'n special. Ain't no amount money come befo' that. 'Specially when we talking 'bout a mu'fucka who ain't even banging right. I'm fit'na break this nigga off sum'n proper."

Heemy relaxed a little, feeling like a mountain had been removed off of his shoulders. It felt good to know that his big homie had enough faith in him to not only hear him out, but to investigate and verify everything that he told him. He laid the Tech on his lap and exhaled a sigh of relief. "But I'm saying, though, what all Sonny said? And did he talk to Rahmello and tell him that I came to see him?"

"Hell nawl, he ain't told that nigga shit. And as far as the homies, they don't know shit either. I ain't told 'em. Sonny said to keep it under wraps til' he touch down. Then after that," he pulled out a spiky pair brass knuckles with a four-inch blade sticking out the top, "it's fit'na get real Sonny 'round this mu'fucka. You feel me? Mu'fuckas better have they mu'fuckin' sunglasses on."

"That's what Sonny told you?" Heemy perked up. "He said that he was coming home?"

"Hell yeah, that nigga said he coming home. Said he just got word from his granddaddy, and that his grandaddy told him he passed the test, whatever that's supposed to mean. Anyhow, his granddaddy told him that he should be home in a few more days. Said sum'n 'bout they found the witness on his case, and that the mu'fucka fit'na get dealt wit'. You feel me? So being as though that's the only witness on the case, they ain't gon' have nothing else to hold him on. Oh yeah, and another thing," Snot Box continued as he sparked his Philly back up, "Sonny told me about the situation wit' them YBM niggas. He said that's another thing that's fit'na get dealt wit'. So, like I said befo', nigga, knuckle up and guard ya grill. Me and the homies gotcha back. You feel me?" He held his fist out, and Heemy gave him a pound.

"A'ight, but what's the deal wit' the party?" Heemy asked. "Did Sonny shut it down, or is it still on?"

"Man, that party on like a mu'fucka. You feel me?" Snot Box laughed. "You see the homies dipped down, got the all-white whips lined up and down the driveway. Shit, nigga, we fit'na to show out. You feel me?"

"Yeah, homie, I feel you." Heemy cracked a smile. He was looking at the shiny white Escalades that were parked up and down the cobblestoned driveway. There had to be at least ten of them. They were parked bumper to bumper, with big shiny rims and sparkling chrome grills.

Vrrrrrm! Vrrrrrm! Vrrrrrm!
Heemy grabbed his iPhone from the center console and looked
at the screen. "Yo, Mello just sent me a text message. For some
reason he keeps telling me to come up to the house, so he can show
me sum'n. Now, you sure Sonny ain't call this nigga and tell him
about me coming up to the jail to see him?"
"I'm positive, homie, trust me," Snot Box replied, looking
Heemy square in the eyes. "Sonny ain't told that nigga shit. As far
as Rahmello know, he got the homies right where he wants us. But
that's cool, though, that's just the way I wanna keep it. Sonny'll be
home in a few mo' days."
"But I'm saying, though, should I go up there and holla at him?"
"Why wouldn't you? If he called you any other time, you
woulda went. So, go now. And don't say or do nothing that'll put
him on point. I wanna keep his ass right where he at. You feel me?"
He reached over to open the door, but forgot about Heemy locking
it. "Well, damn, homie..."
"My bad," Heemy said as he reached down and deactivated the
locks. "A nigga ain't know what he was walking into. Mighta had
to blaze my way up outta this muthafucka."
Snot Box shook his head and laughed. "Well, Sonny sho'nuf
wasn't bullshitting. You definitely a down ass nigga." He laughed
some more and then pushed open the door. After climbing out the
truck, he spun back around to face Heemy. "And remember, Blawd,
whatever you do, don't do or say nothing that'll wake him up. His
stupid ass thinks he two steps ahead, so let him keep on thinking
that. That element of surprise a mu'fucka. You feel me?"
"Yeah, homie, I feel you." Heemy chuckled. "How many times
you gon' ask me?"

***

Back at the County Jail

After hopping in the shower and scrubbing away the filth from
the mop closet, Sonny was in desperate need of something that
would relax him and ease his mind. He hadn't touched a drug since

the night he was arrested, but at this point, a nice smoke out session was exactly what the doctor ordered.

So, after twisting up a nice fat Dutch, he threw a towel over his cell door and extracted the water from his toilet bowl. The toilet was the safest way to get bombed out in a cell.

The suction from the drain of an empty toilet was so strong that all he had to do was hunch down in front of the toilet and blow the smoke inside. Then after that, he could fall back and chill, without ever having to worry about someone catching a whiff of the stinky Loud smell.

The more and more he smoked, the more he thought about Rahmello and the awkward position his brother placed him in. The story could only end one of two ways, and both scenarios were like a dagger to the heart. He never wanted to be in a situation where he had to kill his own brother. But if he didn't, he knew his brother would surely kill him.

It was a lose, lose situation, one he seemingly could not avoid. The thought, alone, damn near brought tears to his eyes.

"Come on, Mello, man. What the fuck is you doing, dawg?" Sonny mumbled under his breath. He inhaled the sweet, sour smoke and then blew the smoke down into the sewer drain.

When Heemy first told him about Rahmello's betrayal, he didn't want to believe it. But at the same time, he'd never known Heemy to be a liar.

So, after handling A.J., Sonny hopped on his cell phone and called Grip. He figured, at the very least, his grandfather would have an idea as to what was going on. He told Grip everything that Heemy told him, and his grandfather released a long heavy sigh.

Grip didn't want to come right out and say it, but he did mention the conversation he and Rahmello had the night before, where Rahmello indicated there was somewhat of a tension between him and Sonny.

He also revealed for the first time that Olivia was the secret witness in Sonny's case. He then went on to explain that necessary measures were being taken in order to have her eradicated from the situation, and that his release from custody would be sooner rather than later, predictably within the next few days.

Sonny's brain was in a stupefied boggle. How could Olivia be the witness in his case, when there was no way she could have possibly known about the night he and Sheed killed Biggs down in South Philly? Moreover, if Rahmello knew Olivia was the secret witness, why would he wage war against his own family, solely for the sake of protecting her?

Then on top of that, go against the grain and cut a side deal with Juan, knowing Juan played a role in the murder of their father and then turned around and orchestrated the ambush at his funeral? There had to be more to the story, and Sonny was determined to find out what it was.

After disconnecting his phone call with Grip, Sonny reached out to Triple OG, Snot Box. He remembered what Heemy said about Rahmello flying in a bunch of homies from all around the country, so he knew Snot Box had to be one of them.

Snot Box confirmed everything Heemy told him, but made it pellucidly clear that he and the homies had no idea that Rahmello was planning on making a move against him.

As far as he and the homies knew, Rahmello only had beef with some Mexican nigga named Diablo, and they were flown in for extra support and manpower.

He further indicated that Rahmello made mention of his new Columbian connect, and that his plan moving forward was to make them all millionaires.

It was then, that Sonny realized exactly what his younger brother was up to. Rahmello knew he wasn't strong enough to wage war by himself, and that his only chance to come out on top was to get an army behind him. And who better than the Block Boys, every last one, from the east to the west?

But Rahmello wasn't stupid. He knew the Block Boys were loyal to Sonny. So, in order to carry favor and get the homies have his back, he knew he needed to be in a position to feed them, which explained the reason he reached out to, and linked up with Juan.

Sonny hit the Dutch once more and then flushed it down the toilet.

Sky high, he got up from the floor and moved over to the sink at the front of his cell. After splashing his face with a handful of water, he looked at his reflection in the mirror and shook his head slowly.

"Damn, little bro, after everything we been through, you really gon' stab me in the back, just to take my muthafuckin' spot?" he stated out loud, speaking as though Rahmello could hear him. "That bitch of yours is telling on me, more than likely because you told her to do it. How else would she know about that situation wit' me and Sheed, other than the fact you musta ran ya mouth and told the bitch everything I told you? I trusted you, nigga. I was loyal to you. I showed you love. I took you off the streets when you was scrambling and starving, and this is how you do me? Me? Ya muthafuckin' brother? The nigga that woulda killed and died for you? That's some fucked up shit, dawg. That's some fucked up shit."

He splashed his face with another handful of water, then he hopped up on his top bunk. He kept the towel on the door because he didn't want to be bothered with. The collision course between him and Rahmello had already been set in motion, and with only a few days left until it was time to be released, he knew that it was imperative to clear his thoughts and not allow his emotions to dictate his actions.

The love for his brother had regressed into a wicked feeling of hatred, and hatred was the number one enemy to a soldier on the battlefield.

That was another valuable lesson that had been taught to him by his late father. It was during the time he was still reeling over Mook being killed by Grip.

He mentioned to Easy how much he hated his grandfather, and how he wouldn't stop applying pressure until Grip was dead. Easy checked him, quickly.

Looking his son square in the eyes, he said, *"Never hate your enemy, Sontino, never. It will only affect your judgement."*

Frustrated, Sonny closed his eyes and massaged his temples. He was thinking about Easy and how it would have broken his heart to see his sons going through it. But at this point, there was nothing Sonny could do. Had Rahmello left any room for forgiveness, Sonny would have given it to him, but he didn't. He slipped up and stepped out of line, so now he had to get spanked. It was as simple as that.

Vrrrrm! Vrrrrm! Vrrrrm!

The buzzing of his Samsung Galaxy sent a shock wave through his pillow. He lifted his head, then he reached down inside of the slit and scooped it out.

Looking at the screen, he saw that the caller was Alexis. He hadn't heard anything from her in the past few hours, so naturally the sound of her soft voice was something he assumed would relieve his mind of the bullshit.

He threw in his ear buds and accepted the call. The reception on his phone was somewhat sketchy, so every other second, Alexis' face was blinking in and out of view.

"Aye, yo, Lexi, hold on right quick" Sonny said as he scooted down toward the edge of his bunk.

He held the phone in front of the window, hoping to get a better reception. The two bars jumped to three, and Alexis came into clear view. She was dressed in all-black, with a black hoody pulled up over her head. The second Sonny noticed, he knew something was wrong. It was almost a quarter past nine, and according to what Alexis told him earlier that day, her and everybody else who was leaving from La Casa Moreno should have been heading out to Nahfisah's party by now. But there she was, dressed in all-black as opposed to being dressed in all-white.

"Sontino, I can't hear you. What did you just say?"

"I was telling you to hold on. My phone was fuckin' up, and I could barely see you," Sonny replied, as he moved a little closer to the window. "But what's up, though? What'chu wearing all-black for? Ain't you supposed to be going to my sister's party?"

"I was planning to go, but I can't. Something just happened that I need to take care of," Alexis spoke in a voice that was all business, nothing even close to the sweet sound Sonny was expecting.

"Yo, where you at right now? It's dark as hell in the background."

"I'm up the block from ya peoples house."

"My peoples house? What'chu mean, La Casa Moreno?"

"Umm-hmm."

"But, what'chu doing up the block? Ain't no houses up there, it's just a bunch of woods."

"Listen, Sontino, I love you too much to keep playing these games with you."

"Games? What games? You're confusing me right now, Alexis. What the fuck is going on?"

"All I can say is that when you come home next week, there's a few things we need to sit down and talk about."

"Next week?" Sonny shot her funny look, wondering how she knew the intricate details of his case. "Yo, who the fuck you been talking to? And who the fuck is that standing behind you?" He lashed out when he caught a glimpse of the big, black, bald headed man that was roaming about in the background.

"I'm not even try'na go there right now, Sontino. Just know that I love you, and that I'm out here riding for you."

Click!

"Yo, Alexis? Alexis? Fuck!" Sonny shouted in frustration. He dialed her number right back, only to be greeted with the sound of her voice mail.

Tap! Tap! Tap!

"What?" Sonny snapped out when he heard the sound of someone knocking on his door. "Can't you see I got the muthafuckin' towel up? That means step the fuck off!"

"I already know, brozay. But this some serious shit," he heard his young bul, Sleepy, announce from the other side of the door. "I wouldn't be knocking on the door if it wasn't. I'm telling you, Sonny, you need to see this."

Flaming mad, Sonny hopped down from the top bunk and violently snatched the towel off of the door. "What is it, Sleep? What the fuck I need to see?"

After looking around to make sure nobody was watching, Sleepy pulled out his iPhone and slid it under the door. Sonny picked it off the floor and looked at the screen. The only thing he saw was Sleepy's Facebook page.

"Fuck you got me looking at'cha Facebook shit for?" Sonny asked him.

"Nah, bro, you gotta scroll down on my news feed. The ol' head we sent that video to, he just sent you a message back."

Sonny's nostrils began to flare. He'd been so caught up in the bullshit with Rahmello, and now Alexis, that he forgot about the video he sent to Alvin of A.J. getting fucked in his ass with the broom stick.

Gritting his teeth, he placed the towel back over the door and then hopped up on the top bunk. He scrolled down the news feed and found the message Sleepy was talking about.

Actually, it wasn't a message, but a video from Alvin. He appeared to be sitting in his cell with two of his goons behind him. Sonny popped in his ear buds, then he pressed down on the *play* button.

"Sontino, I'ma keep this shit straight to the muthafuckin' point," Alvin stated like the boss he was. "Clearly, you don't understand how real this shit is. I told you time and time again that I am, and already was, everything that you're try'na be. But all that talking shit is over and done with. Now is the time that I show you." He held up a stack of pictures, flashing them at the camera one at a time.

Each picture was a snap shot of Sonny's mother, whether she was coming or going from her house, or simply just sweeping the sidewalk in front of her salon.

"I got another stack of pictures for you," Alvin said as he held them up to the camera. This time, the pictures were snap shots of Nahfisah and Imani. He even had pictures of their new house in Willow Grove, and the new Maserati that Rahmello bought her for her birthday. Looking straight into the camera, he shook his head slowly.

"See, you got this thing about you where you think you a boss. Nigga, you a fucking peasant, a nobody ass nigga, who only got a chance to a shine because niggas like me is locked the fuck up. But like I said all that's irrelevant now.

"When I first heard about what happened to my daughter, my initial reaction was to murder ya whole family. But because my grandbabies woulda been left out in the cold, with nobody to care for 'em, I let it slide. But at this point, I don't even give a fuck!" he shouted at the camera. The rage inside of him had bubbled into a blind fury that he could no longer hold back. "You touched two of mines, now I'ma touch all of yours! Believe that! So, dress warm, muthafucka! It's 'bout to be a cold winter!"

Sonny's entire body began to shake, as the video came to an end. He punched in the numbers to mother's cell phone, hoping to get Annie on the line, but the phone just continued to ring. Her, Keyonti and Imani were all alone at the house in West Chester, with nobody there to protect them. It was clear from the pictures that Alvin knew the address, so who was to say he didn't already have a team of killers driving out to the house? Or even worst, had a team of killers already inside?

"Come on, Mom, answer ya fuckin' phone," Sonny said, as he anxiously bit down into his bottom lip. His heart damn near burst out of his chest when her answering machine came on. "Fuck!" He pounded his fist against the wall. Thinking as fast as he could, the only name that popped up in his mind was Savino's. He was still salty about his lawyer going behind his back and selling keys to Rahmello. But now was not the time to be sweating over the bullshit. He punched in the numbers to Savino's phone and prayed to God that he answered.

Ring! Ring! Ring!

"Who the hell is this?" Savino's voice came over the line.

"Aye, yo, Mario, it's Sonny," the passion of his voice came out in a rapid spew.

"Sontino?"

"Yeah, man, it's me. I need you to drop whatever you're doing and drive out to my mom's crib. Right now. I need you to get her and the kids outta there."

"Wait, what? Hold on, Sontino. I'm gonna need slow down a bit and say exactly what it is that you're trying to tell me."

Sonny took a deep breath and then spelled it out for him nice and slow. "Drive out to my mom's crib. The one in West Chester. Get her, my daughter, and my niece, outta there. And I need you to do it right away. Like, right now."

"Say no more, Sonny. I'm on it," Savino said as he hopped up from his sofa. He snatched his keys off the coffee table and shot out the front door. He could tell by Sonny's demeanor that something was extremely wrong, so he added a little pep to his step. When he reached his Range Rover, he hopped inside and pressed the push start. "Alright, man, I'm backing out my driveway. Is there anything else you need me to do?"

"Yeah," Sonny said as he exhaled a deep sigh of relief. "Make sure you take a gun wit'chu."

Chapter Twenty-Three

Heemy cruised up the cobblestoned driveway, then he dipped around the water fountain and coasted over to the west wing of the house. The first thing he noticed when he pulled up and came to a stop was Rahmello. He was dressed head to toe in a crispy white, Louis Vuitton linen set. His white-on-white, Louis Vuitton high-top pikes were fresh out the box, and as always, he was looking like money. His neck, wrist and earlobes were smothered in diamonds, and a big fat Cuban cigar was dangling out the right side of his mouth.

He flashed Heemy a smile and then gestured towards the two Lamborghinis that were parked alongside one another. Each car was cocaine-white with black rims and dark tinted windows. The doors were flipped up on both cars, showing off the buttery soft interiors. From the steering wheel to the dashboard, the two front seats and the center console, everything was chocolate and cream, silky and smooth like a Little Debbie's Swiss Roll.

"So, what'chu think?" Rahmello said as he removed the cigar from his mouth. He cracked up laughing and stretched his arms out wide. "You ready to start looking like the boss you is, nigga? Well, get'cha ass up outta that truck and come enjoy somma this mutha-fuckin' luxury!"

Heemy was completely caught off guard. Were one of the Lamborghinis for him? And if so, why was Rahmello being so nice all of a sudden? Tossing these questions around in his mind, Heemy killed the engine and hopped out of his F-250. He was dressed head to toe in nothing but Gucci. His all white, two-piece, linen Gucci suit was tailored to perfection, concealing the outline of his bullet-proof vest and the shoulder holster that was tucked underneath. His black necktie was covered in white G's, and a single red rose was sticking out the top of his lapel. He wasn't the type to wear a lot of jewelry, so he kept it simple with an iced-out, big face David Yurman and a blinged out pair of white diamond, solitaire earrings. He looked at the two Lamborghinis, and then brought his gaze back to Rahmello.

"So, you're saying that one of these is for me?"

"You muthafuckin' right, one of these is for you," Rahmello replied, embracing Heemy with their Fo' Hunnid handshake. "You earned it, my nigga. If it wasn't for you, and the way you stuck by me, I woulda never even made it to this level. So, it's only right that I show my lil' nigga some love. This shit ain't about me, dawg...this shit is about *us*," he pointed back and forth between them, "Mello and Heemy, the *new* bosses. From here on out, we doing is shit *our* way. Now, gawn and pick whichever one of these muthafuckas you want. We rolling out in about ten more minutes, and I still got sum'n else that I need to show you."

Heemy walked over to the first Lamborghini and stuck his head inside. As a young nigga growing up in North Philly, dead broke without a pot to piss in and a window to throw it out, he never imagined that he would one day possess sometime so exclusive. It was almost like a dream. "Yo, you serious right now?" He backed away from the Lambo and shot Rahmello a skeptical look. "This muthafucka run about a quarter mil. And you just giving it to me?"

"Ain't nobody giving you shit," Rahmello replied as he walked over and stood directly in front of him. He reached inside of his pocket and pulled out an iced-out Cuban link with a Block Boy charm. He held it in front of Heemy's face and looked him dead in the eyes. "You earned this shit, bro. The car, the chain, and everything else that you're destined to get ya hands on. And about that conversation we had earlier today, I was wrong for that, my nigga. I was outta line, and I apologize. I shoulda never even said that dumb-ass shit. If a nigga got beef wit'chu, he got beef wit' me. So first thing in the morning, we going dead at them niggas, all of 'em. They touched one of ours, so now we gotta touch back and show these muthafuckas what it's hittin' for. Not only them, but the entire city for that matter. We gotta take this shit back to the way it was when...when—"

"When Sonny was home?" Heemy finished the sentence.

"Yeah," Rahmello replied in a somber voice. He took a deep breath and exhaled slowly, knowing that he fucked up by going against his own family. The love for his brother was still there, but

252

he had gone so far against the grain, that there was simply no turning back. Not at this point, anyway. His only option was to finish what he started, whether he wanted to or not. "Speaking of which," Rahmello placed the necklace over Heemy's head and left it dangling around his neck and shoulders, "follow me around back. I need to show you sum'n."

As they took off walking toward the pool house, the side door of the mansion swung open and Nahfisah appeared in the doorway.

She was dressed in a mid-thigh Coogie dress that was mainly all white, except for the soft pink streaks that were swirling all around it. Her suede and leather Guisseppe pumps had her long shapely legs looking good enough to eat, and the diamonds on her neck, wrists and earlobes were shining so bright, it appeared as though she were decorated in blue lasers. A white and pink, Coogie handbag was draped over her left shoulder, and her diamond encrusted Hello Kitty iPhone was clutched in her right hand.

Heemy looked at her and shook his head slowly. For some reason Nahfisiah was looking prettier than he remembered. He wanted to tell her how much she meant to him and that he was sorry for the way he treated her, but because Rahmello was present, he decided to keep it to himself.

Nahfisah noticed the way Heemy was looking at her. She'd been thinking about him just as much as he'd been thinking about her. But instead of telling Heemy how much she loved and missed him, she shot him an ice-grill and then looked over at Rahmello.

"What's up, Nah? You almost ready?" Rahmello asked as he slowed down and came to a stop. He chuckled under his breath when he peeped the way Heemy and Nahfisah were looking at one another. The two of them were always arguing and fighting, so why would tonight be any different?

"Yeah, I'm ready," Nahfisah replied, cutting her eyes at Heemy. She rubbed the tip of her nose and let out a light snort.

"Aye, yo, hold up," Rahmello said as he took a step closer. He squinted his eyes and saw that the tip of her nose had a light red tint. "Fuck is you standing there snorting and sniffing for?"

"Huhn?" Nahfisah looked at him with a shocked expression. She rubbed the front her nose and tried to play it off like she wasn't high. Unfortunately, her runny red nose and glossy wide eyes were a clear indicator that she'd been snorting cocaine.

"*Huh?*" Rahmello retorted. "What'chu deaf all of a sudden? Fuck is you standing there snorting and sniffing for? You been fucking wit' that shit?"

"Who? *Me?*" Nahfisah pointed at her chest. "Boy, don't be coming at me like that."

"So, what'chu looking all high for? Eyes all glossy. Nose red. Standing there snorting and sniffing and shit."

"Dang, why you coming at me like that?" Nahfisah screwed her face up. "A bitch can't smoke a blunt for her birthday? Shit."

"A blunt?" Rahmello looked at her sideways. "Fuck a blunt gotta do wit'cha nose being all red?"

"Oh, that's probably just my allergies," Nahfisah proffered a weak excuse. "Them Mexicans came by the house this morning to cut the grass, and the smell of the grass must've triggered my sinuses."

Right away, Heemy knew that she was lying. The two of them had been together that entire morning, and not once did the landscapers come by her house to cut the grass.

Nahfisah noticed the way Heemy was looking at her, and rolled her eyes. "Mind ya business, little boy, 'cause wasn't nobody the fuck talking to you. I was talking to my *brother!*"

"Yeah, whatever," Heemy shot back, shaking his head in disappointment.

"Now," Nahfisah rolled her eyes at him once more and looked over at Rahmello, "like I was saying: them Mexicans came by the house to cut the grass, and the smell of the grass musta triggered my dag-gone allergies. And if you don't believe me, look." She reached inside of her Coogie bag and pulled out a subscription of Benadryl. "I even had to drive out to the drug store to get me some medicine."

Rahmello looked at Heemy, who was still shaking his head, then he turned back around to face Nahfisah. He didn't know what was going on between the two of them, but he could tell something was wrong.

It was almost as though they were hiding something from him. Gritting his teeth, he looked at his Patek Philippe and saw that the time was 9:11 p.m. He wanted to pry a little further to see if he could get Nahfisah to admit that she fell off the wagon, but because she was so adamant that she hadn't, he knew he would only waste more time. So instead of accusing her of something that he already knew, he decided to keep it moving. He was already a few minutes behind and still needed to show Heemy what he had in the back yard.

"So, what's up, Nah? You wanted to holla at me about sum'n?" Rahmello changed topics.

"Alexis," Nahfisah said as she held up her iPhone. "I called her like three times, but for some reason, she's not answering. I was wondering if we could wait a little longer until she gets here."

"Wait for who? *Her?*" Rahmello replied with an attitude. He had strong disdain for Alexis, because he knew she was dealing with Sonny. In addition to that, she was always snooping around and acting funny. He couldn't say for sure, but his gut feeling was that Alexis had been keeping tabs on him. "Nizzaw." Rahmello shook his head *no.* "Ain't nobody catering to her muthafuckin' ass. She knew that we were leaving the house at a quarter after."

"But I'm saying, though, can't just wait like another ten minutes?"

"I wish the hell I would. She better drive her ass down there. She knows how to get down to Penn's Landing. And if she don't, she better Google that shit."

"But that's my girl," Nahfisah shot back. "And besides, me and Flo already told Alexis that we were riding to the party in her car. We can't just leave her like that."

"Sure, you can," Rahmello replied as he continued walking and gestured for Heemy to follow. "Just tell Flo that she's riding with me, and that you're riding in the car with Heemy."

"What?" Nahfisah scoffed. "Don't nobody wanna ride wit' him. How come we can't ride in one of the Escalades with you? Olivia told me that she ain't even going. So, it's not like you ain't got enough room."

"First of all, I'm not riding in one of the Escalades. The Escalades is for the homies. Me and Heemy rolling out in the twin Lambos." He pointed back at the two Huracáns. "Tell Flo she can hop in the second one, and you hop ya ass in the first one. The first one is Heemy's."

"Get on my damn nerves!" Nahfisah stomped her foot as she dipped back inside of the house. "Come on, Flo! Rahmello said we gotta ride with them. For all that, I shoulda brought my own goddamned car!"

"Come on, Blawd, lemme show you what I need to show you, so we can get up outta here," Rahmello said as he led the way toward the back of the house

When Heemy stepped into the back yard and saw how dark it was, he automatically became suspicious. All of the lights were turned off, including the lights in the pool house. He had never seen the back of the La Casa Moreno so dark. The only sliver of light was the yellowish gleam from the crescent moon that was beaming down from up above.

Placing his right hand over his holster, Heemy continued following Rahmello across the yard and toward the pool house. He was still uncertain as to whether or not Rahmello knew about his trip to the county jail. So, for safe measures, he unfastened the latch on his holster and placed his hand on the butt of his Glock 19.

The only reason he didn't pull it out was the fact that Rahmello was walking in front of him and not behind. That, alone, gave him the upper hand. Because if shit got funny, at the very least he could tag Rahmello in the back of his dome before anyone else got to him.

"So, what's up dawg? What'chu wanted to show me?" Heemy asked as they approached the pool house. It was a tan and white, two-story house surrounded by an Oakwood veranda. "And what's up wit' all the lights being turned off? What's that about?"

"Ssh," Rahmello replied with his index finger placed in front of his lips.

He pulled open the gate to the veranda and slowly made his way up the porch. He glanced around the back yard and then looked up at the big house. He was checking to see if Olivia or anyone was snooping from one of the windows. Satisfied that nobody was watching, he removed a set of keys from his side pocket and unlocked the front door.

Heemy was growing more antsy by the second. With his hand over his holster, he glanced around the back of the house, just waiting for somebody to hop out from behind the shadows. He didn't even care that Rahmello could see that his hand was on his pistol. He was ready to blast if need be.

"Damn, homie, what'chu looking all uptight for?" Rahmello flashed him a sadistic smile. "What'chu scared of the dark?"

"Naw, fam, I ain't scared of shit. I'm just wondering why you asked me to come back here."

Rahmello shushed him once more and then twisted the knob and pushed the door wide open. "I hope you got a strong stomach, 'cause shit a little crazy in here. I'd hate to see you throwing up and fucking up all that white shit you wearing."

No sooner than he said it, the deadly aroma of fresh blood came swooping out the house. It was coppery and rank, similar to the smell of a slaughter house. Rahmello stepped inside of the living room and gestured for Heemy to do the same.

Gritting his teeth, Heemy stepped inside of the house. He turned back around to make sure the door stayed open, but Rahmello waved him off. "Nah, don't do that," Rahmello shook his head. "Close that muthafucka and make sure it's locked."

"Man, its darker than a mu'fucka in here. The only light we got, is the little bit of light that's coming in from the outside."

"So, what. I 'on't want nobody coming back here and seeing what's going on in this muthafucka. Now, close the door."

Heemy did as instructed, and Rahmello turned on the living room lights with the clapping of his hands. Asshole naked and nailed to the living room wall were Shabazz and Aziz. The two men were beaten to a pulp and drifting in and out of consciousness.

The nail gun that was used to pin them against the wall was laying on the hardwood floor. Right beside it, was a chromed out .45 with a pearl white handle. It was speckled with burgundy blotches of blood and peeking out from underneath a bloody red towel.

"Yo, Mello, man, what the fuck?" Heemy blurted out, looking back and forth between Shabazz and Aziz.

They were nailed against the wall, side by side, similar to two men being crucified. Their feet were bound together, one on top of the other, with a long bloody nail sticking out the middle, and their arms were stretched out wide, palms in, with bloody red nails poking out the back of their hands.

Shabazz was knocked out cold, and Aziz could barely hold his head up straight. He attempted to mumble something to Heemy, but the only thing that came out was a gibberish slur. His swollen head lollied to the side as he broke down crying. He'd been a loyal soldier for the Moreno Family for well over twenty years, and never imagined that things would end this way.

"Yo, Mello, man, this shit ain't cool," Heemy protested. "This is Shabazz and Aziz. They're a part of the fam."

"Not my family," Rahmello replied with a straight face. "They're a part of Sonny and Grip's family. To me, these muthafuckas ain't shit."

"Yo, that's crazy, bro, straight up. This whole beef situation between you and Sonny is some bullshit. You mean to tell me y'all niggas can't figure this shit the fuck out? We better than this, bro. We a family."

Rahmello shook his head and smiled. "Not anymore, we're not." He removed a red flag from his pocket, then he reached down and grabbed the .45 off the floor. Looking Heemy dead in the eyes, he began wiping the blood from the pistol. "The love and loyalty that I once shared with my brother, that shit is over and done wit'. It'll never go back to the way it was. From here on out, it's all about making history, a *new history,* where you and me can stand on our own two feet, independently, with nobody to answer to except for ourselves. But in order for that to happen," he aimed the pistol at Heemy's face, "I need to know what side of history you wanna be on. Is ya loyalty with me? Or is ya loyalty wit' Sonny? Because it can't be both, Heem. It's gotta be one or the other, no in between. So, what's it gonna be?"

Heemy looked down the barrel of the .45, then he looked at the trigger guard, where Rahmello's finger was stuffed into one side and curling out the other. He could feel the sweat forming across the front of his forehead, the increase of his heart beat, the taste of his bottom lip as he licked it, then he anxiously bit down into it. He took a deep breath and gritted his teeth.

"So, what's it gonna be?" Rahmello repeated the question, looking at Heemy with a raised brow. "Me or Sonny?"

Heemy took a deep breath and exhaled slowly. His first reaction was to go out like a G, standing firm on his own principles. But at the same time, he knew that it was better to go along with the plan and prove to Rahmello that he was all in.

"Last chance," Rahmello said as he cocked back the hammer with the tip of his thumb. "Me or Sonny?"

"It's just like you said, bro," Heemy flashed him a fake smile, "this is history in the making. It's time for niggas to make they own way and determine they own destiny. Fuck Sonny."

Rahmello nodded his approval, then he pulled back on the trigger. But instead of a fiery loud bang, the only sound that came from the pistol was a meek, hollowly *Click!* The gun was empty. But yet and still, Heemy did not flinch. He didn't even blink an eye. He just stood there staring at Rahmello with a blank, expressionless face.

"My muthafuckin' nigga," Rahmello cracked up laughing, impressed by Heemy's resolve. He reached down inside of his pocket and removed the ten-shot clip he extracted from the .45 about an hour earlier. He stuffed the clip back inside of the gun and then passed the gun to Heemy. "Now, finish these muthafuckas off," he said as headed out the front door. "And if I was you, I'd be letting that shit spark from the porch. That blood spatter a muthafucka."

Heemy looked down at the .45 in his right hand. He then looked over at Rahmello, who was already halfway across the back yard. He cocked a bullet up into the chamber, and aimed the barrel at the back of Rahmello's head. It was the perfect opportunity to take him out and avoid a full-blown war. He pressed down on the trigger, but before he squeezed, a strange news coming from the back the house snatched his attention.

Confused and caught off guard, he swung the barrel at Shabazz and Aziz, only to see that both men were still knocked out cold.

"Psst! Heemy!"

"Yo, who the fuck is that?" Heemy bellowed. He swung the .45 toward the dining room where he heard the whispering. "Whoever it is, you better make ya'self known, 'fore this bitch start barking."

"Calm down," the voice whispered. "It's Alexis."

"Lexi?" Heemy squinted his eyes, noticing the contrast of her silhouette in the midst of the darkness. She stepped out from behind the shadows in the kitchen and approached him slowly. Heemy lowered the fo' pound and took a step closer. "Yo, Lexi, what the hell is you doing back here?" He looked at her from head toe. "Dressed in all-black like a mu'fuckin' ninja? What the fuck is going on?"

"Ssh!" Alexis looked at him with big wide eyes, placing her index finger in front of her lips. "Stop talking so loud. Rahmello might hear you. *Al chekèl,"* she spoke in her native Creole, telling her bodyguards, Pierre and Toiussant, to check out and guard the front door.

When the two, giant sized Haitians, blacker than night and bigger than Terry Crews, emerged from the shadows, Heemy took a step back and lifted up the fo' fever.

"No, Heemy, don't!" Alexis shouted as she stepped in front of the gun. "They're with me!"

"Aye, yo, Lexi, *what* the fuck is going on?" Heemy shot back. Pierre and Toiussant breezed right past him. They posted up in front of the door, so big and bulky, that it was hard for Heemy to see outside to the front porch. He looked at the two men and then brought is gaze back to Alexis. "Yo, somebody better start explaining what the fuck is going on. Sonny know you out here?"

"Listen, just act like you never seen me," Alexis pleaded with him. "The only reason I announced my presence is because of them." She pointed back at Shabazz and Aziz. "Here, gimmie ya gun." She grabbed the .45 from Heemy's hand and fired two shots into the ceiling.

Blakka! Blakka!

"Fuck you do that for?" Heemy looked at her like she was crazy.

"So, Rahmello could hear it. He told you to finish them off, right? Well, good, as far as he knows they're dead. Now, gawn and go. I'ma need you to keep your eyes on Nahfisah."

"But—"

"Don't but, Heemy, just listen to me. Keep your eyes on Nahfisah. Make sure that she's safe. And when the time comes, all of this will make sense to you. Now, go." She looked past him and told her bodyguards to step aside, so that Heemy could leave. "Soti nan rout la."

The two men created a lane at the front door, not once taking their eyes off the back yard. Heemy looked at Alexis for further explaining, but she shook her head *no*. "Just trust me, Raheem, please. And don't say anything to Rahmello about me and my men being back here."

Heemy took a deep breath and sighed. None of this was making any sense to him. It seemed as though everybody had their own agendas, inadvertently leaving him caught up in the thick of it all. Shaking his head, he turned around and headed out the front door.

"And Heemy," Alexis called out behind him.

"Yeah, Lexi, what's up?"

"Be safe."

Askari

Chapter Twenty-Four
Nahfisah's Party

"Don't fuck no bitch that's fucking wit'cha dawg, that's law. If you come up, don't forget about ya dawg, that's law. I'ma street nigga, so it's fuck—the law. If you broke, nigga, that should be against, the law".

The two-hundred-foot yacht that Rahmello rented out for Nahfisah's birthday party was the perfect scene for a good time. He and his crew were on the upper deck, holding a meeting in the dining area and down below on the lower deck, Yo Gotti and his Memphis crew had the party goers going crazy.

The music was bumping, the people were dancing and boss-sized bottles of Ace of Spades with shiny bright sparklers were being rolled out on solid gold carts and passed around to any and everyone who wanted to drink like a boss.

There had to be at least five hundred people in attendance, and those who weren't fortunate enough to make it on deck, were doing their thing on the Delaware Avenue pier—blowing on the sticky icky, popping bottles and enjoying themselves just as much as the people on the mega sized boat.

It was all love, and that's just the way Rahmello wanted it. It was time for the city to know and recognize the emergence of a new era. *The New Block Boy Movement!*

"So, this is the thing," Rahmello said as he looked around the room full of big homies. They were seated at the roundtable in the middle of the room, one at a time, passing around a dinner tray full of goodies. Sprawled out on top of the tray were the eleven iced-out Block Boy chains that had been dropped off by Mikey Millions a few hours earlier. There were also eleven, custom-made Rolexes for each one of the big homies, accompanied by an iced-out pinkie ring with the Triple B's spelled out in quarter-cut diamonds, resting on an icy bed of glistening white baguettes.

Rahmello looked around at the homies trying on their new jewelry, and couldn't help but to break out smiling. He had them exactly where he wanted them.

"So, this is the thing," he repeated himself, eliciting everyone's attention. "As you all can see, this is a new day, a new time and on the strength of what we stand for and represent, it's only right that I bring my niggas along for the ride. And trust me when I tell you, when it's all said and done, they gon' be talking about us the same way they speak about Big Meech, Harry O, and all of the bosses that came before us. No longer are the days when niggas like my brother can sit back and eat, get fatter than a muthafucka, while the rest of the family's scrambling for crumbs. That's a dub. From here on out, whatever we do, we do it on the same level. We ride on the same level. We *fly* on the same level. We travel on the same level. Whether it's court side at the NBA Finals, or front row at the MGM watching Mayweather get busy, we do it on the same level. *Ain't* no difference. Now, as far as my brother?" He shrugged his shoulders and leaned his head to the side. "I'm pretty sure we can all agree he did things a little bit different. I mean think about it. When Sonny was around, it was all about him. New Mansion for Sonny. New Phantom for Sonny. New record label for Sonny. New club, new sports bar, new real estate company for Sonny. And what did we get?" Rahmello asked as he looked around the room, seeing that the homies were nodding their heads in agreement, all of them except for Heemy. He was standing by the window, looking down at the lower deck, with his back to the meeting. Rahmello noticed, but he brushed it off as though he didn't take it as a sign of disrespect. It was, however, something he planned to speak to Heemy about at a later time. For now, it was all about finishing his speech. He got up from his seat at the head of the table, and slowly began to walk around the room.

"I'ma tell you what we got—*shit!* Not a goddamned thing. A few of us mighta touched a bird or two, but other than that, what did we get? It's niggas in here right now, that's still living wit' they muthafuckin' mom. I ain't even gon' talk about the homies that's locked behind the wall. So, what do we do?" He paused for a couple of seconds, allowing his words to sink in. He circled the room twice, then he returned to his seat at the head of the table and sat back down. Leaning back in his chair, he kicked his Louis Vuitton Spikes up on top of the table. "Not only that, but where do we go *from here?* Don't nobody know? A'ight, fuck it, I'ma tell you." He pulled his feet back, then he leaned forward with his elbows propped up on the table. Pointing at the ceiling with both hands, he looked around the room and smiled. "Straight to the muthafuckin' top, baby. Straight to the top, and I'm the nigga that's gon' get us there. All I ask in return is that every man seated at this table gimmie his loyalty. My enemies become your enemies. My wars become your wars. And if that's what y'all willing to do, then I promise on my muthafuckin' flag that by this time next year, every nigga seated around this table gon' be a muthafuckin' millionaire. Now, is you niggas wit' me, or what?" The entire room went crazy, as everybody professed their loyalty.

"Hell yeah, we wit'chu!"

"Fa'sho."

"Nigga, you know what it is. Straight to the top, baby."

"Block Boy the fuck up!"

"Bdddddddddddat!"

"Woooooo!"

These niggas some fuckin' weirdos, Heemy thought to himself, as he stood in front of the window listening to everybody celebrating. He cut his eye at Snot Box, and noticed how the big homie was celebrating louder than everyone else. He was bouncing around and talking so much shit, that it was hard for Heemy to decipher whether or not he was still ryding with Sonny.

Maybe Rahmello's proposition was just too good for this nigga to turn down? Or maybe he's thinking about double crossing Sonny in order to get closer to Rahmello?

All of these things were going through Heemy's mind as he gritted his teeth and turned back around to look out the window.

Down below, on the lower deck, Nahfisah and Flo were sitting at the bar talking and nodding their heads to the music.

The ride from La Casa Moreno to Penn's Landing was a rough one for Heemy. After talking to Alexis, he hopped in the Lamborghini, where Nahfisah was already inside waiting to leave.

As the twelve-vehicle procession line cruised through the front gate of La Casa Moreno and trailed up the dark hilly road, Heemy began spilling his heart out to her. He told Nahfisah how much he loved and cared about her, and how he was sorry for treating her so harshly.

"*Boy. Bye,*" Nahfisah replied with an over dramatic scoff. She flicked him off with the back of her left hand, then she reclined back in her seat with her Chole shades pulled down in front of her eyes.

Heemy left it alone and continued driving. The car was silent for the next twenty minutes. He didn't even look in Nahfisah's direction. He just stared straight ahead, leaned back in his seat, whipping the Lambo with his right hand. But when they stopped at a red light on Broad and Spring Garden, he looked out the corner of his eye and saw that Nahfisah was hunched forward, snorting a line of coke from the back of her hand.

"*Yo, what the fuck is you doing?*" Heemy snapped at her. He pushed Nahfisah's hand away from her face, and she smacked him across his. "*I knew ya ass was lying about some goddamned allergies! Talking all this shit about you turned ya life around. Bitch, you still out here fucking wit' that shit!*"

"*Nigga, you ain't my goddamned daddy! I can do whatever the fuck I want! And if a bitch wanna powder her nose, I'ma powder my fucking nose.*" She reached down inside of her Coogie bag and pulled out a Newport cellophane wrapper that was halfway filled with raw. After rolling it open, she sprinkled some of the blow on the back of her wrist.

"*Shawty, you must be out 'cha fuckin' mind.*" Heemy said as he reached over the leather console. He snatched away the cellophane wrapper and tossed it out the window.

Nahfisah threw a hissy fit. She reached out to scratch him, but was quickly pinned against the passenger's side door. Heemy's hand was wrapped around the front of her neck. She struggled to break free, but it was no use. His death clutch was way too strong.

"*Pussy, I'ma get my brothers to kill you!*"

"*Yeah, yeah, yeah, I know,*" Heemy replied in a sing-song voice. "*Heard it all before.*"

The traffic light turned green, but Heemy failed to notice. It wasn't until he heard the blaring of the car horns behind him that recognized the light was green. He released his hand from Nahfisah's neck and continued driving eastbound on Spring Garden. An awkward silence filled the car for the remainder of the ride. Nahfisah was zoned out in her own thoughts, and Heemy was zoned out in his. Neither one spoke another word.

"Damn, Nah, you gotta shake that shit," Heemy mumbled under his breath, still looking at Nahfisah from the upper deck window. He took a pull on his Black & Mild and inhaled deeply. He was so stuck on Nahfisah that he didn't see Rahmello when he came over and stood right beside him.

***

"In the club, got them bottles on replay. Try'na break a record like a DJ. That's a hunnid fifty bottles in one niiiiight. I get it, bitch, act right. Act right. Act right. Money don't fold, that's that act right. Act right. Act right. Niggas playing games, get that act right."

"Yo Gotti and dem got this shit *poppin'!*" Flo said, as she nodded her head to the music. She simply could not take it anymore. Her and Nahfisah were seated at the bar, while everybody else was out on the dance floor having a good time. After knocking down the last of her double shot of Henny, she hopped down from the bar stool and motioned for Nahfisah to do the same. "Come on, bitch, we can't be doing this stressing shit. Especially on a night like this! All these niggas in here, and you stressing over this muthafuckin' *young bul?* Girl, you better hop up of that nigga's dick and slide down another one. Matter of fact, to hell with this shit." She reached out to grab Nahfisah from the bar stool. "It's ya birthday for crying out loud. Ya ass gon' *have* you some fun!"

"Uhn-uhn, gurl, I'm fine right here," Nahfisah told her, as she pulled away shaking her head *no*. "Go do ya thing and come back."

"You sure?"

"Yes, Flo, I'm sure." Nahfisah smiled at her, knowing her girlfriend was dying to shake her ass on the dance floor. "Go 'head and do ya thing. I'ma be right here."

"Well, in that case? *Deuces!*" She chucked up her two fingers and made her way to the center of the deck, where everybody was crowded around the stage.

In a matter of seconds, she was wedged in between two chicks—feeling on asses and titties and loving the feeling the two girls rubbing on hers brought. Then suddenly, just like that, in the snap of a finger, the music stopped playing. The entire party looked up on the stage at Yo Gotti.

"Errybody, pull out y'all mu'fuckin' cell phones," Gotti dictated in his thick, Memphis drawl. He waited until the dance floor was covered in a sea of white lights and then slowly nodded his approval. "A'ight, now, where it's gawn down at?"

"*In the DM!*" The entire crowd screamed back in unison.

Gotti chuckled, then he looked back at his DJ. "Gawn and drop that shit, mane." The *Down in The DM* baseline erupted from the speakers and the crowd went crazy.

"*I seen ya girl post her BM. So, I hit her in the DM. All eyes, yeah I see 'em. Yeah, that's ya man, I hate to be him.*"

Looking at her best friend, Nahfisah cracked up laughing. She wanted to go out and join her, but she was too stressed out and depressed. Not only that, but disappointed in herself for being so weak.

At the first sign of tribulation, she was already back to using drugs. All of her skills and coping mechanisms to refrain from getting high went right out the window. It hadn't been an entire day, and she'd already snorted an eight ball and a half. The only good thing about her relapse, was that the little bit of coke she had left, Heemy threw it out of the window.

From what she learned about herself during her time at rehab was that her two main triggers were abandonment and rejection. Both triggers were pulled back like a rubber band when Heemy blamed her for his friends being killed. Then, for him to just sit there seething while she cried her eyes out, was yet another thing that drove her over the edge.

"There you go, butterfly. I've been looking all over for you," Bushnut said, as he approached her with a dozen white roses. Here." He handed them to Nahfisah. "Now, you know Daddy's been missing you, right?"

***

"This shit definitely wasn't a part of the plan," The Reaper said, looking around the parking lot full of people dressed in all-white. He was seated on the passenger's side of his tinted-out minivan. The triple back MPV was parked along the edge of the Front Street Pier, about a football field away from the yacht.

A couple of spaces down, surreptitiously tucked behind the tinted windows of a Pepsi blue Crown Vic, were Killah Kye and Keeno. And right beside them, sitting all alone in his burgundy Infinity, was Doo Dirty. He was dozing off and nodding out from the *Nut Shit* he'd just snorted. The rest of the crew didn't know about it, but his secret dope habit was growing stronger by the day.

"Yo, hand me them binoculars," The Reaper said to Kia, who was seated right behind him. She handed over the binoculars, and The Reaper placed them against his eyes. "I told this stupid muthafucka to do something that'll let me know it's him," The Reaper seethed, adjusting the sights on the binoculars.

He was looking around the lower deck trying to locate Bushnut. When he couldn't find him, he set his sights on the upper deck. Looking through the windows, he saw a bunch of niggas dressed in all-white with icy bright jewelry. They were popping bottles and spraying champagne as though they'd just won a championship.

"Yo, it's a lot of people out this mu'fucka," Murda Mont stated from behind the steering wheel. He was slouched back in the driver's seat with a stockless AK-47 resting across his lap. "It's gotta be at least a thousand people out here. You think that's a good thing, or a bad thing?" he asked The Reaper, who was still scoping out the yacht.

"Is what a good thing or a bad thing?"

"All these mu'fuckin' people that's out here." Murda Mont pointed around the pier. "The way I see it, they just a bunch of tattle-tales waiting to happen."

"Not necessarily," The Reaper spoke slowly. "It's actually sum'n that we can use in our favor."

"Sum'n that we can use in our favor?" Kia stated from the back seat. "And how you figure that? 'Cause I ain't down wit' leaving no muthafuckin' witnesses. That shit ain't a good look."

The Reaper lowered his binoculars, then he turned around in his seat to face her. "The more people the better, especially when the shots start ringing and everybody's running around ducking for cover. That's the perfect distraction in any event the cops roll up. It'll be so many people running around, bleeding and screaming, that the cops won't know who to tend to first. And what does that do for us?"

"It gives us the opportunity to get away." Kia smiled at him, nodding her understanding.

"Now, let me see what's up wit' this dumb-ass nigga Bushnut," The Reaper replied, spinning back around in his seat.

He returned the binoculars to the front of his eyes and adjusted the sights. He swept the binoculars back and forth, but still no Bushnut. The Reaper didn't realize it, but he was parked on the wrong side of the yacht.

The bar, stage and dance floor were all on the opposite side, allowing the party goers to have a clear view of the Delaware River and the Philadelphia skyline that glistened from the horizon.

Mumbling under his breath, he accused Bushnut of being the dumbest muthafucka on two legs.

"Fuck is that, the anchor?" The Reaper stated aloud, but was actually talking to himself. He was looking at a thick, rusty chain. It was hanging down the hull of the ship, connected to an iron claw that was gripping the third rail of the lower deck. It was so long that it dipped down into the water. "Nah, man, that can't be no anchor, not hanging off the side of a muthafuckin' yacht," he blurted out, zooming in to get a better look. Suddenly, the chain began to wiggle and shake, and emerging from the water was a skinny, green object that appeared to be a man. He was naked from the waist up and covered in tattoos. His entire back was the image of a scaly, green dragon. It was detailed with razor sharp wings and eagle-like talons that were ripping the flesh from the man's back. Slowly and intensely, the creature of a man began climbing up the rusty chain. "Nah," The Reaper shook his head in disbelief, "it can't be." No sooner than he said it, Diablo looked back in his direction, almost as though he were looking The Reaper dead in his face. He flicked out his long, reptilian tongue, then he continued climbing up the chain.

Trembling with rage, The Reaper dropped the binoculars. He felt the teeth marks on the front of his neck where Diablo tried to kill him, then he gripped up his sawed-off shotty and climbed out of the van.

"Yo, Double R, where you going?" asked Murda Mont. He was leaned forward with the choppa clutched in both hands. "Want me to come wit'chu, or what?"

"Nah, Mont, I'ma handle this shit myself."

"But what if you need one of us to back you up?" Kia asked him. She whipped out her twin .45 Kimbers and hopped out of the van ready to blast.

"Trust me, Kia, I got it," The Reaper said as he took off jogging. "Just be ready to do y'all thing when I send the party y'all way. I'm 'bout to burn this muthafucka down."

***

"Hola, papa?" Chee-Chee answered the phone on the first ring.

He was sitting in the cockpit of Juan's helicopter, looking up ahead at the bright lights from the yacht. The stealth, black chopper was sleek and smooth, so quiet that for the past twenty minutes he and Sisco had been circling the yacht from a hundred feet out, not once being detected. The side door was pulled wide open, fully exposing the .50 caliber Gatling gun that was screwed into the floor. The long, husky barrel was aimed out of the window ready to wreak havoc.

Equipped with a thousand-round drum and bullets the size of fingers, it was more than capable of flipping an elephant. So, clearly, hollowing out the ship in a matter of seconds was nothing. The only thing stopping it from happening was the green light from Juan.

Chee-Chee and Sisco had been patiently waiting for the jeffe's call. They now had it.

"Ju in position, Chee-Chee?" Juan asked from the comfort of his indoor swimming pool.

He was stretched out on rubber float sipping on a cold glass of iced tea. Right beside him, comfortably reclined on a float of his own, was Felix Dubois from France. He was tongue kissing back and forth with the two beauties he flew down from South Korea.

The word was out that Big Angolo had passed away, and that Grip's ascension to the head of the throne was essentially inescapable. The only way to offset what appeared to be inevitable was to reach out to the remaining bosses who weren't a part of Grip's super pact and persuade them to band together in order to establish a powerful front that could take him head on.

That's exactly what Juan planned to do. He already had Felix on his side, so that was one boss down. Now, he had to prove to the remaining bosses how serious he was. And what better way to do it than to hit Grip on his home front and weaken him from the inside out.

"Si, Papa. I'm 'bout a hunnid feet away," Chee-Chee replied. "Ju tell me when, I get it done."

"Do it."

***

"What's up, brozay? You a'ight?" Rahmello asked, as he placed his hand on Heemy's shoulder. Behind him, the homies were going crazy—dancing on the table and spraying one another with champagne. "You seem a little out of it tonight. What's up wit' that?"

"I'm straight," Heemy replied, exhaling a cloud of smoke. He looked at Rahmello for a brief second, then he returned his gaze to Nahfisah.

"You sure?" Rahmello looked at him with a raised brow. "I know you ain't trippin' about the shit that happened in the pool house. I was only fuckin' wit'chu, bro. You seen the gun wasn't loaded."

"Nah, bro, we good." Heemy flashed him a fake smile. "I'm just soaking it all in, you feel me? This is a big step we taking, moving forward. I just wanna make sure I got my mind right."

"Absolutely," Rahmello agreed. "As my second in command, I wouldn't have it any other way." He reached down inside of his pocket and pulled out a Rolex and a Triple B ring. They were the only two left on the tray after the rest of the big homies had taken theirs. "Here." He handed Heemy the watch and ring. "You strapped now. You all the way ready."

"Ready?" Heemy shot him a quizzical look. "Ready for what?"

"You see this shit right here?" Rahmello smiled at him, holding up his Block Boy chain. "This mu'fucka means sum'n, Heem. It means that I'm untouchable, and the same goes every mu'fucka that's wearing one. It means that we represent the elite, the best of the best. When niggas see this chain, this mu'fuckin' ring and watch they gon' know, Heem. Them niggas gon' know."

Sparking up the Dutch in his hand, Rahmello looked out of the window and took a deep breath. He was staring at the Philadelphia skyline. The glowing buildings illuminated the horizon, reflecting off the still waters of the Delaware.

"Everything you see," he pointed at the sky-high buildings, "all of that belongs to us now. Every block, ever alley, every Ave, every strip. We the new bosses, my nigga. The city gon' have to respect it, or check it."

Heemy could hear everything Rahmello was saying, but his attention was on Nahfisah. She was sitting at the bar talking to a light skinned nigga that was dipped in diamonds. Initially, she rolled her eyes and flagged him off. But when she looked up at the upper deck and saw that Heemy was eyeing her from the window, she pulled him in close and began kissing him passionately.

"Yo, pardon my soul," Heemy said as he stormed away from the window.

Rahmello called out behind him, but Heemy continued walking. He shot past the homies and barged through the door that led downstairs to the lower deck. Confused, Rahmello looked out of the window and saw Nahfisah standing by the bar getting freaky. It was then, that he put two and two together.

"I *knew* them muthafuckas was creeping on the low!" He cracked up laughing, then he took a pull on his Dutch Master. "Big sis done went and got this nigga wide open."

As he exhaled the Loud smoke, his iPhone began vibrating in his pants pocket. He pulled it out and noticed Olivia was calling. She'd been acting weird that entire day, and he didn't know why.

At the last minute, she claimed her stomach was hurting and that she'd rather stay home instead of going to the party. He offered to leave a few men behind, but Olivia shut it down, telling him that she needed rest and didn't want to be bothered with.

"Sup, Mami, you good?" Rahmello asked, after accepting the call.

"Ay, dios mios!" Olivia's voice came booming through the phone. "Ay, dios mios! Ay dios mios!"

"What the fuck? Yo, Oli, what's wrong?"

"Rahmello, help me! They came to get me!"

"Came to get'chu?" His heart dropped into his stomach. "Somebody's inside of the house?"

"Ay, dios mios! I can hear them!" Olivia cried. "They just shot Heldga!"

Rahmello's entire body began to shake and tremble, as the thought of his family being violated sent chills down his spine. "Yo, where my son at? You got him?"

"Yes, baby, I just got him from the nursery. *Oh-my-God-I-can-hear-them-coming-up-the-stairs!*"

"Oli, calm down." Rahmello had to think fast. "Where you at in the house?"

"The hallway," Olivia cried, doing her best to not wake a sleeping Omelly. "About four doors down from our bedroom. Baby, I'm scared. I can hear them coming. They're almost up the stairs."

"Fuck!" Rahmello shouted, eliciting the attention of everyone in the room. "You remember when my grandpops showed us the safe room?"

"Yeah, baby, I remember." Olivia cried some more. "The one he showed us on the night he went missing."

"Right. Now, hurry up and run down there. When you step inside, I'ma give you the combination to the other door."

"Baby, I'm scared."

"Just do like I told you, Olivia. Damn!"

The room Rahmello was referring to was dead smack in the center of the hallway, nearly two doors down from he and Olivia's bedroom. It was tucked behind a door that appeared to be a regular one. But on the other side, instead of a bedroom, there was nothing but a small vestibule and a steel gray door.

Behind the steel door was a secret room that was similar to a bunker. Grip had it structured solely for situations like this, knowing that a day would possibly come where his enemies breached the front gate.

Biting down on his knuckle, Rahmello listened closely as Olivia ran down the hallway. A few seconds later, he heard the loud sound of a woman screaming. She was talking in a foreign language, possibly French.

"Pa kate'l alè!"

"Don't hurt us, please!" He heard Olivia's voice, followed by the sound of her cell phone crashing against the hard marble floor. At that point, every sound that came through the phone was muffled and distant. "Please, not my baby! No! Leave him alone!"

"Iley, yo, Oli? *Oli?*" Rahmello snapped out. He could tell by the way she was begging and pleading that the people inside of the house must have gotten to her before she made it to the safe room. "Fuck!" Rahmello shouted in frustration, smashing his phone against the wall.

He took off running, with everybody staring at him. A few of the homies made an attempt to run after him, but Snot Box stopped them in their tracks.

It was time for Rahmello to be taught a lesson.

***

"Yo, my man, the ship's packed to capacity, ain't nobody else getting on," said one of the two bouncers who was guarding the entrance to the yacht. Stretched out before him was the twenty-foot ramp that connected the yacht to the edge of the pier. He folded his arms across his chest and shook his head from side to side. "I don't know what'chu coming up here for, you ain't getting in."

"Is that right?" The Reaper hissed at him. He was halfway up the ramp, with his sawed-off shotty tucked behind his right leg.

"Hell yeah, that's right," said the second bouncer. "And even if it wasn't, you still don't meet the dress code. This an all-white party, and you're dressed in all-black. You better take ya ass on somewhere."

Boom!

A blast from the shotty lifted the man clean off of his feet, turning his all-white shirt into a bloody red honeycomb. The first bouncer attempted to run, but went flying over the ramp and into the water when another blast rearranged his midsection.

The Reaper ran up the ramp with the shotgun smoking.

When he barged through the double doors that led to the lower deck, he looked up and saw Rahmello running down the stairs. He leveled the shotty, but before he could let off a clean shot, Rahmello disappeared into the thick of the crowd.

For some reason, the music stopped and everybody bum rushed the bar. Clutching the shotty with both hands, The Reaper moved through the crowd unnoticed.

***

"What the fuck is this?" Heemy said, as he approached Nahfisah and Bushnut. They were standing in front of the bar kissing and groping on one another. *"Nahfisah?"* Heemy grabbed her by the arm, snatching her away from Bushnut. "Fuck is you doing? What'chu think I'm a fuckin' nut?"

"Little boy, if you don't get outta my goddamned face," Nahfisah snarled at him. She pushed him in the chest and pulled her arm away.

Bushnut looked at Heemy and laughed. "Damn, youngin' the bitch done chose. Ya lost, my gain. That's just a part of the game, baby boy. Accept it."

Raging mad, Heemy looked Bushnut dead in his eyes. There was something about him that was familiar, but he couldn't quite put his finger on it. Then it hit him.

He knew exactly where he remembered him from. He was twenty pounds heavier and seemed to be touching some serious paper, nothing close to the scrawny, broke crackhead he remembered. But yet and still, it was him.

"Beaver Bushnut?"

"The one and muthafuckin' only." Bushnut rubbed his hands together, loving the recognition. To him, there was nothing better than the look on a muthafucka's face when they saw the way he bounced back from his crack addiction. "I know who you is, young buck. You Treesha's son. I've been try'na catch up wit'chu. Wanted to see if we could sit down and talk business."

"Talk business?" Heemy twisted his face.

He gave him the once over and noticed the chain around his neck. Specifically, the iced-out Mr. Peanut that was glistening from his torso. A light bulb flashed inside of Heemy's head. He dug down inside of his pocket and pulled out the bag of dope that he'd taken from Smitty. He looked at the *Nut Shit* stamp, then he looked at the iced-out charm, comparing the two together. *Nut Shit?* Heemy licked his lips and took in a deep breath. *Beaver Bushnut? The YBM!* He squeezed the bag of dope in his hand, making a rock-hard fist. Then in one swift motion, threw a hook so vicious that it sent Bushnut crumbling to the hardwood deck.

Whop!

"Raheem, what'chu do that for?" Nahfisah screamed at him. She swung the empty shot-glass in her hand, but Heemy mugged her in the face, and she fell flat on her ass. Everybody stopped dancing and looked over at the bar.

"Bitch-ass nigga!" Heemy gritted his teeth, stomping Bushnut in the face. He grabbed a bottle of Spades from the bar top and cracked Bushnut upside the head.

Crack!

Using the edge of the broken bottle, he stabbed Bushnut repeatedly. The music stopped playing, as everybody crowded around the bar.

Yo Gotti and his people hopped off of the stage, with his bodyguards leading the way. In a matter of seconds, he was downstairs in the bowel of the vessel safe and sound.

Heemy's suit jacket was covered in blood, but he didn't care. Gritting his teeth, he stabbed Bushnut over and over, slicing him across the face and head. After stabbing him a few more times, he buried the bottle deep inside of Bushnut's neck. Exhausted, he whipped out his Glock .19 and aimed the barrel at Bushnut's face. Slipping his finger in the trigger-guard, he heard Rahmello shouting his name.

"Aye, yo, Heemy! *Heem!*"

Heemy looked up and saw Rahmello barging through the crowd. His light skinned face was flush red and glistening with tears.

"Heemy, man, we gotta go! It's Olivia and Melly! Somebody's try'na kill 'em!"

Nostrils flaring, Heemy aimed the gun in Rahmello's direction. Rahmello looked at him with big, bulging eyes, shaking his head *no.*
"Heemy, what the fuck is you doing?"

Boca!

***

Still moving through the crowd unnoticed, The Reaper spotted Rahmello. His first thought was to decorate the deck with his gooey hot brains. But doing so, would only defeat the purpose. He needed Rahmello alive so he could take him to the three hundred keys that he received from Juan. So instead of aiming the shotgun at the back of Rahmello's head, he aimed the gun at Heemy. He attempted to let off a shot, but Heemy beat him to the punch.

Boca!
The fiery, loud burst lit up the night, and The Reaper went stumbling backwards. He let off a shot from the pump, but instead of hitting Heemy, who was still shooting at him, the bullet tore through the face of the woman that was standing right beside him. The entire crowd erupted in fear. All at once, they stampeded the exit, crying and screaming, pushing one another and doing their best to avoid being shot.

***

A chunky spray of slimy warm blood splashed Rahmello in the face, as Flo fell in his arms with the top half of her dome missing. The unexpected weight of her dead body sent him crashing to the deck. He looked up at Heemy, and saw that he was still shooting at the dark-skinned man with the the sawed-off shotgun.

The man appeared to be hit, but he wasn't dead. His shotgun was still flaming, and Rahmello could feel the heat of the gunfire.

Thinking fast, he pulled out his .45 and strapped Flo's body across the back of his shoulders. The thickness of her bloody warm body was exactly what he needed to shield himself from the gunfire. Moving as fast as he could, he crawled across the deck on one hand. His other hand was squeezing down on the .45, tearing up the legs of the people who stood in between him and the exit. He would stop at nothing to make it home to his girl and son.

***

Boca!
Heemy let off another shot, but the rush of the crowd knocked him off balance. He tripped over a bar stool and stumbled to the floor. He popped back up with the Glock .19 ready to spit, but the stampede of people was so thick that he couldn't find his target. He looked all around, but the dark-skinned man with the shotgun was nowhere in sight. The only thing he saw was a deck full of people crying and screaming, all of them doing their best to make it off of

the yacht. He then remembered Nahfisah. He looked around the crowded deck, but could not find her.

"Nahfisah!" he shouted over the loud cries, praying she wasn't one of the people who'd been trampled by the stampede. Or even worse, one of the people who'd been hit by a stray bullet. "Nahfisah, where you at?"

Suddenly, a sweeping gust of warm air shot throughout the deck, as everybody looked up in the sky. A black helicopter was hovering the yacht.

At first glance, Heemy assumed the helicopter was a ghetto bird, one of the many that belonged to the PPD. But when he noticed the Gatling gun that was sticking out the open side door, he hit the deck and crawled up under the bar.

Bdddddddddooooooom! Bdddddddddooooooom!

The Gatling gun went to work, tearing up everything in its wake. The glass from the upper deck window rained down like a hail storm, causing Heemy to cover his head. He could hear the sound of the homies shooting back, but their counter attack was minimal at best. Their semi-automatic weapons were no match for the brute force of the Gatling gun. The upper deck was decimated in seconds.

Bdddddddddooooooom! Bdddddddddooooooom!

The crowd of people were right back to shouting and screaming and doing their best to make it off of the yacht. A few of them even dove overboard, in a last attempt to get away from the gunfire.

Heemy looked around the deck, searching for Nahfisah. He spotted her. She was standing against the rail at the rear of the deck, covered in blood, shivering and shaking and watching the horror with big wide eyes.

"Nahfisah, get down!" Heemy shouted over the Gatling gun. He continued shouting, but it was no use. The sound of the rapid fire was so loud that he couldn't even hear himself.

All around him, people were being torn to shreds. The sea of people dressed in all white was now a burgundy canvass of mayhem. He attempted to crawl out from underneath the bar, but jumped back when one of the homies from the upper deck came crashing down right in front of him. His headless body was twisted like a pretzel.

The pineapple-sized hole in his stomach was gushing out guts, and Heemy could see the whiteness of his ribcage.

"Nahfisah, I'm coming!" Heemy continued shouting. The Gatling gun was tearing up the exit, so he figured it was the perfect time to make his move. As he crawled from underneath the bar, he spotted the dark-skinned man with the shotgun. He was making his way toward Nahfisah with the shotty aimed at the side of her face. Heemy popped up and took off running. *"Nahfisah, get down!"*

***

Diablo was scaling the rail of the deck with a demented grin on his face. The sight of all the killing had him hot and antsy. His only regret was that the pain and suffering was being caused by someone other than himself. Yet and still, he was determined to have fun. The woman he'd been looking for was only a few feet away, standing all alone trembling and crying. He stuck out his long, slitted tongue and flicked it up down, taking in the sweet scent of his prey

"I told ju, mija, dat next time I would get'chu. Ju will soon know why dey call me Diablo."

***

The Reaper aimed the shotty at the helicopter and let off a round. *Boom!*

The chopper swayed and rocked, but that was it. The Gatling gun was still booming, chopping people down left and right.

"Umm!" The Reaper grimaced, as he reached for the bullet wound on his left shoulder. Grinding his teeth, he tightened his grasp on the shotgun and looked around the deck for an exit route. He saw none. He did, however, see the man he was looking for. He was scaling the rail of the deck, creeping toward a woman who was crying in the far back corner. He raised the shotty and took off running.

"Remember me?"

***

"Agh, shit!" Heemy shouted when he slipped on a patch of broken glass and hit the deck hard. He dropped his gun and popped back up searching for it. He scoured all around the deck, but he couldn't find it. He looked back at The Reaper and saw he was a few steps away from Nahfisah. Disregarding the gun, Heemy continued to running toward her.

What the fuck is that? Heemy thought to himself when another man popped up behind Nahfisah. His mouth was wide open like he was ready to bite her. His teeth were long and sharp and curled at the end like the tusk on a wild boar.

"Remember me?" He heard The Reaper shouting. He looked in his direction, then he looked back at Nahfisah, just as the monster of a man was ready to take bite. The monster looked at The Reaper and shrieked.

"Eeeeeeiiiiiii!"

The Reaper fired.

Boom!

Heemy and Nahfisah went flying over the railing.

Splash!

Chapter Twenty-Five

"Hello? Mrs. Moreno? Is anyone home?" Savino called out from the doorway.

He was standing on the front porch to Annie's house looking at the bashed in front door. It was cracked down the middle and nearly knocked off the hinges. Her Mercedes-Benz S550 was parked in the driveway. The back-passenger's side door was pulled wide open, and halfway hanging out the door was a blood-covered car seat.

"Something's extremely wrong here," Savino mumbled under his breath, looking back and forth between the house and car. He pulled out his .38 Special and slowly pushed open the front door.

He stepped inside of the living room and saw the room had been ransacked. The black, suede furniture was slashed open and flipped over. The coffee tables and lamps were shattered to pieces and the 60" flat screen that hung on the wall was slanted at an awkward angle. A penny-sized bullet hole was placed in the center.

"Mrs. Moreno?" he called out in a shaky voice. "Kids?"

There was no reply. The only sound he heard was the whimpering of a wounded animal. Clutching the .38 like his life depended on it, he slowly made his way toward the sound. It seemed to be coming from the kitchen.

As he moved through the dining room, he saw the condition of the room was similar to the ransacking of the living room. The crystal chandelier that once hung from the ceiling was laying on the floor, and right beside it was the dining room table. It was cracked down the middle and smeared with blood. The dining room chairs were scattered all around and laying on the floor, sprinkled with blood, was a baby doll and two stuffed animals.

"This is bad," Savino mumbled under his breath, thinking about Sonny's daughter and niece. "Kids?" he called out some more, but this time barely above a whisper. "Mrs. Moreno? This is Mario Savino, Sontino's attorney. If you guys are in here, you can come out now. You're safe."

Again, there was no reply. The only thing he heard was the whimpering of the wounded animal. Swallowing the lump in his throat, he continued making his way toward the kitchen.

"Jesus Christ!" he shouted at the top of lungs when he turned on the kitchen lights. The entire kitchen was covered in blood. There was blood on the floor, blood on the walls, blood on the cabinets, blood on the ceiling. Blood was everywhere. The refrigerator, the stove, the dishwasher and microwave, all of them were covered in blood.

Uuugggrrrr! The wounded animal began to growl.

Savino couldn't see him, but could tell that the sound was coming from the other side of the granite island in the center of the kitchen. He tightened his grasp on the rubber-grip handle and slowly made his way toward the sound.

When he reached the other side of the island, he looked down and spotted Rocko. The oversized Rottweiler was looking up at Savino with blood shot eyes. The bullet holes embedded in his face and shoulder were oozing out blood, and with his two front legs snapped in half, he was using his hind legs to push himself forward.

Still determined to defend his family to the bloody end, his razor-sharp canines were clamping up and down, biting at the air, desperately trying to latch on to Savino's leg.

Uuugggrrrr! Urf! Urf! Uuugggrrrr! Urf!

Savino took a step back and aimed the barrel between the dog's red eyes. There was nothing left to do, except put the dog out of his misery. Taking a deep breath, he pulled back on the trigger.

Boc!

Rocko's brains went scattering across the floor, and Savino dropped to his knees crying like a baby. In a twisted, weird way he felt somewhat responsible for what he now realized happened to Sonny's mother and children. Had he only made it there sooner. Shaking and trembling, he pulled out his cell phone and pressed down on the number that Sonny called him from.

Ring!

"Yo, Savino, holla at me," Sonny's voice boomed through the phone. "Are they safe? Did you get 'em?"

"Sontino, I don't know how to tell you this" Savino sobbed.
"Tell me, what?" Sonny shouted at him. "Did you get 'em or not?"

"Your mother? The kids? They're, they're gone."

"Gone? Fuck you mean they gone?"

"Sonny, they're gone. And there was nothing I could do about it."

***

Nahfisah popped out of the water gasping for air. Heemy pushed her body up on the pier and then gripped the ledge with both hands and pulled himself out of the cold Delaware.

Soaking wet, he looked down at Nahfisah. She was curled up in a ball, shivering and shaking. Her blue eyes were zoned out in a trance and over and over, he could hear her saying, "No. No. Don't shoot. No. No. Don't shoot."

The pandemonium from the yacht had spilled out onto the pier, and all around he heard the booming of loud gunfire. The helicopter was gone, so the additional gunfire was somewhat confusing. Who was shooting, and why?

"Come on, Nah, we gotta go," Heemy said as he reached down and grabbed Nahfisah by the hand. He pulled her to her feet and reiterated that they needed to leave, but Nahfisah just looked at him with a blank face.

"No. No. Don't shoot. No. No. Don't shoot."

"Goddamnit!" Heemy grimaced, flinching when the zip of a stray bullet whizzed past his left ear. "Come on, Nah, stop bullshitting! We gotta go!"

"No. No. Don't shoot. No. No. Don't shoot."

"Man, fuck this shit!" He lashed out, as he grabbed Nahfisah by the waist. He threw her over his shoulder and took off running, praying they didn't catch a stray bullet.

The parking lot was jam packed with people running and screaming. A chick he knew from the neighborhood was gunned down right in front of him, but he ran right past her. The pinging of bullets bouncing off of every car he ran past made it seem as though someone was shooting at him. But as he looked around the parking lot from left to right, the only thing he saw were people running.

Finally, he made it back to his Lamborghini.

"I shoulda killed his ass when I had the chance," he mumbled under his breath when he saw Rahmello's Lambo was gone.

The two cars were parked alongside one another, but now the only Lamborghini Heemy saw was his. "Ain't even stick around long enough to make sure his sister was safe. Bitch-ass nigga."

Glancing around the parking lot, Heemy pulled out his car key and deactivated the locks. After lifting up the passenger's side door, he pushed Nahfisah inside and then pulled it back down.

Making his way around the front of the car, he heard the pinging of bullets tearing up the Escalade beside him.

Who the fuck is out here chopping at me?

He looked around the parking lot, but it was nearly impossible to identify a specific shooter. He wanted to bust back, but at that point, his only concern was Nahfisah.

He popped open the driver's side door and hopped down inside of the Lambo. Pulling the door closed, he looked over at the woman who had without a doubt stolen his heart. She was rocking back and forth and shaking her head *no.*

"No. No. Don't shoot. No. No. Don't shoot."

"Damn, Nah, you gotta snap outta that shit." Heemy released a long sigh. He pressed down on the push start, gripping the wheel with his left hand.

Tap! Tap! Tap!

The sound of someone tapping on his window made him peek over his left shoulder.

Standing on the other side of the car door was Keeno. A menacing scowl was plastered across his face, and the barrel of his Glock .40 was pressed against the window.

"Yeah, nigga, what's up now?"

Boca!

To Be Continued...

286

Available NOW!
Blood of a Boss V: Blood in my Eyes

About the Author

My pen name is *ASKARI*, but I'm known throughout the city of Philadelphia and surrounding counties as S-Class. Prior to writing books, I was one of the hottest up and coming rappers in the city. This was in the early 2000's, prior to social media. But I still had a strong buzz, blazing mixtapes and rocking clubs from Jersey to New York City. In October 2001, my homie, Peedi Crakk, was signed to Roc-a-fella Records, and being the real nigga he is, he took our entire crew along for the ride. Our sole mission was to lock down the rap game and get our families out the hood. Unfortunately, in February 2003, just as my career was beginning to take off, I was arrested and charged with a murder that I absolutely did not commit. There was no physical evidence linking me to this crime: NO GUN, NO FINGERPRINTS, NO DNA, NO VIDEO SURVEILLANCE, NOTHING!!! The entire case hinged on the identification testimony of one alleged eyewitness, who initially described the shooter as *A DARK-SKINNED BLACK MAN WITH A SUNNI MUSLIM BEARD.* However, as you can see from my pictures, I have a light brown complexion, and at the time of this crime, I was eighteen years old with a baby face. I had no beard whatsoever.

At my trial, the district attorney's case relied exclusively on the testimony of this one eyewitness; the same witness who knew me prior to this incident, but described the shooter as a completely different person. This witness was a convicted felon, currently serving time for an unrelated matter. He did, however, state for the record that he was promised leniency in exchange for his testimony against me. This witness testified that at the time of this incident, he was standing on the corner selling crack cocaine and that he was under the influence of alcohol and drugs. He further testified that he only had a partial view of the shooter's face, as the shooter was wearing a hoody sweatshirt, with the hood up over his head. He also indicated that the crime scene was not well lit. During cross examination, he revealed that after this incident, he went around the neighborhood asking people "What happened?", and that another individual *TOLD* him that I was the shooter. This witness' identification testimony was so suspect and unreliable, that even the trial judge acknowledged there was the possibility of a misidentification.

In addition to shortcomings of this witness' identification testimony, the recording of his 911 call was mysteriously missing from the evidence file. Not only that, but the investigating detectives, for unknown reasons, failed to make an appearance at trial. As a result, they were never questioned about the integrity of their investigation. Even worst, according to police reports, there was at least one eyewitness to this crime who the detectives never interviewed. I made numerous attempts to have my trial counsel locate and interview this witness, but my attorney failed to do so. THIS WITNESS MAY HAVE VERY WELL BEEN THE ONLY OPPORTUNITY I HAD TO PROVE MY INNOCENCE. BUT UP UNTIL THIS DAY, HE HAS NEVER BEEN PROPERLY IDENTIFIED, LOCATED AND INTERVIEWED!!!

Sadly, despite all of the witness' shortcomings and a notable lack of physical evidence, the jury convicted me of first-degree murder. My trial lasted TWO DAYS!!! SMFH!!!!

Man, when I tell you I was crushed.... I couldn't believe it. Moreover, I couldn't understand. How could something like this happen? How the fuck could I be convicted of something that I didn't do? Excuse my language, but I'm angry as hell!! Please, try to understand.

Yet and still, in the midst of the bullshit, I knew that I had to remain humble, positive and prayerful. I knew that I had to remain diligent in my fight to prove my innocence, while at the same time conducting myself as a man, standing firm on the principles that my mother and father instilled in me as a child. I have not wavered, and I never will. I shall and must continue to fight for my freedom; that's just my nature.

I was only twenty years old when I was kidnapped by the system. I was a father of three beautiful children. I was working two jobs and busting my ass in the studio every day, primed to be the next Jay Z. I was also working with the youth in my community as an assistant coach on our little league football team. But I guess none of that mattered. I once seen a civil rights documentary where an ignorant Klansman stated: "When we get ourselves all riled up to hang us a nigger, any nigger will do." It's about to be 2018, and for nearly fifteen years, I've been in prison for a crime that I didn't commit. Maybe to them, I'm just another nigger. SMFH!!!!

You know, it's funny when I sit back and think about my life. I thought that I'd be triple platinum now, captivating audiences with my creativity and word play. I guess I still am, but instead of a microphone, I'm using a pen. Still focused on using my creativity to open the doors that confine me. Whether they be the doors that kept a young brotha locked in the hood, or the doors that currently have a brotha locked behind bars. Either way, I will be free.

To my real family and friends, fans and supporters, I love y'all from the bottom of my heart. Words could never express my gratitude. And to the big homie, CA$H, thank you bro. When I was down and out, sitting in a cell, looking for a way out, I came across *TRUST NO MAN*. In your dedications and acknowledgements, you gave me a new outlook, a new source of motivation. It was then that I picked up a pen, and I'm determined to never put it down.

Always,

Rayshon "ASKARI" Farmer

Submission Guideline

Submit the first three chapters of your completed manuscript to ldpsubmissions@gmail.com, subject line: Your book's title. The manuscript must be in a .doc file and sent as an attachment. Document should be in Times New Roman, double spaced and in size 12 font. Also, provide your synopsis and full contact information. If sending multiple submissions, they must each be in a separate email.

Have a story but no way to send it electronically? You can still submit to LDP/Ca$h Presents. Send in the first three chapters, written or typed, of your completed manuscript to:

LDP: Submissions Dept
Po Box 944
Stockbridge, Ga 30281

DO NOT send original manuscript. Must be a duplicate.

Provide your synopsis and a cover letter containing your full contact information.

Thanks for considering LDP and Ca$h Presents.

Coming Soon from Lock Down Publications/Ca$h Presents

BOW DOWN TO MY GANGSTA
By **Ca$h**
TORN BETWEEN TWO
By **Coffee**
THE STREETS STAINED MY SOUL **II**
By **Marcellus Allen**
BLOOD OF A BOSS **VI**
SHADOWS OF THE GAME II
TRAP BASTARD II
By **Askari**
LOYAL TO THE GAME **IV**
By **T.J. & Jelissa**
IF LOVING YOU IS WRONG… **III**
By **Jelissa**
TRUE SAVAGE **VIII**
MIDNIGHT CARTEL IV
DOPE BOY MAGIC IV
CITY OF KINGZ III
By **Chris Green**
BLAST FOR ME **III**
A SAVAGE DOPEBOY III
CUTTHROAT MAFIA III
DUFFLE BAG CARTEL VI
HEARTLESS GOON VI
By **Ghost**
A HUSTLER'S DECEIT III
KILL ZONE **II**
BAE BELONGS TO ME III

A DOPE BOY'S QUEEN III

By **Aryanna**

COKE KINGS V

KING OF THE TRAP III

By **T.J. Edwards**

GORILLAZ IN THE BAY V

3X KRAZY III

De'Kari

THE STREETS ARE CALLING II

Duquie Wilson

KINGPIN KILLAZ IV

STREET KINGS III

PAID IN BLOOD III

CARTEL KILLAZ IV

DOPE GODS III

Hood Rich

SINS OF A HUSTLA II

ASAD

KINGZ OF THE GAME VI

Playa Ray

SLAUGHTER GANG IV

RUTHLESS HEART IV

By Willie Slaughter

FUK SHYT II

By Blakk Diamond

TRAP QUEEN

RICH $AVAGE II

By Troublesome

YAYO V

GHOST MOB II

Askari

Stilloan Robinson
CREAM III
By Yolanda Moore
SON OF A DOPE FIEND III
HEAVEN GOT A GHETTO II
By Renta
FOREVER GANGSTA II
GLOCKS ON SATIN SHEETS III
By Adrian Dulan
LOYALTY AIN'T PROMISED III
By Keith Williams
THE PRICE YOU PAY FOR LOVE III
By Destiny Skai
I'M NOTHING WITHOUT HIS LOVE II
SINS OF A THUG II
TO THE THUG I LOVED BEFORE II
By Monet Dragun
LIFE OF A SAVAGE IV
MURDA SEASON IV
GANGLAND CARTEL IV
CHI'RAQ GANGSTAS IV
KILLERS ON ELM STREET IV
JACK BOYZ N DA BRONX II
A DOPEBOY'S DREAM II
By **Romell Tukes**
QUIET MONEY IV
EXTENDED CLIP III
THUG LIFE IV
By **Trai'Quan**

THE STREETS MADE ME III

By **Larry D. Wright**

IF YOU CROSS ME ONCE II

ANGEL III

By **Anthony Fields**

FRIEND OR FOE III

By **Mimi**

SAVAGE STORMS III

By **Meesha**

BLOOD ON THE MONEY III

By J-Blunt

THE STREETS WILL NEVER CLOSE II

By K'ajji

NIGHTMARES OF A HUSTLA III

By King Dream

IN THE ARM OF HIS BOSS

By Jamila

HARD AND RUTHLESS III

MOB TOWN 251 II

By Von Diesel

LEVELS TO THIS SHYT II

By Ah'Million

MOB TIES III

By SayNoMore

BODYMORE MURDERLAND III

By Delmont Player

THE LAST OF THE OGS III

Tranay Adams

FOR THE LOVE OF A BOSS II

By C. D. Blue

Askari

Available Now

RESTRAINING ORDER **I & II**
By **CA$H & Coffee**
LOVE KNOWS NO BOUNDARIES **I II & III**
By **Coffee**
RAISED AS A GOON I, II, III & IV
BRED BY THE SLUMS I, II, III
BLAST FOR ME I & II
ROTTEN TO THE CORE I II III
A BRONX TALE I, II, III
DUFFLE BAG CARTEL I II III IV V
HEARTLESS GOON I II III IV V
A SAVAGE DOPEBOY I II
DRUG LORDS I II III
CUTTHROAT MAFIA I II
By **Ghost**
LAY IT DOWN **I & II**
LAST OF A DYING BREED I II
BLOOD STAINS OF A SHOTTA I & II III
By **Jamaica**
LOYAL TO THE GAME I II III
LIFE OF SIN I, II III
By **TJ & Jelissa**
BLOODY COMMAS I & II
SKI MASK CARTEL I II & III

Blood of a Boss 4

KING OF NEW YORK I II, III IV V
RISE TO POWER I II III
COKE KINGS I II III IV
BORN HEARTLESS I II III IV
KING OF THE TRAP I II
By **T.J. Edwards**
IF LOVING HIM IS WRONG...I & II
LOVE ME EVEN WHEN IT HURTS I II III
By **Jelissa**
WHEN THE STREETS CLAP BACK I & II III
THE HEART OF A SAVAGE I II III
By **Jibril Williams**
A DISTINGUISHED THUG STOLE MY HEART I II & III
LOVE SHOULDN'T HURT I II III IV
RENEGADE BOYS I II III IV
PAID IN KARMA I II III
SAVAGE STORMS I II
By **Meesha**
A GANGSTER'S CODE I &, II III
A GANGSTER'S SYN I II III
THE SAVAGE LIFE I II III
CHAINED TO THE STREETS I II III
BLOOD ON THE MONEY I II
By J-Blunt
PUSH IT TO THE LIMIT
By **Bre' Hayes**
BLOOD OF A BOSS **I, II, III, IV,** V
SHADOWS OF THE GAME
TRAP BASTARD
By **Askari**

297

Askari

THE STREETS BLEED MURDER **I, II & III**

THE HEART OF A GANGSTA I II& III

By **Jerry Jackson**

CUM FOR ME I II III IV V VI VII

An **LDP Erotica Collaboration**

BRIDE OF A HUSTLA **I II & II**

THE FETTI GIRLS **I, II& III**

CORRUPTED BY A GANGSTA I, II III, IV

BLINDED BY HIS LOVE

THE PRICE YOU PAY FOR LOVE I II

DOPE GIRL MAGIC I II III

By **Destiny Skai**

WHEN A GOOD GIRL GOES BAD

By **Adrienne**

THE COST OF LOYALTY I II III

By Kweli

A GANGSTER'S REVENGE **I II III & IV**

THE BOSS MAN'S DAUGHTERS I II III IV V

A SAVAGE LOVE **I & II**

BAE BELONGS TO ME I II

A HUSTLER'S DECEIT I, II, III

WHAT BAD BITCHES DO I, II, III

SOUL OF A MONSTER I II III

KILL ZONE

A DOPE BOY'S QUEEN I II

By **Aryanna**

A KINGPIN'S AMBITON

A KINGPIN'S AMBITION **II**

I MURDER FOR THE DOUGH

By **Ambitious**

298

TRUE SAVAGE I II III IV V VI VII

DOPE BOY MAGIC I, II, III

MIDNIGHT CARTEL I II III

CITY OF KINGZ I II

By **Chris Green**

A DOPEBOY'S PRAYER

By **Eddie "Wolf" Lee**

THE KING CARTEL **I, II & III**

By **Frank Gresham**

THESE NIGGAS AIN'T LOYAL **I, II & III**

By **Nikki Tee**

GANGSTA SHYT **I II &III**

By **CATO**

THE ULTIMATE BETRAYAL

By **Phoenix**

BOSS'N UP **I , II & III**

By **Royal Nicole**

I LOVE YOU TO DEATH

By Destiny J

I RIDE FOR MY HITTA

I STILL RIDE FOR MY HITTA

By **Misty Holt**

LOVE & CHASIN' PAPER

By **Qay Crockett**

TO DIE IN VAIN

SINS OF A HUSTLA

By **ASAD**

BROOKLYN HUSTLAZ

By **Boogsy Morina**

BROOKLYN ON LOCK I & II

Askari

By **Sonovia**
GANGSTA CITY
By **Teddy Duke**
A DRUG KING AND HIS DIAMOND I & II III
A DOPEMAN'S RICHES
HER MAN, MINE'S TOO I, II
CASH MONEY HO'S
THE WIFEY I USED TO BE I II
By Nicole Goosby
TRAPHOUSE KING **I II & III**
KINGPIN KILLAZ I II III
STREET KINGS I II
PAID IN BLOOD **I II**
CARTEL KILLAZ I II III
DOPE GODS I II
By **Hood Rich**
LIPSTICK KILLAH **I, II, III**
CRIME OF PASSION I II & III
FRIEND OR FOE I II
By **Mimi**
STEADY MOBBN' **I, II, III**
THE STREETS STAINED MY SOUL
By **Marcellus Allen**
WHO SHOT YA **I, II, III**
SON OF A DOPE FIEND I II
HEAVEN GOT A GHETTO
Renta
GORILLAZ IN THE BAY **I II III IV**
TEARS OF A GANGSTA I II
3X KRAZY I II

DE'KARI

TRIGGADALE I II III

Elijah R. Freeman

GOD BLESS THE TRAPPERS I, II, III

THESE SCANDALOUS STREETS I, II, III

FEAR MY GANGSTA I, II, III IV, V

THESE STREETS DON'T LOVE NOBODY I, II

BURY ME A G I, II, III, IV, V

A GANGSTA'S EMPIRE I, II, III, IV

THE DOPEMAN'S BODYGAURD I II

THE REALEST KILLAZ I II III

THE LAST OF THE OGS I II

Tranay Adams

THE STREETS ARE CALLING

Duquie Wilson

MARRIED TO A BOSS… I II III

By Destiny Skai & Chris Green

KINGZ OF THE GAME I II III IV V

Playa Ray

SLAUGHTER GANG I II III

RUTHLESS HEART I II III

By Willie Slaughter

FUK SHYT

By Blakk Diamond

DON'T F#CK WITH MY HEART I II

By Linnea

ADDICTED TO THE DRAMA I II III

IN THE ARM OF HIS BOSS II

By Jamila

YAYO I II III IV

Askari

A SHOOTER'S AMBITION I II
By S. Allen
TRAP GOD I II III
RICH $AVAGE
By Troublesome
FOREVER GANGSTA
GLOCKS ON SATIN SHEETS I II
By Adrian Dulan
TOE TAGZ I II III
LEVELS TO THIS SHYT
By Ah'Million
KINGPIN DREAMS I II III
By Paper Boi Rari
CONFESSIONS OF A GANGSTA I II III
By Nicholas Lock
I'M NOTHING WITHOUT HIS LOVE
SINS OF A THUG
TO THE THUG I LOVED BEFORE
By Monet Dragun
CAUGHT UP IN THE LIFE I II III
By Robert Baptiste
NEW TO THE GAME I II III
MONEY, MURDER & MEMORIES I II III
By **Malik D. Rice**
LIFE OF A SAVAGE I II III
A GANGSTA'S QUR'AN I II III
MURDA SEASON I II III
GANGLAND CARTEL I II III
CHI'RAQ GANGSTAS I II III

KILLERS ON ELM STREET I II III

JACK BOYZ N DA BRONX

A DOPEBOY'S DREAM

By **Romell Tukes**

LOYALTY AIN'T PROMISED I II

By Keith Williams

QUIET MONEY I II III

THUG LIFE I II III

EXTENDED CLIP I II

By **Trai'Quan**

THE STREETS MADE ME I II

By **Larry D. Wright**

THE ULTIMATE SACRIFICE I, II, III, IV, V, VI

KHADIFI

IF YOU CROSS ME ONCE

ANGEL I II

By **Anthony Fields**

THE LIFE OF A HOOD STAR

By Ca$h & Rashia Wilson

THE STREETS WILL NEVER CLOSE

By K'ajji

CREAM I II

By Yolanda Moore

NIGHTMARES OF A HUSTLA I II

By King Dream

CONCRETE KILLA I II

By Kingpen

HARD AND RUTHLESS I II

MOB TOWN 251

Askari

By Von Diesel

GHOST MOB II

Stilloan Robinson

MOB TIES I II

By SayNoMore

BODYMORE MURDERLAND I II

By Delmont Player

FOR THE LOVE OF A BOSS

By C. D. Blue

BOOKS BY LDP'S CEO, CA$H

TRUST IN NO MAN

TRUST IN NO MAN 2

TRUST IN NO MAN 3

BONDED BY BLOOD

SHORTY GOT A THUG

THUGS CRY

THUGS CRY 2

THUGS CRY 3

TRUST NO BITCH

TRUST NO BITCH 2

TRUST NO BITCH 3

TIL MY CASKET DROPS

RESTRAINING ORDER

RESTRAINING ORDER 2

IN LOVE WITH A CONVICT

LIFE OF A HOOD STAR

www.ingramcontent.com/pod-product-compliance
Lightning Source LLC
Chambersburg PA
CBHW070555260626
47161CB00002B/609